Time Of Reckoning

One of those rare novels of suspense that go beyond thrills and a breakneck pace to reach the heart of a deeply emotional question of right and wrong.

D0826915

Other books by Walter Wager

TELEFON
SWAP
VIPER THREE
SLEDGEHAMMER

Time Of Reckoning

Walter Wager

PLAYBOY
PAPERBACKS

To Martha Winston and Richard Parks,
whose taste and charm are surpassed only by
their wisdom and diligence.

TIME OF RECKONING

Copyright © 1977 by Walter Wager

Cover photo copyright © 1981 by PEI Books, Inc.

Published simultaneously in the United States and Canada by Playboy Paperbacks, New York, New York. Printed in the United States of America. Hardcover edition published by Playboy Press in 1977. Library of Congress Catalog Card Number: 77-22548.

Books are available at quantity discounts for promotional and industrial use. For further information, write to Premium Sales, Playboy Paperbacks, 1633 Broadway, New York, New York 10019.

ISBN: 0-872-16857-3

First Playboy Paperbacks printing January 1978.
Third printing July 1981.

AUTHOR'S NOTE

This is a work of fiction about imaginary people and deeds. Unfortunately, it is inspired by certain terrible acts done by monstrous individuals whose membership in the human species must be a source of embarrassment to *almost* all of us. There are some—here as well as in the lands that were ruled by the Nazis—who are capable of the same oppression and mass murder today.

There are also many good people, real ones. Among them is the able Einstein Medical School professor who gave technical advice on drugs, etc., for this book, Dr. Theodore Smith. I hope that I have used it accurately, for he is not only a perfectionist but also my splendid cousin.

Time Of Reckoning

1

The heat and the stink of the gasoline fumes in the slow-moving tank were—as usual—almost nauseating, and the thirty-cylinder roar of the powerful Chrysler engines didn't help either.

"Tinker Bell . . . Come in, Tinker Bell," Arbolino chanted angrily into the microphone.

The awful blast of the 75-millimeter cannon less than a yard away battered his senses like a blow from a baseball bat, punching through his thickly padded headset as if it were a cheap pair of children's earmuffs. The thirty-six-ton Sherman lurched —just a bit—under the recoil, and Lieutenant J. M. Arbolino braced to avoid banging his head against some goddam piece of metal. He'd commanded this rolling fortress since Patton's armored fist smashed the German forces ringing Bastogne, and now—four months later and more than three hundred miles into Hitler's Reich—Arbolino still hadn't quite figured out how to avoid cracking his head on *something*.

He heard the clatter of Stark and Guber reloading the 75, and then—suddenly—the staccato hammering on the hull that always frightened him. His head knew that the three-inch armor could stop the enemy's 7.92-millimeter machine-gun slugs, but his stomach was never wholly convinced.

"Ho-ly shit!"

He couldn't help it. Arbolino had completed two years at Columbia before the draft grabbed him, but the rude language wasn't his fault. They all spoke that way in the goddam army, with the exception of Corporal Jerry Jeff Atkins, whose father was a minister in a northern Alabama region so pious that it was known as the Buckle on the Bible Belt. Atkins rarely said anything, but he hummed a lot of swell gospel songs. That's what he was doing now as he worked the tank's .30-caliber

Browning, punching out four short savage bursts before he silenced the Kraut machine gun firing down from the guard tower.

That didn't help Arbolino's spirits at all. He saw at least five more such towers ringing this side of the camp and—if Intelligence was right for a change—the defenders were those goddam S.S. fanatics.

"Hacksaw . . . Hacksaw," the commander of a nearby Sherman appealed over the radio.

Arbolino ignored him, called again for the fighter-bombers they'd been promised.

"Tinker Bell, this is Hacksaw."

There was no reply, only crackling static.

"Panzerfaust, ten o'clock," Arbolino announced professionally when he spotted the German bazooka unit beside the gate. The thunder of the 75 filled the hull again, and the S.S. antitank team ceased to exist. There would be other crazies rushing out to die senselessly, Arbolino thought grimly. It was plainly *Götterdämmerung* time in the Ol' Third Reich, and those goddam P-47s were nowhere in the sky.

Shiiit.

"This is Hacksaw . . . No sign of our wonderful goddam air support, but we don't need them anyway. Crank 'em up and pick your spots. We're goin' in!"

Arbolino's tank dismantled the gate, and nine other Shermans bulled their own entrances through the wire fences. The infantry behind them charged through these gaps and—in the great tradition of ground forces under fire—gunned almost everything that moved. The tanks helped, but it was the frantic, panting foot soldiers who had to snuff out the snipers and the idiot holdouts and the suicidal Wagner fans who charged out tossing grenades. The fighting was savage and bloody. When the surviving S.S. finally stood with their arms raised in a sullen herd, Arbolino sighed and led his crew out of the cramped misery of the massive metal box.

There was something wrong with this place.

Something that he couldn't name spooked the young lieutenant, and there was a strange nasty taste in Arbolino's mouth as he stood up in the commander's hatch, his fingers gripping the handle on the swivel-mounted .50 as if the heavy machine gun were some sort of icon.

The rest of the crew climbed down, stretched and mumbled as they always did. Cotler took a leak—as he always did. The kid from Ardsley was a first-class driver, but his kidneys weren't really cut out for pushing a tank that couldn't do more than twenty-two or twenty-three miles an hour. Atkins stood up front, sipping water from a canteen in his left hand while his right held the carbine that he "wore" like a watch. The thin country boy carried that weapon everywhere, and the others kidded him about that. They weren't joking now. It was as if they all sensed that there was something creepy here.

Arbolino saw them first.

"Jee*zus,*" he said and he swung the machine gun as if they were a threat.

They weren't.

There were scores of them—gaunt, ravaged, shuffling scarecrows in tattered uniforms. Not S.S. uniforms, something very different. Men, women and children with dazed-crazed eyes moved warily around the corner of a nearby wooden building. The human tide inched forward toward the tank, hesitated and stared. Arbolino had never seen such desperation as that frozen on those faces, and he told this to Captain McInerney when the intelligence officer drove up in a jeep a moment later.

"What the hell's going on here, Mac?"

"It's a murder factory, a slaughterhouse!"

McInerney's frowning driver shook his head. "Nah, I worked two years in a slaughterhouse," he said in a choked voice. "I never seen anything like this in my whole life."

Arbolino pointed at the gaunt, frightened herd. "Mac, who are these people?"

The intelligence officer didn't answer.

"In my *whole life,*" insisted his driver hoarsely.

It was crazy, like some weird fugue or a film whose sound track had slipped out of sync.

"They butchered thousands every week," McInerney suddenly announced in that flat Boston accent. "Men—women—kids. Thousands and thousands! Jesus, Jesus, Jesus."

"Why?"

It was obvious that McInerney hadn't even heard the question.

"They starved them, shot them, gassed them—burned them

like cordwood," he half-screamed. "Dante's inferno—go see
for yourself!"

Arbolino walked back to his crew, told them what the intelligence officer had said and gave the order. "Mount up."

Cotler climbed back inside to drive, and Arbolino took up his
position at the .50 again. The others sat on or hung on to the
hull as the big tank crawled forward. The mob of gaunt prisoners drew back in naked fear. The Sherman clattered past them,
moved on into the center of the camp. *There* was the building
where the Nazis gassed people, a lanky infantryman from Baltimore explained helpfully, and *that* was the place where the
bodies were incinerated like garbage.

"Thousands?" tested the tank commander.

The foot soldier nodded.

"Every week?"

The rifleman's helmeted head bobbed again, and the tankers
looked at each other in silent shock.

"Hundred fifty, maybe two hundred thousand, I hear," the
infantry sergeant said. "There's a whole damn pit full of bodies
down beyond them barracks."

They reached it ninety seconds later. It was just as the NCO
had said.

There was a huge hole in the ground, longer than a football
field and half as wide.

It was filled with corpses.

Hundreds and hundreds of those pitifully thin bodies—more
than a thousand, for sure—lay piled and intertwined. It might
have been more than two thousand, Arbolino thought. There
was no way to count this, no way to cope with the incredible
impact of this nightmare vista.

Stark began to shake, and then he threw up. He had three
Purple Hearts for wounds taken in North Africa and Normandy, and he had a Bronze Star he'd earned in the Ardennes
—and he kept vomiting. He'd never seen anything like this.

At that moment the lieutenant noticed the child. He hadn't
seen him approach, but suddenly he was there—a little desperate boy of three or four in scraps of cloth. He whispered something, and Guber understood.

"He's hungry," translated the gunner.

The child raised his left hand, pointed to his upper arm.
There was a number on it, tattooed. The tankers gave him the

bars of bitter chocolate from the emergency rations in the Sherman, and he ate ravenously, chewing blindly like an animal. The Americans watched him, and Atkins offered the boy his canteen. In a little while the child stopped drinking and politely returned the metal flask. Guber asked him a question, and the boy pointed to the pit.

"His parents are in there, lieutenant."

Arbolino swore, and then the child pointed again, at the building behind them. Corporal Jerry Jeff Atkins reacted first, swiftly and instinctively. His carbine pointed at the second-floor window, snapped. The S.S. sniper tumbled out, and the Alabama country youth's weapon sounded twice more. The bullets tore at the falling body, confirming those years of duck-hunting experience. Atkins lowered the carbine, bent down awkwardly to put his arm around the little boy. He tried to comfort the child, and he did his best to fight back the tears that furrowed the dust on his face.

It was Atkins who wept, who hummed his gospel song and cried. The three-year-old just looked at them from somewhere inside his head, watching with the gutted eyes of a burned-out old man.

"Hacksaw, this is Tinker Bell," squawked the radio.

Arbolino glanced up, saw the dots moving in from the horizon. "Seven . . . eight . . . nine," he counted aloud.

The goddam air support had arrived.

2

There's no official record of exactly what Captain McInerney said over the radio that gray afternoon, but somebody back at division must have believed him, because the ambulances and trucks loaded with food arrived just after dawn the next morning. They drove all night, a big convoy of more than a hundred vehicles. The medics and the GIs and the cooks surveyed the incredible situation swiftly, went to work at once. They did an excellent job, even if they were too late to save ninety-eight of the ex-prisoners who died quietly of hunger and disease in the dark hours.

The general reached the camp at noon. Three silver stars, pearl-handled pistols and balls of brass. The toughest son of a bitch on wheels—that's how he had once described himself to a snotty *Time* magazine reporter on the eve of the Normandy breakout, and he wasn't kidding. He wasn't joking now either. He arrived in a covey of armored cars and goggled motorcycle outriders, jumped out of the staff car before his aide could open the door.

"Let's hear it," he ordered bluntly.

A stocky major stepped forward to report.

"No bullshit," warned the general as his eyes swept the scene.

"No, sir."

The major told what had happened, how Arbolino had led the armored attack to the edge of the camp and spearheaded the final thrust through the enemy defenses.

"Get him."

Somebody found the young lieutenant, and he tried to stand strong and tall as he described the previous day's battle. It wasn't easy, for he hadn't been able to sleep.

"So you were the point, and you decided you weren't going to wait for the air support?" the general challenged.

"That's it, sir."

"And who the hell gave *you* the authority to ignore orders, sonny?"

Arbolino looked at him with red-ringed eyes, fought down a yawn and resisted an impulse to hit him.

"Nobody gave it to me. I took it. It goes with these," the lieutenant said, pointing to the gold bar on his left shoulder.

The general grinned—the big one that those *Stars and Stripes* photographers loved. "Bet your ass it does," he agreed.

"The air support was late, sir," Arbolino added. He couldn't quite understand why the general was smiling.

"The goddam air support's *always* late," the general said, then jerked one finger at his aide. "Get the goddam box. We've found ourselves a gen-u-wine goddam soldier."

Arbolino was wearing a new Bronze Star fifty seconds later when the general asked that he guide him around the camp.

"*Me,* sir?"

"Why not? You took it. It's yours."

Now the general noticed the pitifully thin child who stood a few feet behind the lieutenant, who hadn't left Arbolino's side since they'd met at the pit.

"Can I bring him, sir? They killed his parents, and he's sort of adopted me. He's scared, general."

"Bring him."

They drove around the camp slowly in the staff car, with a radio command truck tagging along as it always did. When they emerged from the crematorium, the aide reported a message from a Colonel Duckingham—he'd halted his armored task force until the infantry trucks could catch up.

"Tell that dumb shit to keep moving!"

The aide translated smoothly with a speed born of experience. "Please radio Colonel Duckingham that it's imperative that he continue the advance according to schedule," he told the communications sergeant.

The general didn't utter another word for the next forty minutes. He had a reputation as a man who talked freely—sometimes too freely—but he didn't speak again until they'd completed the grisly tour.

"This isn't the only butcher shop," he told Arbolino fiercely when they'd seen it all. "The British took one just as bad at a place called Belsen, and there are more the Russians found. Do you know what those Krauts who lived near the Belsen camp told the British?"

Arbolino shook his head.

"Said they had no idea this sort of thing was going on—no *fucking* idea. Well, they're not going to pull that crap on me," the general vowed.

He turned to his aide again. "Marty, I want all those food trucks emptied—fast. Send every one of them into the nearest town, and bring the whole crowd out here. Everybody—every goddam man, woman and child from thirteen to a hundred and thirty. I want those innocent bastards to see this."

There was chaos in the town of Dachau when the trucks first arrived, and the mayor protested indignantly and made several references to the Geneva Convention until a certain Captain Begelman—whose father was a lawyer in Akron—explained that the general was an angry, ruthless man who might well order the entire community bombed into rubble. That would come after all the adult males had been machine-gunned in the main square, an event that would be preceded by the hanging of the mayor. Of course the general hadn't said any of those things, but Begelman had a flair for the theatrical.

The convoys rolled back and forth between Dachau and the death camp all afternoon and late into the night, and resumed the next morning at first light. The last truckloads of stunned civilians were at the gas chambers early that afternoon when Arbolino's tank detachment received orders to move.

East.

Fast.

They were to help mop up the last remnants of enemy resistance, to hammer their way through to meet the advancing Soviet juggernaut that was grinding west across Czechoslovakia. The Russians had already taken a burning Berlin after bloody street fighting, Captain McInerney told Arbolino.

"They say Hitler's dead," he reported.

"Whoopee," Arbolino replied sarcastically.

"Don't you give a damn?"

The tank commander shrugged, gestured to Stark to climb

into the Sherman. "I give a damn about this kid," he said, nodding toward the nearby child.

"What's he got to do with Hitler?" challenged the irritated intelligence officer. "Hitler's dead! Don't you guys care?"

Cotler finished urinating, started to button his pants. "Piss on Hitler," he said.

"Piss on his grave," agreed Guber cheerfully.

Then the two of them got into the tank, and the boy moved closer until he stood only inches from the lieutenant. Arbolino took his hand, not knowing quite why.

"The whole damn war'll be over in a couple of days!" McInerney exulted.

"What war is that?" asked Cotler.

Now Atkins hurried toward the Sherman, carbine in one hand and a small book in the other. He waved the leather-bound volume tentatively, glanced at the child and hesitated a moment before he spoke.

"He's Jewish, isn't he, sir?"

"I think so."

"It's my Bible, lieutenant. It's a Christian Bible, and it's in English. Would he mind . . . would it be right if I gave it to him?"

"Sure . . . Say, you got any cigarettes?"

"Don't smoke, sir, but Guber or Stark might have a pack."

"I want all of them, every pack we've got. They're for him."

The intelligence officer's frown signaled his bewilderment.

"Why in hell are you giving cigarettes to a three-year-old?"

"He can buy things with them," Arbolino explained. "Food, candy, shoes. You speak German. You tell him."

Atkins returned with seven packs of Camels, four Chesterfields.

"You know that it's against regulations to give this stuff to German civilians?" the captain asked.

"You going to stop me?"

"No, lieutenant."

McInerney gave the cigarettes to the child, said something in German and then added a pack of his own.

"I'm not a louse, you know," he declared defensively.

"Never thought you were. Thanks, Mac."

The intelligence officer half-smiled, pulled another packet of

Old Golds from his pocket. "Smoke too much anyway," he lied.

Arbolino patted the child's head. "Tell him we have to go, Mac. We're soldiers, and we take orders, and the orders are to move out."

The intelligence officer translated, and the child nodded in comprehension.

"Doesn't he talk?" McInerney asked.

"His name is Ernst. That's practically all he ever told us."

The solemn-faced boy put out one hand, and Arbolino shook it in farewell.

"Keep an eye on him, Mac."

"You can bet on it."

Arbolino mounted the tank, then remembered as he lowered his legs into the commander's hatch and tossed the Bible to McInerney. "He can read that when he learns English—if he wants to."

Cotler started the engines, and their roar made it difficult for Arbolino to hear the intelligence officer's reply.

"What?"

"He'll be okay. There'll be all kinds of relief outfits here in a couple of weeks."

The tank began to move.

"Someone'll take care of him!" McInerney shouted over the din.

The other Shermans fell into line, and the armored column clattered out of the concentration camp, heading east. Arbolino was still thinking about the child some thirty-five minutes later, when he heard the sounds, peered up at four flights of P-47 fighter-bombers skimming the horizon. Breaking all precedent, the goddam air support was on time.

Maybe somebody would take care of the boy after all.

3

Somebody did.

First it was the U.S. Army. That was before it was fashionable to bad-mouth the U.S. Army and everything else American, so everyone agreed that the U.S. forces which liberated the concentration camps did a bang-up job of feeding, clothing and rehabilitating the thousands of survivors—including a three-year-old boy named Ernst. No one felt self-conscious about using words like "liberate" and "rehabilitate" that extraordinary spring. The prevailing emotion in Los Angeles and London, Toronto and Paris, New York and Amsterdam was joy.

Joy that the war in Europe was done.

Joy, and astonishment.

The enormity of the massacres in those camps was hard to believe, and the numbers were almost impossible to comprehend. More than five million Jews and an even greater total of Russians and other Europeans—perhaps seven million—had been exterminated by the Third Reich. Films of the camps were shown around the world, and people blinked and gaped and wondered how a highly civilized people like the Germans could do this.

Well, according to all reports.

It had been done systematically and efficiently, and quietly. Many Germans hadn't known what their government was doing, and many others hadn't wanted to know. More than a few did know, took an active role in the industrialized inhumanity of the murder factories. That took a while to sink in —on both sides of the Atlantic.

It finally did.

Joy and astonishment, and rage.

The intelligence services of the nations that had joined to fight fascism were already at work. Purposeful professional teams of British, Russians, Americans, French, Poles, Dutch, Canadians, Norwegians, Yugoslavs and others had been in action for months—hunting. That was also before government security agencies and counterespionage organizations were casually despised, exposed and taunted as threats to decent folk. Naïvely confident that they represented right, agents of a score of Allied intelligence units continued to track down the criminals.

What do the police call them in American TV shows? The *perpetrators*—that's it. They hunted the *perpetrators* of the mass murders committed between 1939 and Hitler's fiery death in the Berlin bunker—the war criminals. The top Nazi officials were easy. Goering and Goebbels had the good taste to commit suicide, and the other prominent figures proved relatively simple to catch. No, *apprehend.* Quite a few of the *perpetrators* were *apprehended,* including a lot of men and women who insisted that they had merely obeyed orders from the higher-ups. They explained that they had run the murder machine and the death camps only at the command of bigger people, for they themselves were *little* men and women who never made policy. There were many who said this, and to hear them tell it the Third Reich was largely a nation of dwarfs and trolls.

The hunt continued.

Preparations for the war crimes trials began.

The fighting against the Japanese continued halfway around the world. Obviously unable to cope with U.S. air power, the military leaders in Tokyo effectively dispersed the notion of the superior wisdom of the East by continuing a hopeless struggle. Buoyed by a set of patriotic clichés and schmucky slogans, they proudly refused to end the bloodletting until terrible nuclear weapons charred Hiroshima and Nagasaki. Atom bombs back to back top almost anything, they discovered, even the idiocy of fanatical old men with a lot of medals.

Arbolino and Stark, Guber and Cotler and Jerry Jeff—and their tank—were busy with the "occupation" of a town called Gotteszeil in eastern Bavaria. It was a pleasant community that hadn't been battered too much by the war, and what made it especially attractive was the fact that there had been only two or three Nazis in the entire population. One was a man named Otto something, who'd died of bleeding piles just before the

Americans arrived with all that chocolate and food and other goodies. This might seem hard to believe, but who would doubt the word of a shapely and affectionate young woman lying beside you? Every member of Arbolino's crew—with the exception of Jerry Jeff—ran into such congenial companions that balmy autumn while they waited for the U.S. Army to confirm that their overseas combat service added up to enough "points" for the trip home. The fine young women of Gottes-zeil were sad when the crew left in November.

The general died in December.

He never knew that they were going to make a terrific motion picture about his life, with George C. Scott in the title role. He would have felt a lot better about checking out in a dumb-ass automobile accident if he'd heard about Scott, but back in December of 1945 nobody appreciated what a swell actor George C. Scott would become. The general never doubted that they'd eventually do a picture—a *major* motion picture, as they say—about his greatness, but he was worried that some pretty boy like Robert Taylor might get the part. Unaware of George C. Scott's big potential, the general was rooting for John Wayne right up to the moment of that stupid car crash.

Strange as it may seem, news of his death didn't really cause that much excitement in the alphabet camp where the little boy waited. Ernst called it the alphabet camp because it was run by an organization named UNRRA—the United Nations Relief and Rehabilitation Agency—and the thousands of uprooted survivors of the murder factories were known as DPs. Ernst could tell you that DP meant Displaced Person, for he was a bright child with an intelligence superior to that of most boys of his age. He could also tell you his age, and his number. He'd memorized the number they'd put on his arm.

It was through that number that a social worker connected with some Jewish welfare outfit found out who he was. According to the central registry of concentration-camp prisoner numbers that the efficient Nazis had kept in Berlin, his full name was Ernst Beller and his father had been a chemist. Now someone had to discover whether Ernst Beller had any surviving relatives, any family who would take him.

Both parents—dead.

All grandparents—dead.

Three aunts and eight cousins—dead.

It looked as if the boy would spend the rest of his childhood in some camp or public institution. Then, in the last week of June—some fourteen months after the tanks had smashed into Dachau—Ernest Beller was notified that he was going to join his Uncle Martin in America.

4

Uncle Martin had once met Freud.

Sigmund Freud, the one with the cigar and the mother number.

Really.

It wasn't that surprising if you knew that Uncle Martin graduated third in the class of 1925 at the U. of Vienna med school and went on to become a full-fledged psychoanalyst. Even his few enemies had to admit that there wasn't a therapist in his age group who was more fledged than Martin Beller. Now he had a thriving practice in New York City, a large and high-ceilinged apartment on Central Park West, a small potbelly and a fine head of whitening hair that went nicely with his dignity. He also had the open admiration of his wife, Greta, the respect of his colleagues and a good deal of his patients' cash.

He was no phony. A stocky man who wore his soft Austrian accent as a badge of honor, Dr. Beller was a dedicated therapist who'd settled comfortably into the Manhattan scene back in '38 and helped quite a few people since. He never got into bickering with Jungians or analysts of other schools, but he never doubted the classical Freudian theory for a minute. After all, if he'd always wanted to put the blocks to his mom, why wouldn't everyone else? There is, of course, a great deal more to the theories of the late Sigmund Freud, an undoubted genius. Martin Beller knew the whole bit.

His wife was no dummy either. What she didn't know about Beethoven, Mozart, Brahms, Mahler and postimpressionist art you could tattoo on your big toe, and still have enough room left for Greta Beller's excellent strudel recipe. She was hip to the stock market and real estate too, handling the family investments. Both of the Bellers were warm and kind, and so was their daughter, Anna. It would be a cliché to say that Anna was a pretty ten-year-old with lovely hair and sparkling eyes. Well, Anna *was* a pretty ten-year-old with lovely hair and sparkling eyes—and glasses.

They all welcomed Ernest, gently.

They all loved him, warmly.

They all nurtured him, genuinely and compassionately. Despite the analyst's injunction that they must be careful not to smother the child, both adult Bellers gave the boy a great deal of both physical and emotional affection, and his cousin celebrated him as the brother she'd never had. It was easy to do, for he was a cheery, bright, congenial lad who enjoyed company and learned everything quickly.

"He's a Beller all right," the analyst's wife said proudly one Friday afternoon in June as they were packing for a weekend at Fire Island.

"He has a good mind," her husband agreed warily.

"Good mind? He's going to be brilliant, Martin," she insisted. "He learned English in seven months, and now he has the vocabulary of a ten-year-old. He's only six, you know."

"I know, Greta. Let's not push him though. He's been through a lot of trauma."

She paused in her packing, tensed. "Is there something wrong, Martin? He seems so—so well adjusted."

"He probably is," Dr. Beller answered reassuringly. "No, I don't see anything wrong, but there could be problems later. I won't predict that there will be, but . . ."

"There might be," she finished. "I understand. We've got to do everything to help him forget that camp."

The therapist nodded, shrugged. "It isn't that easy, Greta."

"He never talks about it."

Dr. Beller nodded again. "He may be suppressing it—for now. Let's see, dear."

She resumed the packing, stopped. "What about that number on his arm? Couldn't it be removed? Every time I see it my stomach knots up."

Dr. Beller saw that his wife was close to tears. "Mine too, Greta," he admitted.

"Then think of how he must feel!" she groaned.

He put his arm around her and comforted her before he called in their nephew.

"Ernest," he began—using the "more American" version of the boy's name—"you're starting school in a few months."

"I know, uncle. I'm looking forward to it."

He was so direct, appreciative, solid.

"Aunt Greta and I were talking about the number on your arm."

For a second—just a split second—the analyst thought he saw something flicker in that plump happy face. Maybe not.

"Yes, uncle?"

"Well, the children will all be Americans and they won't understand about the number. They might see it in gymnasium, and they might say something." Martin Beller still said it the way he used to in Vienna—gimm-nah-seum.

The boy was still smiling. "I guess they might," he agreed.

"Ernest—would you want to have the number removed? It wouldn't be difficult."

The child considered, decided. "No, thank you, uncle."

"It wouldn't hurt," said his aunt. She was struggling very hard to avoid crying.

"You wouldn't have suggested it if it did. I know that, auntie," he answered pleasantly. "It's kind of you, but it won't be necessary."

His eyes flickered to the door.

"Is it the Yankee game?" guessed Beller.

"I was listening on Anna's radio."

A moment after he left, Greta Beller started to cry quietly.

In the third week of September 1948, Ernest Beller joined the first grade at one of New York's finest and most progressive private schools. The Dalton School was located across town on 89th Street between Park and Lexington avenues, and Ernest Beller made the journey each day with his cousin by bus. It was Anna who reported on his first gym class—*phys. ed.* in her jargon.

"Terry Gold told his sister," Anna explained, "and she told me in the cafeteria. A couple of boys asked him what was that on his arm, and he said it was a number. They asked why, and he said he'd been in a camp in Germany."

"Oh, my God," sighed Greta Beller, who hadn't been in a synagogue for at least thirty years.

"They asked if it was a concentration camp," Anna continued, "and he said yes. Then they asked him what it was like, and he told them it was terrible."

"What else did he say about it?" Dr. Beller probed gently.

She shook her head. "Nothing. He said he didn't want to talk about it anymore, and then it was time to play basketball. Terry told his sister that Ernie's pretty good for a kid who never played basketball before."

Ernie Beller did well at the Dalton School during the next nine years. He was always in the top quarter of his class, among the better athletes in basketball and sufficiently popular to be elected vice-president of the eighth grade. His adjustment to the American scene was excellent, and there was no sign of any residual trauma. He did discourage prying questions about the horrors of Dachau, but that was certainly understandable. Greta Beller made a point of encouraging his "cultural interests" via tickets to the best plays and concerts, and found him a first-class piano teacher. Despite all his other activities, Ernie was a good boy who always found time for his hour of practice each afternoon.

At 3:40 P.M. on the day before his fifteenth birthday, Ernie Beller was on his way home from school when a group of poorly dressed boys stopped him in the street. They were all bigger than he was, and two carried bicycle chains. A third swung a small bat, and he was the one who demanded Ernie's watch and money. The boy from Dachau didn't hesitate, not for a moment. He'd heard of friends slashed and beaten by such muggers, and he had no doubt that this gang could be equally vicious.

He reached into the open garbage pail beside him, jerked out two empty quart bottles and smashed the bottoms off against the apartment house wall.

The muggers froze.

"I'll kill you," he said in a voice that was cool and factual.

"Hey, man, you crazy?"

"I'll kill you," he promised.

He wasn't joking.

It was absolutely clear that this neatly dressed prep school kid with the short haircut was ready to cut them to pieces, to gash and gouge with the ferocity of a homicidal street fighter.

"He's *crazy*," judged the leader of the attackers, and they retreated—very carefully.

When they were out of sight, Ernie Beller dropped one of the broken beer bottles back into the trash and, taking no chances, carried the other until he was only twenty yards from his own building. As he entered the apartment house, he said hello to the uniformed doorman and predicted that the Yankees would win the evening's doubleheader against Boston. When he unlocked the door to apartment 12A, his aunt was having coffee—strong Viennese coffee capped with whipped *Schlag*—with an old friend.

"Good afternoon, Frau Gehferlach," he said politely to the visitor.

His aunt beamed, proud of both his memory and manners. He excused himself, and ninety seconds later the two women heard the first notes of Mozart's Piano Sonata no. 7 in C Major, the one they say he wrote for the daughter of Mannheim orchestra conductor Cannabich in 1777.

"That's rather *good,*" Frau Gehferlach complimented as she reached for another strawberry jam torte.

His aunt looked at him at the piano that was framed in the doorway at the other end of the living room.

"Yes, Ernest is a *good* boy," she ratified in a low confidential voice.

She didn't want to speak too loudly. Ernest was so cheery and unselfconscious, and she didn't want to do anything that might disturb him.

5

John F. Kennedy and Ernie Beller both did pretty well in 1960. The American people told the senator from Massachusetts that he could move into the White House in Washington, and Harvard told the boy from Dachau that he could share a suite in Lowell House in Cambridge. Beller entered Harvard at seventeen. You could, too, if you had S.A.T. scores above 730, averaged twenty points a game for the basketball team of a fine private school and had a nationally known psychoanalyst as your adoptive father.

Lowell House, with its bells and blue dome, is one of Harvard's most attractive dormitories. All right, nobody's knocking Dunster or any of the others. Such petty rivalries certainly didn't afflict any of the members of the class of '64, who were united in their quiet pride in the new U.S. president—class of '39—and their conviction that plenty of Radcliffe girls put out, even if they were all high-school valedictorians. Whatever history may say about JFK, Ernie Beller discovered at least two intelligent young women at the sister school who confirmed this estimate. One was a nineteen-year-old blonde from Dallas who knew a great deal about Henry James, Herman Melville and contraception.

That was 1960, the year that Johnny Mathis and the Kingston Trio each had three "gold" albums and almost nobody cared about Vietnam. Ernie Beller and his lanky WASP roommate—a bright and modest lad whose family owned something like one-ninth of downtown Baltimore—wore Levi's and tweed jackets and spoke earnestly about the civil-rights movement. Nineteen sixty-one proved to be a startling wipe-out for Mathis and the Kingston Trio, and the civil-rights movement didn't fare that well either. Would you believe that the heavy hitter that year was Mantovani? No joke—five smash LPs on London. Beller was working his way through the *Kama Sutra* with a passionate Brecht-Ionesco-Dürrenmatt-Beckett fan named Linda. She was the avant-garde theater buff who got Beller involved with the Harvard Drama Club, a connection that became so intense that he seriously considered a stage career.

Uncle Martin talked him out of it.

"I hear you're a splendid actor, Ernest," he congratulated genially, "and I hope you'll continue as long as you're at college. Acting out is healthy—but not always commercial."

"I haven't really made up my mind, uncle."

"No reason to rush it. I'm just telling you—man to man—that I've had some top actors and directors on my couch, and they all agree that it's a hard way to make an unreliable living. Think about it."

Ernie Beller nodded, reflected sensibly through the middle of 1962, when Johnny Mathis came back strong with four successful albums and merry middle Americans were singing along with five lilting Mitch Miller platters. The Beatles were still working Liverpool delicatessens when Uncle Martin heard the wonderful news that Ernest was going to apply to medical school.

"Do you think he'll be an analyst?" Greta Beller asked her husband hopefully.

"I think he'll be a first-year medical student—if he gets admitted," Dr. Beller replied with a chuckle.

Three medical schools accepted Ernest Beller, and in September of 1964—a dynamite year for the Beatles, Harry Belafonte, Andy Williams and Lyndon Baines Johnson—he began at the College of Physicians and Surgeons of Columbia University. He could have commuted each day to the massive medical complex overlooking the Hudson, for the school on the Upper West Side of Manhattan was only twenty-five minutes from home. Rather than waste even this time, he chose to share an apartment on 170th Street off Broadway with two other students. Beller worked hard, got grades that put him in the upper fifth of his class—and rarely spoke unless questioned. Very few people at P&S even noticed him until the incident in the anatomy class.

"Good morning, ladies and gentlemen," Professor Fiske said with his usual sly grin. "Welcome to Anatomy One. We're going to be working with human bodies."

Everyone knew that Fiske was a prurient prick, so nobody was surprised that he picked on the buxom brunette from California. With Eden Morris's prominent contours, it was difficult not to notice her.

"Have you had much experience with human bodies?" he teased. "*Dead* human bodies?"

"None at all."

His glittering eyes danced up to the next row, and he furtively checked the seating plan. "How about you, Mr.—Beller? Have *you* ever seen a human corpse?"

"Thousands," Ernest Beller answered flatly.

The class laughed.

"I'm not talking about war movies," Fiske snapped angrily.

"I'm not either."

Nobody chuckled this time. They stared.

"And just where did you see all these corpses, Mr. Beller?"

For a moment—a bright lurid instant—his mind's eye filled with a dazzling, terrifying view of that pit. It was very real, even to the point of the American tank crew standing beside him.

"In a hole at Dachau—a big hole with two thousand corpses."

The entire class gasped, gaped.

Fiske wouldn't yield.

"Come, come, Mr. Beller," he chided patronizingly. "You're much too young to have served in the army unit that liberated Dachau."

"You're right, professor. I was only three years old, but I remember the bodies quite clearly."

There was another collective gasp, and a young woman somewhere at the rear of the room began to weep softly. Fiske shook his balding head twice, swallowed his embarrassment and—surprisingly—his compassion. No one knew that he had it.

"I'm sorry, Mr. Beller," he said truthfully.

"So am I," Beller replied.

The anatomy class went on smoothly, and so did Ernie Beller. It wasn't just that he never spoke of his awful wartime experiences after that, but rather the warm and friendly way he related to the other students. By the end of that first term, he was relating very nicely, too, with Eden Morris at least twice a week.

Nineteen sixty-five was a swell year for Ernie Beller, the investors in *Fiddler on the Roof* and the Rolling Stones, who hit it big on both sides of the Atlantic—and the Pacific—with "Satisfaction" and "Out of Our Heads." Large crowds of small-ish girls gave Herman's Hermits no privacy at all, but this hardly affected Dr. Beller's nephew, whose taste ran to the Juilliard String Quartet, Jean-Pierre Rampal and almost any-thing Ella Fitzgerald ever recorded, especially Gershwin and Arlen. Other students smoked grass and marched to protest all kinds of things, but Ernest Beller had his hair cut every six weeks and did his own thing. He had neither the time nor the desire to change society, since his third-year studies and the work in the clinic kept him very busy.

To put it bluntly, he wasn't that lively.

Pleasant and intelligent? Yes. He was almost as smart as Eden Morris. The slight gap in their grades wasn't the reason that she left him for the husky intern from Oklahoma. Ernest Beller was a bit too low-key, a trifle too introverted for her. Leo Durocher may not have been exactly right when he told the sportswriters that nice guys finish last, but Ernie Beller came in second and that wasn't nearly good enough. He found a bright-as-a-button and cute-as-a-kitten laboratory technician named Sally Anne who was emancipated, very clean and deeply concerned about the global threat of overpopulation. She was easy to love—in more ways than one.

It wasn't easy to leave her when he got his M.D. that bright June day in 1968, and their intimacy continued during the first months of his internship at Bellevue Hospital. That's why she possessed a key to his East 29th Street apartment that steamy August night. She knew that Ernie would be on time for their 7 P.M. dinner date, for he was as punctual and organized as a man could be without being unpleasant. She was some-what surprised when no one answered her ringing, but she shrugged and let herself in to wait. She was even more sur-prised to find Ernest Beller seated before the television set, completely focused on the news broadcast.

". . . believed to have crossed the frontier from Syria," Walter Cronkite reported in that sincere and magical singsong. "The raiders were armed with automatic weapons, explosives and axes, and damage to the kibbutz was considerable."

You could see that clearly. The film of the blasted homes and the ruined school was a tribute to the skilled cameraman attached to the CBS News bureau in Jerusalem. Of course, he'd had a lot of experience shooting this sort of story, and that surely helped.

Now he panned neatly to the screaming women.

Great sound.

"Thirteen of the fatalities are said to have been women and children," Cronkite announced while an engineer seated twenty yards away from him in the building on West 57th Street in Manhattan prepared to run the Esso commercial. The agency that handled Esso's advertising could get very nasty if the tape wasn't rolled *exactly* on time.

They were loading bodies into ambulances, and the women were still screaming.

"Israeli authorities report that four of the terrorists were slain, but an estimated eight or nine others got away in the darkness."

Then they rolled the Esso tape—*right* on the button.

"Awful, awful," Sally Anne Lennard said, and he nodded as he turned to face her in the doorway.

"More dead Jews," he replied.

"The men who did this will be punished!" she said.

He looked at his watch, rose and reached for his tie on the doorknob.

"Someone will make them pay, Ernie!" she insisted emotionally.

He considered this notion soberly, for six or eight seconds. "Whom did you have in mind?" he asked as the sincere voice from the box explained the great care that Esso took to avoid screwing up the environment.

She didn't know how to answer.

There were times when it was hard to tell whether Ernie was joking or serious, and this was one of them.

6

Almost everyone figured that when Ernest Beller completed his rotating medical internship he'd go on to a residency in pediatrics, and marry Sally Anne. They were all wrong. His aunt still hoped that he'd take advanced training in psychiatry and wed some wealthy Jewish girl whose family had a good collection of pre-Columbian art. She was wrong too. He was actually fond of pre-Columbian, but his plan didn't call for him to marry anyone right now. When he told this to Sally Anne, she cried a bit and took a higher-paying job at a fine new medical center in Los Angeles, where the weather was a lot better and the street-crime rate significantly lower.

On the face of things, it was logical for Ernest Beller to go into pediatrics because he had an obvious and extraordinary gift for treating children. He was not only exceptionally skilled in diagnosing and coping with their medical problems, but the kids trusted him. All the kids—Irish or Italian, Chinese, black or Hispanic, poor or middle-class—loved Dr. Ernie. Why they called him that or why they were so crazy about him didn't really matter, but he was a hero to the younger girls and boys and he would have made one helluva pediatrician.

He chose pathology instead.

His plan required it.

The dictionary definition of "pathologist" is "one who makes postmortem examinations, diagnoses morbid changes in tissues removed at operation, et cetera." The root lies in the Greek word *pathos,* which Webster's New Collegiate views as "a combining form meaning suffering, disease, passion." That fit Ernest Beller precisely, although no one knew it.

"What does it mean, Martin?" Greta Beller asked her husband, whom she respected deeply—especially his mind.

"What do *you* think it means?" responded the psychoanalyst automatically.

"Death. He's choosing death over life! Don't laugh, Martin."

Dr. Beller didn't laugh, which was a good thing, for his wife was, as usual, intuitively correct. He told her that he'd speak to Ernest about it, and he did when his nephew came uptown for Sunday brunch less than forty-eight hours later.

"I'm afraid your aunt's a bit disappointed you didn't choose psychiatry," the analyst said with a chuckle that was only half-true. "I've heard you're very good with children, and that's a growing area for therapists."

Ernest Beller smeared more cream cheese on the thin dark bread, covered it with two slices of smoked salmon.

"I love kids all right," he admitted, "but I've discovered I find the lab more challenging. You could say that by working on some dead people I'll be helping keep other people—including kids—alive."

You could also say that Ernie Beller had become a top-notch liar. Watching his warm smile as he chewed, it was impossible to discern the plan that was slowly evolving behind those big bright eyes. Neither his uncle nor his aunt nor Sharon—the trim brunette who taught Puerto Ricans and Haitians "English as a second language" by day and spent nights and weekends with Ernie Beller—had any idea that he was getting ready for something extraordinary. Sharon Gresham, who was extremely fond of dry white wines, Italian movies and carnal contact with Ernie Beller at least seven or eight times a week, was terribly disappointed when he told her that he was joining the army and going overseas.

Three years.

He didn't have to serve, for the Vietnam War was almost over. He also didn't have to explain his reasons, and he didn't. The army was glad to cooperate with such a well-trained and competent pathologist, so Captain E. Beller's request for assignment to the U.S. ground forces in West Germany was approved without question.

It was all going well.

He'd been studying German for a year, and he'd polish his language skills further in the Federal Republic—the Fourth Reich. During the last weeks before reporting to the military hospital in Virginia, he spent many hours completing his research on West 43rd Street. He checked and rechecked the annual news indexes at the *New York Times,* then studied the microfilms very carefully for the detailed information he needed. He seemed to be in excellent spirits, and even the murder of a dozen Israeli athletes at the Munich Olympic Village didn't appear to depress him.

It was a question of numbers.

He couldn't afford to mourn for the twelve.

His duty was to avenge the *six million.*

Neither his preparations nor his plan were quite complete, and when they were he would have to move with the greatest care and precision. He would have to be efficient—just like the monsters who'd run the death camps. When he boarded the air force transport for Frankfurt that crisp October morning, Captain Beller (E) was cheerful and confident.

He had every reason to be.

After all, he'd been preparing for this for twenty-seven years.

Three hours after Ernest Beller's jet took off—at 11 A.M. on October 28, 1972, according to the CIA security entry log—a stocky pink-faced man named William Harper passed through the outer gates of the Central Intelligence Agency headquarters compound in Langley, Virginia. He was driving a 1971 Chrysler with D.C. plates and he was frowning. Nine minutes later he entered his office on the fourth floor of the huge drab building, and he was still frowning.

"Colonel Shulman," he growled as he strode past his secretary, "and get Parks too."

"What?" she asked.

"Shulman and Parks. You deaf?"

"Would it help?" she wondered hopefully.

She knew that it wouldn't. Nothing ever did when he was in a mood like this, and he was almost always in this kind of seething rage when he returned from those weekly meetings of Working Group Six at the Pentagon. Parks and Shulman arrived, and she buzzed them in immediately.

"Hobbits!" the shirtsleeved man behind the desk swore.

"What did he say, Alan?" Parks asked the marine corps colonel who'd entered with him.

"He said hobbits," reported Shulman, who was known for his memory as well as his expertise in jungle warfare.

"Fuckin' hobbits. The whole damn Pentagon is overrun with hobbits. It's Tolkien territory!" Harper raged.

Richard Parks, who had the curliest hair and the sharpest mind in the class of 1961 at Duke, nodded in recognition. "He's saying that they're living in a fantasy world," Parks translated with a still boyish grin. "You ever read any of the Tolkien books, Alan?"

"The only fiction I read is the *Congressional Record*," answered the colonel. "Hey, Bill, you want to tell us what the hell's wrong—*please?*"

Harper put on a pair of horn-rimmed glasses, took them off and placed them on the desk.

"The masterminds of the intelligence community have decided to go along with our friends at State on that business in Khartoum, so we're not going to do anything about those bastards who took out the ambassador," he said.

"Chicken, huh?" demanded the marine veteran.

"The whole room was full of feathers," Harper confirmed. Then he smiled slyly.

"There's more?" Parks guessed.

"A little. *Officially*, we're going along. I had a drink with the director last night, and he had an idea we might do something *un*official. Something quiet, if you know what I mean."

"What *do* you mean, Bill?" Shulman wondered.

Harper swiveled in his big leather chair, looked out the window for several seconds before he replied.

"Where's Merlin?"

"Jeezus Christ! Merlin?" Parks exclaimed. "You said something *quiet.*"

The colonel nodded twice. "Great idea," he approved.

"*Quiet?* Merlin's quiet like Mack the Knife!" Parks protested.

"You didn't read that either, Al," Harper told the colonel. *"Threepenny Opera.* Now where's Merlin?"

"Hong Kong. If you send him after that bunch that hit the ambassador—"

"Not the whole bunch," Harper soothed. "Just the Number One Pistol—as a lesson."

"Last word was they were all in Cairo," the colonel volunteered helpfully.

Parks stood there shaking his head in frustration.

"No sweat," judged the man behind the desk. "Wherever he is, Merlin will find him. Merlin's real good at finding people."

He was right.

Merlin found the man three weeks later, and the entire matter was settled quietly. As a matter of fact, the only noise generated was a single scream uttered just before the man who had slain the American ambassador to the Sudan disappeared below the surface of the River Nile.

7

Everything changes, but not necessarily for the worse. By the end of 1972 the Recording Industry Association of America had certified as "gold" two Aretha Franklin albums, two each by Elton John and Joan Baez, a pair of Tom Jones LPs and three featuring the rich voice of Roberta Flack. John Denver was just starting to get some attention, which is more than Ernie Beller could say. Captain Beller didn't want any attention, however, so he didn't have any promotion men or public-relations crew out hyping his efforts. Stationed at a U.S. Army base near Munich, he was seeking anonymity.

His efforts were not entirely successful. The other physicians didn't practice nearly as much on the rifle and pistol ranges, and they didn't spend any of their spare time taking hand-to-hand combat or "silent killing" courses with the Special Forces detachment. The energetic Green Berets of the Second Special Forces Group were delighted to teach him how to garrote with a piece of wire and kill with a single knife thrust, and they were impressed with how quickly he mastered booby traps and high explosives in the demolition training. They were no dummies, and they knew that the other doctors viewed them as embarrassingly gung-ho and violent jocks. Captain Beller respected their dedication and their skills, and they liked him for that.

The other doctors at the hospital thought he was a bit odd —especially the Jewish ones. They recognized his fine work as a pathologist, but they wondered about his unusual attitudes toward Germany and the Germans. Some of his colleagues put aside the past, mixed casually with the local population and took local girls as bowling partners, mistresses or wives. Others were coldly aloof, and a number were openly bitter. Beller wasn't any of these things, as far as anyone could see. He appeared to be completely neutral and dispassionate, almost uninterested in either the past or the present of this place and its people.

"My old outfit liberated the camp, you know," Phil Feldman blurted angrily across the lunch table one August afternoon.

Beller looked at the mustachioed surgeon, blinked. "What?"

"The outfit I was with back in the States—the Forty-fifth Infantry. It was the Third Battalion of the Forty-fifth that busted in back in forty-five, you know."

There were some people who found Feldman's habit of ending sentences with "you know" irksome, but Beller wasn't one of them. He respected the Californian's gifts as a surgeon.

"Broke in where?" Beller asked.

Major Feldman scowled impatiently. "The camp near Dachau, where they butchered two hundred and eighty-eight thousand people. What kind of a Jew are you, Beller? Doesn't it interest you?"

The pathologist sipped his coffee, and nodded. "It certainly does, Phil," he replied truthfully.

"It's less than twenty miles away, goddammit. What the hell's the matter with you? Why don't you go over and face a little reality?"

"I'll go—when I'm ready," Ernest Beller pledged.

He went to many places in Germany between August 24, 1973, and October 5, 1975, when he boarded the plane that took him home for discharge. He visited Berlin, Hamburg, Frankfurt, Düsseldorf, Bonn and other cities—but never the haunted *Konzentrationslager* just east of the old city of Dachau. He spent several days in each of the urban centers, shunning the usual sights and tourist attractions and spending hours instead in local libraries and municipal offices and *certain* bars. These were always near the town prison, and Beller never wore his uniform in these establishments.

It was all part of his plan.

He also wrote an extraordinary number of letters to various branches of the federal government in Bonn, and kept all the replies in a locked metal box.

That was also part of his plan.

So was his decision to join the staff of the Office of the Medical Examiner in New York City when he returned to civilian life. On the afternoon of the November Monday that Dr. Ernest Beller performed his first autopsy for Manhattan's harried taxpayers, Colonel Shulman dropped by Harper's office at CIA headquarters to say farewell. He was glad to be returning to regular duty with the marine corps, and he wasn't hiding it one bit.

"We'll miss you, Alan," Harper assured him.

"Miss you boys too. Not the paper pushers, but you've got some damn fine troopers out in the field—men who won't let you down."

Colonel Shulman had a tendency to make brief, inspiring speeches, some of which had earned him excellent ratings in "leadership."

"You mean agents such as Merlin," Harper guessed accurately. "Just got a message from Istanbul. He's in the hospital there."

"And what about the Bad Guys?" Shulman had great gut instincts.

"He blew two of them away," Harper reported, "and there's another one who left at least a fifth of blood in the alley."

"See what I mean?" the marine asked. "You can count on guys like Merlin to get it done."

A lot of people at the agency did.

Merlin was violent, but he did get things done.

Special things.

"You gotta hand it to Merlin," the colonel said with a macho chuckle, "and if you don't, he'll take it."

A veteran dissembler whose skills had improved steadily since he first seduced the freshman homecoming queen at Stanford, Harper forced out a laugh and wondered what to say to this hearty combat commander.

"Bet your ass," he volunteered hopefully.

It worked, and Colonel Shulman was smiling toothily as he left the office. Harper returned to the photos of the African general and the affectionate Swedish blonde who was charging the CIA $1000 a week to keep him happy. Perhaps congressmen and journalists might nit-pick about the morality of the operation, but there was one thing no one could argue: The pictures were excellent.

8

Was it Kafka, Telly Savalas's agent or Richard M. Nixon who said that you can't trust anybody? Well, you can't. Your own mother could sell your letters to the L.A. *Times* or the *Daily Mail*. Less than sixty days after Harper studied those expensive pictures of the expensive blonde, the African general screwed everybody—the woman, the CIA and himself. He went on a malt scotch bender, and while he was bombed out of his head he was bombed out of his palace. An air force colonel dropped a couple of five-hundred-pounders on the presidential compound, and before you could recite the number of the general's Swiss account there was a brand-new Numero Uno in the People's Democratic Republic and the Swedish Embassy gave the yellow-haired lady political asylum. Harper took it philosophically, recognizing the fact that giving political asylum is the national sport of Sweden, where there isn't much else to do most of the year.

The whole number didn't bother Ernest Beller one bit, and he was just as cool when Elizabeth Taylor split with Richard Burton again in late February. He was busy with his own thing —doing autopsies, stealing chemicals and official stationery and polishing his German. The plan was shaping up nicely, and he was so pleased that he decided to tell his uncle about it.

No, Ernie Beller wasn't crazy.

Well, not *that* crazy.

He was actually a lot loonier, but not *that* loony. Unlike a lot of criminals, he didn't want to get caught—*yet*. One—or even three if the BBC had a panel show going—could debate whether he wanted to be caught at all, but that probably wouldn't be nearly as much fun as those swell documentaries on bird watching in the Orkneys.

It was all a matter of timing, and he could wait. Ernest Beller was as good at waiting as Merlin was at finding, and the right moment finally came on a Sunday in May. The Yankees had won their first doubleheader all season the previous evening, and the *Times* reported that the Wolverhampton Wanderers had upset Tottenham Hotspur—leaving them in a dead tie with the Birmingham Armpits in the First Division (English League) of British football. Encouraged by these omens and goaded by the fact that he had almost no time left, the shrewd pathologist went to visit his uncle.

Close-up: Ernest Beller.

Very earnest Beller, speaking sincerely.

"I've got a plan, uncle. I've been working on it for a long time," he confided. "It's the murderers, the men who killed all our people in those camps. Not just our people, millions of others too. Someone has to punish them—the war criminals."

His uncle stared at him intently.

"I've given it a great deal of thought," explained the Dachau survivor, "and I accept the fact that I can't go searching for them. If the Israelis and the other intelligence agencies haven't been able to find Martin Bormann and the rest, I'll have to settle for the ones who've already been caught and put in prison in Germany. There's no death penalty in the new Germany, uncle. Isn't that progressive?"

The elderly analyst didn't answer.

Ernest Beller reached into his jacket pocket, took out Jerry Jeff Atkins's battered Bible. "A soldier gave me this at the camp. An eye for an eye and a tooth for a tooth," he continued grimly. "I'm going to Germany next week for the international pathology conference, and I'm going to break into those prisons. I know exactly which war criminals are in which prisons, and I've planned carefully how to get in. I have all the equipment, everything."

Martin Beller looked horrified. He plainly understood the plan.

"I'm going to kill them, uncle. I'm going to avenge the six million!"

At that moment Greta Beller entered the room.

Close-up: Martin Beller, desperate.

"How is he?" she asked.

"I've just been talking to him about my plan to go to Germany," Ernest told her.

She shook her head. "He wants to say something. It's tragic. Since the stroke he can't speak or write or even move his arms," she lamented.

Ernest Beller looked at the man in the bed, sighed. "Tragic," he agreed. "Will he ever speak again?"

"Nobody knows. He's a prisoner in his own body, seeing and hearing but completely unable to communicate. Look at him. He wants so much to say something."

The older man's face was contorted with effort, and he was breathing heavily as he tried—so hard. He failed, and a tear trickled from his left eye.

"Martin, Martin liebschen," she called out sympathetically. "He's crying," she sighed as she turned to her nephew. "I haven't seen him cry in thirty years."

"Thirty-one."

It just slipped out. The thirty-first anniversary of the American liberation of the camp had passed a month earlier, and Ernst Beller hadn't said a word about it to anyone—till now.

"What?" she asked.

"Nothing."

She shook her head again, and accepted.

"Ernest, when are you leaving and how long will you be gone?"

"Friday. The conference runs for a week, but I may drive down into Italy later with a friend who teaches at Johns Hopkins. She has relatives in Florence."

His aunt nodded tolerantly, as he knew she would. It was so easy to fool these emancipated liberals with casual reference to a sexual jaunt, for everything they believed pressed them to accept such a yarn as a normal "healthy" explanation.

The lips of the man in the bed quivered, but only a crude Cro-Magnon grunt emerged. It was a pitiful sound for a man who spoke four languages, knew the works of all the great philosophers and social scientists and writers of Western civilization right back to Aristotle.

"Good-bye, uncle. Please try to rest."

"We'll watch a little television this evening—the educational station, of course," Greta Beller said softly as her nephew reached for the doorknob. "He can't stand all the violence on the commercial stations."

"Who could?" Ernest Beller asked piously a moment before he kissed his aunt good-bye.

When he'd gone, she turned to her stricken husband. Tears were seeping from both eyes now, orbs swollen larger than she'd ever seen them before. Something was bothering or hurting poor Martin, but there was no way to determine what it might be. Whatever it was, it was terrible.

9

Latitude 13 degrees 25 minutes east.

Longitude 52 degrees 31 minutes north.

There is a great and famous city on the green bank of the Spree River, a metropolis divided by a wall and an ideology. South of the Baltic, east of the Elbe and west of the Oder, it was a strategic location even before it became a major cultural and business center. Born as a Hanseatic trading town in 1237, it grew into the industrial center of Prussia under Frederick the Great five centuries later and nearly died on the night of February 3, 1945, when the U.S. Army Air Force burned out a thousand acres in the gut of the city.

It's all different now.

The whole place has been rebuilt into a sleek and jazzy modern city, and the planes that fly in are DC-8s and Boeing 727s instead of General Jimmy Doolittle's B-17s or the Royal Air Force's heavies. The aircraft that land don't even touch down at the same field now, for Tempelhof has given way to the newer Tegel Flugplatz on the other side of town.

The city is Berlin—East and West and full of eye-catching contemporary buildings and groovy shops and assorted overt and covert employees of at least half a dozen powers cool-warring it up neatly. The western section of the sprawling metropolis is sealed off from the Marxist acreage by twenty-eight miles of concrete wall, land mines and armed East German guards who have AK-47s and bad posture—either of which can kill you. The setup is ridiculous, something only a cloak-and-dagger writer or Vanessa Redgrave could love.

Ernest Beller didn't love it and didn't hate it either as he looked down at the city from six thousand feet. It is one of the many ironies of the second half of this wacked-out century that West Germany's efficient airline, Lufthansa, is barred from

flying into Berlin by Moscow's merry minions. The Pan Am jet
bringing Dr. Beller and half a dozen other pathologists into
Tegel kissed the runway exactly on time. It was a fine morning
in early June, and Ernest Beller noticed the splendid legs of
the short-skirted "ground hostess" who guided the disembark-
ing passengers to the baggage-claim area.

Beller didn't notice the overhead camera, however.

Frank Wasserman did.

Mr. Wasserman had an advantage, of course. He was trained
to spot cameras and photoelectric cells, assorted "bugs" and
electronic eavesdropping devices and all types of people who
might be following him—up to size 48 long. Mr. Wasserman's
other advantages included looking the way Robert Redford
would if he were five inches taller, and shooting the way Clint
Eastwood would love to shoot. None of this was obvious, and
Mr. Wasserman looked like another pleasant U.S. tourist as he
walked past Dr. Beller and the other medical types.

Mr. Wasserman was almost never obvious.

It didn't go with either his self-image or his line of work. Mr.
Wasserman was leaving the baggage pickup as the pathologists
arrived, having flown in on Air France sixteen minutes earlier.
Following the porter who was carrying his matching tan can-
vas-and-leather suitcases, Mr. Wasserman paid no attention to
Beller strolling along in conversation with a Canadian woman
on the staff at McGill. Just for the record, the Man with the
Plan wasn't aware of Wasserman either.

Neither of these clever, good-looking and ruthless men
knew that the other was alive.

Not yet.

With lots of parks and greenery, Berlin is much more attractive than most cities, but Wasserman hardly noticed the scenery as the taxi wove through the Mercedeses, Opels and VWs
flowing steadily toward the center of the city. He wouldn't be
able to enjoy anything fully until he'd picked up the kit, and
he felt naked and defenseless all the way to the Hilton on
Budapesterstrasse.

If Watergate broke your heart, the Berlin Hilton should re-
vive your faith because it's exactly what a Hilton should be.
Tall, mindless modern architecture, great elevator service,
dandy ice cubes, three restaurants *and* three bars *and* a roof
garden *and* a café *and* The Starlight Room on the top floor

combine in an utterly standard skyscraper hotel. For those who look out, it offers interesting vistas of East Berlin across The Wall and/or West Berlin's chic Kurfurstendamm, dazzlingly lit at night.

But it wasn't night and Wasserman had seen the Ku-damm at least a hundred and forty-two times (not counting legal holidays). He knew its banks, boutiques, antique shops, art galleries and fashionable clothing stores and, if so inclined, could recall that the street was two and a quarter miles long and one hundred and seventy-seven feet wide. Having just hung up his clothes in Room 927, he took only a single long look out at the view before he left to make the pickup at the leather-goods shop nine blocks away. He wasn't interested in the leather suits in the nearby Berliner Ledermoden or the alligator bags at Croco on the Ku-damm. The store he sought was a small one on a side street. The sign in the window said Alexander.

"Good-day," said the bespectacled man behind the counter, who recognized Wasserman's clothes as American.

"Good-day. I've come for a suitcase left for repair," Wasserman answered as he automatically eye-swept the shop.

"Herr Prinz?"

"No, King."

For a moment Wasserman wondered whether this man was Alexander, but he brushed the question aside and handed over the claim check.

"You weren't due in until tomorrow," grumbled the man who might be Alexander as he pulled the canvas-and-leather bag from under the counter. It was the junior version of the two suitcases that sat in Room 927 at the Hilton, an exact kid brother.

"You speak Russian?" Wasserman asked as he picked up the bag. The weight of it was encouraging, suggesting that they had kept their promise—for a change.

"Naturlich."

"Then you remember Chekhov's great line in *War and Peace*—"

"What?"

"Piss off, sonny!"

"Chekhov didn't write *War and Peace!*"

Wasserman swung the bag, looked around the shop. "He

would have if he had the time," he told the man behind the counter. "Say, Alex, where's the back room?"

"Tolstoi wrote *War and Peace!*"

Wasserman nodded agreeably. "You know, you're beautiful when you're angry. Now where the hell's the back room?"

There was a hard edge in his voice that the clerk with the Hamburg accent couldn't ignore, so he nodded toward the curtain behind him.

There was a sturdy wooden table in the back room. The man who'd just arrived in Berlin—his fourth trip here in seven years—put down the suitcase, opened it.

Close-up: big smile.

Close-up: contents of the bag. One .357 Magnum. One long-barreled .22 assassin's gun. Two screw-on silencers. One sniper's rifle, with scope—to be assembled. Incendiary, explosive, gas and concussion grenades—four of each. One 9-millimeter Uzi submachine gun, the wooden-butt model, 25.2 inches long, six hundred and fifty rounds a minute. Fourteen of the thirty-two-round staggered box magazines. Chopped liver wasn't all that the Israelis made well, Wasserman thought. He'd ordered this gun because it was a standard infantry weapon of the West German Army, which would make it easy to get/steal more ammo. There were also extra clips and shells for the other guns, shoulder holster and belly holster and a fiberglass bulletproof vest. He took off his jacket, tie and shirt and put on the bulletproof vest. He buttoned the shirt over it, knotted the tie and strapped the shoulder holster into place. The Magnum barely fit, and he drew it three or four times before he was sufficiently satisfied to slip on the jacket.

"Tolstoi also wrote *Anna Karenina!*" the man behind the counter announced triumphantly when Wasserman returned to the front of the shop.

"I just came for a suitcase—not a goddam lecture on Russian literature."

"Which brings up *another* point, mein herr. You owe me two hundred and thirty-two deutschmarks for the suitcase."

One glance showed that the argumentative man in the glasses wasn't kidding.

"You've gotta be crazy. I don't need your suitcase. We both work for the same people, and you know the only reason I'm picking up this bag—"

"I don't know why you're taking the suitcase, and I don't want to know," interrupted the Tolstoi scholar. "All I know is that I paid a hundred and forty-four—all right, a hundred and forty—marks for that item myself, and I expect a fair profit. How'm I going to pay the rent and the taxes? You pistols come in here, and you don't give a damn about me at all."

"You're right—and you're crazy."

"I'm a businessman. Do you know how many months behind our company is in paying my expense accounts? Do you realize—"

"Shut up. Here's your two hundred and thirty-two marks," Wasserman said irritably and slammed the money on the counter.

The businessman counted it as Wasserman headed for the door.

"There's tax!" he cried out shrilly.

The man with the .357 under his left arm ignored this hysterical appeal, marched out and headed back toward the Hilton. He was on the Ku-damm four minutes later, when he heard the unpleasantly familiar sound.

It wasn't a pneumatic drill or jackhammer.

Some son of a bitch was working an automatic weapon. Right in the commercial center of Berlin.

Unless the "Kojak" series was shooting on location, Wasserman thought as he peered toward the noise, the Tourist Office and the Chamber of Commerce were going to be furious. There was another burst of firing—louder and nearer. Sensible folk on the street dodged into doorways or dropped behind cars, but Wasserman was professionally curious. The battering sounded like one of the British short-barreled Sterlings, and he wondered who in hell would be gunning up a main shopping street in the middle of the day.

He saw the black Audi sedan tearing through the traffic, the bright June sun glinting on something metallic jutting from the right front window. The person who was holding that something was squirting off bursts at storefronts and other vehicles—including a luxurious green Mercedes 450SL that erupted into flames when bullets ripped its fuel tank. Now the mobile machine gunner spotted Wasserman, swung his weapon and poured bullets that barely missed.

Wasserman didn't.

He dropped into the shooter's crouch and drew the Magnum, all in one choreographed motion. The .357 boomed twice. It was almost mechanical, but not quite. There was a lot of reflex in it, but some hatred too. His first round missed the racing car. His second destroyed about one-quarter of the machine gunner's face.

There was another face staring ferociously from the rear seat behind the recently deceased gunman. It was that of an attractive young brunette woman. *Click.* Wasserman's mind photographed it, just as it had been trained to do. Five years from now—if he was alive—he'd retain that image along with the silhouettes of Sov tanks and Red Chinese jets and those torpedo boats the French sold to the Egyptians. Not given to philosophizing, Wasserman didn't think about this but simply fired another shot that gouged a hole in the trunk of the receding Audi a moment before it spun around a corner.

Good idea. Wasserman jammed the Magnum back into the shoulder holster and did the same thing. He hurried around the corner—another corner—to flee the area before the capable Berlin police might arrive to ask questions. The evening news broadcasts would surely say something about who the homicidal maniacs in the Audi were, and there'd be an account in both the *International Tribune* and the U.S. Army paper on the stands in the morning.

It was nearly noon by the time he'd left the bag in his room, but he wasn't ready for lunch yet. Putting on a pair of tinted sunglasses, he took a taxi to the Amerika Haus at 21–24 Hardenbergstrasse. It was one of the best U.S. cultural centers in Europe, and the blonde at the information desk near the door wasn't bad either. She was Fraulein Cassel, according to the nameplate that didn't quite mask her healthy physique—not to mention her alert and intelligent demeanor.

"Mr. John Siegenthaler," he said politely.

"The music collection?" she tested in a voice that carried a lot of Chicago.

"No, audiovisual," he replied with the approved countersign.

"May I tell him who's calling?"

She had a very nice smile, and her swell posture did a lot for her.

"Frank Wasserman."

She dialed a number, passed on the name and invited him to enter the second door on the left. It was not marked "audiovisual" but "film research" was close enough. There were some charming Laurel & Hardy and Bogart posters on the wall of the inner office, and a mirror that had to mask the closed-circuit TV camera. The person behind this desk was a sturdy-looking chap in his late twenties, and he scanned Wasserman's passport before pressing the buzzer that opened the door behind him.

"What the hell are you doing here?" demanded the woman behind the large plastic-and-metal desk. She was black, very pretty, in her thirties and mad enough to spit. If she didn't, it was only because she was a lady with an M.A. from Yale.

"Hello, baby," he replied pleasantly. He was determined to be pleasant, and he knew that it wasn't going to be easy. She was full of questions, and they would all be hostile. "Wasserman. Frank Wasserman. Says so right here on my passport," he answered and waved the green plastic folder.

"Don't crap me, mister," she ordered bitterly. "I want to know what you're doing here. This is a delicate station, and I can't afford to have some cowboy come in and shoot the whole town up."

She'd be annoyed when she heard about the man he'd killed on the Ku-damm. It had never taken much to ignite her temper.

"You're looking great, Diane. Where's Siegenthaler?"

"I'm Siegenthaler, you bastard. Now let's get two things straight, mister. We don't want you here, and we don't need you here!"

Maybe there was something in the air that made everybody crazy here, the man whose passport said Frank Wasserman thought. It could be some kind of air pollution. What else would explain all the hostility?

"Don't holler," he advised.

"I'm the station officer, and I'll do what I goddam please," she practically screamed back. She'd put on five or six pounds, without any harm.

"Just checking in. Right, you're the station officer and I'm touching base the way I'm supposed to."

She glared, jammed a filter-tipped cigarette in a holder that contained another filter and reached for a match. Before she

found the pack, the man with the Magnum flicked his gold
Dunhill and lit her cigarette.

"What are you doing here? Why wasn't I notified till this
morning that you were coming?"

"Crash Dive," he answered. He pulled a small Canary Island
cigar from his pocket, bit off the end.

"Crash Dive? What's that?"

There was no way that he could tell her. "You can ask the
deputy director for Ops," he replied evasively and lit the cigar.
"It's his deal, Di."

"I should have guessed that you'd show up. Last week that
creep Duslov checked into town. He's as violent as you are."

The man who wasn't Frank Wasserman puffed.

"Andrei Duslov?"

"The same. He's attached to their part of the Allied Kommandatura over on Kaiserwerther Strasse. As if that isn't
enough, those Maoist crazies in the Lietzen-Stoller gang have
been shooting up the town. They ripped off a bank on the
Ku-damm about an hour ago."

Now *that* was interesting.

"I thought you gave up smoking, Di."

"Screw you!"

"You did for three years while we were married—very
nicely, too. You were a wonderful wife."

She stood up, and he thought she was going to throw something.

"I'm not your wife anymore. That was all over twenty-six
months ago. I'm the station officer, and this is my turf. I expect
some respect."

He nodded, puffed again on the dark Don Diego. "You want
me to salute, Di?"

Ms. Diane McGhee pointed at the door, jabbing her right
index finger like a dagger.

"Throwing me out again?" he asked.

"I never threw you out, you bastard. I should have."

He nodded in assent, started for the door.

"Level with me, are you going to make waves?" she questioned somewhat less stridently.

"Do my best not to," he promised.

He always did his best not to, she reflected after the door
closed behind him—but he always made waves.

Crash Dive?

What the hell was that? He wouldn't tell her, of course. He still had the same arrogance, the same determination to go it alone and do it his way. Just because they'd code-named him Merlin, the son of a bitch thought he could do anything.

10

If you'd boogie over to Fasanenstrasse 7–8, almost anyone at the Berlin Tourist Information Office there would tell you that the city has some dandy "meeting and congress" halls—great for conventions or really big bar mitzvahs. There's the Deutschlandhalle with sixteen thousand seats, the Sportpalast that can handle up to eight thousand and the Neue Welt that's real neat for groups no bigger than eighteen hundred. Smallest of the lot is the modern-modern Kongresshalle, designed by an American architect named Stubbins, who penciled in a 1260-chair hall but also provided lecture rooms, conference halls, closed-circuit TV and simultaneous-translation gear for five languages —plus several bars, restaurants, urinals and a lot of parking space. All these made it irresistible to the World Pathology Conference, and that's why Dr. Ernest Beller spent the afternoon there.

For the record, the building is kind of funny-looking— strange, anyway. The structure peers out from beneath a concrete slab with an odd double slope, which is why some jocular Berliners refer to it as "the pregnant oyster." Of course, Berliners have a wonderful sense of humor and are nice to visitors, which is a terrific help if you're surrounded by Communists armed to the eyeballs and aren't too sure exactly what U.S. foreign policy might be next year—or what British foreign policy is this year. France doesn't have any, which makes it simpler. Since there were more than seventy delegates from Marxist countries and no trouble was likely, Beller and the other pathologists from the West could ignore the ignoble political realities and concentrate on tissue sections and similar juicy delights until the day's session adjourned for a big welcoming 6 P.M. reception tossed by the local medical association.

Dynamite hors d'oeuvres.

Cocktails only so-so.

The man whom the CIA called Merlin was already several drinks ahead—on the other side of town. He'd been cruising carefully selected bars and strip joints since three in the afternoon, checking out hookers and hustlers and hipsters who might know where to find Bernard.

Blue Bernard.

He'd earned the name as one of the pioneers in Berlin's dirty-film business, having produced more obscene movies than almost anyone else in Western Europe during the previous decade. His "blue pictures" had earned him much more than a great deal of money. Blue Bernard was no hack porno prince, he was an "auteur," a creator. He also did some pimping and dope wholesaling on the side, just to keep in practice. According to the word around town, he shunned heroin as vulgar and supplied cocaine for the more affluent. At least that's what Merlin was told by the gay procurer with dyed red hair who suggested that Blue Bernard might be filming in a certain warehouse near Checkpoint Charlie, transit point to East Berlin.

"A class operation, that's what he said," Merlin told Bernard after the two burly guards had admitted him to the "studio."

"That's the only way I know," Bernard admitted with a shrug. "Go first cabin, or don't go at all."

It was a lie, of course. Bernard had done a big bunch of grubby things since he got his start as a seventeen-year-old back in 1945, stealing food from military depots. Bernard had always lied a lot, but with charm.

"Move it, Helga," he ordered as he offered Merlin a splendid Cuban cigar.

It was hard to tell which one was Helga. There were two very large women—perhaps two hundred and fifty pounds apiece—wrestling under bright lights in the middle of the "studio." They were covered with mud, and nothing else.

"Cinéma vérité," Bernard explained seriously. "With everybody and his uncle doing porno pictures these days, I had to get into something different. Can't just run with the pack."

"It's never easy for the true creator," Merlin confirmed.

Bernard puffed on his own large cigar, gestured invitingly

toward the cut-glass decanter filled with Asbach Uralt. Merlin poured himself an inch of the fiery German brandy.

"You see what those weird Swedes did to Bergman?" Bernard demanded. "Just over some lousy taxes. If someone could do that to a genius like Ingmar Bergman, you think I'm safe?"

Helga—or was it the other one—grunted loudly.

"Keep it down, will you?" Bernard snapped. He was a small, sharp-featured man, quite bald and rather vain about his hands, which he waved around considerably. "This is only a run-through, dammit."

"You in town for the Jerry Lewis Festival?" he asked as the American enjoyed the cognac.

"Among other things."

"Can't understand why his own countrymen don't recognize what a genius that man is—another Buster Keaton," Bernard said. Then he leaned closer to Merlin, spoke confidentially.

"You probably think those two are lesbians, *nicht wahr?* They're not. Helga can be very affectionate. She was a math teacher in Goslar. Eats practically nothing. It's a pituitary problem, they tell me."

Merlin finished his Asbach Uralt, decided against another.

"Now the other one—she's *kinky.* Well, my friend, it's good to see you back in Berlin. Despite those goddam terrorists, it's still a great city, isn't it?"

"Unique. Listen, I can see that you want to get back to the creative process. I just stopped by to say hello, and to ask whether you might help me with a little matter."

Bernard blew a sensational smoke ring. "What are friends for?" he asked grandly.

"Those terrorists—"

"Animals!" Bernard judged scornfully. Blue Bernard still believed in the old-fashioned German virtues of discipline, thrift and respect for private property. Unlike a number of people whom he was too decent to mention, *he* never ripped off other narcotics dealers' stashes or beat up their female employees.

"I'm—*interested*—in those people," Merlin said.

"A-ha!" The bald man's clever, nervous eyes flashed and skittered around like a schoolboy's hand-held camera.

"You might hear something, Bernard. You have many

friends and admirers, and they might hear *something,*" the American pressed cautiously in an insinuating tone.

"Possibly. I heard *something* just before you arrived," Bernard acknowledged. "A black Audi was found out in Charlottenburg early this afternoon. It had been stolen last night. There was a dead man in the front seat, with a large piece of his face missing."

"Moths?"

"Not according to the *polizei.* They have witnesses who saw a tallish man—about your size—blast him on the Ku-damm just after that bank was hit. The dead man was Egon Lietzen, Willi's brother."

Willi Lietzen was one of the senior terrorists, high on "wanted" lists all across Western Europe.

"You heard this on the news, huh?"

"It hasn't been broadcast yet. The bullet that killed Egon came from a large handgun."

Merlin flipped open his jacket. "Like this one?"

Bernard smiled appreciatively. It was a pleasure doing business with honest professionals. "I'll ask around. If I hear anything—"

"The Hilton. Room nine twenty-seven. Frank Wasserman."

"Danke, I have such a bad memory for names."

Merlin puffed on the corona. "Excellent cigar. There are two more small matters . . ."

"That's what old friends are for," Bernard assured him again.

"I'd like to pass a message to a Soviet officer at the Kommandatura. It's important that no one else get it—only Andrei Duslov. I'd bet that he lives in East Berlin, spends his days on this side of the wall. He's likely to be wearing a lieutenant's or captain's uniform—Red Army."

"But he's KGB? I've heard of him—a hard man."

Bernard shouted for more mud in German, turned back to his guest. Merlin had saved his life—or at least eleven years of it—when he helped Bernard avoid a jail term on some serious criminal charges back in 1970.

"What is the message?"

"I want to meet him tomorrow at four P.M. in the Dahlem Museum—in front of the Dürer portrait of Jerome Holzschuher."

"Shall I say Frank Wasserman?"

"Say the man who didn't kill him in Rio last year. He'll remember. No tricks. Please emphasize that—nicely."

Bernard bristled. "Have I ever spoken rudely to anyone? Now what about the final item?"

"I hate to impose," Merlin apologized.

"Please."

It was time to talk money.

"It is just possible that I might need some help for a few hours—in a week or two. Men such as those you have guarding the door."

"No problem."

"With automatic weapons," Merlin added. "There is a distinct possibility that automatic weapons might be required."

"They're familiar with several types of submachine guns. Do you have any preferences?"

They could have been selecting swatches of cloth at a Saville Row custom tailor's.

"I'm not fussy. I'll pay for them, of course."

"Preposterous," Bernard replied indignantly.

"A thousand marks a man."

"*Two* thousand—no charge for the ammo."

Merlin succeeded in stifling a chuckle, relit his cigar. One of the ponderous wrestlers was groaning as the elegant bald man walked his visitor to the door, and Bernard shook his head sadly. "Recommended by Fellini—both of them," he said.

"Federico Fellini?"

"His cousin, Murray. Does all his casting. I met him in a whip store in Milan last Christmas."

They shook hands, and Merlin thanked him again. "I'm not really sure that I'll need those fellows," he said as he handed over one thousand marks as a deposit, "but you never can tell."

The filmmaker stuffed the money into his pocket without counting it, his mind obviously on other things. Sincere concern dominated his face as he looked up at Merlin, put his hand on the American's shoulder. "Take it from me," he said earnestly, "the way things are today, two men with submachine guns can always come in handy."

Merlin took it—all the way to the Hilton, where he began to laugh as he entered the lobby. It was encouraging to know that half the tarts, thugs and criminals in Berlin would be looking for the terrorists. Unlike Murray Fellini, Blue Bernard and his people delivered.

So did the Canadian woman, the brunette who taught at McGill. Ernest Beller took her to dinner at a "rustic" Westphalian restaurant named Heckers Deele, and then to the Wertmüller film she'd missed in Montreal. It was called *Seven Beauties*, focused on how far a man will go to survive. Beller found the concentration-camp scenes troubling, especially when the male star said, "How did the world get like this? We all get killed and nobody says anything."

Beller was still thinking about this when he awoke beside the still-sleeping Canadian the next morning. He looked at his wristwatch, saw that it was only ten minutes to seven.

Too early to telephone the prison in Hamburg.

There was a man named Otto Kretschman in a cell there, and in four days Ernest Beller was going to kill him.

11

There was absolutely nothing new in the newspaper that called itself the *International Tribune*. Merlin was appalled as he read about another ferry sinking, drowning 204 people in the Ganges, another crippling strike by British manicurists, another terrible fire in a Chicago nursing home, another corruption scandal in Japan and another awful attack by Moluccan "freedom fighters" who had blown up Amsterdam's main sewage plant. Commandos wearing gas masks and hip boots were ready to fight their way in if the guerrillas didn't accept the government's final offer of three pounds of chocolate each and a month at the best hotel in Aruba—Modified American Plan.

"We recognize the sincerity of these misguided young men," the Dutch prime minister had told the press, "but we cannot compromise on basic moral principles. They'll have to pay for their own lunches. On the laundry—we're willing to negotiate."

The Dutch had guts, Merlin reflected as he finished dismembering half a grapefruit at the table that room service had brought. The West German authorities—fine chaps who offered great pension programs and top burial benefits—would have caved in on both the lunches and the laundry. They'd given that last group of hyperactive Palestinians six-packs of Löwenbräu, four different kinds of wurst and cuckoo clocks from the Black Forest. Merlin sipped at his second cup of good coffee, looked at the telephone. The whole idea behind breakfast in his room was not to miss the call. Duslov would—compulsively—make some change in the rendezvous, but it was unlikely that he could resist the temptation to meet once more.

The goddam phone didn't ring until ten to twelve.

"The crap is three feet deep in Amsterdam," a familiar voice blurted.

"Good morning, Bernard."

"Just got a phone call. Toilets backing up all over town there. Hippies blame the whole thing on the CIA, of course. No offense."

"Bernard—please—what about the appointment?"

"An hour earlier, three o'clock, same place. He said the same thing you did."

Merlin tried to remember, but it was still too early in the day.

"What?"

"No tricks."

Taking no chances, Merlin entered the handsome Dahlem Museum on Arnimalle at 2:30 to scout the building for traps. He wasn't the least bit surprised to find Duslov, only a few yards from their meeting place.

"Sorry to keep you waiting, Andrei," the American said with the slightest trace of sarcasm.

"I got here at two," the Russian replied in a tony BBC accent. "Had to check out the place for hanky-panky, and I wasn't going to waste the opportunity to enjoy all this glorious art. Just look at that Dürer!"

Merlin recognized the celebrated painting immediately. "Portrait of Jacob Muffel—that's the one on the hundred-mark note."

Duslov winced in his splendidly tailored blazer. "Only a capitalist-materialist such as you would equate art with money," he said scornfully.

Duslov was high enough in the KGB so they overlooked his exotic passion for non-Russian art. If he had a weakness, this was it.

"Magnificent," he judged warmly. "A treasure house, that's what this is. Only an asshole like you would set a meeting for our dirty business in such a place of beauty!"

"I only did it because I figured this was one of the few places you wouldn't be enough of an asshole to kill me," Merlin answered truthfully.

"Bang on," Duslov agreed. He was a trim, sandy-haired, blue-eyed man who might be forty but was surely professional.

Light on the Red rhetoric and heavy on the logic, he was among the best of the "illegals" operating abroad for the Committee for State Security. He'd actually gone to Oxford for two years when his mother was assistant agricultural attaché at the Soviet Embassy in London, and still took a keen interest in The Race. (See boat race: Oxford v. Cambridge.)

"I don't think much of your principles," Duslov confided, "but your analysis is bloody sound. Shall we go on to the Titian in the next gallery? There's a rather nice Raphael madonna too."

"I don't have any principles, Duslov," the American said as they walked, "but I've got a proposition for you. It is dirty, tricky and likely to cause several deaths."

"Naturally. I didn't think you'd waste my time with anything else," the Russian answered. He paused, took a long look at a Holbein the Younger portrait and sighed in satisfaction.

"It will be in our mutual interest."

"I should certainly hope so, old chap. Whom are we doing? I certainly hope it isn't another of those dreary Nazi conspiracies. I've had it right up to *here* with those, some time ago."

"Would I waste your time on one of those tired Nazi revival schemes? I'm not talking about a bunch of old slobs in trusses. I'm talking about a brand-new line, the latest thing on the market. How're you fixed for Maoist crazies?"

"Lietzen-Stoller?"

Merlin nodded.

"Why?"

"They're bad for real-estate values. I hear they blew up one of your bookstores downtown here last month. Hooked up with your Chinese chums, aren't they?"

"*Your* Chinese chums. What have you got in mind?"

Merlin shrugged.

"Nothing fancy. Let's find 'em and kill 'em."

Duslov wasn't ready to commit himself. "Would you like to see the Ravensburg Virgin in the sculpture gallery?" he fenced. "Fifteenth century, quite good."

Merlin shrugged again. "If you like. There hasn't been a virgin in Ravensburg in five hundred years, or at least I never found one. Say, do you know the story about the seven-hundred-pound lady gorilla in heat in the Central Park Zoo?"

"Don't be vulgar. Tell me, how would you suggest the work be divided—if."

"If Yuri likes the idea," Merlin completed.

Yuri V. Andropov was a bespectacled middle-aged man whose very name often inspired migraine headaches, coughing fits and sweaty palms. He was a top member of the Politburo with *two* keys to the executive toilet, and head of the KGB.

"He'll love it," assured the American. "Since your operation in West Germany is covert and you'd rather not have your illegals burned, I assume that you'd want to keep contact to a minimum. The same would go for all the clowns being run by the East German Democratic People's Lovable Marxist Eat-Your-Prunes-and-Shut-Up Republic."

Duslov looked up at the ceiling, wondered whether this could be the result of watching too many talk shows or was it excessive exposure to situation comedies?

"Please . . . please go on . . . simply," he appealed.

"We'll handle the killing. You wouldn't want to get involved in that anyway. Be lousy for your image with the student revolutionaries. Your crowd can help find them, and we'll finish the job."

"Only one connection: you and me."

"Deal?"

The Russian flicked an imaginary bit of lint off his lapel. "I'll let you know—day after tomorrow, two o'clock."

"Up by the Rembrandts on the first floor."

Duslov's eyes gleamed in anticipation of the two dozen Rembrandts, and he wondered whether the American might be more civilized than he'd suspected. Prevailing opinion at both Oxford and KGB headquarters was that the Yankees were oafs, but how could you be sure? The fact that they'd embraced the dribblings of Jackson Pollock and tinned veg—they'd call it soup cans—of Warhol wasn't entirely convincing. One visit to the Met on Fifth Avenue in New York had alerted Duslov that these capitalist dummies weren't such dummies.

"Take care of yourself," he advised Merlin as they parted. "Berlin can be just as dangerous for Americans as Istanbul."

Good old Andrei always had to have the last word, and the CIA man smiled pleasantly to show that he didn't mind this all-too-human imperfection. It was amusing, but not surprising, that Duslov knew about the incident in Turkey.

"I'll be careful," Merlin promised.

And he was. He checked several times to see whether the Mercedes taxi bringing him back to the Hilton was being followed, and when he entered his room he made another sweep with the scanner that looked like an electric razor. He slid open the plastic face, flicked the switch. The red bulb glowed, confirming that the detector was working. Then the dial swung, and he knew that there was a tiny FM transmitter somewhere within twenty feet of where he stood. It was well concealed, but Merlin had considerable experience, and finding was what he did best. It took eight minutes to find it, only seconds to decide to leave it alone. The model was a standard Japanese device sold to a number of intelligence services, so common that private detectives and industrial spies in a dozen countries used these regularly.

There was no way of immediately determining whose "bug" this was, but Merlin was in no hurry. Knowing that it was here would let him manipulate the listeners until he didn't need them anymore, and then he would destroy them and their toy with the dazzling efficiency that had earned him his name. He prowled the room searching and sniffing for other hostile hardware, assumed that there was some device in the phone and walked to a nearby post office to make the call to Frankfurt. The brief, noncommittal conversation with "Frau Braun" about shipping the "Italian typewriter" took less than ninety seconds. The "Italian typewriter" would be very useful, Merlin reflected as he wandered out into the warm afternoon sun.

The sun was still shining strongly when Duslov made his call fifty minutes later, but he didn't feel it. There was no air conditioning in the KGB's East Berlin headquarters, but everything about this place was chilly. The old building itself, the armed men at every floor and the damp cellar all radiated cold. There was no choice, however. This massive basement housed the Russian communications center that offered "secure" lines to Moscow, and Duslov certainly wasn't going to talk about this on a phone likely to be tapped.

"That is what he proposes, general," Duslov concluded.

There was a long pause. General Zimchenko was never one for quick decisions, a major reason he'd survived this long.

"What do you think, Duslov?"

Some senior commanders might have said "recommend," but Zimchenko was neither that polite nor that hypocritical. He didn't give a crap about what policy a subordinate might favor, since he made all the decisions. He was wary, but no phony. Unlike many other KGB chiefs, he'd never bothered with those new "management and personnel" courses.

"I'm inclined to view the project favorably, general."

The noise from Moscow was definitely a growl. "View the project favorably? Can't you talk straight? You sound like one of those damn toe dancers in the Ministry of Foreign Affairs. I think that overexposure to all those decadent paintings is rotting your mind!"

"Please, general," Duslov said as he watched the whirring scrambler attachment beside the phone.

"Socialist realism isn't good enough for you, huh?"

"We've been through this several times, general. Why don't we decide on the American's proposal?"

There was another odd sound—definitely rude. "I've decided. We'll go along—very carefully. If anything goes wrong, we'll blame them. Should be no problem with that. Even their own press blames the CIA for everything from clap to earthquakes."

"That's true."

"And if it works, we'll be rid of those Chink-loving lice who've been sabotaging proletarian solidarity."

Duslov recognized the quote from last week's *Pravda*, guessed that the skirmishes on the Manchurian border were getting worse.

"Keep me informed, Duslov. Watch your step. This is the same bastard who took out my wife's nephew in Turkey. When the job's finished, let me know where you do it."

"Do what?"

"Bury him," the general snapped impatiently and slammed down the phone.

Why did generals always want to kill people, Duslov wondered. He sighed, thought about the odd American whom he almost liked. Well, he wasn't going to worry about the CIA operative or any other Yankee. Duslov certainly wasn't worrying about Dr. Ernest Beller, for—like Merlin—he didn't know that there was such a person who would be flying to Hamburg to commit an act of violence.

On Pan American Airways flight 615.

Taxiing down the runway for takeoff right now.

12

The loud, insistent noise of the Teletype dominated the small room, making Beller frown as he tried to concentrate on the news reports unreeling before his narrowed eyes.

"What's up, frenn?" demanded the bulky man who loomed oppressively half a step behind the doctor's right shoulder.

"Urban guerrillas hit a police station near Buenos Aires this morning. Bazookas and explosives."

"Anybody kilt?" The accent was definitely deep Dixie. Like the speaker, whose heavy presence and booming voice made the room even more crowded, it could hardly be ignored.

"Nine police and seventeen guerrillas."

The Teletype seemed to stutter ever more loudly.

"Use' to be good country—*cattle* country, an' now it's ass-deep in Reds. Worse'n New Yawk."

A thin man in expensive German business clothes and gold-rimmed spectacles entered the room, silently joined Beller in absorbing news of the latest Mexican earthquake as the machine hammered on mindlessly.

" 'Course New Yawk's dirty too," the hearty southerner volunteered cheerily. "One thing you gotta say 'bout Hamburg —clean streets and plenny a tail. *Know* what Ah mean?" He had the chuckle of a lewd Santa Claus.

"The Reeperbahn area's famous for that sort of thing," the pathologist acknowledged. He started for the door.

"Nothin' beats a creep on the Reep. Strippuhs by the yard, bare-ass nekked right to their toes. Every damn kinda hooker you can 'magine. Over hunred of 'em in a great big cat house licensed by the gummint. Call it Err-ozz Centuh."

"Not Err-ozz. Ear-oss," Beller corrected as he tried to circle the beefy barrier.

"Been there too, huh?" smirked the fat man. "Found me a

dandy club called Madame Pomp-a-door. Two real big blondes with gallon jugs, best Ah *evuh* saw. Five, six littul chicks from Tie-land. Only tongue they spoke was French, know what Ah mean?"

Beller half-smiled politely.

"We shooah don't have all this wall-to-wall pussy in Austin!" the other American declared.

"And we don't have snipers at our university here in Hamburg!" the patriotic German executive broke in icily.

Beller took advantage of the confrontation to slide out into the hotel lobby. The Atlantic was Hamburg's finest, where sophisticated film tycoons such as Otto Preminger and obscenely rich oil sheiks' horny sons would stay when visiting the historic Baltic port that was West Germany's second largest city. Everything about the ornate lobby—from the lofty ceiling to the gleaming shoes of the green-jacketed bellboys—was posh. The stately-stolid exterior of the pre–World War II hotel didn't pretend to be contemporary, but the bathrooms were dazzlingly modern in their hardware, and Beller enjoyed the view of the Aussen-Alster lakefront. Water and the feel of the sea were basic ingredients in Hamburg's special charm. Dr. Beller liked the Elbe River, the two Alster "lakes" and the huge bustling port. He enjoyed the three hundred thousand buildings that survived the Allied bombing and respected the rather dashing new architecture, and he certainly had nothing against the two million residents of this prosperous metropolis.

Except Otto Kretschman.

Actually, Kretschman was an involuntary resident housed in a cell on the third floor of the massive old Kaiserwald Prison. The pathologist couldn't remember why they'd named a penal institution within the city limits as if it were in a king's wood, but he knew what Kretschman had done and where. The former S.S. officer had been in charge of the gas chamber that Hitler's regime had used to slaughter so many thousands—at Dachau.

That's why he was going to be first.

Hitler? Nobody mentioned Hitler, the doctor mused as he strolled out to look at the pleasure craft only two hundred yards away. The small boats made a pretty scene, and when he turned the other way he saw the impressive spires of Saint

Jacobi, Saint Katherinen and Saint Petri thrusting skyward. There was the pierced neo-Gothic tower of Saint Nicolai, tallest of all. Dr. Beller appreciated beauty in churches, music, women and other natural wonders—but he wondered why no one in Germany ever mentioned Hitler.

Were they trying to pretend that he'd never existed?

Were they so fearful of guilt that they couldn't even speak his awful name?

Why did that word—those two syllables—choke in the throats of so many who hadn't even been born when those terrible deeds were done?

These were the thoughts that zigzagged through Ernest Beller's mind as he walked away from the hotel, swinging the brown leather briefcase in the breeze. Hamburg was more than sixty-five miles up the Elbe from the Baltic, but there was still a taste of sea in the air. He walked for a long time until he came to a restaurant with a view of the port, and he was careful to order the local specialty—eel soup with ham bone and five kinds of fruit. The pathologist didn't mean to eat another meal in this city, and it would be a shame to miss the eel soup for which Hamburg was justly famous.

After he paid his check, he went to the men's room to put on horn-rimmed spectacles of clear glass and a false mustache. Checking his disguise in the mirror, the Dachau survivor was surprised to find that the mustache resembled Hitler's. He shrugged at the irony, went out to flag down the taxi that took him to Kaiserwald. Surrounded by twenty-eight-foot walls topped with guard towers, this big gray building looked exactly like what it was—a German penal institution built in 1912 —though it had been modernized slightly in 1956.

The chief warden was waiting for him.

"Everything is ready, Herr Doktor," he announced in German when Beller was ushered into his office.

He spoke German because the forged letter from the Ministry of Justice about Dr. Frohlich's research was written in German, and "Frohlich" was supposed to be an official from the health service in Berlin.

"There are only seven inmates here who meet your specifications," the chief warden apologized.

"They've all been here at least fifteen years?"

"Correct. One of them's been inside since nineteen forty-nine. You probably never heard of him—Otto Kretschman. Before your time, eh?"

"A bit," Ernst Beller lied.

He was Ernst Beller now, not Ernest.

Dachau, not Harvard.

"Interesting project," judged the chief warden. "Psychometric testing of long-term inmates to study the effects of prolonged incarceration."

The technical jargon flowed easily from this husky brown-eyed man's mouth. He was one of the new breed of administrators who'd replaced old-fashioned jailers in the progressive new Germany. He wore a sport jacket and a snappy tie, and there was no doubt that he had a master's degree in penology or sociology.

"Not study," Beller corrected. "Measure. That's why it must be done in each man's cell without any distraction."

"Of course."

The first was a narcotics trafficker who'd slain a customs inspector in a shoot-out down at the port, wounded two policemen before he was subdued.

The second was a sardonic pimp who'd disfigured one whore, crippled another in a Reeperbahn row that scared the hell out of the Spanish consul, who just happened to be busy in the next room.

The third was a bank robber who'd used too much explosive on a vault door, setting off a building collapse and inferno that claimed the lives of three firemen.

Kretschman was the fourth.

"I wish to protest," he said angrily.

What little hair he had left was graying, and he was fat and sulky after years of too little exercise and too much starchy prison food. The wide blue eyes were still the same and Ernst Beller recognized them immediately. Without warning, it was Dachau again and a little child was looking at a younger Otto Kretschman in boots and black Schutzstaffel uniform ordering prisoners into *that* gas chamber.

It was terrifying.

"I am an S.S. officer, and I demand to be treated with the respect to which a captain is entitled."

It was weird, hearing today's Kretschman speak but seeing the other one—a bizarre "voice-over" that resembled a poorly dubbed foreign film.

"I am an S.S. officer," he repeated—and Beller wasn't afraid anymore. The flashback ended.

"Of course, captain," he agreed easily. He told a series of well-rehearsed lies about the purpose of the "tests," assured Kretschman that the results would inspire the authorities to improve the living conditions of long-term inmates. It was fascinating to see how Kretschman still responded—after all these years—to reference to "the authorities."

The doctor asked several questions, took notes on the answers and went through a couple of rigmarole exercises that simulated measuring alertness, eyesight, reflexes and muscular tension. Then he told Kretschman to roll up his sleeves, lie down and touch his left ear with his right index finger—at the count of ten. As the S.S. man counted aloud, Beller opened the briefcase and removed the hypodermic he'd concealed in the hollowed-out memo book. It was a very small model made for research on children, but it held more than ten cubic centimeters of Pavulon.

"Six . . . seven . . . eight . . ."

At nine the pathologist plunged the needle into the S.S. man's arm, and Kretschman winced—but he didn't stop counting. He obeyed orders. "Ten," he said. After he'd touched his left ear with his right index finger, he opened his eyes.

"What was that test with the needle, doctor?" he asked respectfully.

It was now seven or eight seconds after the curare compound had entered his bloodstream. In twenty-two seconds he would be paralyzed, and in less than an hour he wouldn't be at all.

"Ability to cope with surprise and pain," Beller said. "No problem for a trained officer, I see. Would you now touch your right ear with your left index finger, please?"

The ex–S.S. man obeyed, and Beller glanced at the watch on the prisoner's wrist. Nine seconds to go.

"Captain Kretschman, I have something confidential to tell you. Your contributions to the Third Reich have not been forgotten. There are people who remember, and I am one of them."

The Nazi began to smile, but that changed as the curare hit his central nervous system. He tried to sit up, failed.

"You are dying, captain. You have lost the power to move or speak, and in something less than an hour your breathing mechanism will fail. Curare does that. Actually this is a synthetic curare developed as a muscle relaxer, and it's going to relax you right into your grave."

The wide blue eyes radiated bewilderment.

"My name is Ernst Beller. My parents were among those butchered at Dachau. I was there too."

The executioner recited his number, the building in which he'd been quartered and the date his parents perished.

"I know that you won't tell anybody, captain. Just think about it. You're the first. I have others on my list, but I'm honoring you because of my special feeling for Dachau. Goodbye, captain."

Beller left the cell, asked that Kretschman be allowed to rest for an hour—as he had with the first three. Then the doctor went through his charade with another inmate, and left thanking the chief warden for his cooperation. At 5 P.M. Dr. Beller was on a train heading south, somewhat disappointed that he'd be missing this evening's *Lohengrin* at the Hamburg State Opera. He wondered which fine tenor would sing the title role of the knight of the grail, and whether it would be as easy to kill the others.

Then he thought about his uncle back on Central Park West, and made a mental note to send a postcard from Frankfurt. Sick people and shut-ins always appreciated such gestures, and Ernest Beller knew that his aunt and uncle would be glad to hear how well the conference had gone. He certainly didn't want them to worry. That would be inconsiderate.

13

"He'll see you now," Miss Rasmussen said crisply.

Donna Rasmussen was a person to be treated with respect. She was not only the executive secretary to the deputy director for operations of one of the largest and sneakiest organizations in the world, but she was also the best female bowler on the entire CIA headquarters staff. Penny Levine had beaten her in 1974, but had been out of competition since being transferred to Buenos Aires.

Miss Rasmussen shook her head of blonde Minnesota curls toward the steel door, and Harper and Parks went in to face the deputy director. John Smith—people made jokes about his name—sat in a high-backed swivel chair behind a large desk that was ostentatiously devoid of papers. A standard General Services Administration pen stand, two multiple-button phones and a yellow legal pad stood out on the gray plastic top like blocks of color in a Mondrian print. There was nothing on the walls but a Friends of the Earth calendar. Smith cared about the environment, his daughter's chances of getting into Vassar and a great many things he couldn't discuss with his wife or his dentist. He was one of the first to have the new windows installed—the glass panes with the fine metal grids that blocked laser eavesdropping.

"Jackpot?" he guessed.

"No, Crash Dive," Harper said. "Merlin wants a Cyclops run."

Cyclops was the special computer programmed to handle all the terrorist groups, deeds, methods and relationships around the world. Everything about Cyclops was top secret.

"What kind of run?"

"Full scan on the Martians, including film and still photos. He says he needs it right away—urgent."

"He always wants everything right away, doesn't he?" Smith grumbled. "He's barely toilet-trained."

Harper shrugged, accepting the fact that Merlin's style annoyed a lot of headquarters executives.

"What's he going to do with it?"

"Something crazy," Harper said, irked by the fencing and enjoying the opportunity to lay it right on the line with the fussy deputy director.

"That's for sure," Smith agreed. "He never does anything like anyone else. Hasn't he seen all this stuff?"

"Twice," Parks offered with barely concealed hostility, hoping the deputy director would veto the run.

Smith looked at him, shook his head. It was tough enough to run agents like Merlin without coping with righteous types like Parks.

"Anything else, Bill?"

"Our audiovisual lady in West Berlin wants to know what the hell he's doing in her backyard. Very steamy Telex."

Smith leaned back, intermeshed his fingers thoughtfully. "What're you going to tell her?"

"I'll say he's taking a leak. After all, he's barely toilet-trained."

The deputy director solemnly chose to ignore this provocation. "She's a very capable person," he thought aloud, "and she's doing an outstanding job running a very difficult station."

Harper was about to reach for his pipe, looked around and saw no ashtrays. "She's the Eiffel Tower," he declared archly.

"That's a Cole Porter lyric. You're the tops, you're the Eiffel Tower!" Parks volunteered.

These bright young men were hard to take.

"What are you saying, Bill?" Smith asked patiently.

"She's doing such a terrific job that we had to send in Merlin. If you don't want to bruise her feelings, let him finish this mess —his way—and he can get the hell out of there!"

Harper wasn't the sort you could let talk to one of those goddam committees on The Hill, the deputy director reflected, but he was good at problem solving and thought clearly. Merlin had always done things—very difficult things— his way, and it was unrealistic to expect him to change. The Berlin unit and the other teams in West Germany had been unable to stop the Martians their ways—all the usual ways.

"Give him the Cyclops run—in the burn canister."

Harper would have sent the material in the special container anyway, for it was standard procedure to ship such highly classified information in the cans that would incinerate all contents if tampered with or improperly opened.

"You know she isn't going to take this?" Smith asked almost casually. "What do you think she'll do?"

"Something crazy," Harper judged.

The deputy director didn't conceal his puzzlement.

"Well, she was married to him for three years, wasn't she?" Harper reminded.

"Not as crazy as Merlin," calculated Smith. "I'll bet on that."

Harper believed in humoring top management, but he certainly wasn't going to take that kind of a sucker bet. "I'll get back to you on Jackpot tomorrow," he promised, and hustled out before the nervous deputy director could change his mind.

The two canisters left Andrews Air Force Base on the regular Monday-night courier flight, and Tuesday afternoon Merlin found the message slip asking that he call Mr. Siegenthaler. He didn't have to look very hard, for the clerk at the Hilton handed him the envelope. It is/was a credit to the fine CIA training at The Farm—that special educational facility tucked away in a corner of Camp Peary, Virginia—that he didn't call. Only a schmuck would use a nonsecure line in a city as "hot" as Berlin.

He went.

"These came in from Bonn for you," the station officer announced as she pointed to the two packages wrapped in heavy green plastic. She was making a genuine effort to stay cool, and Merlin was impressed. It would be interesting to know what she really felt, and even more interesting to hear how she knew he was at the Hilton since he hadn't told her.

"Thanks. Sorry to bother you."

He wondered whether she knew that there actually was a man named John Siegenthaler, a hip and influential newspaper publisher who might not enjoy having his name used for agency cover. She probably knew. She was terribly well read, and dynamite on both crossword puzzles and double-crostics. Steve Sondheim used to call her for help with words, people said.

"No bother."

What the hell was Crash Dive?

He looked at his watch, thought how beautiful and desirable she still was to him.

"Five o'clock," he reported. "Buy you a drink?"

What was he up to with that damn Duslov? She hadn't passed *that* on to Washington yet, and the thought that she might still care about this wild man was disturbing.

"Some other time. Keep in touch, Mr. Wasserman."

"I will."

He wouldn't.

He never had. That wasn't the way Merlin did things. Nobody ever knew where the hell he was or what this son of a bitch was doing, but he got things done in his own mysterious and private way and they all accepted him as Merlin the Magician.

Fraulein Cassel was leaving her receptionist's desk as Merlin walked out, and he gallantly held open the street door for the healthy young blonde. Healthy—she was built like a brick . . . library. That sounded *nicer,* Merlin thought as he appreciated her substantial physical endowments. He decided to stroll along with her, and within two blocks discovered that she'd completed high school in Evanston, Illinois, and returned to Germany with her mother four years ago when her American father died.

"They met when my dad was stationed here in forty-nine," she explained, "and I was born here. As President Kennedy said, *Ich bin ein Berliner.*"

His trained eyes automatically swept the shopping street ahead as they turned the corner, registered the young man cruising toward them on the motor scooter.

"That was fourteen or fifteen years ago," she added. "I guess the city's changed quite a bit. They've done a wonderful job of rebuilding, and that's certainly helped the tourist business."

She didn't ask him what he was doing in Berlin.

Merlin liked that.

"I'm told there's more crime in the past year or two," he replied.

"Not just here," she defended.

The fellow on the scooter was picking up speed.

"Everywhere," Merlin ratified. "That bothers me. One thing I can't stand is a breakdown in law and order—any kind of violence."

The man on the scooter ripped a purse from the arm of an elderly woman, roared toward them at top speed.

"It has to be stamped out," Merlin insisted sincerely.

As the scooter passed them, Merlin thrust the two packages into her hands, picked up a trash can and hurled it at the rider. The thief was sent flying into the plate-glass window of a delicatessen, and lay—unconscious and badly cut—sprawled among the assorted wursts and beer bottles. People were screaming. Merlin took back the packages without breaking his stride.

"That's what we have police for. It's up to them to protect us from thugs," he said coolly—and then he invited Fraulein Cassel to join him for dinner. She glanced at the shattered window, shrugged and suggested a pastry at the Hillbrich instead because she had an appointment for seven o'clock.

The atmosphere at the chic *konditorei* on Rankestrasse was excellent, and so was the sacher torte.

Her name was Freda.

She lived alone, and she was free for dinner tomorrow night, at half-past seven. It would be a great dinner, Merlin thought as Freda Cassel stepped into the taxi he'd flagged, and there was a definite possibility of a dandy breakfast too. He was humming as he returned to his hotel.

Some thirty-five hundred miles or so west—about fifteen minutes by ICBM—Greta Beller was also in good spirits. Not *that* good, but better anyway. Her husband's health was improving. Dr. Esserman had said that it would be a positive sign if Martin showed some symptoms of recovery—any kind of recovery—within the first three weeks after the stroke. It was nineteen days now, and Martin had just articulated—barely—his first word.

Ernst.

One word, with tremendous effort.

Ernst—a beginning.

"What about Ernst?" she'd asked, but her husband hadn't been able to say anything more.

He probably would in a week, or a month. There was no way to predict when, or what he might say.

14

While the city may not quite compare with such cultural centers as Paris or Florence or Leonard Bernstein, there are plenty of nice things to say about Frankfurt am Main. For two things, it was never invaded by Genghis Khan, and Elizabeth Taylor never got married there. Third, it was in a local research institute that Dr. Paul Ehrlich discovered the arsenic "wonder drug" arsephenamine, for which he got the Nobel Prize in 1908, and a lot of free drinks and sandwiches. Arsephenamine was good for syphilis, and Ehrlich was great for Edward G. Robinson, who did the role on the silver screen.

What's more, Frankfurt's on a river and that's dandy if you like sailing boats or watching barges. The Main runs into the bigger and splashier Rhine farther west, and the Main is also the reason for Frankfurt's name. Legend and travel writers concur that this spot is the easiest place to cross the river, a view apparently confirmed by the fact that the Romans built a bridge and a fort here about two thousand years ago. Before they could collect much in the way of tolls, the legions had the stuffing kicked out of them by the Celts—the horde, not the Boston basketball team. Then the Alemanni—a rough crowd with pagan gods, fur shirts and no barbers—whooped out of the tall timber to eject the Celts. This was obviously not too great a combination, because the Franks stomped the Alemanni and grabbed the river ford. That made it the Franks' Ford, or Frankfurt.

Scout's honor.

It really happened that way, about A.D. 500.

Ernest Beller had learned all about that and the eleventh-century customs house and the twelfth-century imperial mint and the first Frankfurt trade fair, in the thirteenth century, during his earlier visit in 1974. That had been a reconnaissance mission. He had scouted the terrain and the enemy's defenses, as had his ancestors who'd sent men to spy out the land. It was somewhere in the Old Testament. Beller remembered the quotation from his readings of Jerry Jeff Atkins's worn Bible, but couldn't quite place it this sunny day as he prepared to go into battle again.

Combat ready.

That was one of the proud expressions of the tough Special Forces troopers. Beller didn't have a heavily armed "A" team of Green Berets with him to take this objective, but he had no doubt that he could do the job alone. It was a demolition mission. The target to be destroyed was Dr. Egon Berchtold. Beller had done a good deal of research about the Nazi movement and era, and he suddenly recalled that a Josef Berchtold had edited the *Voelkischer Beobachter* and commanded the S.S. back in 1925. Perhaps they were related.

It didn't matter, Beller thought as he enjoyed the hot lather on his face. He finished shaving, carefully rinsed and dried the straight razor and washed his face of the last traces of soap. The bathrooms in the old section of the Parkhotel were bigger than those in the new annex added in 1970, and Beller preferred the old-fashioned space and comfort to the razzle-dazzle of the "modern" building. Both had floor-heated bathrooms and three-band radios and TV sets, the German businessman's notion of "international luxury standard." This was still the commercial heart of Germany, still the business and banking center of the nation. The first Rothschild bank had been launched here in 1798.

There were no Rothschilds here anymore.

There were practically no Jews of any sort in Germany, Beller reflected grimly as he buttoned his shirt. Berchtold had helped see to that. The room seemed to close in, and for a moment the pathologist felt a wave of dizzying fury. He had to get out—out of the room, out of the hotel itself. He quickly knotted his tie, slipped on a light jacket and picked up his slim black attaché case. He felt a bit better when he stepped out onto the Wiesenhuttenplatz three minutes later, but he didn't really escape that hemmed-in sensation until he reached the green and open area that was Frankfurt's famous Zoölogischer Garten. It was only a mile—perhaps less—from the hotel, but the zoo seemed much farther than that from the bustling center of town.

"Exotarium, *bitte?*" asked the ticket vendor.

Still not focused, Beller hesitated.

"You wish just the zoo, mein herr, or also our wonderful Exotarium?"

The man had recognized Beller as an American.

"Two marks—zoo. One and half more for Exotarium. Animals not in cages in Exotarium. Very modern."

Beller paid the higher price, wandered in and walked through the main section of the zoo until he found himself facing a tiger. He sat down on a bench, watched the huge cat pacing for a while and then unlocked his attaché case. He took out the top file, relocked the leather box and flipped open the manila folder.

The face in the first photo hit him like a club.

Egon Berchtold—monster.

The pathologist hated all the murderers in all the files in his case, but he felt a special enmity toward this degenerate. Yes, this man was a physician—like Beller—who had betrayed his ancient oath to serve humanity and committed unspeakable experiments and atrocities upon prisoners at Ravensbrück. He'd been the right hand of Professor Karl Gebhardt, Himmler's boyhood friend who rose to lieutenant general in the S.S. and directed the horrors committed by obedient Nazi physicians at a dozen camps. Dr. Gebhardt had been hanged by the neck until dead on 2 June 1948, the photostat of the *New York Times* clipping said, but Berchtold had gotten off with a sentence of life imprisonment.

There was another clipping on Berchtold, an item in the U.S. Army's *Stars and Stripes.* Gas-gangrene wounds. That's what he'd done to young Polish girls, let them fester and swell up with poison—and die. Berchtold had killed so many Polish girls that the S.S. had promoted him to the rank of major, *Sturmbannführer.* Now it was Sturmbannführer Berchtold's turn to die.

How could a fellow doctor do these things?

Ernest Beller studied the photo of the hawk-faced man in that terrible uniform, flipped to the picture of the Barbarossa Prison. The Holy Roman emperors had been crowned in and

ruled from Frankfurt for centuries, and this penal institution
had been named for one whose memory still warmed German
historians and patriots. Charlemagne had once governed from
this city, but it was Barbarossa, more warlike, for whom the jail
was named in 1935. That was the Hitler era, and Hitler had
designated the attack on Russia "Operation Barbarossa." Perhaps that explained it.

But *how* could a physician commit these atrocities?

Beller looked at the photo of the sturmbannführer again,
wondering so intently that he didn't notice the guide approach
with the group of tourists. "The Frankfurt Zoo is one of the
finest in Europe," the guide announced. "There are many
excellent zoos in Germany. We are interested in such educational projects, and you have probably heard of the big one in
Berlin. We believe that ours is better, and I think you'll agree
after I've shown it to you. Please follow."

They did, leaving Beller alone in the hot morning sun. He
thought about what the guide had said. It was true. The cities
of Germany had more first-class zoos than those in other European centers. Why? Did that explain why this civilized nation
had been so efficient at caging millions of people, at building
those human zoos?

"Who knows?" the bitter boy from Dachau said aloud.

He shook his head, aware that talking to oneself was not a
good sign. He locked his papers away, stared at the tiger. Beller
decided that he didn't like zoos. It wasn't that he disliked
Germans, for he was, or had been, German himself, but he
disliked zoos. Uncle Martin would probably attribute it to
childhood trauma, he thought as he walked aimlessly and un-
seeing past the animals, and Uncle Martin was probably right.
Whatever the reason, Ernest Beller knew that he'd never visit
another zoo again.

He bought a small box of dark chocolates on the way back
to the hotel, and when he was alone in his room he opened the
box and—quite deliberately—ate three of the dark rich can-
dies. Then he took a small bottle from his toilet kit, drew the
hypodermic from its hiding place and injected the Digilanid—
very carefully—into the bottoms of nine pieces on the left side
of the box. Digilanid was a water-soluble digitalis compound
that in this dosage would be fatal for a person with heart
problems.

Berchtold had survived two minor heart attacks in 1969 and 1972.

And he loved chocolate.

Ernest Beller had done his homework well, had cultivated a medical assistant from Barbarossa back in 1974. He'd met several of the prison staff at a bar near the jail, loosened their tongues with drinks and encouraged them to gossip. He knew the Digilanid ought to work, but he had to check on one more detail first.

The Hauptbahnhof, Frankfurt's central railroad station, was only three blocks from the hotel. Frankfurt itself was a major communications hub, and this station handled trains from scores of cities in Western Europe. That traffic explained why the Hauptbahnhof news kiosk carried papers from many places—including Hamburg. Making his way through the streams of travelers, Beller bought two Hamburg dailies and returned to his room to examine them.

There it was.

A little item on page twenty-two, down at the bottom.

Otto Kretschman had died in his sleep at the age of fifty-eight of *natural causes,* less than a year before he would have been released.

They didn't suspect a thing. It was safe to go ahead, and Ernest Beller went—to Barbarossa Prison.

It looked like a warehouse for people, a large box—rectangular and four floors high—that filled an entire block. Beller could see where they'd repaired the damage caused by a couple of errant U.S. Army Air Force thousand-pounders. While Frankfurt hadn't been pounded nearly as badly as Hamburg or Berlin, some sections of the city had sustained plenty of damage. The quaint old Sachsenhausen area on the other side of the river and the neighborhood around the vast I. G. Farben headquarters building were barely touched, but the streets around the Goethe-Haus und Museum on Grosser Hirschgraben near the main square and the area where the prison stood weren't that lucky. The repairs were still visible if you looked for them, especially on the north face of the jail.

"The exterior may not be too impressive, Herr Holstein," admitted the assistant warden, "but we've spent—excuse me —you people in Bonn have spent more than three million marks in the past four years to reequip our educational and athletic facilities. That's why we're always so glad to welcome anyone from your department. Would you like to see our woodworking shop?"

Herr Holstein, who looked twenty-five years older than Ernest Beller in his gray wig, smiled politely with an expression that suggested chronic constipation. It was a great part, and the would-be actor enjoyed playing it.

"You are too kind," he replied. "We only do our job. That's what we dull bureaucrats are supposed to do, *nicht wahr?*"

His slight accent suggesting Westphalia was nearly perfect.

"I wish that I had time to inspect," he continued, "but I only have an hour or so before my train. As I wrote, I'm here on the Detweiler matter. The investigators in the Office of the Special Prosecutor believe that this old doctor you have may know something. You're familiar with the Detweiler business, of course."

"Only via the television news," lied the assistant warden with an apologetic chuckle. "Terrible, isn't it?"

There was no Detweiler affair. The letter on the forged stationery of the Ministry of Justice had transmitted a yarn about charges that a biology professor at the University of Cologne had committed war crimes in Ravensbrück; Herr Holstein—legal assistant to the deputy minister—would arrive to question this Berchtold, who'd worked at that camp.

"It's the times," soothed the pathologist. "My own grandchildren hardly read at all. How is this Berchtold? He's had heart sickness, I understand."

"He seems all right now. We've got him assigned to helping in the infirmary. Does quite well, they say. Hard to believe he did those things."

This man and so many others didn't want to believe it, and that angered Ernst Beller. The anger helped with the role.

"I trust that you're not questioning German justice," Beller demanded harshly.

"Oh, no. Not at all. I'm certain that the trial was entirely *correct*—and so was the judgment," the prison official blurted.

Two guards brought Berchtold into the room, and the assistant warden left hastily so that the important functionary from the federal government could proceed.

"Sit down, Dr. Berchtold. My name is Holstein. I'm from the Ministry of Justice in Bonn."

The monster sat down.

"We're conducting an investigation into the wartime activities of a Dr. Wilhelm Detweiler, and I'm sure that you'll cooperate with the authorities."

"Of course."

Beller opened his attaché case, took out a folder—and the box of candy. He ate one—from the right side.

"Terrible habit," he confessed. "I'm trying to lose weight. Here—you have some."

The former sturmbannführer hesitated.

"You'll be doing me a favor. You can eat them all, if you like. My wife would be delighted," Beller said heartily.

Then he began the questions about the nonexistent Detweiler, stretching out the inquiries until the monster had consumed eight of the nine treated pieces. Beller counted carefully as he "took notes" on a large pad.

"So you never saw this man at Ravensbrück?"

"Never. Of course, it was a large installation."

"Did you ever hear of him—anything at all?"

"Not before today, Herr Holstein. I give you my word."

Beller managed not to laugh at this obscenity, thanked him and watched the guards take him away.

The pathologist was back in the Parkhotel within thirty minutes, and as he tipped the bellboy who'd carried his luggage to the front door he glanced at his watch.

The digitalis would be working by now. It would start blocking the normal electrical conduction in the heart, and the monster would begin to feel nausea.

Would he recognize the first symptoms?

Would he taste the fear?

The bellboy loaded the two suitcases into the rented car, and Beller put the attaché case on the front seat. The gray BMW was a well-built car, a standard model that wouldn't stand out too much in anyone's memory. The last of the poisoned candy had been flushed down the toilet, and the burned ashes of the box were swirling in the same sewer. It was time to go.

Dr. Beller drove carefully, sorry that he hadn't had the opportunity to enjoy Frankfurt's famous Palm Garden. Ernie Beller appreciated—no, enjoyed—flowers, and this was one of the most splendid displays in all Europe.

Traffic slowed to a crawl near the former I. G. Farben headquarters, currently the HQ of the U.S. Army's V Corps. The Americans had renamed it to honor a dead general named Creighton Abrams, but that wasn't on Beller's mind as he drove.

He was thinking of the sturmbannführer.

In a few more minutes the bastard would be vomiting, and then he'd *know.* He was a doctor. Even if he hadn't practiced in years, Berchtold could not help but identify the chilling signs.

Heart attack!

He'd be screaming for help—just as those Polish girls had.

Beller finally reached the autobahn heading east, slid the BMW into the swift stream of cars. He turned on the radio and heard the latest single of an emphatic German rock group named Kraftwerk, a driving "heavy metal" sound probably meant for younger ears. After the Caterina Valente ballad that followed, the announcer noted that it was 6 P.M.

Egon Berchtold would be hallucinating by now, and the orderlies in the prison infirmary would be struggling to hold him down. Who had held down the victims of those grisly medical experiments in Ravensbrück? the pathologist wondered. Who had responded to their fear and agony?

Beller found himself driving faster. It was easy on this fine road. Everybody was cruising along at seventy-five and the pace was hypnotic. Mile after mile, record after record, the avenging doctor raced through the growing darkness. Nearly two hours slipped away—somehow—before he broke the spell and pulled off at a gas station to refuel. As the attendant gave him his change, Beller checked his watch again and nodded.

The heart palpitations were reaching their peak, and the pump in the sturmbannführer's chest was bucking and twisting wildly. Berchtold would be terrified, sweating, chalky, scared frantic. Within a matter of minutes the monster would be dead.

"Good," Beller thought aloud.

"What?" asked the attendant.

"Nothing. It doesn't matter."

The pathologist was smiling as he drove off into the night. He'd found a station broadcasting the Bach Partita in B-flat Major, the Wanda Landowska recording made in 1936. The road was straight, the night was cool, the music was lovely, and

the monster was dead. Egon Berchtold? He was a doctor—like
Ernest Beller—and he had the same initials. For one moment
the pathologist wondered whether they might have anything
else in common, whether he himself might harbor some
deeply buried demon such as the one that let/made the other
physician do those hideous things.

No, it was just a coincidence about the initials.

It was merely an interesting coincidence.

15

"Meet Heidi," Blue Bernard said.

"Pleasure to meet you, ma'am."

"Charmed," Heidi answered.

Some people might have considered Heidi a freak, for a 195-pound transvestite in a parody of a Courrèges gown is a bit unusual and certainly stands out in a crowd.

Not this crowd.

Merlin looked around the screening room at the bizarre group Bernard had assembled, decided that it resembled the mob you'd get at a wedding between Dracula's dentist and one of those ladies who run the enema-and-flogging ads in porno publications. There was a large Danish blonde in a black leather suit, carrying a riding crop that she swung with casual expertise. There were a couple of Asian hookers—probably from Malaysia or Indonesia—pretty creatures with serene dimpled smiles. Three or four gay young men—or was one a woman?—and a cluster of hard-faced types who might be enforcers for some narcotics tycoon trailed an elegant sixty-year-old grande dame—who herself trailed the expensive scent of something that cost $80 an ounce.

"How good of you to come," Bernard said politely.

"I hope this will be amusing," answered the madam of two of the most expensive brothels in Berlin.

"Her late husband was an admiral," Bernard confided a moment later. "Supply department. Left her a piss pot of money. She's only in business to avoid ennui, if you know what I mean."

Before Merlin could answer, a Persian or Lebanese gentleman wearing about $1200 of the best clothes Roman tailors and bootmakers can offer slid into the room. He glanced at a scar-faced Greek and a husky Bavarian, blinked and forced out a thin smile.

":They're armed," Merlin observed.

"You'd be, too, in their business. The import trade is quite competitive," explained the porno prince. "As a matter of fact, their organizations had some active disagreements only last Easter."

"Nice funerals?"

"The best. I myself sent over four hundred marks' worth of flowers in ten days. Ah, here's Sandor and his talented daughter."

More pleasantries.

"What does she do best?" Merlin asked when they were out of earshot.

"Women, I think—but that's not what I meant. Did you notice their hands? No? *Pity.* They're the best pickpockets in the country. They have twenty or thirty people out on the streets working for them—all good craftsmen. It's a quality operation."

A brunette beauty with a rhinestoned eye patch arrived with a fat man who had a Doberman on a leash, striding haughtily past three blank-faced types who wore the impersonal expressions of taxi drivers but were actually car thieves. A dozen other raffish folk sauntered in, and when they were all seated Blue Bernard addressed the meeting.

"I want to thank all of you for coming on such short notice, and I assure you that we won't keep you too long. You're all busy, hard-working people, executives with many responsibilities of your own. I appreciate your willingness to help, and I celebrate the generous aid of old and good friends."

The admiral's widow inserted a three-inch joint in a jeweled cigarette holder, lit it and drew deeply on the best Thai stick money could buy. She eyed Merlin appraisingly as if he were a prize bull, making no effort to conceal her carnal evaluation. The CIA man smiled, turned his attention back to Blue Bernard as a tall albino slipped in and dropped into a seat in the last row.

"Better late than never, Erwin," Bernard said archly. "Well, I'll turn the floor over to my friend, Frank."

"We're going to show you some film," Merlin declared.

"Something *interesting?*" said the madam in tones that a Marlene Dietrich might use to seduce a Greek shipping millionaire.

"I hope so. If you're not entirely immune to money, it should be interesting. I myself would not find fifty thousand marks boring."

She blew the smoke out, nodded benignly like a gracious countess—who moonlighted as a nymphomaniac

"I wish to find these people, and they do not wish to be found."

"Is it a game?" asked the brunette with the eye patch.

Merlin shook his head. "Not the way they do it," he said. "These people kill. Roll the film."

The room went dark, and the face of a towheaded young man abruptly flickered onto the screen.

"Willi Lietzen . . . age twenty-nine . . . height about five feet ten . . . weight one-sixty . . . born in Düsseldorf."

Fast dissolve.

Medium shot. Daylight. Exterior. Pan with Willi Lietzen in a crowd of students, first marching . . . then shouting . . . then throwing rocks at the police.

"Active in communist youth groups at University of Bremen, and then started his own Maoist unit at law school here in Berlin four years ago. Clever, tough, knows three languages, believes in random violence to shake up the government and the system. He's the planner, and he's killed at least seven people in the last two years."

Jump cut.

Close-up. Female face.

"Marta Falkenhausen . . . twenty-six . . . top student in political science at Humbolt University . . . daughter of Colonel Sigmund Falkenhausen, who worked with Oskar Dirlewanger in Poland . . . reported to be Willi Lietzen's girl friend . . . known to be an excellent shot. Bagged three policemen in Munich just after Christmas."

It was the face Merlin had seen staring hatefully from the back of a black Audi on the Ku-damm. Now the camera pulled back to show Marta Falkenhausen waving her arms as she addressed some rally. She didn't enjoy being photographed. The sequence ended with her making an obscene gesture at the cameraman.

Merlin heard the tinkle of an airy laugh in the dark room, and he knew that it came from the admiral's widow.

Jump cut.

Long shot. Night. Exterior.

Runners carrying torches charging over a hill in some track-and-field competition.

Tighten and freeze focus on a heavy racer with thick legs and shoulders.

"Werner Buerckel . . . age twenty-seven . . . star athlete at high school in the Saar . . . son of a miner . . . very strong but not exactly a mental giant . . . worked in the mines for six years . . . killed one man with his bare hands and more than a dozen with explosives. He's their demolition man, bank vaults or buildings or people. Said to carry explosives with him all the time—like a security blanket."

"How disgusting!" Heidi wheezed hoarsely from somewhere on the right side of the audience.

"Is he crazy?" asked a Hungarian-flavored voice as the film changed to show Buerckel in a street fight between two hostile groups of young demonstrators.

"He looks *very* strong," someone noted shrilly, almost hopefully.

"He *is* strong, and some doctors might call him crazy. I'd say he's completely loyal to Willi Lietzen, and dangerous. This is the man who bombed the Soviet Friendship Bookstore in the middle of the afternoon, not at night, when it would be empty."

The next face was almost swarthy, wide.

"The late Paul Stoller. Political assassination was his bag. You may remember that several schoolkids were maimed the day he tossed the grenade at the mayor. His politics were so extreme that he considered Stalin a Nazi—and Mao too. Great chess player, they say."

Now the screen blossomed with the face of the machine gunner Merlin had slain.

"He's dead too, shot escaping from that bank robbery a week or so ago. Willi Lietzen's kid brother, full of cheap slogans and free-floating hostility. Hated everything from ice cream to ball-point pens and sunny afternoons—a creep."

Someone in the back of the little theater yawned loudly, but Merlin—and the film—continued.

Paul Grawitz, who stole and drove cars.

Fritz Kammler, an army deserter who knew how to handle and repair the basic infantry weapons used by the West German ground forces.

Karla Lange, who had an advanced degree in electrical engineering and was rumored to be connected with an Arab terrorist organization in Vienna.

"Terrible hair," a woman's voice said.

Karla Lange was very plain, to put it generously.

"She has several scars on her body," Merlin continued. "She was burned in a fire when she was only nine."

*"Fab*ulous!"

This was not a healthy group, Merlin told himself, and hardly representative of the sensible new breed of decent post-Hitler Germans who believe in generous health insurance and pension programs and free trade unions. He told himself that twice, and then he called for the lights.

Blue Bernard thanked everyone, touched lightly on the fifty thousand marks again and blew the audience a big kiss of appreciation. The admiral's widow blew one back—at Merlin, flashing a look that guaranteed a visit to her place would surely be interesting. Merlin waved airily, wondering what the folks in the deputy director's office would say when they heard he'd committed fifty thousand DM—sixty-five thousand if you included Bernard's commission.

The admiral's wife had a pink tongue, Merlin thought as he left the screening room—a little pink tongue like a cat. Well, she was probably no stranger than some of the people who taught school in northern California or served on the London County Council last year. Merlin rarely wasted time with words like "strange," for they were subjective—like rich, virginal or anthropomorphic. "Prunes"—now that was a word Merlin could handle. "Shoe" was another.

All right, she was strange.

Merlin didn't care.

Would you call those college-trained executives in button-down shirts and discreet ties—the dedicated public servants who told him whom to track and destroy—*normal?* They were so spaced out on patriotism and official procedures and forms in quadruplicate that they probably considered Merlin odd, he thought as he watched the eye-patched brunette wiggle out with her escort.

Marvelous wiggle.

"When will you have the stills?" Bernard asked.

"I was hoping that you might know someone who could run them off—without too many questions."

The last phrase struck Blue Bernard as funny, so he smiled. "I know such a person. He printed those splendid photos of the Danish blonde and the three men in chains, the ones they sell outside the big hotels for twenty marks a pack. He never asks questions, and he's fast."

"Has his lab in the back of a truck," Merlin joked.

"How did you know? We'll get the pictures of these thugs out within twenty-four hours. . . . Mario, *stop* that!"

One of the departing moviegoers was fingering a .32 in his belt, eying a business rival with obvious hostility.

"Don't be an idiot, Mario. Must you embarrass me every time I invite you anywhere?"

Mario left scowling, and Bernard shook his head. "You see the sort of animals with whom I have to deal? Is it any wonder that I've got to kick ass a lot?" he grumbled to the American.

"Can't get good help anywhere," Merlin agreed and handed over eight hundred marks "for expenses." Blue Bernard would take a commission on the still pictures, of course, but he'd probably charged his own mother for his baby photos. Merlin wasn't going to fret about such minor details, for his mind was already focused on the 10 P.M. rendezvous. The imminent delivery of the Italian typewriter was reassuring.

So was walking out into the street, for it reminded Merlin of the hundreds of thousands of law-abiding Berliners who constituted more than ninety-five percent of the city. They might violate a traffic regulation or cheat just a bit on their taxes, but they didn't sell dope or make obscene films or kill people. It was unfortunate that Merlin could walk among these proper burghers and still be so far from them, and someday he'd have to think about that more. He might even consider doing something about it, as his former wife had so often suggested.

Someday.

Not tonight.

He walked into the Ballhaus Resi at 9:51, just a trifle early, as always. He couldn't help it; they'd trained him to take this precaution and it had saved his life at least twice. Situated at Hasenheide 32 at the corner of Grafenstrasse, the Resi is a Berlin institution like the Brandenburg Gate or Spandau Prison. The Resi is a dance hall, one of the best-known in the city. The Walterchens Ballhaus over on Bulowstrasse is known as "the widow's ball" because its patrons are "mature" and the women here ask the men to dance—sedately. The Resi is known as "that telephone place." It offers a water show with colored lights and a stage show locals consider quite lively, but what makes the Resi's repute are the telephones and message chutes on each table.

Especially the telephones.

The place seats some eight hundred at numbered tables. One or three walk in, check out the tables that each seat five and select someone who looks attractive. You can then send a written invitation to dance to "the short lady in the blue dress" at table 46, or you can direct-dial her via the phone on your table. It's simple, but clean—and it works. Berliners and visitors come here to find dancing partners, drink beer and develop meaningful relationships of all sorts—even respectable. The tone is wholesome and cheery, honest.

Merlin sauntered in, let his eyes adjust and then scanned the tables just as if he were seeking a trim young woman whose skills included the fox-trot. There seemed to be quite a few already dancing to the fourteen-piece band, and many others, in twos and threes, sitting and waiting. There—over at table 19—was his "contact," drinking beer and smiling and chatting with a buxom Swabian nurse who was simply crazy about "swinging Berlin." Now they were dancing.

Merlin found an empty chair at table 37, mumbled something to the two computer programmers already seated and pretended to listen to their bawdy jokes about the rumps of the women at the next table. A waiter took his order, delivered a large stein of dark beer. Merlin checked table 19 again. The son of a bitch was still dancing. Now the phone on his own table rang, and a female voice invited him to join the fun.

"Table thirty-four—I'm in pink."

The woman looked pleasant, about thirty and probably nonhomicidal. Clean breath and good disposition were important, but the nonhomicidal part was decisive for Merlin these days.

He hung up the phone, began to rise—and then it rang again. One of the computer team answered it eagerly, then handed the instrument to the American.

"Who is this?" asked a voice he knew well.

"Merlin. When did you get in?"

"It's a charming place, isn't it?"

The CIA man glanced across at table 19, saw his "contact" grinning.

"It's a noisy goddam tourist trap," Merlin said, "and you picked it. You always pick lousy places with crowds of people —*always.*"

"There's one too many now."

Merlin got the message immediately, finished his beer and left—with the woman in pink at table 34 glaring at his back. He walked two blocks down Grafenstrasse, turned right and stepped into a doorway. He listened tensely, heard nothing.

Rubber-soled shoes.

The man who was following him had to be wearing them. He would be quiet, and he'd be armed.

He was.

At that instant a husky man in his thirties seemed to step out of nowhere, a frown on his face and a 9-millimeter P-1 handgun in his fist. The weapon was only half-drawn, but that gave Merlin little comfort. He felt even more distress three seconds later when the man pointed the pistol right at his stomach.

Who the hell was he?

Russian?

One of his ex-wife's loyal troops?

Maoist crazy?

Commercial mugger?

Merlin never got to ask. He didn't get shot in the gut either. Another man—who'd been sitting at table 19 less than four minutes earlier—stepped out of the darkness. Like most of the people Merlin knew, he too had a handgun. It wasn't one of the West German weapons made at the new Walther plant at Ulm, it was an American-manufactured .357 Magnum, good for punching holes in walls or disemboweling people.

The man with the .357 Magnum hit the man with the 9-mm. Walther on the back of the head, hard.

The man with the Walther fell forward, breaking his nose bloodily on the sidewalk.

It was fast and ugly, and almost silent.

"And you always hit people too hard," Merlin continued as if the telephone conversation hadn't been interrupted.

"You're welcome."

"Didn't I say thanks? Okay, let's get him off the street."

They dragged the unconscious stranger into an alley, searched his wallet. According to his papers, this man was a thirty-eight-year-old television repairman named Manfred Hassel, owner of a 1974 Opel and a resident of the Charlottenburg section of town.

"What do you think, Angie?"

Angelo Cavaliere, who had learned most of the ways of the world during three years in U.S. Army Military Intelligence and nine in the agency, shook his head contemptuously.

"TV repairmen never carry nine-millimeter Walthers," he said. "They all pack Smith and Wesson thirty-eight Specials like the Japanese police. This guy's a phony. He's not bad on tailing, though."

Merlin paused in his rifling of the wallet. "We work for the same company. You can trust me," he appealed.

"I saw him pick you up outside the hotel at four. He's got some good moves, must be a pro."

It was nice to know that Angelo Cavaliere—sometimes referred to as the Italian Typewriter—was covering the flanks. Cavaliere, a dark-haired man who combined substantial shrewdness with the reflexes of a cobra and a huge collection of still photos from horror movies, was a skillful and unobtrusive colleague who knew how to operate in Germany. His family had wanted him to become a doctor, but Angie hadn't enjoyed the sight of blood—so now he was earning $24,000 a year as a secret agent.

He was not cruel.

Some employees of certain cloak-and-dagger organizations might have been angered by the failure of the wallet search, and when the man with the bleeding face moaned they might have done something intemperate—such as kick him in the belly or left ear. Angelo Cavaliere wasn't that sort of barbarian. The good Jesuits hadn't brought him up that way at all. When the stranger who wasn't a TV repairman named Manfred Hassel groaned a second time, Mr. Cavaliere suggested that they put him in a large trash can, and they did. Then they pushed the lid on, and headed for the street. Merlin spoke when they reached the end of the alley.

"Angie—"

"Yeah?"

"We've got to stop meeting like this."

"It wasn't my idea," Cavaliere said defensively.

Then Merlin walked out onto the street and turned back toward the Hilton—with his protective shadow not far behind. As Merlin picked up speed, he checked his watch again and began to walk even faster. Fraulein Freda Cassel, who worked at the Amerika Haus and served great breakfasts, was waiting in her bed—and Fraulein Cassel didn't enjoy waiting.

16

Everybody gets born, but there are a million ways you can do it. Some are born rich, others premature, quite a few as Chinese, and a few theatrical types check in as Siamese twins —on the cusp between Libra and Scorpio. It is better to be born in the summer because you'll have a bigger chance of survival.

Merlin was born American, lucky and optimistic—a trifle too optimistic. Freda Cassel was not in bed when he reached her small but pleasantly furnished apartment. It was a good eleven or twelve minutes before she got into bed, but when she put her head on that flowered pillowcase she surely did her best to make up for lost time. Uninhibited, strong and joyfully physical, she celebrated their new intimacy with an exultant enthusiasm that was also tender. She was more than qualified to work at the U.S. cultural center, but the history of American jazz and musical theater wasn't all that she knew very well, Merlin judged as he finally slid off into deep sleep shortly before two in the morning.

He didn't dream at all.

He was that contented, that sated.

The smile was still on his face when the smell of coffee and the softness of her warm lips awakened him at five after eight. She wriggled easily out of his sleepy efforts to embrace her, announced the time and suggested that he could just squeeze in a shower before breakfast. Neither the lavender-scented soap nor the almost wholly transparent shower curtain surprised him, for they fit this splendid and sensual young woman. He was thinking about her unabashed animality while toweling himself dry.

"Wow!" she said.

Merlin looked up at her in the doorway.

"What a body!" she admired.

"I get a lot of compliments on my tits," he admitted.

"It's your boyish legs. For a man of your age—"

"I'm twenty-three—and a half."

"You're crazy," she said happily, "and breakfast's ready."

Orange juice, sausages and eggs, rolls and coffee.

"Just like home," he approved between chews.

"You can take the girl out of Chicago, but you can't take the Chicago out of the girl. More coffee?"

"No, thanks. Freddy, you're a wonderful woman."

He'd almost said "girl," but remembered that some contemporary females found the usage inflammatory and/or patronizing. He didn't know that much about this lady yet. *Lady?* Christ, that was another word that got young women pissed.

"I hope you haven't got the wrong idea about me," she said as she rose from the table.

"What do you mean?"

"Just because we made it on the second night—"

"Perish forbid," Merlin assured her. "Freddy, I think you're a person of class and distinction."

"I'm no easy lay," she said en route to the sink with the dishes.

"I am."

She shook her head. "I'm twenty-six, and I have no social diseases—and I'm no saint."

Merlin looked impressed. "How'd you like to run for vice-president?" he asked.

"And I don't lie!"

"There goes your political career. Are you sore about something, honey?"

The way she was charging back to the table was definitely menacing, but she didn't hit him. She picked up the coffee cups, glared at him from about two feet away. "I don't tell people phony stories about doing research for a TV documentary about the Joe Louis–Max Schmeling fight!"

"The second fight. We're going to dramatize it. Diana Ross is playing Louis," Merlin said amiably.

"And Barbra Streisand's doing Schmeling, I suppose?"

"Dynamite idea. Can I help with the dishes?"

She replied from the kitchen. "You can tell me why the hell

you're wearing some kind of bulletproof vest and why you carry a gun, you son of a bitch!"

"For a moment there you sounded just like my ex-wife," Merlin noted truthfully. "You go to Yale?"

"You go screw yourself, Frank Wasserman—or whatever your name is. Is it really Frank Wasserman?"

"A rose by any other name would smell as sweet. That's Shakespeare, hon," he volunteered.

The clatter of dishes announced that she was still furious.

"I'm an insurance investigator," he "confessed" abruptly. "New Haven Mutual wants me to bring home a man who heisted nearly six hundred thousand in diamonds and jelly beans from a triplex on Park Avenue. I've traced the gent here, and he's got some rough friends. That's why I go heavy."

She stood in the doorway again. "Is that the truth?"

"Honest Injun," he swore effortlessly.

"And your name is Frank Wasserman?"

"On my mother's grave."

He didn't tell her that his mother's grave was empty because the old lady was in such terrific shape that she'd just won a trophy as the best female tennis player over sixty in the entire state of Florida. Freddy Cassel hadn't asked, and it didn't matter that much anyway. What counted was mutual trust and respect, and a lot of good clean sex never hurt either. As a matter of fact, the idea occurred to Merlin a moment later when they embraced, but she had to get to work.

He could wait until evening.

So long as she believed his story everything would be all right.

The hot June sun and Lady Luck were both smiling when the intelligence agent and Freddy Cassel reached the street, for a taxi appeared at once, a nice surprise in this quiet neighborhood with light traffic. The Hilton was on the route to the Amerika Haus, so they had barely completed plans for the evening when he kissed her and stepped out into the glare. He watched the cab roll off into the herd of vehicles that thundered through the heart of the city.

"Well?" asked the cabdriver as the taxi pulled away from the Hilton.

"It's going well," Freddy Cassel said with a smile.

"He doesn't suspect?"

"Not a thing," she guaranteed as the cab turned off the Ku-damm toward 21–24 Hardenbergstrasse, where she had to be at that receptionist's desk in seventeen minutes. She was, as usual. The director of the Amerika Haus liked Freddy Cassel, who was always on time and did her work so well and so cheerfully. If only all the staff were like her his life would be so much simpler.

17

"Eins . . . zwei . . . drei . . . vier, eins . . . zwei . . . drei . . . vier," the tall bald man chanted as he jumped and clapped his powerful hands over his head rhythmically.

Sigmund Falkenhausen did an hour of exercises every morning, and another hour each night. In between he tossed in some of those Canadian Air Force routines pitting muscle against muscle, tension techniques designed to keep him fit. Some people might call him a physical-fitness nut. He had been called much worse by the judge who sentenced him in 1952, and the epithets uttered by the racially impure "mongrels" who testified against him certainly couldn't be published in either the London or the Nippon *Times*. Those hysterical outbursts by vengeful non-Aryans hadn't really touched him, and today the jokes of the guards about his rigorous regimen of calisthenics didn't reach him either.

Colonel Falkenhausen *knew* that he was right.

He always had been, and always would be.

He was stronger, smarter, better in every way—for he was a member of the Master Race. History would surely confirm him and his actions, and now it was only a matter of time until the weakness and stupidity of the current German government and the mongrelized Americans and Britons brought the whole tottering structure crashing down in disaster. Another war with the Slavic swine—perhaps a nuclear holocaust— might be necessary to prove that Der Führer was correct in every detail, but it would come. There was, after all, nothing wrong with purification by fire. Der Führer himself had spoken of this; and if the fire was the ball of heat produced by a hydrogen bomb, that didn't matter. Sigmund Falkenhausen didn't believe in the tooth fairy or Father Nicholas, but he was confident that a marvelous new Nazi world was coming.

Men such as Brigadeführer Oskar Dirlewanger were still free, working and planning for that great day. They'd never captured *him*. The major general was too wily, too sly an old poacher to be trapped in the nets of the fools who'd been hunting him since the collapse in 1945. Even Himmler had called Dirlewanger "an original." What if he *had* spent 1935–37 in prison for some "offenses against a minor," and what if his later units consisted of convicted thieves, poachers and petty criminals drafted from a dozen German prisons? They'd served the Reich well, butchered more than twenty-five thousand Red guerrillas and sympathizers—lots of civilian sympathizers—in White Russia. The Dirlewanger Brigade had proved its toughness in the final cleanout of the Warsaw Ghetto in 1944, killing so well that the command was increased to a full division—a Waffen S.S. division—and Oskar got the Knight's Cross.

Then he'd vanished like smoke.

There had been rumors a few years back that he was training "shock units" for the Egyptian Army, and other stories that he was in Spain or Argentina. Wherever he was, one could be sure that shrewd old Oskar was preparing men and weapons for the next offensive. He wasn't sitting around getting fat and sloppy. He was staying fit, mentally and physically. You could bet on that.

"Eins . . . zwei . . . drei . . . vier," he repeated, enjoying the trickle of sweat running down his back. This was good, healthy Aryan perspiration, reminding him of the hard work and victories of the past. All the lies the vermin had told the scummy International Military Tribunal at Nürnberg couldn't change that truth, that glory.

The other prisoners in the gymnasium looked at Falkenhausen, said nothing. Like most of the guards, they thought that the former colonel was probably dangerous and surely mad. They were common criminals, unable to comprehend Sigmund Falkenhausen's profound commitment and philosophy. They could be taught. Dirlewanger had started with jailbirds, welded them into a crack security outfit feared by millions. Many lies and slanders had been spread about the brigade, Falkenhausen brooded without missing a beat, but his pride in the unit's achievements was much too strong to be shaken by the filthy innuendos of dirty little men.

Nothings such as Kraus.

The ex-colonel eyed him contemptuously, staring furiously at the prison guard who derided the Dirlewanger division as "rabble who could only murder women and children." Rolf Kraus delighted in repeating the ugly lies of his father, a stupid man who'd been an artillery *Feldwebel* with one of the Wehrmacht units chewed up in the Ukraine. It was no wonder that Germany had lost the war, Falkenhausen told himself, with lousy sergeants in howitzer batteries mocking the contributions of glorious S.S. detachments.

"Eins . . . zwei . . . drei . . . vier."

"What's the matter, colonel? Can't you count any higher than that?" Kraus challenged.

The other prisoners laughed. They didn't fully understand why Kraus despised Falkenhausen and everything he represented, for the guard had never spoken to them of the shame. His father had returned with one arm and the bitter conviction that the horrors committed by the "elite" Nazi "security" outfits had dishonored the German Army, had degraded the Wehrmacht's tradition by making it an accomplice in evil. The armor of those Teutonic knights that stood in a dozen museums now "stink of the criminals who tainted Germany's place in military history," the artilleryman had told his son again and again, and it would not be easy to erase the stain. It could not be glossed over or ignored, and until it was faced squarely the shame could not be expunged.

That's why Rolf Kraus hated Sigmund Falkenhausen.

Shame.

"Time to knock it off, old fella," the guard said a moment later.

That wasn't true. Colonel Falkenhausen had a mental clock that told him he still had a full two minutes, and he was fed up with this nasty harassment. Falkenhausen had been doing his exercises day after day—month after month—year after year —and he knew his rights. He had a full hour. That was in the *official* regulations, the *written* rules.

"Eins . . . zwei . . . drei . . . vier," he called out in righteous defiance.

The other inmates scattered, sensing what was to come. They all realized that Falkenhausen was some sort of haughty fanatic, a seething compulsive ready to explode at any time.

They'd heard about the horrible deeds, how Dirlewanger had injected Jewish women with strychnine so his staff officers—including Falkenhausen—could enjoy watching their death throes as an appetizer before dinner. That's why he was a leper among these burglars, swindlers and street brawlers, even more of an outcast than the child molesters.

"Move your butt, stupid."

That was when Falkenhausen went crazy.

In a single wild leap he was upon the guard, and before Kraus could raise his hands the screaming ex-colonel began to beat him savagely. He knew how to hurt with his hands and feet, and he was in top physical condition, like a man a quarter of a century younger. He punched, kicked, smashed and battered Rolf Kraus to the ground, enjoying the release of the hostility that had been pent up for so many years. He heard the shouting somewhere nearby, but ignored the noise to concentrate on his enemy. Yes, it was good to hit and hurt the enemy again. Let them all see what a fit and trained S.S. officer could do, even at this age. Sigmund Falkenhausen moved in for the kill.

Blackness.

It was as if someone had pulled the plug on the only lamp in the room.

The "someone" was a pair of guards named Hegel and Sprenger, who produced the instant darkness by hitting Falkenhausen with clubs. Hegel struck him in the pit of the stomach with the traditional MP's thrust to the solar plexus, and Sprenger slammed him across the back of the head—twice.

Total blackness.

Tuesday, 4:58 P.M.

Bright sunshine.

Thursday, 11:10 A.M.

Same location: the bulky Franconian castle known as Schloss Gillenstein, set on the edge of a green forest overlooking Nürnberg. A prison for "difficult cases" since the reign of Kaiser Wilhelm, this turreted redoubt wasn't nearly as historic as Schloss Rosenau near Coburg or the tenth-century castle at Pottenstein. It was at least four centuries younger than the great fortress at Lauenstein. Nürnberg's most famous castle is the twelfth-century Kaiserburg, and Gillenstein's only claim to fame outside this region of northern Bavaria is that this is where some of the Nazi war criminals were kept during their 1946 trials before the International Military Tribunal.

Sigmund Falkenhausen knew Nürnberg well, and not because of its fine medieval structures or its reputation as the toy capital of Germany. He had been here several times for those fantastic mass rallies the führer would address in the vast Zeppelin Wiese, and he had roared with the others—thousands of others—when the deranged spellbinder had promised them that they would rule the world. It wasn't going to happen today, or tomorrow either.

Unless Dirlewanger helped him to escape.

Even after all these years, Falkenhausen couldn't believe that the general had abandoned him. His commander would inevitably return to break him out, to free him to join the new and surely successful crusade to conquer the planet for the Aryan race. Even now in this cramped cell, his gut and head still hurting, Colonel Sigmund Falkenhausen lived on his faith that the S.S. comrades would come.

Let the prison psychiatrist laugh or doubt.

The others had not forgotten Sigmund Falkenhausen.

The ex-colonel wasn't entirely wrong. There were several people in West Germany—and a few in Israel, Argentina, Britain and the United States—who remembered him quite clearly. One of these was a man who'd checked into Nürnberg's Crest Hotel—near the entrance to the autobahn—a day earlier. He carried a tape recorder, a letter from the features editor of the Manchester *Guardian*, a handlebar mustache and the faintly tired clothes of a working but not too well-paid journalist. His speech confirmed that he was a British journalist with a college degree from some lesser university, not Oxford or Cambridge.

"One of those red brick places," guessed the manager of the ninety-room hotel on Münchenerstrasse.

He, too, wasn't entirely wrong.

There was some red brick up at Harvard, plenty in surrounding Cambridge.

At 11:10 A.M. on this warm June morning, Geoffrey Donald Cuthbert parked a hired gray BMW sedan just below the eighty-four-foot-high walls of Schloss Gillenstein. The prison might not be the biggest castle in Franconia, but its walls were impressively lofty and it had a great moat. A moat is almost useless without a drawbridge, and Gillenstein had a fine metal-studded and -striped model that still worked. Walls made of huge blocks of stone and a functioning drawbridge were two things about this place that Ernest Beller would remember.

"We pull it up every night and lower it in the morning," the warden said as they sipped coffee in his office. "Damn thing makes a lot of noise. We grease it, of course."

"Of course."

Why was the warden looking so uncomfortable?

Did they suspect?

"Even with a grease, it makes one terrible clatter," the man behind the desk rambled on, his eyes darting about uneasily.

Why was he stalling?

Was it a trap?

"God's will, I suppose," he told the pathologist. "It may seem old-fashioned, but I'm a religious man. I take my God seriously. Brought up that way. Solid Catholic education."

Beller nodded, thought about his own upbringing. His uncle and aunt had leaned over backward not to "impose" any formal religious beliefs on the orphan, fearful lest anything resembling dogma or rigid rules might "inhibit" his "free and natural development."

"I never had much religious training," Beller said. "My—my father was a doctor, and I suspect that religion seemed a bit antiscientific to him. No, *un*scientific—almost medieval."

"God will forgive him," the warden predicted benevolently. "Now about this Falkenhausen whom you want to interview . . ."

"Yes?"

The warden shifted in his chair, blinked twice. "You know that modern penology tells us that there's no such thing as a prisoner beyond redemption, Mr. Cuthbert?"

The avenger nodded.

"Well—this Falkenhausen—he's *difficult.* I can't remember another case quite so complex in my career."

What the hell was he saying?

"I don't believe in capital punishment, you understand, but this inmate really strains my progressive thinking. I try to view him with Christian charity. The best I can do is to wish that he were in a mental facility, some institution for the criminal insane."

Beller wasn't sure about what was happening, but it wasn't supposed to happen like this.

"When can I see him?"

"He's violent," continued the warden. "Violent and dangerous. He attacked one of the guards two days ago, without warning. Beat him badly. He might have killed him if two other correction officers hadn't intervened."

"Yes?"

"He's *vicious*, Mr. Cuthbert."

"I don't understand what you're saying."

The warden cleared his throat. "You can't see him. He's in an isolation cell. No visitors for at least a month. That's my decision, and nothing will make me change it. I'm sorry."

"But I've come all the way from Bonn. You promised—"

The warden stood up, signaling his desire to end the discussion. "I must apologize. You'll have your interview—in August or September. There's nothing that urgent about this, is there? He's not going anywhere, you know."

"I could be dead by then," Beller pleaded, "or he could."

"Not him. He's as healthy as a young ox, and a lot more trouble. I'm asking that he be transferred. Well, that's it. I regret the inconvenience."

The prison official spoke as he was walking—no, herding—Beller to the door. The words were courteous enough, but the tone had become perfunctory and the doctor sensed that further talk would be useless.

"Keep in touch, as they say in American films," the warden told him in his best public-relations manner.

He'd failed.

Beller wasn't discouraged, of course.

There was always Plan B.

18

It was all a matter of timing.

He'd learned that from the Special Forces men, the experts in demolition and guerrilla. If you found that the defenses ringing the target had changed, the assault team had to change the plan of attack. If the weapons weren't right for this situation, the commander of the strike force had to select and acquire new weapons.

Improvise.

Then hit the target at the precise moment when the foe was weakest, was least ready to cope.

Beller had a number of weapons and identities and plans, so now it was a question of using one of his alternative schemes. The conversation with the warden at Gillenstein had suggested which to select—the one he'd originally scheduled for The Bitch.

Now it was a question of timing.

Within forty minutes after Beller returned to his hotel, he'd checked out the various Catholic churches in this city of 510,000. The most beautiful and impressive Catholic house of worship was Saint Lorenz across the Pegnitz River, a Gothic structure begun in the thirteenth century and adorned by a splendid rosette window and a superb wood-carving by the great Veit Stoss—both famous throughout Germany. Damaged in the Allied bombing and rebuilt with funds donated by an American whose ancestors left Nürnberg more than two centuries ago, Saint Lorenz would surely—*almost* surely—be where the warden would be on Sunday morning for the noon mass.

It had to work. Beller enjoyed a satisfying lunch of Nürnberger bratwurstel—the grilled local sausages—and sauerkraut with dark beer at a restaurant appropriately named Bratwurst-Hausle on the town square, then wandered out to enjoy the city. He had nothing to do until Sunday morning, and there was no point in wasting his time. The former home of celebrated painter Albrecht Dürer was interesting, but Beller enjoyed the toy and doll museum on Karlstrasse just as much. He'd always had a special fondness for toys. The Nürnberger Philharmoniker was giving an all-Haydn concert in the ultramodern Meistersingerhalle "dedicated to victims of fascism" that evening, and performed so well that Beller got a particularly good night's sleep. Some might prefer Bruno Walter's interpretation of the Allegretto movement in the *"Military"* Symphony no. 100, but this one seemed sound and left Beller quite satisfied.

After breakfast he found himself thinking about the toys again. It was childish, of course, but he smiled just thinking of them and headed downtown to the city's well-known toy shops. Mechanical toys—along with the pocket watch, the clarinet, gun casting and the first geographical globe—were invented in this nine-hundred-year-old trading center, and the local toy shops were still among the best-stocked in Europe. No one knew Ernest Beller here, so the doctor spent fifty happy minutes, without the least embarrassment, enjoying the diverse and complicated delights of the big Spielwarenhaus Virnich on Luitpoldstrasse. For some reason that he didn't remember, he hungered for toys the way some little boys lust for candy. It was an appetite that could hardly be sated, one almost surely linked to the nightmare of his early years. The exact origins of the obsession could probably be identified by six or seven thousand dollars' worth of psychotherapy, if one wanted to make the investment.

Ernest Beller didn't. All he wanted was to kill certain people, and to enjoy the simple pleasures of the toys.

When he'd watched or touched or tested almost every item in the store, he walked on to the shop named Herbst at 17 Gibitzenhofstrasse.

Trains.

That was the specialty here. His eyes gleamed as he entered the store and saw the first wonderful display. Sensing a possible sale, a clerk threw a switch and the freight began to move. It was five minutes to eleven.

At four minutes before eleven, another freight train rolled

into sight. Beller couldn't see it, for it was more than three hundred miles west of Nürnberg, near a large industrial city. Others watched it slow down for a curve. They wore the coveralls of track workers, three men who didn't belong to any of Germany's powerful unions but rather to a group that Merlin and his CIA colleagues called the Martians.

Willi Lietzen.

Paul Grawitz, who stole cars.

Werner Buerckel, explosives expert.

Lietzen held a small walkie-talkie to his ear, nodded. "Here they come," he said.

The train that swung around the curve was headed by two diesels, hauling some nineteen flatcars loaded with brand new Volkswagen sedans, a multicolored mix of Rabbits and Dashers. There was another car, a green Opel that sat motionless on the track. As soon as the train engineer saw it, he slammed on the brakes. The freight lurched and shuddered to a grinding halt less than ten yards from the sedan. Son of a bitch! The scared and sweating railroader stared at the Opel, swallowed the last of his shock and fear and stuck his head out of the cab to get a better look. He saw the trackmen.

"What the hell's going on?" he asked angrily.

"It's a revolution!" Willi Lietzen explained as he produced his gun. "Get down immediately and you'll be all right."

The engineer hesitated for several seconds, not realizing that Willi Lietzen spoke literally. Since the railroader didn't climb down immediately, he wasn't all right.

He was dead.

Lietzen shot him between the eyes with a 9-millimeter automatic. The leader of the Martians wasn't that great a marksman; it was just a lucky shot. A moment after the corpse fell out, the assistant engineer scrambled down hastily. Buerckel and Grawitz climbed up, moved quickly through the automobiles. Each VW had one window open a bit because of the summer heat. The terrorists slipped their brown-paper-wrapped packages inside the sedans, racing against time.

"Fifty-two," Buerckel reported when he climbed down from the train.

"I told you to prepare at least a hundred," grumbled Lietzen.

"Ran out of stuff."

Lietzen shook his head. Ran out of brains was more like it. Surely Che and Mao had had better helpers than these simpletons.

"Then get some more—*please*. Okay, Paul, let her roll."

After Buerckel had moved the Opel off the tracks, Grawitz set the train in motion—leaped off just as it got under way. Even as he jumped, the chief of the Martians was busy with his walkie-talkie. Two cars pulled up less than ninety seconds later. Karla Lange was at the wheel of the black Fiat, Marta Falkenhausen in the station wagon. Lietzen looked at his watch.

"Everything all right?" Karla Lange asked.

"We'll know in about twenty seconds. Cover this moron, will you?"

While the women pointed submachine guns at the dazed assistant engineer, the three men stripped off their coveralls and stuffed them into canvas airline bags.

"Five seconds," Marta Falkenhausen announced in expectant tones.

"What do we do about *him?*" Buerckel wondered.

"I *told* you, Werner. Handcuffs. Remember?"

At that instant the first bomb went off with a flash of noise and fire. The other incendiary weapons blew up in swift succession, wrecking the cars on the train, charring shiny new VWs into twisted hulks. It was all right, Werner thought, for Willi had explained that much of the VW stock was owned by the corrupt and exploitative West German government.

"Wünderbar!"

Whatever people might say about Marta Falkenhausen, she was no anal-retentive. She was always generous in complimenting others' good work, whether it was blowing up a building or shooting a policeman. That was one of the main reasons that Werner Buerckel liked her so much. She knew just as much political theory as Lietzen did, and yet she didn't have to put comrades down all the time. Well, almost all the time. Even Willi Lietzen was smiling now as he watched the train recede, trailing smoke from the burning autos.

The train kept rolling.

"May I help you?"

Beller looked up from the moving toy freight, saw the sales

clerk hovering politely. The pathologist checked his watch. Eleven minutes. He'd been enjoying this countertop exhibit for eleven minutes, and now they were getting just a tiny bit impatient. The clerks at Herbst were used to adult males who were fascinated by the toy trains, and they certainly never crowded these "children of all ages." This particular employee really thought that the man in English clothes might be ready to buy.

"No, thank you," Beller said. "You've got some very fine trains here."

"Best assortment in Bavaria, people tell us. I can see you're a train buff, sir. Why don't you look around? We don't pressure people to buy at Herbst, you know."

"I'll be back."

The truth was that Ernest Beller was a little embarrassed as he stepped out into the street. His mind knew that there were many men on both sides of the Atlantic—probably on both sides of the Pacific, too—who were still fascinated by toy trains. Their wives probably kidded them about it, wondered why they spent so much money on those elaborate model railroad setups in the spare room or cellar. Still, the very phrase "toy trains"—a misnomer—made Beller feel childish.

He felt better a minute later. He found a Bible in the bookstore across the street, thought with his eyes closed about the quotation that had been bothering him since Frankfurt. Spying out the land? *There* it was. Right, the land was Canaan. Book of Numbers, of course. Chapter 13, verse 17.

Ernest Beller didn't waste the time to look up the Old Testament admonition about "an eye for an eye, and a tooth for a tooth."

He knew that one by heart.

19

Something was happening to Ernest Beller.

He wasn't clear in his mind as to just what it was, but something was fermenting—down deep. It didn't have a name yet. Perhaps his uncle could identify it or give it a label. Uncle Martin was a well-trained analyst who had both a great deal of experience and considerable intuitive skills. He rarely spoke of this intuition because his colleagues were so sure and so proud that their work was scientific, that their way was as precise and orderly and measurable as the methods of other physicians who dealt with infections or tumors. It had taken them decades to win the acceptance and respect of the others who had X rays and laboratory tests to detect their enemies, who could count things and prove things.

The pathologist thought about this as he walked through the streets of the old section of Nürnberg that Saturday morning. He remembered the few occasions when his uncle had spoken about the intuition—the "trained intuition." All kinds of doctors came to use it sooner or later, he'd confided. Not wildly, but shrewdly and intelligently. Even though they didn't talk about it with lay people, it was understood in the profession and was nothing to be ashamed of really.

Poor Uncle Martin.

Now he couldn't talk at all.

If he could, he'd surely do something to interfere with Ernie's vengeance. No, it wasn't vengeance but rather punishment. Uncle Martin wasn't the least bit religious and took the Bible as interesting folk myth, and if you spoke of "an eye for an eye" he'd likely say something about hating your father. So far as Ernie knew, he didn't hate either of his parents, whom he'd last seen in *that* pit—just the beasts who'd put them there. Yes, that summarized the Third Reich. The beasts had put the people in the pits—a weird reversal.

Something was happening to Ernest Beller, and whatever it was, it was bothering him. He could feel it, like the menace in a house your stomach senses is really haunted. Something was making him walk faster than he wanted to or needed to, and something was pushing him into a part of the city that he'd already explored. Pausing to avoid being pulped by a Würtzberger beer truck, he thought carefully and wondered why this *thing* seemed murky. He was still confident that logical step-by-step analysis would produce the correct answer.

It had something to do with the warden.

The man who ran the prison at Schloss Gillenstein had made some remark, planted some seed that was now putting out roots. Beller could feel them sprouting and growing in his unconscious, growing stronger by the second. Religion. Yes, that was it. The warden had spoken of his strong religious training and convictions, and now Ernest Beller wondered why he himself had been given neither. What had he missed? Was this the reason that he felt alone and outside, unable to enjoy the communal warmth shared by those who had religious identities?

He was sweating now.

His throat was dry.

The pathologist hurried on, caught himself just before he would have collided with an elderly woman turning the corner. The dark glasses and cane said that she was blind. Goddammit, Beller thought, I could have knocked her sprawling into the traffic.

She sensed his nearness, coughed. "Would you accompany me across the street?" she asked in matter-of-fact tones devoid of self-pity.

"Of course."

He tried not to ask the question, failed.

"Was it the war? Who did this?"

The white-haired woman smiled. "I lost my sight only nine years ago, long after the war. No, it wasn't American or British bombers, young man. It was God."

God, again.

God and some odd quest for guilt were a strange combina-

tion, Beller brooded after he left her. No, he didn't feel guilty.
They had asked for the bombing. They had blasted the cities
of other nations first, and he certainly had no doubts that the
aerial punishment was justified. God—*any* god—would sanc-
tion such just retribution. The tribunal that had called those
gory official deeds of the German government "crimes against
humanity" was right, but Beller was strangely relieved that
this woman in her seventies hadn't been blinded by Allied
airmen. As a rational person, Ernest Beller realized that it
would be less than fair to blame all Germans for the horrors.

He would have to keep that in mind.

Suddenly he was there, facing the strange magnet that had
drawn him to this place. It wasn't U-shaped at all, but formed
in the outline of a six-pointed star. The Jewish symbol over the
door of this nineteenth-century building marked it as a synagogue, the only one left in this city of more than half a million.
There had been several in Nürnberg before the "non-Aryan"
population was slaughtered in the Holocaust. Now there were
a few hundred Jews instead of many thousands, and these
survivors needed but one place of worship.

Beller heard the chanting, froze. The sounds of the ancient
song drifting from an open window paralyzed him.

It didn't make any sense. Ernest Beller had no religious
education, hadn't even visited synagogues except for some
fifteen or sixteen weddings and funerals. Still, these five-thou-
sand-year-old prayers seized him. Dr. Ernest Beller, who was
Phi Beta Kappa at Harvard and ranked in the top quarter of
his class at Columbia's medical school, was a prisoner of a god
whose very language was a mystery to him.

Now he heard the high voice of a young boy, and he guessed
that there might be a bar mitzvah service in progress. Beller
had never made this ritual passage to manhood, hadn't
thought about it seriously until his visit to Gillenstein. This
prayer of affirmation—it had to be that—held him hypnoti-
cally, touching something that the medical scientist hadn't
known existed. Only vaguely aware of what he was doing, Dr.
Ernest Beller walked to the temple and opened the door.

The sight dazed him.

There were only thirty or forty people in the chamber. The
walls were almost bare, and there were none of the trappings
of a wealthy, healthy congregation. These were the survivors,

the ones who had endured. These were the stubborn ones, who wouldn't go and wouldn't die—yet. Most of them were in their fifties or sixties, but Beller hardly noticed them. His eyes locked on the splendor of the Torah, and the thirteen-year-old boy in silken prayer robe nearby.

Shaken by a complex torrent of emotions that had nothing to do with any book he'd ever read or course he'd ever taken, Beller stared helplessly. It was, somehow, awesome. It was also frightening, this powerful mystery for which no one had prepared him. He would surely reason all this out sensibly in due course, but he wasn't ready to cope with this now. Dr. Beller looked at this scene he'd never forget, nodded and closed the door.

Too much.

He walked away with dry lips, eying the storefronts for a bar where he could buy a stein—perhaps two or three—of cool beer. Even after the third glass he couldn't understand why he had reacted so strangely, why these trappings and ceremonies and chants should move him. Dr. Ernest Beller didn't believe in these things, and he didn't believe in "racial memory" either. Besides, the Jews weren't a race; it was the Nazis who'd said they were. These questions bothered him all of Saturday afternoon.

The man who arrived at Schloss Gillenstein at 11:45 the next morning was a lot more calm. He wore the robes of a Catholic priest, but his serenity wasn't that of a human who knows that he has found the true faith. His was the peace of an executioner who has watched his main adversary drive away. Beller waited a few minutes after the warden's car disappeared from sight, then presented himself at the prison gate.

The guard was embarrassed. No, this was not the time to visit an inmate.

The cleric was understanding but insistent.

The captain was summoned, and he apologized for the "situation." Visiting hours began at 2 P.M., and whom did the good father wish to see? Falkenhausen? Impossible. He'd *broken the rules*. The captain wasn't going to describe the bloody assault, for that might offend the sensibilities of a man of the cloth. These clerics were so spiritual, so unworldly.

The priest was undiscouraged. He'd come a long way at the

request of the prisoner's ailing sister, a woman who might soon
be "joining her maker." He'd given his word. He was on his
way to a nearby monastery, and had little time. Wasn't the
captain a good Christian? Surely the warden was, for the father
at Saint Lorenz in the town had mentioned his piety.

"Ten minutes," yielded the uneasy captain.

"God will bless you, my son," pledged the man wearing the
large wooden cross.

Beller glanced down at the moat for two or three seconds
before he entered the old castle. Narrow corridors, stone floors
and walls—all the standard features of medieval fort-homes.
Falkenhausen was in a cell on the fourth floor in a tower. That
suited the plan perfectly.

"Who are you?" Falkenhausen asked warily.

"The father brings word from your sister."

"What sister?"

"And your nephew, Oskar," Beller added swiftly.

The vicious old man's eyes gleamed in recognition.

Dirlewanger hadn't forgotten.

"Please come in, father."

Perhaps Falkenhausen wasn't a complete psychopath after
all, the captain thought. He'd never heard him say "please"
during these many years. In fact, the senior guard had half-
expected the beast to insult—maybe even assault—the man of
God. Was it possible that there was still some shred of decency
in this savage that could be redeemed?

Could he dare to leave them alone?

"Please sit down, father," Falkenhausen invited.

The animal sounded almost civilized—for the moment.

"I'll knock on the door in ten minutes, captain," Beller said.
"Ten minutes—no more."

Captain Mecke hesitated. If something—anything—went
wrong . . . if this violent prisoner attacked the priest, the
warden would surely hold him, not Falkenhausen, responsible.

"I'm not certain that—"

"It'll be all right."

Shit, Mecke thought. These priests thought that everyone
was a goddam angel. Mecke was a Protestant, and he wasn't
about to have *his* career ruined because some simple-minded
son of Rome believed all men were good at heart.

"You have my word," Falkenhausen said.

He sounded normal enough. The captain shrugged, left the cell.

"I bring greetings from your friends, your *old* friends," Beller began.

"I haven't heard from them in a long time. I'm not complaining, mind you, but it's been a terribly long time."

Beller nodded benignly.

"They have not forgotten you, my son. Your comrades have been busy with *important new work.*"

Was the man really a priest? Falkenhausen didn't dare ask. The S.S. didn't question. The solemn oath of the S.S. was loyalty and obedience.

"Oskar?" The name leaped from his lips before Falkenhausen could stop it.

"Not far away. He needs you—now."

Falkenhausen almost shouted with joy. It was all happening, just as he'd dreamed. "I'm ready," he declared as he snapped to attention.

"Of course. Your friends have been watching and waiting for a long time. Now it is time for you to join them. Nothing can stop you."

It was wonderful. Nothing could stop him, just like the old days.

"I see that the small window up there has only one bar. Here is a specially hardened file," Beller said as he reached under his robe to draw it from the sheath taped to his right leg. "When the others sleep, you are to file through. You must be done by three in the morning. Is that clear?"

He was no priest. There was a toughness in his voice that was far from clerical.

"And then?"

The visitor smiled, pulled up his cassock to expose a long length of cord wrapped around his waist.

"This is nylon rope, light but strong. It measures ninety feet. We'll be waiting with a car."

"Oskar?"

"There's no time for questions, colonel. Here's the rope. Hide it in your bedclothes till you need it."

Then Beller banged on the metal-studded door, and twenty-five minutes later he was back in his British-journalist clothes, checking out of the hotel. It was too bad that he couldn't wait around to make certain, but that would be too risky. The church bells were ringing as he guided the BMW onto the autobahn, and when he looked back at the city the view resembled one of those quaint scenes on picture postcards. It was easy to see why so many tourists found Nürnberg charming.

Shortly before 8 A.M. the next morning, the new shift of guards arrived at Schloss Gillenstein. One of them was Kraus, and he was the first to notice the short length of white rope—perhaps fifteen or twenty feet—hanging from the tower window. He looked down quite automatically, saw the body floating face down in the moat. Even without a view of the features, Rolf Kraus recognized the corpse.

Sigmund Falkenhausen.

The Nazi criminal was dead, and one tiny bit of the stain on the honor of German warriors was just a little dimmer.

20

"I don't think it's very funny," Duslov said belligerently as Merlin entered the men's room, "and you can tell your people that."

What the hell was he talking about?

"Would you mind if I took a leak?" Merlin fenced as he walked to the urinal.

"I suspect that you may be *personally* responsible for this provocation," the KGB agent announced angrily.

Merlin shook his head, unzipped his trousers and began to dispose of some of the Moselle he'd been drinking. After imbibing half a bottle of excellent Piesporter, he was in no mood to wrangle, but there was probably no way to avoid it.

"What provocation?" he asked reluctantly.

"Don't tell me that naming one of your ear-splitting rock groups KGB was an accident. I'm no child."

No, he wasn't. Duslov was one of a large number of dirty-minded middle-aged men. Merlin found no comfort in the fact that the Soviets were just as paranoid as his own countrymen. It wouldn't help to point out that the "B" in KGB was a talented guitarist-composer named Mike Bloomfield, or that the group had been named by some puckish record company executive. There was nothing you could do about paranoids except vote against their reelection and hope your brother didn't marry one. Merlin zipped up his pants, strode to the basin to wash his hands.

"I thought you called this meeting to talk business, Andrei."

"I did. I'm keeping my part of the bargain. I'm behaving *correctly*."

Merlin reached for the soap. "Terrific. Do I get three guesses?"

"I have heard that these people—"

"What goddam people, comrade?"

To call Duslov's smile patronizing would be an absurd understatement.

"The Martians—a rumor about their next operation. Their last was quite a success, wasn't it?"

Merlin rinsed his hands, tore off two paper towels. "A smash. Now what's this about their next number?" The American's face showed no trace of the elation within him.

"They are planning a big bang," Duslov confided. "Explosives, I presume. Those precise words were used. 'A big bang.'"

Merlin balled up the towels, flipped them accurately into the open bin. "Thanks a heap, comrade. Got to admit I'm impressed by your fast service, Andrei. . . . Mind if I ask one question?"

"Go ahead."

"Do we *have* to meet in weird places like this?"

The Russian grunted, turned to leave. "Remember what I said," he ordered. "Jokes about the KGB are hardly conducive to good relations. This sort of behavior isn't my idea of detente."

"Detente in the *crapper?*"

At that moment a dentist named Pfalzheimer from Ulm— a lovely town—walked in, and Andrei Duslov left. Merlin guessed that Dr. Pfalzheimer was some kind of a germ nut because he washed his hands *first*, but the CIA man's attention turned to Freddy Cassel as soon as he left the lavatory. She was clearly the prettiest woman in this Funkturm Restaurant, even lovelier than the panoramic night view of Berlin that sprawled beneath this exotic dining place in the radio tower, high over the fairground. For a few seconds she was all he saw, and he smiled as he returned to their table.

"She says he had a meeting with Duslov," Harper told the deputy director, nineteen hours and twenty-three minutes later.

Time flies—west to Langley.

"*Andrei* Duslov," Parks chimed in unnecessarily.

"Son of a bitch?" asked the deputy director.

"Only man I know whose mother wears a flea collar," Harper answered.

The deputy director had barely learned to cope with the righteous assassins and the hostile press, and he wasn't about to endure stand-up comics. Maybe Congress was correct. Perhaps the whole goddam place was turning into some sort of existential nut house.

"He was seen with Duslov *before*," Parks said.

"What do you think, Bill?"

Harper smiled enigmatically at the deputy director, hoping to impress him with his cool. That was the way you got salary increases, and Harper could use an extra $3500 a year. "Think he's doing his number—the one we sent him to do, John."

"Metaphor?"

"Metaphor—terrible situation. Rotten name, too. They'll probably tag the next damn mission Dangling Participle. Can't you say something to that clown who picks the code names?"

"His uncle's a senator. Bill, why is Merlin playing games with the Sovs?"

Cool.

Harper wasn't going to admit that he had no idea, that he didn't understand Merlin any better than anyone else did.

"He's doing it his way, John. All the other ways didn't work, remember. Three whole networks, and it isn't over yet."

The deputy director frowned unhappily. "Bill, you don't think our lady in Berlin knows about Metaphor?"

"Metaphor? She doesn't even know about Crash Dive!"

Harper misinterpreted the deputy director's gloomy look. Smith wasn't afraid. He was dismayed. He stood up, stepped to the window and stared out for ten or twelve seconds.

"Why should we be in such desperate haste to succeed, and in such desperate enterprises?" he quoted. "Thoreau. You've read Thoreau, Bill."

Harper nodded, but it was a lie.

He'd never read a word of Thoreau, not one.

21

The man who might be "Alexander" attacked the moment that Merlin entered the luggage store.

Bam!

Just like that.

"Sixteen and a half marks!" he shouted.

Maybe it was the dye in the leather that produced this hysteria. But whatever it was, Merlin was in no mood to sympathize.

"You owe the tax! Sixteen and a half marks, mein herr!" the madman insisted.

Could Marx be right? Was it really inevitable that rampant capitalism would lead to this?

"I've come to use the phone," Merlin said in calm and reasonable tones.

"Not until you pay the tax!"

Merlin lit a cigar, blew out a perfect smoke ring. "Of course," he agreed. "By the way, do you know a good orthopedic surgeon?"

The man behind the counter hesitated warily. "Why do you ask?"

Merlin put away his silver lighter. "Because after I give you the goddam sixteen and a half marks I'm going to break off your arms and beat your face in with them."

"I'm not afraid of thugs."

The American nodded, blew another smoke ring. "Whoever said I'm a thug? You don't have to be afraid of me, friend. I'm no thug. I'm an *assassin.*"

Merlin flipped open his jacket to show the .357 Magnum, and the German held onto the counter to avoid falling. He wasn't afraid, but he could barely avoid soiling his trousers.

Merlin placed the money on the glass counter, smiled. "Should have sent you a check last week," he said pleasantly.

"Don't worry. I rarely kill people on Tuesdays, except in months ending in R."

"This is June."

"So you can stop sweating. Now I'd like to ask you for a favor. I've got to talk to Bonn on a secure line, and—for reasons of my own—I'd like to use yours."

"I'm not asking any questions," assured "Alexander."

He was intensely curious as to why the American wasn't using the phone at the "audiovisual" unit at the cultural center, but he sensed that it might be unhealthy to inquire. He'd seen many operatives pass through this shop, and something in his lower intestines told him that this man *was* one of those who killed. He handed Merlin a key.

"It's in the back room. Lower left drawer of the desk."

Merlin put down a fifty-mark note.

"I hope this will cover the charges—and the tax."

No doubt about it. He was just the sort who would break off your arms and smash in your face with them.

And then he'd do worse.

"That's too much, mein herr. You're too generous."

"My only weakness."

Merlin went to the back room, locked the door and opened the drawer. Sitting on the edge of the desk, he dialed the number of the CIA "country central" in the German capital.

"Atlas," a woman said.

"Mr. Herbert Stoltz," Merlin recited.

"Traffic?"

"No, mail room."

Challenge, sign and countersign—all correct.

"Mail room."

"This is Merlin. What have you got for me?"

At that very moment, Ernst Beller was back at work.

Stuttgart: the modern and well-equipped Gablinghofen Women's Prison. The institution had been named after Dr. Ingeborg Gablinghofen, noted social psychologist who'd played a major role in progressive penology and insisted "There's no such thing as a bad woman"—right up to the moment that her twin granddaughters set her on fire. Gablinghofen had the third best women's basketball team in the country, and a wonderful contemporary-arts program. A portly police inspector from Bonn—who had a B.A. from Harvard and memories that made him homicidal—was following Matron Krondorf down a second-floor corridor.

"What's the file?"

"Crash Dive," Merlin replied.

"Just a second. . . . Right. You wanted all print-outs on the Martians."

"Anything at all."

"That's about all this is."

Matron Krondorf, who didn't weigh an ounce over 180 and was all muscle, coughed and stopped outside the cell. "They called her The Bitch of Belsen," she recalled in the tones you'd use to discuss an obscure Egyptian pharaoh. "There was talk of setting dogs on prisoners, and lampshades made of human skin."

Beller sniffed importantly, looked splendid in his uniform and waved his briefcase at the cell door.

"At once, Herr Inspektor," *said the intimidated matron.*

"Falkenhausen. One of your Martians is a woman named Marta Falkenhausen . . . age twenty-six."

"Spare me the urinalysis," Merlin interrupted. "I know about her kidney stones. What else?"

"Her father was a war criminal, S.S. officer. Sigmund Falkenhausen. Died on Sunday—trying to escape from prison."

Merlin sensed something.

"Where?"

"Gillenstein near Nürnberg. Old castle for bad types."

The matron shook her finger at Inga Diessen twice before she remembered that this gesture might be misconstrued as an old-fashioned threat. It was against the rules to intimidate an inmate, and Matron Krondorf always obeyed the rules. That was why she wouldn't leave Frau Diessen alone with any man — even the inspector.

"We have reason to believe that the death of Martin Simon may not have been an accident," *Beller repeated.* "He was a witness against you and others in 1946, and if you will cooperate now—"

"Answer the inspector," *ordered the matron, who had no idea that Martin Simon had just sold his barbershop in San Diego and was living in retirement within sight of the Pacific.*

Ignoring hunches was something Merlin had learned not to do.

"What happened?" he asked as he looked around for an ashtray.

"Rope apparently broke, and so did his neck. They found him floating face down in the moat."

Apparently.

"Probably nothing to do with your problem," guessed the man in the "mail room."

Probably.

"I have no information about that dirty little Jew-liar," Inga Diessen *said in a hoarse, unpleasant voice. "I'm glad that he's dead, and I'm sorry I didn't finish him off myself. I never did one-tenth of the things he said, never!"*

"There were other witnesses," Beller *noted.*

"All filthy Zionist Red liars!"

Merlin tapped off the ash into the wastebasket.

"Anything else?"

"Hard to say," answered the man in Bonn. "Sigmund Falkenhausen wasn't the only war criminal to die in prison this month, you know. I keep the Trash Bin file, routine stuff on that crowd. There was an S.S. officer named Berchtold—Ravensbrück creep—who kicked off in Frankfurt just a couple of days before."

"Cause of death?"

"Would you believe a heart attack?"

Merlin wouldn't. Something strange was going on. He couldn't name it yet, but he could feel it.

"I don't think it means anything," judged the "mail room" agent in Bonn. "Got to be careful to avoid going paranoid about these funny coincidences."

What was so funny?

Beller could see that he'd have only a single chance, just a couple of seconds. He was alert, ready to strike. He'd brought the weapon originally planned for Sturmbannführer Falkenhausen, the gas device he'd loaded so carefully in the medical examiner's lab in Manhattan after midnight. He'd never been able to test it on humans, but there had been a caged rat. Now he remembered how well and how swiftly the cyanide had slain the rodent, and he felt confident that it would take care of The Bitch.

"Please note in the inmate's records that she has refused to cooperate with an important investigation," Beller said, signaling that the interview was finished.

The weapon was highly recommended. According to the Special Forces intelligence experts, KGB hit men had slain two anti-Soviet Ukrainian exiles in Frankfurt with this same type of gun.

"I certainly will," promised the matron, and she turned to open the cell door.

That was it—his only chance.

Beller whipped out the fountain-pen-that-was-really-a-gas-gun, thrust it right under Inga Diessen's nose and squeezed the trigger. The cyanide struck at once, and she was reeling as he officiously hustled the matron out and slammed the cell door behind them.

The Bitch was dying—swiftly.

"Any others?" Merlin asked.

"Yeah—guy up in Hamburg. Dachau grad. Yeah, in eleven days we've got three stiffs."

Four.

Merlin wouldn't hear about Inga Diessen's demise for nearly three days, but that hardly counted. He was a man who played hunches. Nine times out of ten—well, seven out of ten—he was right. Now he was restless and tired of waiting, so he guessed that these deaths were part of a pattern. —

He was right.

He also thought that these murders were the work of the Martians, and if he could find the pattern and discern the plan he might track them down.

He was wrong.

He didn't suspect that one avenging survivor of the camps was carrying out a brilliant and psychotic crusade, but that didn't matter. Dr. Ernest Beller was suddenly in danger, for Merlin was a master tracker.

The hunt was on.

22

"I feel funny in this outfit," Angelo Cavaliere said as the brown Ford moved toward Nürnberg.

"You don't look funny," Merlin replied.

They were both in U.S. Army uniforms, and the car was painted with American military insignia.

"Why do I have to drive?"

"Because you're the junior officer," Merlin explained between puffs on the cigar.

Merlin's shoulders were adorned with the gold leaves of a major, while his companion's tunic carried the bars of a second lieutenant.

"And why am I the junior officer?"

"Because I'm taller. Don't you ever go to the movies? The taller guy is always the senior officer, and better-looking."

"Shit," complained the man behind the wheel. "When I was in the army I was a goddam captain," he added as he accelerated to pass a bright yellow VW. "Why was I demoted to second john?"

"Filthy language. Captains don't say 'shit,' kid."

"I knew plenty who did," he argued.

"Not in *my* army. Maybe in the U.S. Army, but not mine. We're a classier outfit. . . . Hey, off to the right. That's the big stadium where Adolf the Asshole used to hold his big rallies. Take a look."

The driver sneaked a swift glance, flicked his eyes back to the highway.

"Where'd you get these uniforms and the car?" he asked.

"You want me to drive?"

"Bet the goddam army doesn't know about it."

Merlin didn't bother to answer. It was hardly rare for CIA personnel to operate in military uniforms.

"I was an air force colonel once," he reminisced.

"Not a *real* one. I was a *real* captain. . . . Say, you know anybody in Nürnberg?"

Merlin shook his head, dropped some ash out the window in vicious defiance of West German regulations against littering. "I used to," he answered, "but he had an accident."

"That figures." No one could dispute that there was a remarkable rate of attrition among the people Merlin knew—even casual acquaintances.

The center of the city loomed ahead now.

"I wasn't supposed to take this deal," Cavaliere grumbled. "I was set to go on leave. They had Ken Kaufman set for this number, but he got hurt."

"I asked for you, Angie, 'cause you're the best."

"Horse shit."

It was difficult to believe that a Phi Beta Kappa from Holy Cross would speak this way.

"What happened to Ken?"

"He was stomped by an NBC crew in the Senate Office Building. They were charging down the hall to catch some admiral who'd been testifying about how the Sovs have more toothpicks or nail files than we do, and Ken was in the way. Out-and-out case of hit-and-run. Those NBC crews are mean. We're retaliating, of course. We're not going to tap their phones anymore."

"Fair is fair."

"Not really," Cavaliere said frankly. "I used to think so before I joined this circus, but not anymore."

The traffic was heavy, confirming West Germany's wonderful economic boom.

"Sir," Merlin told him. "Second johns say 'sir' to majors."

"Major Knowlton—right?"

"You got it. And what's your name, lieutenant?"

"Bonomi, John G. You want me to sing out my goddam serial number?"

"I think I prefer your Irving Berlin medley."

The man behind the wheel cleared his throat. "There's no business like show—"

"Let's hear the serial number," Merlin interrupted. "Say, did you ever hear the joke about the seven-hundred-pound lady gorilla in heat in the Central Park Zoo?"

"*I* told you that joke in Algiers eight months ago. Christ, how long has it been since we met? Three years? Four?"

"Long time. Why?"

A traffic light stopped them, and Cavaliere turned to look at the man beside him. "Four goddam years, and I don't even know your real name. It was Kraft—Gilman Kraft—in Algiers. In Tokyo it was St. John—something St. John—you were a liquor dealer. Diamant—Linc Diamant—in Athens. Four goddam years, and I don't know your real name."

"I like you, Angie, so I'll tell you the secret."

"Yeah?"

"I don't have a real name."

There was no point in getting angry with Merlin, so Cavaliere turned on the radio and listened to some women called The Silver Convention chant a vigorous invitation to "boogie" with dedicated disco delight. The two men didn't speak until they reached Schloss Gillenstein.

"You think these Krauts are going to buy this story?" Cavaliere asked as he turned off the engine.

"They don't have to. We're giving it away."

Ever since Attila the Hun and his crowd speared, spit and slashed their way across Central Europe, Germans have always treated military men with respect. This was an early form of preventive medicine, since it was soon and widely noted that individuals who were less than deferential ran up major medical and dental bills and also tended to die young. The Germans had a lot of practice fighting with other tribes and nations and with each other, doing so well that their Thirty Years' War between 1618 and 1648 is regarded by historians as a prime example of moronic religious butchery. There were some swell battles with the Swedes and the Spaniards and the French, which proved so popular that the Germans took on the French four or five times more during the next three centuries. The Germans developed a genuine talent for weaponry, military organization, rousing slogans and splendid discipline. As any of the many fine and peace-loving Germans will confirm, it is a goddam lie that war used to be their country's national sport. It was always a science, with great-looking uniforms. Germany has given the world some of the most important scientists, including Count von Zeppelin; Heinz Zipper; that Gutenberg fellow who invented movable type; and Albert Einstein, who invented the movable physicist—moving himself right out of the Fatherland because the Institute for Advanced Studies at Princeton seemed more promising than becoming a bar of soap.

Anyway, the prison guard who escorted the two American officers to the warden's office was *very* deferential. Warden Sauer wasn't deferential because he hadn't quite gotten over the notion of Yankees as "occupation forces," but he was polite and courteous.

"Sauer," he introduced himself briskly.

"Major Perry Knowlton, and this is Loo-tenant John Bonomi. U.S. Army Criminal Investigation Division, suh."

Merlin put just a touch of a southern spin on the "suh." It was real neat.

"There was a call from the federal police in Bonn, major. I've been expecting you."

Merlin gave him an excellent imitation of a sincere smile, one so good that even Angie Cavaliere was impressed.

"Like to show you our I.D., suh. Army regulations."

The warden almost snapped to attention.

He understood regulations.

"Certainly," he beamed, and studied the expertly forged cards. "Would you like some coffee—or tea?"

"Mah-ty kind of you, suh. Been one helluva drive, if you'll pah-don mah French."

Cavaliere hoped that Merlin wouldn't overdo it, remembering his tendency toward excess. The impostors sat down, and Sauer ordered the coffee.

"It's the Falkenhausen matter, I understand," he said a moment later.

"Falkenhausen, Sigmund. Former colonel," Merlin chanted in his best military style.

"Not my favorite inmate," Sauer confided. "Don't quote me on that in your report, major."

The warden wanted to let these Americans know that he was no baby. He'd been around, and he was aware that army CID types always made reports—*written* reports in *quadruplicate*—on such investigations. Peter Sauer didn't want his personal views on that savage in anybody's official files—in *quadruplicate*.

"Course not," Merlin pledged. "Bad apple, huh?"

"Terribly difficult. No one ever came to see him, you know, not even his family. Until the week before he died, Falkenhausen hadn't had a visitor in seven years. I looked it up."

He tapped the file on his desk in his best bureaucratic manner. Let the Americans know that Peter Sauer went by the book too.

"There were two in the last five days of his life," Sauer continued crisply. "Our doctor says that he fell to his death in the small hours of Monday morning. He was found floating in the moat, drowned."

"Great moat you got."

"Thank you, major. It's quite historic. I suppose you want to know about the two visitors."

"Youah readin' mah mind, suh. Get this down, loo-tenant."

Cavaliere clicked open his ballpoint, prepared to take notes on the pad fixed to his clipboard. The coffee arrived at that point, interrupting the conversation for more than a minute. There was a whole number with sugar and cream and dumb small talk that filled a good eighty seconds.

Merlin didn't press. He waited for Sauer to resume his recitation.

"On the previous Thursday morning, shortly before noon, a British journalist named Geoffrey Donald Cuthbert sat in the chair that you occupy now. He was on assignment for the Manchester *Guardian*. I had received a letter requesting cooperation. It was signed by . . . ah, here it is—Mervyn Nashby, features editor. Requested an interview with Falkenhausen."

"Ah see."

"You may, if you wish. Take a look."

Merlin scanned the letter, sat back and sipped at the delicious black coffee. "Thank you, suh. Now how much time did this Cuthbert spend with youah prisoner?"

"He didn't. Falkenhausen's visiting privileges had been suspended two days earlier for violating regulations. He'd assaulted a member of my staff."

"Bad apple. Gettin' all this, Bonomi?"

"Yes, sir."

"Would you like more sugar, major?"

"No, suh. Just more talk."

Sauer added another lump to his own cup, continued.

"Herr Cuthbert was disappointed, but I could not bend the regulations. Rules are rules, *nicht wahr?*"

"Damn right. So he left?"

"In a gray BMW, I believe. I saw his car from my window. Then on Sunday a priest came—when I was at noon mass. A guard captain—well, the father persuaded him to let him see Falkenhausen on some family matter for ten minutes. The inmate was in good health and secure in his cell when the priest left. The captain has been reprimanded, of course. I'm as religious as the next man, but I can't brook exceptions to the rules. We're not running a kindergarten here, major."

Merlin put down his cup. "Noticed how sharp and disciplined your men are, warden. Sort of thing a military man spots raht off the bat," he commended.

"We are still investigating how Falkenhausen got the nylon rope that he used for his escape effort."

Merlin lit a cigar, offered another to Sauer, who explained that he no longer smoked.

"S'pose his friends provided that rope, huh?"

Sauer's thin lips compressed even tighter. "I hope that *I* don't have any friends like that, major. The rope had been tampered with—very cleverly. Whoever provided it wanted Sigmund Falkenhausen to die."

Merlin wasn't half as good a thespian as Ernest Beller, but he could handle small parts adequately. He was best at little bits of "business."

"Mercy, mercy—what a way to go! Think it could have been that fellah in the priest suit?"

The American was no idiot. Sauer had been wondering whether the "father" was legitimate, decided that he probably was.

"We are checking into that situation, major. Our records show that Father Johann Tesbach came from Berlin, and we're looking for him now. Thus far there is no reason to suspect him of any impropriety."

Merlin stood up abruptly, thrust out his hand manfully. "Wanna thank you, warden. 'Preciate your fine cooperation. Your folks in Bonn'll get copies of ouah report, a'course."

Sauer wanted to inquire as to just what this investigation was all about, but he wouldn't show that sort of weakness. He walked his visitors to the outer office, watched a guard escort them down the corridor out of sight.

"You on duty the Sunday morning that the priest came?" Merlin asked casually at the drawbridge.

The guard nodded.

"He left in a gray car?"

"I'm not sure. I think so. It wasn't a big car—and it might have been gray."

"What did he look like? Tall? Fat? Old?"

The guard shrugged. "I didn't notice, sir. There was nothing special about him, so I guess he was just—sort of ordinary."

Merlin thanked him, and the two impostors drove off in the khaki Ford with the fake U.S. Army markings.

"A journalist who didn't get near him and a priest nobody knows—that's some combo," Cavaliere judged.

"I was right. It *wasn't* an accident!"

"Doesn't prove a goddam thing, major. . . . Say, are you listening to me?"

"He was hit!" Merlin exulted.

"You're getting kind of bloodthirsty in your old age—*sir.*" The "lieutenant" behind the wheel was still not convinced that the Martians had any connection with this death.

"He was *hit!*"

There was nothing you could do with Merlin when he got into one of these states—except wait for it to pass. Cavaliere had been through these scenes nearly a dozen times, enduring the exuberance that came when Merlin sensed that his gut-hunch might be correct. The happy smile he wore right now confirmed that he was in such an irrationally joyous mood.

"All right, he was hit. Whoopee."

"Whoopee!" Merlin agreed.

"And hurrah for our side and God Bless America. Once again your fantastic intuition has prevailed over lesser minds, and I am profoundly honored to work with you, major. Now what the hell do we do, *sing?*"

Merlin turned to face him, still beaming. "Angie?"

"Yeah."

"Do you know any Harold Arlen?"

"I know the one from *Wizard of Oz*. Yeah, 'Somewhere Over the Rainbow.' Will that do?"

It did just fine, and the Irving Berlin medley that followed as they swung onto the autobahn was just as dandy.

23

Frankfurt.

That's what the sign over the air terminal said.

"Don't worry."

That's what Cavaliere said as the two CIA agents walked from the plane toward the building.

"I'm not sure they took me seriously," Merlin brooded aloud. "What did you tell them?"

"I told them to alert all U.S. and West German military bases that the Martians may pull a raid to grab the explosives they need for their next operation. They ran short during that train job, so they'll move fast to steal more—somewhere."

"Take it easy," advised the lieutenant as they neared the entrance to the building. "You're Merlin, a heavy hitter. People respect you, Merlin. You're no bullshit artist."

"I hope they alerted the Germans. . . . You think people respect me, Angie?"

"They love you. You're adorable."

"Don't get fresh."

A British couple in tweeds, utterly indifferent to the eighty-degree weather, looked at them curiously.

"It's all right. We're engaged," Merlin assured them—and the uneasy English hurried away.

"I think your wife still cares, Merl," Cavaliere said while they waited for their bags. "She asked about you when I checked in last week."

"Ex-wife. No, she cares about Crash Dive. Her ass is burning because she doesn't know what we're doing."

Cavaliere lit a cigarette. "What the hell *are* we doing, Merlin?"

"We're going to jail," the man in the major's uniform said as he saw his suitcase.

"This sounds like Monopoly."

"That's capitalism for you. Let's go."

Some seventy minutes later they were in the office of the warden at Barbarossa Prison. He reported that the demise of Egon Berchtold had come after a heart attack, and the cause of death had been certified by the institution's physician.

"Berchtold had been suffering from cardiac problems for several years," he explained, "and there was nothing suspicious about this final incident."

"I'm suspicious about everything. You get that way in my business, warden, so please humor me."

Warden Schnapp didn't want any trouble. He had dedicated his life to this highly functional principle, winning promotions over a number of less canny civil servants in the process. Still, he was a bit defensive about this foreigner doubting the ability and expertise of his staff.

"Are you questioning our doctor?" he asked stiffly.

"No, but I'd like to."

Dr. Wessler was a plump man with very little hair, a white jacket and only six years to his pension.

"My examination indicated all the classic symptoms of cardiac failure, major. I've dealt with many such cases in my career, and I can assure you—"

"Doctor," Merlin broke in as "sincerely" as he could, "I'm not doubting your skill or experience. I don't know much about these matters—my business is criminal investigation. That's my profession. As one professional to another, I wonder whether anything could simulate those classic symptoms."

The physician and the warden exchanged puzzled glances.

"Did Berchtold have any visitors just before he died? A priest, perhaps?"

Warden Schnapp's laugh was almost contemptuous. "In all the years that man was here, he never attended services once. He sneered at religion as weakness."

The physician nodded, explained that Berchtold had often expressed these views while working as an aide in the infirmary.

"Anyone else?" Cavaliere wondered.

"*Very* good, lieutenant. As my assistant said, were there any visitors at all?"

Trouble? After all these years?

"Is there something wrong? I have a feeling that you're not being entirely . . . *candid,* major."

Merlin sensed the weakness, moved in for the kill.

"You're damn right I'm not, warden," he said in blunt soldier's tones. "This is a joint U.S. and German investigation—and it's classified. You aren't going to be difficult, are you?"

Schnapp stammered, babbled and stopped just short of cringing. He wasn't afraid of these Americans, but if they were working with the security services of the Federal Republic and if they complained to those intolerant and officious bastards in Bonn, there might be an *official inquiry.* The warden called for the log book of visitors.

Nothing suspicious, thank God.

"Just a civil servant named Holstein down to check on the Detweiler matter."

"What Detweiler matter?"

The impudence of this foreigner might have outraged some men, but Schnapp controlled himself and telephoned the assistant warden who'd been on duty. He explained that it was something to do with a man who'd allegedly committed crimes at Ravensbrück.

"Crimes?"

"War crimes . . . I think," mumbled the assistant warden.

Merlin's gut sent him another message.

"Call Bonn—please."

That was when the argument—no, the difference of opinion —erupted. It was amputated a few minutes later when Schnapp's broad-bottomed secretary announced the telephone call for Major Knowlton. "It's Hamburg, major. Kaiserwald Prison."

Schnapp couldn't make out much from the terse conversation, but the CIA operative laid it all out, rather unpleasantly, as soon as he hung up the phone.

"Curare. There was a prisoner named Otto Kretschman doing time up at Kaiserwald. Long time. He died just a couple of days before Berchtold, and the doctor up there thought it was 'natural causes'—just like you did here. It was curare."

"I don't see the connection, major," Schnapp said.

"Hear it. That son of a bitch up in Kaiserwald was an S.S. murderer who ran the ovens at Dachau. Ever hear of Dachau?"

The warden's face froze.

"It's near Munich," Merlin hammered. "They used to kill people there."

"I know about Dachau."

Merlin shook his head. "No, you don't—but that's not the point. They did an autopsy on Kretschman, and they found curare. Now I'm asking you to consider—very seriously— doing an autopsy on this animal Berchtold."

The doctor was rubbing his hands together. "He's been buried, major."

"What the hell do you think they did to Kretschman, candied him in preserves?"

The warden was visibly intimidated. Merlin's brutal manner had prevailed.

"We'll need a court order to dig up—"

"Get it. If you can't, I'll phone Bonn."

For a moment Cavaliere thought that Warden Schnapp might throw something, or burst into tears. It was a toss-up.

"We're staying at the Frankfurter Hof over at Bethmann-strasse," Merlin announced as he rose to leave.

"A fine hotel," volunteered the physician. He was trying to be helpful, really. He was a decent person who'd never committed any war crimes or other offenses, and he was also a bit nervous about this startling situation. "They serve excellent *rippchen* in the Stubb in the cellar," he added.

"Thank you, doctor," Angelo Cavaliere said briskly before Merlin could turn even nastier.

The pork ribs were as good as the physician promised, and the buxom waitresses in nineteenth-century dress went well with the historic decor. The sauerkraut and the local Henninger beer—stein after stein—helped pass the time, and when the spies were finished with dinner they drank fiery Steinhager till midnight.

The first phone call, the one that awoke them, came at twenty minutes to nine. There was a Manchester *Guardian* and there was a features editor named Mervyn Nashby, but there was no Geoffrey Donald Cuthbert—not anymore. He'd been dead for nearly two years.

"Whoopee!"

The second phone call reached them at five after eleven.

"We have secured the order to exhume the remains, major," Schnapp reported. "Would you like to be present when the coffin is opened?"

"No, thanks, I've seen enough corpses."

He put down the phone, saw Cavaliere eying him appraisingly.

"Too many, Angie—and this number isn't over yet."

"You're figuring on more stiffs?"

"I think the Martians are."

They read several newspapers, discussed relative merits and tastes of the Munich weisswurst versus the Westphalian blutwurst or the spleen sausage named *milzwurst* popular along the Danube. They soberly debated whether to order Hanoverian bouilonwurst or the juicy saiten sausages of Stuttgart, finally settled on Frankfurt's popular zeppelinwurst. Despite all their efforts, they were acutely bored by half past two.

"We won't hear anything for a couple of hours," Cavaliere declared suddenly, "so I'm going out. Want to come along?"

"Where?"

"It doesn't matter. I'm going bananas locked up in this suite."

"It's the cigar smoke, isn't it? Admit it. You hate it."

The "lieutenant" waved away a cloud of Canary Island tobacco, made up his mind not to renew this discussion they'd had so many times. "Merlin, I just want out. See you in an hour."

There was no reply until he reached the door.

"What are you going to do—walk around like some jerk tourist?" challenged the shirtsleeved "major."

"Maybe I'll get laid. You coming?"

"No, I've been laid."

It was impossible to maintain a friendly conversation with Merlin when he was in one of these tense-compulsive moods, so Cavaliere left with the hope that things would be different when he returned.

It was almost 4:30 when he reentered the suite. Merlin was sitting up in bed, pointing his gun at the doorway.

"Any calls?" Cavaliere asked casually.

"No."

"Mind aiming that piece somewhere else? I'm your friend, good ol' Angie—remember?"

Merlin put down the gun, smiled pleasantly. "Where'd you go?"

"Natural History Museum. Saw a terrific sixty-six-foot skeleton of a prehistoric diplodocus."

Merlin digested this exciting news slowly. "That's necrophilia, Angie. You go to jail for that."

"What's necrophilia?"

"Laying the dead."

Cavaliere threw his jacket on a chair. "I didn't lay anybody —or anything."

Merlin reached to refill his glass with beer. "Better luck next time," he consoled.

Maybe it was getting to Merlin—the pressure and the violence and the crazy passion of the pursuit.

No, he'd talked like this before when there was nothing to do but wait.

They drank and watched television until five minutes to seven, when the telephone rang. A very stiff Warden Schnapp reported that laboratory tests indicated that the corpse of the late Egon Berchtold contained strong traces of some digitalis compound, and digitalis was a substance that could both simulate and stimulate a heart attack.

"How much digitalis? Enough to kill him?"

"Probably. I must say, major, that this came as a surprise to—"

"It's okay," Merlin said happily.

"We have no idea yet how this digitalis—"

"Holstein."

It took several seconds for the warden to understand. "Are you suggesting that a government official—"

"There is no Holstein, sonny. No Detweiler affair either. You've been had. But don't feel bad—you were had by experts. It isn't your fault."

Now that was a decent thing to say, even if it was a goddam lie. It might help the warden steal an hour or two of sleep during the long hours until the offices opened in Bonn the next morning. Merlin didn't particularly like Schnapp, but the warden probably had a wife and children whom suicide might leave destitute.

"These people are professionals, warden. They've pulled the

same kinds of stunts at other prisons. Let me know what you hear from Bonn tomorrow."

Merlin wasn't smiling when he hung up the phone.

He was grinning—totally.

"Digitalis?" Cavaliere asked.

"Right."

"Curare up in Hamburg?"

"That's it, Angie. Digitalis, curare, and a trick rope in Nürnberg."

Cavaliere whistled softly. "Jeezus K-rist."

"I don't think so, Angie. I don't think he makes house calls anymore. . . . Sorry, Angie. Didn't mean to hurt your feelings."

"I don't bad-mouth *your* Lord."

Sister Cecilia had warned him about the shallow faith of all those Protestants, but Merlin said a lot of things in jest that he didn't mean. Still, he ought to respect the beliefs of others.

"I apologize—won't do it again. Give you my goddam word. Dinner's on me."

Cavaliere didn't ask the question until they reached the elevator.

"Where are we going?"

"Any restaurant in town."

"No, *tomorrow*. You think the Martians are knocking off war criminals in prisons, right?"

"I *know* it."

"There are dozens of war criminals, maybe hundreds, still doing time all across Germany."

"I know that too."

The signal indicated that the elevator was nearing their floor.

"So where do we go next, Merl?"

The elevator door opened, and they faced a very attractive person in a very short skirt and a sweet smile.

"That's" what I don't know," Merlin responded—and he smiled back.

24

"Thirty kilometers to Bonn," Cavaliere read from the road sign as the Ford rolled north the next morning.

Merlin didn't reply. He was enjoying driving for a change, and his mind was on the traffic. He found it relaxing to tune out the Byzantine barbarism of the espionage-and-terror world, to concentrate on a skill that combined mechanical and macho without hurting anyone. There was some risk in a car, but it could be minimized if you drove defensively. Then Merlin realized that he'd grown to do almost everything defensively, and he laughed.

"What's so funny, Merl?"

"I am. Getting funny in the head."

"I thought you were swell back there," Cavaliere said supportively. "When the warden phoned to say that there was no trace of anybody named Holstein at the ministry, you didn't say 'I told you so'—not even once. I was proud of you, Merl."

"You're just saying that so I won't light a cigar."

Cavaliere shook his head emphatically, and semi-truthfully. "Smoke all you want. I know you'll stop if it bothers me. I trust you, Merl."

Merlin laughed again. "You're a member of an elite group —a gang of one," he said, and he pulled out a dark Don Diego.

"They trust you back at Langley. You're Merlin, The Best."

The man behind the wheel bit off the end of the petit-corona, groped for his Dunhill. "Nah, they don't trust anybody, not even themselves. That's the kind of people who get to run big outfits. That's the nature of the beast. They're always second-guessing and third-guessing, and they're always sure that somebody is screwing up." He paused to suck in some smoke.

"I didn't know you were running for office," said Cavaliere.

"What do you mean?"

"Sounds like you're giving a speech, Merl."

"You heard it before?"

"Not this one. Go right ahead."

"Did I mention that the scared people who run big outfits are usually scared that someone will screw up because they don't have that much confidence in themselves?"

Cavaliere shook his head. "No, Merl—but you will."

"I just did. . . . Listen, what about the Taunus?"

Cavaliere's eyes flicked to the mirror. "You mean the green one that picked us up about forty kilometers back? Yeah, still tailing us."

Merlin flicked some ash out the window. "I don't like it," he said after several seconds.

"You didn't complain about the blue van that tailed us the first thirty or forty kilometers out of Frankfurt, Merl."

Obviously busy thinking, the man behind the wheel didn't answer immediately. "I'm getting tired of being tailed," he announced.

"After all these years, Merl?"

"Get a picture and the plate number."

Merlin pulled the Ford off onto the shoulder of the road, and Cavaliere grabbed an expensive little camera from the glove compartment. He squeezed off two photos as the Taunus passed, then recited the license-plate number to Merlin.

"Mind telling me what the hell you're planning?" Cavaliere inquired when the Ford slid back into the traffic.

"And they're generally afraid to make a decision," Merlin said firmly.

"Those guys in the Taunus?"

"No, the people who run big organizations—in all countries —on all planets."

Cavaliere's brow was furrowed now. "What about those fellows in the Taunus, Merl?"

"Don't worry. I'll get to them."

He did—four minutes later. He stopped the Ford by a roadside phone, called the police and reported, in fine German, that three men had stolen a green 1975 Taunus. He gave the plate number, warned that the thieves were heading toward Bonn on this road.

"Ought to do it," he told the "lieutenant" briskly.

It did.

The Taunus resumed the tail position a few minutes later—briefly. Two police cars stopped it some eighteen kilometers out of Bonn, and Merlin guided the Ford into the old university-town-turned-capital without any escort.

"Bonn, gateway to the Rhine Valley, Beethoven's hometown," Cavaliere said when they first saw the river. "Population one hundred and forty thousand. Including suburbs, three hundred thousand. Originally a Roman defense post named Castra Bonnensia, you know."

"You've been reading those damn guidebooks again!"

Cavaliere smiled, almost shyly. "A man who stops learning starts dying," he recited.

"A man who stops watching his ass gets his head blown off," Merlin answered. "Wake up, Angie. You don't think we can trust the BND, do you? They certainly don't trust us."

The man from the BND—West Germany's energetic intelligence apparatus—was tall, nearly forty and had teeth so perfect that they were almost surely artificial. He'd picked the place for the meeting, the restaurant in the ultramodern Beethovenhalle. Merlin had done business with him two years earlier, so he recognized Herr Grad as soon as he approached.

"Good afternoon, major," the BND official said in mechanically casual tones.

Gray.

Everything about him was gray.

His suit, his tie, his eyes—his whole manner—were gray and neutral. There was even a touch of premature gray in his hair, and the frames of his horn-rimmed glasses were—gray. His car was undoubtedly gray, and Merlin nursed the suspicion that if you visited Karl Grad's home you'd find a wife of the same shade.

"Herr Grad, Lieutenant Bonomi," Merlin introduced.

The amenities were important to Karl Grad. He was the kind of German who always shook hands and laughed politely at other people's jokes. Grad never told jokes himself, although he knew scores. He was a serious man who could never be quite comfortable with someone as flip and unpredictable as Merlin. He did his job well, made very few mistakes—a classic example of the competent, ambitious bureaucrat. Much smarter than he let his superiors discern, he had risen inexorably in the BND because he didn't offend or threaten anyone.

"My pleasure, lieutenant. Sit down and enjoy the view of the Rhine. Would you join me in a glass of Schloss Johannisberger?" He was as good a host as he was an executive.

"Don't mind if I do," Cavaliere answered.

"Of course the view's a bit better from the Alter Zoll further up," Grad added truthfully.

A good host? No, a perfect one.

He ordered the wine, asked about their drive from Frankfurt.

"A delightful and scenic journey," Merlin replied archly, "with the special feature of being tailed by a green seventy-five Taunus. Friends of yours, Karl?"

The BND official shook his head.

"Didn't think so. We're guests in this country, and the BND would never be rude to guests, lieutenant. Would you like to talk about the weather, Karl? We've had terrific weather since we arrived. I'm going to tell all my friends about how swell the weather is in Germany in June."

"That's kind of you, major," Grad answered evenly. "Would you like something to eat? Some cold trout, perhaps?"

"Now there's hospitality. Trout would be dandy."

"Thank you very much," Cavaliere added—wondering what in hell Merlin was up to in this elliptical conversation. The talk dawdled on until the wine and food arrived. Grad appeared to be in no hurry to bring up the subject of the list, didn't mention it at all during the lunch.

"Thanks for suggesting the trout," Merlin said as he put down his fork and reached for his wineglass. "The wine was good too, Karl."

"Germany has many excellent wines. If you'd like to try—"

Merlin gestured grandly, and negatively. "No, thanks. I think I'll try the list—if you don't mind."

Herr Grad blinked, reached inside his jacket—giving them the briefest glimpse of a holstered small-caliber automatic—and drew out a plain white envelope.

"There are one hundred and four names," he said noncommittally. Then he put the envelope down on the table.

"And addresses?"

"As your local representative requested, major. Your theory is *quite* interesting."

Merlin scooped up the envelope with one hand, used the other to pour the last of the Schloss Johannisberger.

"It's more than a theory, Karl. Take it seriously."

Grad applied his starched linen napkin to his lips. "We've instructed all the prisons as you asked, major," he assured.

"And the military bases?"

The BND official nodded. "You're *confident* that these people will attempt a raid for explosives?"

Merlin swilled down the wine. "I'm betting on it," he said.

Some one hundred seconds later—at 2:05 P.M., to be precise —a very well-dressed German businessman named Alfred Balser glanced at his wristwatch. It was a gold Rolex, of course. The boardroom of the Chemical Industry Association was buzzing with the conversations of nearly a score of very well-dressed German businessmen—shrewd, successful men whose positions in the community required gold Rolexes and large Mercedes and a thorough knowledge of international trade, currency fluctuation and senior political figures. They were powerful men, top executives in the biggest chemical combines in prosperous West Germany. None of these gentlemen had ever been seduced by the Nazi ideology, for they'd always given their allegiance to the deutschmark.

Balser looked down at Frankfurt nine stories below, then across to the handsome oak door. The lunch had been splendid and the brandy first-class, but where was Heinrich?

"I hope the deal's as good as you say, Alfred," one of the others said jovially.

"Heinrich was very pleased. He'll tell you all about it," Balser replied.

The negotiations with the Soviets had been handled brilliantly, which was no surprise since Heinrich Hessicher had considerable experience in such matters. He was clever, and he was reliable. That's why Balser couldn't understand why he was late.

"He's in the Gents', Alfred. I saw him go in about five minutes ago," volunteered Von Brunnen.

They smoked and chatted, about the usual things—money,

politics, their vacation homes on the Costa del Sol and the latest sex scandal.

Where the hell was Heinrich?

After a few classic scatological jests about toilets and body functions, Balser grew impatient and just a little uneasy. He tried not to hurry as he left the boardroom, but once he was outside he walked swiftly to the lavatory. One booth was closed, and he recognized the expensive Italian shoes below the door immediately.

"Heinrich?"

There was no answer.

"You all right, Heinrich?"

Silence.

"Heinrich? Something wrong?"

No reply.

Balser hesitated, pulled open the door.

There was Heinrich Hessicher, seated on the toilet with his pants down—and a hole just over his nose. It was dripping blood. In the horror of the moment, Alfred Balser didn't notice the large sheet of paper on the floor. The police did when they arrived sixteen minutes later, and they recognized the insignia of the Lietzen-Stoller group before they read the scrawled manifesto.

This was a "warning" from "the people" that no deals with the "Moscow fascists" would be "tolerated." The traditional "Death to the Exploiters and Imperialists!" concluded the note, which a police laboratory technician carefully placed in a large envelope so that it could be checked for fingerprints and other clues. The 4 P.M. news broadcast announced that a building guard had identified Lietzen's photo as that of a maintenance man who'd arrived in coveralls to fix a leak.

Many of those who heard this report were shocked.

At least two—in the uniforms of U.S. Army officers—were angered.

One man took the news with total indifference. The terrorists were as remote and unreal to Ernest Beller as life forms on some distant planet. The whole news broadcast constituted a minor annoyance, an intrusion into the music he was enjoying. Dr. Beller had much more important things on his mind. He was on his way to Düsseldorf, the business center of the heavily

industrialized Ruhr. The two tall buildings on the horizon said
it clearly—the three "slabs" of the twenty-six-story Thyssen
headquarters put up in '57 and the twenty-three-floor alumi-
num-and-glass ode to the Mannesman steel group. Unaware
that Teletypes had already clicked out warnings to every
prison in West Germany housing Nazis who'd committed
"crimes against humanity," he pointed the gray BMW toward
the skyscrapers silhouetted ahead and thought about Monitz.
Thinking about Monitz was always particularly disturbing, for
his crimes touched a special nerve.

He'd slaughtered children.

That had been his job at the camp in Poland.

The Israeli teams that had tracked down Eichmann and
others had been hunting Monitz in thirty countries, but the
monster had been lucky. A journalist visiting a monastery in
Austria had recognized him in 1959, so Monitz got twenty-five
years instead of a burst from an Uzi or a letter bomb like the
one that took out the "respectable businessman" in Bremen a
year later.

Perhaps it was because of the fury that choked him when he
thought about Monitz, whom he would kill in two hours and
five minutes. Or maybe it was due to the "upper" that the
twenty-three-year-old driver of the red Toyota had popped an
hour earlier.

Whatever it was, Beller was less than half a kilometer inside
the city limits when he suddenly saw the red car hurtling at
him. He tried to twist the wheel and slam on the brakes, but
the Toyota was moving too fast. It rammed into the left side
of the BMW, smashing the rear door and back fender. Both
vehicles spun under the impact, and the BMW was hit again
by a green panel truck. That was the last thing the doctor knew
before everything went black.

"Are you all right?"

He opened his eyes, felt nauseated.

"Are you all right, mein herr?"

The man speaking through the window was a police officer.
After a few moments Beller's eyes focused properly and he
managed to speak.

"I—think so."

The policeman helped him out, and Ernest Beller, still
groggy, leaned against his vehicle. It was badly dented, but the

damage didn't seem nearly as serious as it might have been. The expensive BMW was a sturdy machine.

"What happened?" he wondered aloud.

The officer pointed to the red Japanese sedan, knocked over on its side with its whole front smashed. The driver was being laid on a stretcher by two ambulance attendants. "That's what happened," the policeman said. "Not blaming you. We'll figure out who's responsible at the station."

"Station?" Beller asked stupidly.

"The police station, mein herr. You'll have to come with me."

25

Every minute counted.

Every second the danger grew.

Beller knew that he was in jeopardy from the moment the policeman spoke. Not only was there the risk that some clever or lucky officer might find some flaw in his story—some minute error in his papers—but there were all the unpredictable problems that might arise if he arrived at the prison late. The German authorities were methodical, orderly and disciplined. As long as everything went as expected—as it was *supposed* to —they'd go along. If anything broke that neat pattern, they'd be uneasy—perhaps suspicious.

That was the bigger danger.

Beller was due at the prison at a quarter to two. It was 12:25 by the time they reached the station, where he was given a cup of mediocre instant coffee and the bump on his forehead was treated again with a stinging antiseptic that reminded him of the broken skin. The sergeant insisted on giving him a sterile German bandage like a Band-Aid before the questioning began. The avenger thought quickly about the chances of some tiny flaw in his forged papers, realized that there was but one sure and safe way to cope.

He told them that he was Dr. Ernest Beller, showed his U.S. passport and the documents identifying him as a civil servant– physician on the staff of the medical examiner of New York City. There was nothing wrong with these papers, he reasoned, so they had to work.

They did.

The police asked a lot of questions, but very courteously. They clearly respected a fellow public employee, and they addressed "Herr Doktor" with the deference that his professional position demanded. The long tradition of deference to all the many "Herr Doktors"—the hordes of physicians and dentists and lawyers and chemists and engineers and other solid briefcase carriers with vests—affected the tone of the entire examination, but not the questions themselves.

There were many questions, endless questions, all with polite "pleases" and then more questions. There were questions about when he entered the Federal Republic and others about his New York driver's license, and a lot more about the events "immediately preceding the collision."

"It's all routine procedure, Herr Doktor," the sharp-eyed sergeant said at least nine times. He went over each detail again and again and again. He glanced off toward the door to the rear, and Beller sensed that this policeman was stalling.

These efficient Germans were up to something.

He had to make his move—away.

"I want to call the nearest U.S. consul," he said abruptly.

"But you were born in Germany."

Delaying tactics, beyond doubt.

"I insist on my right to speak to the U.S. consul," Beller announced in a slightly louder voice.

"Herr Doktor, *bitte.*"

"Is this a democracy, or still a fascist state?" the pathological pathologist thundered. "You think you can still abuse Jews?"

The sergeant winced. *Gott,* this high-strung foreigner would go screaming to the U.S. papers and television networks—all riddled with people who still held grudges against Germany—and the mayor and the other politicians would go crazy. A young policeman walked in, whispered something.

"Herr Doktor, be calm."

"My senator in Washington will hear about these Nazi tactics!"

Nazi tactics?

"Doktor, we've just had the results of the tests. The driver of the other vehicle was under the influence of an artificial stimulant—a powerful pill. You understand? No way you can be responsible."

Beller's glare was pure hate, 180 proof. "Can I leave this prison?"

There were heaps of apologies, overlapping each other like mounds of leaves. A police car was provided to drive herr doktor to where he could rent a new vehicle, a tan VW Dasher in which he might complete his journey. As Beller drove off, he was disturbed by two things. He was behind schedule, and he was troubled by a senseless feeling that he was being tracked. He checked many times during the next twenty minutes and saw no pursuer, and finally arrived at the impressively modern "penal institution"—fifty-eight minutes late.

"We've been waiting for you."

Something in the warden's tone—or was it the look in his eyes?—suggested sudden jeopardy, and Beller's hand moved toward the bomb under his jacket. The Special Forces demolition experts had taught him well. If these guards moved to seize him, they'd all go with him. The warden glanced again at the letter identifying Beller as a BND agent on official business—Monitz business.

"Why Monitz?"

It sounded like an accusation.

"Warden Wankel, the BND is the security agency for the nation. We do not discuss classified projects with prison personnel."

"I wasn't prying. It was just—after all these years . . . I'll take you up myself."

While they were speaking, the warning message from Bonn was delivered to Wankel's secretary. She started to open it, but then the phone rang and when her conversation with Willi ended she spent a good two minutes adjusting her bra straps to make certain they stuck out and *up*—just right. Willi was so old-fashioned, but a dear. There, they were perfect. She opened the envelope, scanned the message form and stood up quickly.

Then she ran.

Flopping breasts, high heels and all, she ran.

Above, Wankel nodded professionally as a guard opened the metal door to the tier of cells and explained that there were relatively few such barriers on this floor, which held the model prisoners.

"Monitz is a model prisoner?"

"In more ways than one. You see—"

Then they heard the clatter of her high heels.

"Warden—this may be important!" she gasped.

Wankel gestured to the guard captain to open the cell facing them, and simultaneously took the message form from her.

"Hold it!"

The door was already three inches open.

"I'm afraid you can't see Monitz. No one can. This just arrived from Bonn," Wankel announced officiously. He thrust the page at Beller.

"Of course," the assassin improvised quickly. "Herr Wankel, that's why I'm here. No, not to kill Monitz," he chuckled. As patronizing chuckles go, it was Grade A.

The warden smiled back—warily.

"The message is from the BND, and so am I."

"No one can visit him. That's the order."

"Right. I'm here to check out his cell. Get some guards and move him to another cell for an hour while I search to make sure no one's put a bomb in here."

They made Beller stand twenty yards away as they marched the mass murderer out, and ninety seconds later the doctor entered Monitz's cell. The warden had quite a sense of humor. The child-killer's cell was hung with a score of model airplanes, hand-carved in light wood and meticulously painted. He was a "model" prisoner, all right. The guard captain watched from the door as Beller searched—and analyzed. It had to be the powder, the slow-acting poison absorbed right through the skin.

"Where's the warden?"

The captain turned to look up the corridor, and Beller sprayed a tiny puff of the odorless powder across the pillow. In ten or twenty days—depending on his strength—Monitz would fall ill. Within a month after that, he'd die.

"He's coming," the captain replied a few seconds later.

Beller told Wankel that the cell was "clean," ordered him to maintain maximum security for Monitz and pumped his hand twice before he left. The warden beamed when he heard the promise to report to the BND on how well his prison was run. Beller beamed when he walked to his car in the afternoon sun.

It had gone well, Beller thought as he checked for the sign pointing to the highway south.

Everything had worked—and in due course the slow-acting poison would too.

Still, Dr. Beller felt oddly uneasy and looked back several times in his rearview mirror.

No, there was no pursuer in sight.

Not yet.

26

Life is full of surprises.

A gifted Nashville songwriter named Tupper Saussy crafted a splendid little number with that title in 1975, and he was correct. Surprises and smart-ass types such as Klaus Tomburg abound, and there's no way to predict when you'll run into them. Ernest Beller didn't expect either that sunny July morning at 11:05, for his papers were "in order" and his dark suit was entirely appropriate for a junior partner in an important Frankfurt law firm.

"You *can't*, and you *couldn't* anyway," Tomburg told him with a large grin.

The size of the grin wasn't the surprise, for Tomburg weighed two hundred and thirty pounds. He was the biggest and least popular officer on the Kuppenheim staff. Every other guard captain in the German penal system was a wonderful, decent, sincere person deeply concerned about the world's hunger and population and pollution problems, and many of those good chaps had pen pals in Nigeria and Pakistan and southern California. Tomburg was different, a gross glutton with bad manners and an even worse sense of humor.

The others were embarrassed to have such an oaf at Kuppenheim, a provincial prison some twenty-six kilometers north of Baden-Baden. It's a lovely region. Sitting in the Oos Valley between the Black Forest and the fertile Baden vineyards, the luxurious Baden-Baden spa has been known for attracting the affluent since Rome's Emperor Caracalla arrived to try to cure his rheumatism. Kuppenheim isn't known for anything, certainly not its medium-sized penitentiary.

"No, you can't see Herr Dolken," Tomburg said slyly.

"This is a matter of some property he's inherited," Beller insisted, "and I have an official pass signed by—"

The captain's coarse laugh was almost a guffaw. "You probably don't know it, counselor, but Herr Hugo Dolken was sent here for what they used to call war crimes—or was it mass murder?"

Beller blinked behind his thick spectacles several times in a rather good simulation of bewilderment and surprise.

"He killed a lot of people in one of those camps," Tomburg explained, "and now some gang of fanatics is out killing the killers. Funny, uh?"

"I'm here on a real-estate matter," Beller insisted.

"Counselor," the captain sneered, "don't waste your breath. We've had orders that no one can visit the war criminals. That's why you couldn't see Dolken even if he was here."

What the hell was this ape talking about? Dolken had received a life sentence.

"We released that grumbling old fart—no offense, counselor —five or six days ago. Poor health, I heard. His granddaughter came up from Freudenstadt to collect him."

"Ilse—the plump one?" the homicidal doctor improvised.

Tomburg's grin turned into something just short of a leer— about *that* much. "Not fat at all. Slim but very pretty. Good set of knockers for her size."

Then Captain Tomburg belched loudly and Beller thanked him mechanically and turned toward his car.

"Don't blame me, counselor. Ain't my fault if some moronic clerk forgot to notify the rest of the family. . . . Ilse? Nah—it was . . . it was Hanna . . . I think." He belched again—onion sausage.

Klaus Tomburg would never have been promoted to captain if his wife's brother weren't so well connected, but the personnel policies of Kuppenheim Prison weren't what was on Dr. Beller's mind. He had to get a map to locate Freudenstadt, and when he got there he had to find some young woman whose first name was probably or possibly Hanna. Her family name could be anything. That crude slob could even be wrong about Freudenstadt.

It was warm in the midday glare as Beller drove south toward Baden-Baden, but the dark-green woods on the nearby hills helped considerably. The Black Forest had obviously received some more rain than other regions, and wasn't nearly as parched as eastern France less than a hundred miles away.

Shortly before noon he guided the tan Dasher past the ruins of the old castle at Hohenbaden that dominated the valley, and twenty minutes later he bought the map he needed at the newsstand in the lobby of the Bellevue Hotel on Baden-Baden's fashionable Lichtentaler Allee.

Those green-sheathed Michelin guides were terrific.

The Black Forest, locally called the Schwartzwald, stretched a hundred and six miles south from Karlsruhe in the industrial Saar basin to Basel in Switzerland. The Germans had sensibly divided the Black Forest into three parts—the Northern Black Forest, the Central Black Forest and the Southern Black Forest.

There was Freudenstadt, at the southern end of the Northern Black Forest, less than fifty miles down the mountain road from Baden-Baden. It was—praise the Lord—a smallish town with a population of just under fifteen thousand. Yes, it might be possible to find a slim, pretty woman whose name could be Hanna in such a community. Whatever her name was, Beller was hungry and in no mood to wait two hours for lunch. With all the twists and turns on the scenic Hochstrasse—the Black Forest crest road so popular with tourists—it would take at least that long for a prudent driver to reach Freudenstadt.

After lunch of Rhine salmon and onions at a nearby restaurant, Beller began driving south, at less than thirty miles an hour. He had no intention of spinning off one of the endless series of curves into the valley. He meant to arrive in Freudenstadt in perfect health, and then he would kill Hugo Dolken. That story about poor health didn't deceive Dr. Beller. The pathologist had read the reports on Dolken's trial, remembered how tricky and vicious the S.S. dentist had been.

Dolken was alive, but not for long.

It was really very pretty country, and as Beller left the vineyards in the foothills south of Baden-Baden he could see why so many vacationers came to these slopes. The masses of dark green conifers were broken by spaces that lured thousands of German skiers in the winter, and in the summer foreign tourists and hiking enthusiasts poured in to enjoy the natural splendor—and buy cuckoo clocks. This was the scenic Germany they featured in the travel brochures, each town a picture postcard. Buhlerhohe, Sand, Unterstmatt and Mummelsee, with the peak called the Hornisgrinde dominating the horizon.

Two busloads of tourists—one Japanese—slowed Beller as he approached Allerheiligen and the impressive Butten waterfalls, but he squeezed by and reached Freudenstadt at a quarter to four.

The town stood among those now-so-familiar pines on a high plateau where several mountain roads met, and a lot of people—including several guides from the American Express Company and Thomas Cook Ltd.—had called the views "breathtaking." Being obsessed and just a bit near-sighted, Dr. Beller paid little attention to the wonderful panoramas—all four-color jobs that any *National Geographic* subscriber or amateur photographer would adore. The purposeful pathologist did notice that there was a lot of new-look to Freudenstadt, and that there was a big town square surrounded by Renaissance arches. It was certainly the most impressive *marktplatz* in this part of the Black Forest.

Ernest Beller was completely unimpressed.

He was focused on finding a hotel for the night, and a certain dentist who had ripped gold fillings from the mouths of concentration-camp prisoners who were still alive. Witnesses at the trial had testified that Dolken never used any pain-killer, because he enjoyed the screams.

One hundred rooms—sixty with private bath—and a good dining room. That's what the Luz-Hotel-Waldlust at 92 Lauterbadstrasse promised, and even though it didn't offer an indoor pool like some of the others on the edge of town, Beller picked it for the central location. The government travel office had rated this establishment "first-class, superior," a notch above the others even though three of them had indoor swimming pools.

"It's our kitchen," explained the bellboy as he pocketed the tip. "We're famous for our kitchen. The skiers come in the winter, the hikers in the summer—and the sick ones all year round. You've heard of our spa, no doubt. Freudenstadt's water cures are known all over Germany, and in France and Switzerland too."

"It's a charming town," Beller said mechanically.

"We get more hours of sun each year than any other resort in all of Germany, mein herr."

What could one say to such Chamber of Commerce cant? Beller didn't know, so he gestured vaguely and faked a smile and the thirty-year-old "boy" departed. The doctor didn't waste the time to unpack. He reached for the telephone book on the bedside table instead.

Dolken, Stuttgarterstrasse 42.

Gerhardt Dolken had a wine shop, and perhaps a daughter named Hanna. Beller memorized the address, cautiously walked three blocks from the hotel before he asked a man outside a grocery to direct him to Stuttgarterstrasse. Less than fifteen minutes later he stood across the street from number 42. Bottles of Sylvaner and Rulander dominated most of the window display, with some of the fiery Black Forest raspberry brandy grouped in front of a photo-poster of a grinning skier. Beller circled the entire block slowly, remembering what the Special Forces men had taught him.

Reconnoiter the area thoroughly.

Check the traffic flow and possible escape routes.

Find the sentries.

No, there wasn't a policeman in sight.

"Guten tag," the woman behind the counter said politely.

She wasn't pretty, and she was at least fifty. This wasn't the granddaughter, but could be her mother or aunt. Beller paid for a bottle of the raspberry brandy, accepted his change.

"Frau Dolken?"

"Jah?"

She was local all right. The accent proved that.

"You wouldn't have a daughter named Hanna?"

The middle-aged woman with the pursed lips shook her head.

"I met the young lady in Baden-Baden a few weeks ago, at a concert."

Frau Dolken nodded in approval. She respected concerts and all such cultural activities.

"She said that her grandfather lived somewhere near here," Beller tested. *"Hugo* Dolken? A dentist?"

"We're the only Dolkens in Freudenstadt, mein herr. My late husband used to joke about how rare our name is in this part of the country, and now there's only his mother and me left. A dentist, you say?"

"She said."

"No, we're a family of shopkeepers. Sorry I can't help you."

Was she lying?

It wouldn't be surprising, for no one in Germany today would be proud of a war criminal relative.

Another customer entered, and Beller walked out into the fine bright afternoon. The sun was shining—of course—and the clean mountain air was fresh, and Ernest Beller was thwarted.

He was not discouraged.

The sadist would not escape him. It was simply a matter of applying his intelligence to the problem—the same analytical mind that had done so well at Harvard and the Columbia medical school and those other German prisons earlier. If he couldn't *reason* it out, Beller would wait and let his subconscious float the solution up to him. He knew it would work, for it always had. All he had to do was—not do anything, and he'd wake up tomorrow or the next day with the answer. Johnny Mercer, the genial/shrewd southern gentleman who had crafted the lyrics for such gracious and lovely songs as "That Old Black Magic," "Laura," "Too Marvelous for Words" and "When the World Was Young," had once told an interviewer that you couldn't force creative thinking. The answers just came when they were damn good and ready, according to the talented and savvy Mr. Mercer, and if you were really a creator they always came. Dr. Beller recognized that there was much rubbish in popular music, but he also knew better than to ignore the fundamental "country" wisdom of a folk philosopher such as Johnny Mercer.

The solution would come.

It would appear suddenly—clear, logical and simple—within two or three days, and there was no need to sweat it. This was a delightful region, a splendid place to rest and celebrate the wonders of nature. The pathologist felt completely relaxed as he strolled the streets of the pleasantly unhurried city, and he was just as free of tension when he returned to the hotel for dinner. The cuisine posed no threat to the chefs at the Oustau de la Baumanière at Les Baux in Provence or those at Lutèce in New York, but the food was better than good and the half-bottle of Baden-grown Ihringer Winklerberg left him ready for sleep.

The Martians weren't at all sleepy.

Full of histamines, excitement and the crazy commitment that so many people get when they're sure that they're right, the terrorists were sawing the lock off the door of a supply hut at a construction site on the edge of Bremen. They stole four cases of explosives, loaded the boxes into two cars stolen that afternoon and drove south toward the chemical, gas and rubber factories of the industrial Ruhr.

Just before 5 A.M. there was a very loud noise just outside the city of Beckum. Then there were several other explosions that awoke at least a quarter of the 370,000 hard-working residents, civilized burghers who were just as proud of the Shakespeare productions at the City Theater as they were of the fine productivity at the auto, machine and chemical plants. Now a big ball of fire blossomed, and two other red pillars defaced the dawn horizon only minutes later.

Werner Buerckel had done an excellent job of sabotage. The terrorists' demolition specialist had used only one case of explosives to destroy most of a 52,000,000-mark chemical plant. Now there were more fires and the sounds of bullhorns as half a dozen "engine companies" raced toward the blazing factory. The intermittent series of blasts and clouds of choking smoke reminded more than one fire-brigade officer of an unforgettable RAF visit back in late '43, or was it early '44? It had been a terrible winter in the Ruhr.

The terrorists were already a dozen kilometers away, heading east just under the legal speed limit. Despite the explosions and the red glare on the horizon, Marta Falkenhausen was still the only one to congratulate Buerckel on his success.

"*Sehr gut*, Werner," she complimented.

Then Karla Lange—seated up front beside Lietzen, who was driving—remembered how much the explosives man needed reassurance. "Fine work," she chimed in dutifully.

"I only used one box," Werner said in tones edged with pride. "We've still got three left. That's good, isn't it?"

"That's *very* good," Lietzen agreed.

"What are we going to do with the other three?" Buerckel wondered almost childishly.

It was difficult not to laugh.

"Don't worry, Werner," Lietzen replied as he smiled in the darkness. "We'll think of something—soon!"

27

When Ernest Beller awoke the next morning, he was just a trifle disappointed to find that he still had absolutely no idea how to continue his search for Hugo Dolken. There was no reason to panic, of course. The inspiration would come. It had to, for Johnny Mercer himself had predicted that, sooner or later, "Something's Gotta Give."

Nothing did.

After a superior breakfast, the pathologist wandered over to one of Freudenstadt's intensely modern spas, where a proud member of the staff presented a brochure listing all the treatments offered. "Pine extract movement bath; remedial gymnastics; exercises (group therapy); underwater gymnastics (butterfly tub); sauna; Turkish baths; Kneipp (hydropathic) therapy; full, partial and connective tissue massage; underwater jet massage; packs; medicinal baths; respiratory therapy; inhalations; rest rooms; course of therapy by drinking the waters; chiropody; organized gymnastics; breathing exercises; and 'terrain' cures," Beller read aloud.

The incredulity in his voice was obvious, but the spa attendant misunderstood. "You are impressed," he said smugly. "Well, most people are. We use many different sports too."

"Just what medical problems do you treat with all this?" the American physician asked cautiously.

The man in the white jacket handed him another leaflet with a flourish. Before Beller could study it, the attendant began to chant. "Asthma, emphysema, bronchitis, callus formations in the bronchial tubes, diabetes, metabolic disorders, exudative diathesis and pulmonary complaints, degenerative disorders of the locomotory apparatus, cardiac and circulatory diseases and disorders of the bloodstream."

"Wonderful," the American lied with a straight face.

The attendant had merely paused for breath. There was more.

"Spinal ailments, neurovegetative metabolic irregularities, rehabilitation from infarct effects, nervous and physical exhaustion, postaccident and postoperative *and* orthopedic rehabilitation," the man singsonged proudly.

Dr. Beller didn't laugh. It *sounded* ridiculous, but it actually wasn't all that bizarre. The tradition of spas that tried to cope with an extraordinary variety of diseases and afflictions was an old one, and it wasn't limited to Germany. The Germans, of course, had always been particularly vulnerable to odd theories of pseudoscience. Beller wasn't about to judge the merits of this particular establishment, largely because he didn't give a damn.

"If you have any further questions, mein herr, you may telephone for further information," the attendant invited.

There was the answer.

Simple, logical, obvious.

Beller thanked the helpful man in the white jacket, hummed as he walked back to the hotel to call the prison. Thanks to the efficiency of the Federal Republic's modern telephone system, he was speaking to the secretary of the warden at Kuppenheim within ninety seconds. Fraulein Kluger sat bolt upright in her chair when she learned that she was speaking to the deputy director of Penal Research at the Ministry of Social Services, who was plainly *furious*.

"If you people can't fill these reports out properly," Beller snapped in the petulant tones of the outraged bureaucrat, "you cause other departments a *great* deal of trouble."

"I'm terribly sorry," she apologized. "I'll put another copy in the pouch today. . . . Yes, here it is—Hugo R. Dolken—diagnosis: terminal cancer . . . released on compassionate grounds on the ninth to his granddaughter, Anna Griese . . . 107 Mullerstrasse in Freudenstadt. . . . I can assure you that another copy of the full medical report—"

"I can assure *you*, fraulein," Beller roared, "that you people at Kuppenheim will hear more about this."

He slammed down the phone, smiled and reached for his weapons.

The house was the third in a block of typical Black Forest houses, all four stories with beamed fronts in the architectural style so popular in the region forty or fifty years earlier. Beller prowled the quiet residential neighborhood, decided from its cars and small shops that it was lower-middle-class and finally entered the street-floor foyer of 107.

Griese—2B.

The implacable boy from Dachau took a deep breath and nodded. Dolken might fool or bribe those prison doctors, but he would not escape the vengeance of Ernst Beller. For a moment the nameplate over the buzzer blurred, and suddenly the pit—*that* pit with the heaped corpses—filled his vision. It was over in three or four seconds, and Beller was calm as he rang the bell.

"She's not here."

Beller turned to face a thin, crafty-looking old man with a cane.

"I've come to see her grandfather."

The gray-haired man grunted, pointed to the right. "You'll find them both at Hofschuster's—Gruning Terrasse. Eighty or ninety Gruning," he replied with a grin that was somehow unpleasant. He jabbed with the weathered stick again. "That way. Two blocks, then right two more—no, three. They're both there."

Beller couldn't quite make out what the old man muttered after he'd thanked him, so he circled the senior citizen and set off for Hofschuster's. He'd have to be careful, alert for traps.

Just as Dolken would be.

A man who'd been clever enough to trick his way out of prison was no fool, no dozing graybeard worn down by the boredom and confinement of years behind walls. No, Dolken would be more dangerous than the others.

It was exciting. The doctor recognized and labeled the thrill a moment after the adrenaline flushed into his bloodstream, and he stopped dead in his tracks. It was embarrassing. Uncle Martin would have other words, none of them pleasant. The medical terms themselves would be flat and diagnostic, but they would all add up to some kind of mental illness.

"No," Beller said aloud as he turned onto Gruning Terrasse. It wasn't true. He was no homicidal psychotic, no vicious hunter seeking the thrill of the kill. He wasn't doing any of this for personal pleasure or even vengeance. It wasn't that at all. It was that the time of reckoning had come. The legal system had failed to deal with these butchers adequately, and he was merely correcting things. He was doing what thousands—probably millions—of people all around the world dreamed of doing. He was settling the account—at last.

After all those victims.

After all those years.

It was time.

It was time, and it was just—and no one else would do it, so Ernst Beller had to take the responsibility.

Hofschuster—a small brass plaque set in the brick wall of a large three-story building. The sign beside the dark wooden door gave no clue as to what sort of business this structure housed, but there were no police in sight and no unaccounted-for men lingering in nearby cars. The doctor strolled by to the next corner, noted no menace and returned to enter. Wood-paneled walls, a marble floor, lights a bit dimmer than Beller liked. It all added up to something heavy. The atmosphere was almost thick, and Beller found it oppressive. There was a wooden table and a chair, unoccupied.

What sort of place was this?

At the far end of this foyer were two large doors, but there was no one to ask where Fraulein Griese might be. Beller scanned the lobby, walked forward warily to open one of the big swinging doors. He was in a chapel, a large room with rows of pews on either side of a carpeted aisle and a simple crucifix on a pedestal at the far end. There was only one person in the room, a pretty young woman in a simple dark dress and shoulder-length blonde hair. She might have been twenty-three or twenty-five. She was surely in pain. You didn't have to be an analyst to read the suffering in her face.

"Fraulein Griese?"

She looked up, stared at Beller with large sad eyes that seemed to peer right through him.

"Fraulein Anna Griese?" he tested cautiously.

She nodded as if speech might hurt her throat.

"Kurt Nessel," the executioner lied as he glanced around for his target. "I was told that you were here with your grandfa-ther."

She nodded again, abstractedly brushed back a loose strand of that fine gold hair. "I can't cry," she said in numb-choked tones.

It didn't make any sense, and Beller wondered whether she might be deranged.

"I don't mind that nobody came," she continued in that cramped voice, "but I hoped that one or two might . . . Do I know you?"

"No. I came to Freudenstadt to see your grandfather."

She was more than pretty.

She was nearly beautiful, and haunted.

"Here he is," she said.

She pointed at a coffin almost obscured by the pews, and Beller stepped forward to look at the corpse of Hugo Dolken. Was it a deception? Could they have prepared another body —one with a similar face?

No, it was the sadist dentist all right. There was the malformed left earlobe he'd had from birth, and the right pinkie crushed in a 1953 escape attempt merely confirmed the identification. The son of a bitch was dead. He'd cheated Beller, and all the victims.

"I can't cry because I didn't really like him, Herr—I'm sorry, I've forgotten your name."

"Nessel."

"He was my grandfather, but we were all ashamed. He did terrible things for the Nazis—unspeakable things." She shook her head.

Was it anger or pity?

"Was he a friend of yours, Herr—Nessel?"

"We never met. I'm doing research for a book, and I hoped he might help."

She sat down, clearly exhausted. "He had no friends, and he never helped anyone. Maybe some of those other Hitler gangsters were his—I don't know. I don't know anything about my terrible grandfather, except that he's dead and no one has come to mourn him and even I can't cry."

"Fraulein Griese—" Beller began.

"I can't cry!"

Beller stepped forward and put his arm around her.

It was quite extraordinary.

He didn't understand it, but he felt sorry for the monster's granddaughter. He held her firmly but tenderly, and after a few moments he felt the sobs battling deep within her. Muffled gasps and spasms tore at her, but it took longer before he heard her cry. Two or three minutes later the weeping subsided, and Beller offered her his handkerchief.

Even puffy and tearstained, she was lovely.

"Fraulein," he heard himself say, "may I see you home?"

28

It was a hot afternoon and the rented blue Audi moved slowly through the heavy Ku-damm traffic. Cavaliere was pleased to be back in civilian clothes again. He was also puzzled.

"Merl," he asked politely as he saw the bulk of the Hilton ahead, "why are we in Berlin?"

"We're here because *they're* here. I know they are," the man behind the wheel replied confidently.

"*I'm* sure you're right, but what makes *you* sure?"

The light changed, and Merlin smiled, nicely. "My left nut," he explained. "My left nut tells me the Martians are here in West Berlin."

It was going to be one of those crazy Merlin conversations, the migraine specials.

"Well, your left nut's never been wrong," Angelo Cavaliere agreed with a shrug. "Best left nut in the agency, they say."

"My left nut *and* the fact that they've pulled twice as many jobs here as anywhere else during the past year. They've got a burrow here somewhere," Merlin said as he neatly avoided creasing a passing police car, "so all we've got to do is find it."

The entrance to the Hilton garage was only ninety yards ahead, and Merlin said nothing as he maneuvered through the traffic.

"Big city . . . Martians know it cold . . . thousands of German cops and security pros couldn't find them . . . only two of us . . . goddam mess," he summarized after a brief silence.

The son of a bitch could read minds too.

"I know you hate to bother people, Merl," his partner began hopefully, "but Diane's a pretty sharp station officer and she's got a whole gang of experienced troops here, so I wonder whether you think this might be the time to use her—"

Merlin broke right into the thought, at full speed. "No, I think it's time we—you and me—stopped farting around and took the initiative ourselves. It's time to kick some ass," he announced, and he explained his plan. Typical goddam Merlin plan—simple, brutal and practical.

"Do I have time for an aspirin? I'm getting a headache," Cavaliere said truthfully.

Merlin shook his head, turned the Audi into the garage driveway and parked the car. Then it all happened very quickly, exactly as Cavaliere had dreaded. Merlin went up to his room to collect two concussion grenades and a silencer for his handgun. He exposed the hidden "bug," picked up the telephone.

"Operator, this is Mr. Wasserman in nine twenty-seven. I'd like to call Frankfurt. The number is two . . . four . . . one . . ."

He didn't say the next four digits. Instead he tapped the eavesdropping device several times with his ballpoint pen and hung up abruptly. Next he jammed the tip of the pen into the radio-microphone, put the "bug" back where it had been and started for the door. He didn't slow down to answer the ringing phone, for he knew that it was the diligent operator calling for the rest of the imaginary Frankfurt number.

Merlin was smiling as he left. He'd been angry for weeks about being followed and "bugged," and now he was going to eliminate the source of irritation. He would remind them that such disrespect for a veteran of his stature would not be tolerated. Someone was going to get hurt.

Four minutes after Frank Wasserman stepped out of the hotel onto the chic Budapester Strasse, a man in German sports clothes stepped out of Room 933 into the corridor. The watcher in the lobby had reported Merlin's exit, so it was safe to check on what had happened to the "bug." The door of 927 yielded to the man's skeleton key, and it took him less than fifty seconds to place a new "bug" and depart with the damaged model in his left fist.

He didn't see Cavaliere hiding up at the turn in the corridor. He wasn't supposed to.

"Maybe twenty-six or twenty-eight, blonde hair—almost white—about five-nine or ten," Cavaliere told Merlin in the garage a few minutes later.

"Only one?"

"All I saw."

"There'll be more in the room," Merlin computed.

"Nine thirty-three, just up the hall."

Merlin visualized the location, nodded. "Anything else?" he asked.

"He was sort of bouncy."

"Bouncy?"

"Walked on the balls of his feet—like an athlete."

"In five minutes he'll be on the balls of his ass," Merlin promised harshly.

It wasn't standard operating procedure at all, and Cavaliere wanted to point out that there was no certainty that the listeners were Martians. They could very well be Sovs, probably were. Maybe even West German operatives. Shit, it would be a waste of time to argue, Cavaliere brooded as they entered the elevator. Merlin had been simmering since news of the gas attack on the jailed woman in Stuttgart and the destruction of the Beckum petrochemical plant. Now he'd come to a boil. He wanted to smash back, and now that he'd found a foe to hit there was no way that Cavaliere or anyone else could talk him out of it.

Concussion grenades?

Terrible.

"Let's go," Merlin said as they walked out of the elevator on the tenth floor and headed for the fire stairs. The crazy bastard was grinning like some enthusiastic high-school football player. Merlin stepped out onto the ninth floor first, looked around and signaled Cavaliere to join him. When they reached Room 933, Merlin handed his partner one of grenades and then screwed the silencer onto the .22-caliber assassin's gun.

"Don't want to wreck the furniture," he whispered.

He didn't give a damn what the grenades would do to the poor bastards inside Room 933. No, not *poor* bastards, *dumb* bastards, Cavaliere told himself. If they were smarter they'd have seen him.

Jesus Christ. He was starting to think like Merlin.

"Ready?" Merlin mouthed silently.

When Cavaliere nodded, Merlin rapped on the door.

He said that it was "room service"—in a perfect Berlin accent—and a moment later someone warily opened the door, just two inches. Merlin kicked it in instantly, and even as it flew back he hurled in the first concussion grenade. As planned, Angelo Cavaliere threw in the second only a moment later. The two CIA men leaped to either side of the doorway in the hall, dodging the shock waves that would smash the people in the room.

Two explosions—loud.

The first sent the two men inside the room flying, hurling one head first into the plate-glass window with such terrific force that it shattered and cut his scalp open in four places. The other man was literally blasted through the bathroom door, which hung crazily on one hinge. Metal and plastic remnants of a tape recorder and an FM radio transmitter were sprayed around the room like souvenirs of some dead civilization. Dozens of bits of glass from what had been a large mirror littered every surface, and the empty frame of the mirror over the bathroom sink testified that the shock waves had battered the entire suite.

Blood pouring down over his face and ears, the man by the ruined window tried to get up—but fell. The scarlet gush looked weird in that white-blond hair, but Merlin paid no attention to the man's injuries. He walked over, jerked the automatic from the bleeding man's belly holster and put it in his own belt.

"Three minutes," he announced as he turned and walked to close the door to the corridor.

"That guy may bleed to death!" Cavaliere protested.

"We should have brought Band-Aids. Listen, Angie, wrap a sheet around his head while I talk to his friend in the can. If Blondie gets funny, just kick him in the face."

Merlin picked the other dazed man off the bathroom floor, noted that he was bleeding from his ears, nostrils and mouth. His shirt was blown half off, and only his right shoe remained. Merlin dragged him to the sink, turned on the cold water.

"You look disgusting," Merlin said, and shoved the man's face into the water. It only took seconds for the shock of the water—on his face and in his nose and mouth—to jerk him back to reality. His body convulsed in some primeval spasm as it fought to avoid drowning, and he choked and gagged before Merlin pulled him from the bowl.

"You still look terrible. You always dress in rags?" Merlin

baited. He dropped the man onto the toilet, still gasping and bleeding.

"We've got about two and a third minutes before somebody shows up to find out what happened here, chum," Merlin explained, "so you've got one minute—maybe eighty seconds—to tell us who you work for and your mother's maiden name."

The pudgy choking man looked up, coughed. "You mother!" he said venomously.

Merlin picked him up, threw him out into the bedroom like a toy. He crashed into an end table, which broke.

"Seventy seconds—and counting," Merlin noted.

"I think this one needs an ambulance," Cavaliere appealed.

"Merlin, you bastard!"

It wasn't Cavaliere who spoke. It was the half-drowned man sprawled on the floor.

"She said you were crazy, and she was—right," he croaked before the coughs swept all words away again.

"Who said?" Merlin demanded.

The man on the floor wiped the blood from his mouth, gagged again before he spoke. "Same side . . . same side."

Merlin ignored the crude diversion. "Who said? You'd better answer, or I'll drop your cousin here right out the window," he threatened.

The man stared up, furious and defiant. "Station officer."

"Oh, my God," groaned Cavaliere.

"Horse shit. What station officer?" challenged Merlin.

"Merlin—"

"Shut up, Angie. What station officer?"

"Siegenthaler," the man snarled—and then he vomited all over the rug.

Yes, it was the sort of thing she'd do.

Or they could be Sovs who knew the name of the local CIA supervisor. That sort of information was almost impossible to keep secret in major cities around the world, where both sides —and the local security chiefs—knew who ran U.S. and Russian intelligence nets. Maybe these two bleeders were bluffing, weren't CIA after all.

"Crash Dive," the blond with the ruined scalp suddenly sighed. "She said Crash Dive," he remembered.

"Jeezus," Cavaliere said as he wondered whether Merlin would accept this proof that he'd smashed up two of his own operatives and destroyed considerable U.S. government property. Angelo Cavaliere looked around the blood-spattered, blast-battered room slowly, tried to guess what Merlin could say now.

He'd done it, and damn near done in two CIA agents in the violent process.

What could he possibly say?

"One minute," Merlin announced in a shockingly cool voice.

The son of a bitch was still computing.

"You've got about one minute, Angie, to move these gents out of this shambles up the hall to my room. Here's the key." He tossed it, and Cavaliere caught it by sheer reflex.

"What the hell am I supposed to do with them, Merl? These *gents*—whose eardrums and guts you just bombed—need a doctor."

Merlin was already at the door. "They've got an emergency number. When you get them inside my room, they can call for a medical crew—one of our own."

"Hey!" Cavaliere objected.

"Keep them in the can. Don't let them bleed on my bed, will you?"

The dazed duo were both muttering, but nothing that made much sense.

"And where the hell are you going?"

"Hardenbergstrasse, to boot the ass of a very pretty and tricky black lady who caused this whole mess. Meet me there."

Incredible.

After what he'd done, Merlin was righteous—briefly.

Then he was gone.

29

It wasn't just an act. Merlin genuinely believed that the Hilton diaster was entirely the fault of his ex-wife.

She'd always been too nosy, too intellectual, too aggressive to leave him alone. She'd never trusted him completely. She'd tried to manipulate him, using all her knowledge and woman techniques and the sophisticated "personnel" approach of a well-educated administrator.

He gunned the Audi out of the garage, barely controlling his fury. Nobody—man or woman—was going to manage Merlin. Probably thought she was protecting him with a backup surveillance team. Shit, didn't she realize he was sure to spot them? Christ, she was goddam lucky he hadn't killed them both. Neither of them too sharp anyway.

Goddam lucky.

Station officer or no station officer, he was going to beat on her executive butt. Hard. After all these months this woman could still get him angry. It was ridiculous. He had to be careful to handle this confrontation in a totally professional manner, strictly by the book with no trace of any emotional involvement or personal crap. Men tended to favor attractive women, and she was certainly that. She used it. Used everything, except the black thing. Merlin had never known why, and now he didn't care.

He'd never entirely understood her.

She certainly hadn't understood him—not really.

Perfect marriage?

The Audi was half a block from the Amerika Haus when he heard the gunfire. His trained ear identified the rapid-fire weapon instantly. It was the same kind of squirt gun the terrorists had used to spray the Ku-damm his first day in town—an L2A3 Sterling, probably stolen from some British Army depot.

Staggered box magazine with thirty-four rounds of 9-millimeter stuff, 1280-feet-per-second velocity. Infantry job.

Merlin pulled his .357 Magnum, pointed the Audi right at the front door of the U.S. cultural center. He was still forty yards away when they came running out, with the man with the Sterling first to hit the sidewalk. The three others—two male and one female—were dragging a woman who had once been Merlin's. He was stunned for half a second, then extremely angry. He saw the rear door of a brown panel truck open, recognized the face of the woman inside as that of Lietzen's homicidal mistress. Merlin pressed down on the gas pedal, and the man with the Sterling blew away half of his windshield and some key bits of the Audi's pipes and wiring.

The Audi was still moving on its momentum, and the black woman was screaming as they hustled her into the truck. The Sterling hammered again. Merlin had dropped flat on the seat, undamaged except for an ear gashed by shards of glass. He opened the door beside the steering wheel, dived out into the street and rolled over into firing position.

His first slug knocked the machine gunner back against the building, and his second must have hit one woman who was pushing Diane McGhee into the truck. She staggered, and her allies jerked her into the vehicle. Someone threw two—maybe three—tear-gas grenades, and the terrorists raced away with Merlin firing blindly into the choking mist.

He heard a crash, saw his Audi had rammed a parked Toyota and didn't care. With his car dead he couldn't pursue, so he did what he could. He ran into the Amerika Haus, saw Freddy Cassel slumped semiconscious on the floor near her receptionist's desk and charged right past her to the CIA office.

The door was wide open.

The husky security man, Jeff Anderson, was sprawled across the doorway to the station officer's suite. There was blood on the rug—a lot of it. Anderson's shirt was drenched in it, so much that it came through his seersucker jacket. The phone on Anderson's desk had been ripped from the wall, and so had that in the inner office. Merlin ran back, saw Freddy Cassel moving and—dammit—her phone wrecked too. He sprinted up the corridor, saw a door marked MUSIC and pushed it open.

There were seven people seated in front of tables adorned

with phonographs—listening to music. They were wearing headsets, and several didn't even notice Merlin's arrival. Those who did—including a plump fifty-eight-year-old widow who was fond of Aaron Copland's works and younger men who'd treat her badly—almost wet their pants. Merlin was bleeding from his ear, carrying a terribly menacing Magnum and looking as if he might use it at any moment.

There was also an assistant music librarian at a small desk. She had brown hair, falsies and an M.A. in music from Vanderbilt, the Princeton of the South. She knew a great deal about country, jazz, blues, soul, show tunes and even rock—as well as American symphonic, operatic, chamber and liturgical works. She knew little about wild-eyed men with large-bore handguns, however.

"May I help you, suh?" she offered politely.

Merlin noticed that she had lovely blue eyes and some excellent dental work—and a desk telephone. He picked up the instrument, dialed the number of the Hilton swiftly.

"Suh, you can't make outside—"

He waved the gun and she stopped talking.

"Angie?"

"Made the call, Merl. Everything's okay."

"No, it isn't. The Martians just snatched the Black Queen, and the Watchdog's leaking red all over the floor."

It probably made sense if you were good at literary acrostics and crossword puzzles, the woman facing Merlin thought, but this was no time to interrupt to ask.

"Full alert. Notify all our friends and neighbors, local and Bonn. Brown van—no, panel truck—could be an Opel, heading west, maybe three minutes ago. We need a meat truck for the Watchdog to get him to a secure hospital—U.S. Army, not Kraut—and we need a cleanup team to cover here."

"They're on their way."

"Make it fast. In about three minutes we should be ass-deep in local law."

The assistant music librarian, who had kept her hands clasped tightly as she stared at the Magnum, smiled graciously as Merlin slammed down the phone.

"You really aren't supposed to—"

Merlin never heard the end of the sentence. He dashed back up the hall, reached Freddy Cassel just as the high-low-high-low horns announced that police cars were arriving. The Berlin cops were quick, savvy and numerous. Eight men erupted from cars, guns drawn as they moved in warily. Three of those men were pointing weapons at Merlin seconds later.

"Lietzen-Stoller," he told them. "That bastard on the sidewalk was one of them."

The police told him to put down his gun, and he laid it on the receptionist's desk.

"There's a wounded man bleeding back there," he added. The senior cop nodded, and one of the others hurried in the direction that Merlin had pointed.

"And who are you?"

"My name is Frank Wasserman. They kidnapped a woman who worked here—black, pretty, early thirties. Took off in a brown Opel delivery truck maybe four minutes ago."

Three more officers entered, and one was sent to put out a radio alarm. "He's dead," said one of the newcomers with a nod toward the street.

"You kill him?" asked the sergeant.

Merlin nodded, and the sergeant sensed that this was nothing very special to the American who perched on the edge of the desk. Merlin was in no mood to handle more questions, so he decided to cut the conversation short.

"Try Karl Grad, BND in Bonn."

The cop nodded. It was one of *those* messes.

"You have any kind of official identification, Herr Wasserman?"

"No. Just my passport. I'm a furniture salesman."

"I'll bet."

Freddy Cassel opened her eyes, made some sort of sound. Merlin reached down, raised her gently.

"Frank—Frank, they had—guns."

"I know. They're gone. You all right?"

She blinked several times before she answered. "I feel sick —hit me with a gun."

The sergeant ordered one of the police to take her out, and to radio for the ambulance to hurry.

"Tell your men that some friends of mine will be here soon, five or six men in cars and a U.S. Army ambulance," Merlin said.

"All furniture salesmen?"

Merlin nodded.

"All armed like you?"

"Some may be carrying submachine guns. It's a highly competitive business, sergeant."

The policeman almost smiled. By now the corridor was filled with employees and visitors, all nervous and curious. One of those most concerned was the Amerika Haus director, and it was his office phone that the sergeant used. By the time he returned to the lobby, five more "furniture salesmen" were entering the building.

"Merlin?"

"Seal off the back offices, and keep an eye on that cop back there with Anderson."

The other Berlin police looked at their sergeant, who shrugged his assent and turned to the American with the bleeding ear.

"Merlin?"

"My middle name. I have several. Can I take my gun?"

"In a little while. I'm just waiting to hear from my headquarters about this fellow Grad you mentioned. . . . You're bleeding from your left ear, you know."

Merlin thanked him for pointing this out, and then the sergeant offered to get a bandage from the first-aid kit in his car. "Unless you prefer an American bandage," he added as the U.S. Army corpsmen entered with the stretcher.

"Thanks. We'll fix it at the hospital."

Merlin sent the ambulance team back to collect the wounded man, and the sergeant said nothing until the Americans returned with a white-faced Anderson on their litter.

"Just a moment," the police sergeant ordered stiffly.

It could have gotten unpleasant, for no one is supposed to leave the site of a serious crime—in Berlin or anywhere else —until the cops have all the information they want.

"You want to kill him?" Merlin challenged.

"I want to hear from this Grad."

A young policeman hurried in, whispered something to the sergeant, who nodded.

"Take your pistol, furniture salesman. I have been told to extend to you all courtesies as a friend of the Federal Republic."

Merlin scooped up his gun, thanked the sergeant again and

led the medics out onto the street, where a dozen police were holding back a small crowd.

"There's a dead guy on the sidewalk," one of the corpsmen pointed out as they prepared to slide the stretcher into the ambulance.

"No kidding," Merlin responded, and he said nothing more until they reached the emergency ward of the U.S. Army hospital. He was computing. All the while the doctors worked over the wounded man—as the plasma dripped and the scalpels cut and the clamps held pieces of the CIA security man tightly—he computed. He was still calculating and figuring as the needles closed the hole.

Crash Dive.

How did the Martians know?

Who set this up?

Why now?

Crash Dive.

He added, subtracted, divided—again and again.

Where did they have her?

Who had betrayed her?

What did they want?

Merlin thought, analyzed the possibilities over and over with Cavaliere, who'd joined him, and then thought some more. He smoked and paced and smoked, and he cursed now and then.

Crash Dive.

Something added up wrong.

"Crash Dive," he repeated angrily for the thirtieth time.

"You said that. As a matter of fact, you've been saying that every couple of minutes for more than two hours," Cavaliere announced.

"Crash Dive."

The cigar smoke was almost unbearable.

"For God's sake," Cavaliere grumbled, "can't you say anything else?"

Merlin stopped pacing, yawned.

For a moment he stopped calculating and he felt.

Pure wild impulse. No, intuition.

"Metaphor!" he called out loudly.

"Well, you never said *that* before," Cavaliere approved and took another sip of the cold black coffee.

30

"Metaphor!"

"I think I like Crash Dive better, Merl. At least I know what you mean."

Merlin ground out his corona, smiled for the first time in hours.

"Metaphor! Why not?"

"Is there something you forgot to tell me, Merl?"

It wouldn't be anything new.

Merlin never told anybody everything.

"Let's find a doctor," Merlin proposed.

Since his ear was now adorned with a neat bandage, Merlin wanted the physician for someone or something else. Whatever it was, it had something to do with Metaphor—whatever or whoever that was. Cavaliere was confident that Merlin would explain it—most of it—reasonably soon. They found the surgeon who'd worked on Anderson, and that dedicated healer found Merlin's idea appalling.

"That's preposterous. Mr. Anderson is still in serious condition, and I certainly don't intend to endanger his recovery—perhaps his survival—by giving him sodium pentothal."

Dr. Milton Margolis was indignant, a condition not uncommon among graduates of the University of Chicago medical school. He didn't know that Anderson was security officer for the Berlin station, that this CIA unit had been penetrated and that Merlin was gambling that he might recall something—anything—under drug-assisted hypnosis that could give a clue to the Red agent code-named Victor.

"It's just a shot in the dark—a long shot in the dark," Merlin admitted, "but to tell you the truth, I'm just a bit desperate."

"You're a bit crazy," snapped Margolis, who was known for his neat stitching, big mouth and terrific backhand shot. "I don't know just who you are, Mr. Wasserman, but I can tell you no civilian is going to give orders to a major in the U.S. Army."

"You're right, doc. Excuse my dumb manners. May I please use your phone? It's important."

"Keep it short, will you?" Margolis urged in tones that were brisk and officious.

"I want the tie line to Heidelberg. This is a priority call—urgent—to Brigadier General Theodore Brieant at G-two. He's deputy commander, G-two, USAEUR."

Dr. Margolis was surprised and confused, so he did what any well-educated and surprised and confused man would do to cover his embarrassment. He scowled—rather well. He was still making that rotten face seventy seconds later, when General Brieant's aide asked who was calling and was told that it was a Mr. Kraft from Saigon.

"Merlin, you bastard!" General Theodore Sanford Brieant roared into the phone half a minute later. "I knew it was you, you bastard!"

"How's it goin', Ted?" Merlin answered breezily.

"You're the bastard who's been tear-assing all over Germany in a U.S. Army car and uniform! Don't deny it, Merlin!"

Merlin tapped the ash off his new cigar, cleared his throat. "Good to talk to *you,* fellah. Mighty pleased you got your star, Teddy boy. Hope you got my congratulatory wire."

"I'll wire your tool to a fence post! Who the hell do you think you—"

"I'm the man who knows where the bodies are buried, chum. Operation Sinbad? That was way back before you got your star, remember?"

"I'm warning you, Merlin—"

"Don't warn me, and don't waste my time either, if you want to keep that goddam star. You plugged into Ajax?"

Ajax was the central NATO intelligence communications net, with a monster computer at its gut.

"Of course," Brieant answered warily.

"Then put this on the wire. Metaphor. Try the fucking priority classification on that, general."

Major Margolis was shuffling through some X rays, dazed that any mere civilian would dare to talk to a general like that. For a full thirty-five seconds he debated whether Merlin was pretending, or whether the deputy commander of military intelligence for the U.S. Army in Europe was on the other end of that phone.

"Solid Gold," Brieant finally confirmed. "The rating is Solid Gold, highest priority. Is this one yours, Merlin?"

To General Brieant's credit, he didn't ask about Metaphor itself. He remembered how impatient Merlin was with questions he considered prying—a category that started with "How're ya feeling?" and went on from there.

"Yeah, and I need your help."

"Any time," assured Brieant, who knew that Merlin could and would destroy his military career without hesitation. Merlin was the worst. Everybody agreed on that.

"I'm in one of your hospitals, Teddy, and there's a sick guy here who really needs a good dose of pentothal. Clean him out —know what I mean? There's a wonderful doctor here who's been taking care of my friend, and it would be goddam decent of you if you'd tell him to give him this shot. . . . Right. It's for you, major."

Margolis took the instrument, and a great deal of abuse from a general who seemed quite unmoved by the description of Anderson's serious wounds. Brieant pointed out nobly that national security was involved, instructed the surgeon to cooperate fully. Major Margolis did everything but salute as he pledged his allegiance and fidelity, and he was humming a patriotic air as he went to arrange for the drug.

"What the hell was Sinbad?" Cavaliere wondered when they were alone.

"Remember My Lai?"

"Sure."

"Sinbad made My Lai look like an Easter-egg roll."

"So when you told him you knew where the bodies were buried—"

A nurse entered to report that Major Margolis was ready, and that ended the discussion. It didn't terminate Angelo Cavaliere's shock and depression. Even his recognition that the armies of most major countries—and a lot of small ones— had similar massacres and atrocities buried somewhere didn't do that. Cavaliere brooded during the long minutes before the injection took effect.

"What's bothering you, Angie? Metaphor?"

"What's Metaphor?"

Merlin glanced around, whispered carefully. "Top secret."

Everything always was, Cavaliere thought. Even the toilet paper was classified in this weird world.

"Should I close my eyes?" he answered irritably.

Merlin ignored the sarcasm. "Top secret. The Berlin station has been *penetrated.*"

First Cavaliere was frightened. That word—*penetrated*—always flushed terror through his system. Penetrated meant *betrayed,* which meant *dead.* There was a Sov in the woodpile, and that's why Merlin had steered clear of the CIA's local organization. First the shock of fear, then the relief of understanding and finally the Sinbad depression oozed back again.

"He's ready, I think," the army doctor announced.

"Thanks. Major—I hope you'll understand—this is an intelligence matter, and it's highly classified. Could you please step outside for eight or ten minutes?"

The surgeon hesitated, recalled General Brieant's instructions and struggled with his genuine concern for his patient. He looked at the man in the bed, found some encouragement in the regular breathing and visible effects of the earlier transfusion. Hell, those hadn't been mere instructions. They were orders, from a general.

Margolis left and the meticulous questioning began. The initial half-dozen inquiries tested whether the sodium pentothal was working, and then Merlin started probing about various employees—CIA and other—who frequented the Amerika Haus. Angelo Cavaliere could tell from Merlin's face that the interrogation wasn't producing much, but Merlin wasn't discouraged. He kept questioning, thinking and hoping for some tiny clue. When there were no more clever questions to ask, he decided that it was time to gamble.

This was the longest shot of all, but what the hell did he have to lose?

"Victor. Victor," he said into Anderson's ear.

No reply.

"Victor—Victor," Merlin repeated insistently in harsh but intimate tones. *"Victor,* it's time to report."

"What?"

"Victor, Moscow wants to know what happened this afternoon."

And Jeff Anderson began to describe the terrorists' raid.

Merlin was grinning broadly for a full twenty seconds before Angelo Cavaliere grasped the reason for his delight.

"Him?"

"Him," Merlin confirmed.

Jackpot.

It was a fantastic coup. Merlin—that clever, intuitive and violent son of a bitch—had found the Sov agent, and the informer didn't know he'd been identified. Both of the CIA operatives were smiling as they stepped out into the hall.

"He's all yours, doc," Merlin said.

"Fine. Say, I just heard something on the radio. The people who shot Mr. Anderson kidnapped some woman, and they've demanded a million-dollar ransom. Fantastic?"

Merlin stopped smiling. "Keep an eye on Anderson," he told his partner.

"Where are you going?"

Merlin didn't answer. He walked away, somewhat more rapidly than usual.

31

The man in the luggage shop was frightened the instant that Merlin entered.

That was logical, for Merlin's expression and the hunter's tension in the way he moved were bluntly frightening.

"Good-day," the German said hopefully.

"Good-*bye*," Merlin replied and jerked his head toward the door.

It was arrogant and outrageous and didn't make any sense, and "Alexander" was about to say so when he saw the Magnum in the American's fist. Persuaded by the metallic logic, the man behind the counter shrugged and started for the street.

"Where's the recorder?" Merlin demanded.

The intelligent German stopped dead in his tracks, for the muzzle of the .357 was now pointed at his face.

"*What* recorder?"

"The one rigged to the telephone."

The click of the release of the handgun's safety sounded very loud in the quiet shop.

"*That* recorder? *Please*, upper right drawer of the desk. . . . Can I go?"

Merlin considered the "standard procedures."

"If there's another one, you'd better tell me—unless you're a plastic-surgery freak," he warned.

"Behind the counter, next to the cash register," blurted the terrified merchant.

"Don't come back for twenty minutes, and don't make any funny phone calls. I hate jokes," Merlin said.

Fighting down an unpleasant choking sensation, "Alexander" hurried out, and Merlin locked the door with the awareness that the luggage vendor would call his CIA contact. It might take ten minutes, but the German was a competent professional who wouldn't stay intimidated very long. Merlin turned off the recorder behind the counter, removed the cassette from the one hooked to the phone in the back room. He was speaking to the CIA communications center in Bonn ten seconds later.

"Sales manager, extension fifty-nine," he said.

That meant headquarters in Virginia.

"Busy, sir," tested the switchboard operator.

"Try his private line."

Use the secret CIA communications satellite that the air force put up in '73.

"A very large shipment is involved," Merlin added. That was the correct phrase, so he had Smith on the line in the Langley command post in less than two minutes.

"I need troops," Merlin announced.

"We're getting the money. Don't worry. We're taking care of it right now."

Could they really be that dumb at headquarters?

Didn't they know *anything* about terrorists like the Martians?

"I'm taking care of this *myself,*" Merlin said.

He could visualize the scene in Smith's electronically protected office: the scrambler whirling, the tape machine rolling smoothly and at least a couple of desk heroes listening over the speaker phone.

"This isn't your kind of deal, Merlin," Smith reasoned. "We have experienced people who—"

"Shove it. Your people will get her back dead. Don't argue with me. I've got all the goddam chips."

Several seconds of silence followed.

Merlin knew exactly what they were doing.

Smith was trying to figure out the reference, and he was signaling one of those Langley mothers to trace the call.

"Now what the hell does that mean?" Smith finally asked.

"I've got Victor. How's *that* for openers?"

Harper and Parks leaped to their feet, unable to control their excitement.

The wild man had done it. He'd found the Sov infiltrator in the Berlin station.

"That's terrific!" Smith congratulated.

"There's more. Victor doesn't know that we know."

Fantastic.

If Victor didn't realize that he/she/it/who cares had been "burned," the CIA could use the double agent to feed false information to the other side.

"Great work!" Smith exulted. "Listen, here's what we're going to—"

"*You* listen," Merlin broke in rudely. "You'll do it my way, or you don't get Victor."

Parks looked dazed. Not even Merlin talked that way to senior headquarters executives.

"Impossible," he assured Smith, who then glanced at Harper for his opinion.

"He's got us by the nuts, John," judged Bill Harper, who'd always had a gift for language.

Smith closed his eyes to consider the insanity of the situation.

"Merlin," he began soberly, "I know that you have a personal involvement with—"

He never finished the sentence.

You couldn't reason with Merlin.

You certainly couldn't argue with him.

Everyone, even the Chinese, knew what Merlin was like. The bastard always did everything his own way.

"What the hell do you want?" Smith asked warily.

"The Band!"

It figured. The "Band" was the CIA's best assault unit, the vicious varsity of combat types. They knew Merlin from at least two earlier operations, Smith reflected as his stomach twinged, and he wondered whether his ulcer might be returning.

"We'll pay the money, for Christ's sake," Smith pleaded. "You don't need the Band for this."

"All six pieces, day after tomorrow," Merlin ordered.

He knew about Smith's ulcer.

He didn't care.

"I don't think the director's going to be crazy about this," the Langley executive predicted gloomily.

"He doesn't have to be. I'm the crazy one, remember?"

Then Merlin told him where and when to deliver the Band, and what to tell General Brieant.

"Brieant? How much does he know?" Smith wondered in tones laden with jurisdictional rivalry.

"The first three lines of the national anthem and the multiplication table up to eleven. He doesn't know a damn thing about Metaphor or Victor, if that's what you mean."

At least the goddam army didn't know.

That was some consolation.

"I'll try it on the director, but he's going to want more about what you're planning. Isn't there something else I can say, Merl?"

"Happy birthday's always good," the sardonic man in Berlin answered—and slammed down the phone.

Now the entire CIA network in West Berlin would be looking for him—and Victor. His step quickened as he left the luggage shop, for it was only a matter of minutes before armed men ringed the store.

32

It was extraordinary.

Fourteen minutes after Merlin left the store, a portly and subtly creepy man named George Lomas laughed—directly into Smith's face. Devious and dedicated as the agency's chief of counterintelligence should be, Lomas was serious and mysterious and just a trifle paranoid. He was fascinated by puzzles, enigmatic in conversation and rarely smiled.

He *never* laughed.

"Our people in Berlin are looking for him," Smith had concluded—and then Lomas laughed and laughed.

Fantastic.

"Nobody finds Merlin when he doesn't want to be found," chuckled the CIA security executive. "If your people got that lucky, they might also get dead. Merlin does that sort of thing, rather well." The fat man who was always so grim was amused.

"You *like* Merlin?" Smith wondered incredulously.

"No, I respect his cunning, his reflexes and superb animal instincts," replied the man in the button-down shirt and Harvard tie.

Lomas hadn't gone to Harvard, of course. Deception was part of his life-style.

"Should we give him the Band?"

Lomas wasn't smiling anymore. Naïveté always depressed him.

"For Victor I'd give him Barbra Streisand, all the Nadelmans in the Hirshhorn collection and the city of Boston."

The DCI didn't laugh. The director of central intelligence was responsible to the President, and he listened very soberly when Lomas reported to him half an hour later.

"You think he'll deliver Victor?" he asked.

"Merlin kills, but he doesn't lie."

"The Germans aren't going to like this. It's their turf," the director thought aloud.

"They'll hate it," agreed Lomas, who knew that the director was rather hostile toward Bonn's intelligence chief at the moment. It had something to do with recent operations designated Axhead and Carport which had gone sour.

"Wish you hadn't bothered me with this administrative problem, George."

Lomas got the message.

"I never did. Sorry you were out when I came to brief you. Too bad there was no time to wait."

The director smiled benignly, looked at his watch.

It was ten to eleven on Tuesday morning.

At 3 P.M. on Thursday, the regular U.S. military shuttle flight unloaded twenty-nine uniformed men at Tempelhof. The plane was nearly an hour behind schedule, a delay caused by some defective fuel pump at the U.S. air base near Heidelberg. Twenty-two of the soldiers and airmen believed this, and they climbed into a khaki-colored bus with their baggage. The other seven knew that this was a lie, that the plane had been held until their special jet had arrived from Andrews Air Force Base near Washington. They had B-bags, assorted instrument cases and bored expressions, all of which they carried into the van that was waiting for them.

The corporal behind the wheel looked at the chubby officer expectantly.

"Yes?" asked the lieutenant.

"Ira."

"Gershwin," confirmed the officer grumpily.

There was no further conversation as the van rolled out of the airport, and not a word was spoken until it stopped more than twenty minutes later outside the movie theater that served the U.S. forces in West Berlin. Even then only a single word was uttered.

"Wait," the man with the gold bars on his shoulders said.

All seven entered the building with their gear, and the driver unbuttoned his tunic. He seemed even more relaxed than most noncommissioned officers. He wasn't. He wasn't relaxed and he wasn't a corporal in the U.S. Army, and the automatic in his shoulder holster wasn't the standard army gun either. He waited tensely and he watched, and he saw Merlin approach ten minutes later.

It was cool and dark inside.

Thank God for American air conditioning.

Merlin strode through the lobby, opened a door and slipped inside—just a step. He stopped to let his eyes adjust, looked. There on the stage were four men. The theater was obviously also used for live entertainment, and the footlights made it easy for Merlin to recognize the quartet.

"Hey, Luther," he called out as he walked down the center aisle—slowly.

There was no point in taking too many chances. His stand on Victor could have irritated some of those people at Langley.

"Hey," answered Luther, a rangy North Carolinian with a talent for knives and a kid brother playing offensive guard for the Pittsburgh Steelers.

"Don," Merlin said pleasantly to a stocky man seated beside a drum case on the edge of the stage.

"Hey," the demolition specialist replied with a yawn and a tired smile.

Roosevelt Allison didn't wait to be addressed. The trim, muscular black man was a cipher expert, cat burglar and karate black belt—and a fan of Merlin's.

"You're looking *good*, Merl," he announced as he spun the bass case for emphasis.

"Glad you're here, Rosie. You too, Ed."

Ed Budge didn't have to smile, because he was always smiling. Blonde and tan with the regular features of a California surfer, he enjoyed life. He enjoyed driving all kinds of cars exceedingly well, firing a variety of machine guns even more precisely. He flashed the "thumbs up" salute and waved his guitar case.

Suddenly Merlin felt uneasy.

"Just like the old gangster pictures," Budge pointed out cheerily.

Something didn't add up—not quite.

He was less than ten yards from the stage when he drew his Magnum and whirled.

There was a gun pointing at him from the left section of the darkened balcony. It took him a second to spot the night sight, the infrared device clamped to the barrel that let the weapon's owner shoot accurately in the blackness.

"That you, Country?" he challenged in as casual a voice as he could muster.

"Heelll, yahs. How're ya doin', boy?"

Country Binks was—among other things—a sharpshooter. He was the long gun on this team, a hunter who worked from the edges to cover and protect the others. He was also the loving father of three children, a real artist at making pancakes and barbecuing ribs and, like his father, who'd been a justice of the peace in Chisholm County, a keen judge of human character.

"As well as can be expected. Where's Jesse?"

"Here."

There they were—inseparable as always.

Jesse McAlester and his sawed-off automatic shotgun were resting comfortably in the shadows that obscured the right wall of the orchestra section.

That was it, all six. Merlin put his gun back in its holster, stepped forward to speak.

"There's one more," Roosevelt Allison said.

"What?"

"They threw in the Godfather, Merl."

Lomas strode out of the wings backstage, moving almost defiantly and looking a bit like an overfed schoolboy in the tight army uniform.

"Don't you trust me, George?" Merlin demanded harshly.

"Of course I do," Lomas answered a moment before he wedged a cigarette into a stubby holder and groped for his lighter. "Just thought I'd come along to see how the big boys do things. Never too late to learn."

"You don't lie as well as you used to."

Lomas found his slim silver torch, touched the flame to the cigarette, inhaled—and coughed.

"Those summer colds can kill you, George."

The man in the darkness with the shotgun snickered.

"Easy on the melodrama," advised the security chief. "We're going to do it your way. You're in charge. Don't get nasty—please."

It was difficult, but Lomas repressed his impulse to ask about Victor. That would only make Merlin more angry and suspicious, more dangerous.

"Sit down," Merlin finally said and pointed toward the middle of the orchestra section. The men wandered down from the stage, straggled into the eighth and ninth rows of the center block.

"Could you spare a cigar?" asked the black man, who shared Merlin's affection for fine Canary Island coronas. The man who found people pulled two Don Diegos from inside his jacket, and handed one to Roosevelt Allison with a sigh.

"That's about ten, twelve cigars I owe you," Allison noted as he bit off the end, spat it out and lit up contentedly.

"At least."

They liked each other. The cigar number was one of their running routines.

"Merl, what's this all about?" Luther Lartensen asked as he loosened his collar and dropped into a nearby seat. "Hear it's somethin' personal."

"Start the movie," joked the shotgun specialist.

"It *is* something personal," Merlin confirmed, "and we'll start the film in just a second when—aha, here they are."

There were eight noncommissioned officers and a captain, mostly in their late twenties or early thirties. Some were tall and others short, but they all carried gun cases that plainly held rifles. Lomas stood up, stared.

"Mr. Wasserman?" the captain asked.

"Come join the party," Merlin invited.

"Sorry we're late. Got lost trying to find this place."

Merlin looked at the nameplate on the captain's tunic, idly wondered what the "J" in J. Rodriguez was. The sharpshooter in the balcony answered the unspoken question a moment later.

"Hey, Joe," he shouted.

The captain turned, looked up and waved. "Country? Whatcha doing here?"

Now Merlin picked up the faint traces of some Hispanic and southern accent, tried to decide whether Jose Rodriguez was a Texican or perhaps one of the Cuban exiles who'd settled in Miami. Whatever he was, Rodriguez was a dead shot and so were his men. They were the elite marksmen of the U.S. forces in Europe, the army team that shot in competitions. Country had been a member of this unit four years earlier.

"Nobody tol' me," laughed the man in the balcony.

Lomas loathed surprises, and one of the things he liked least about Merlin was that the son of a bitch always had at least two in reserve. The furious CIA security chief shuffled-stumbled across a dozen seats, livid because nobody tol' him either.

"Who are these men?" he whispered angrily.

Merlin gestured, and somebody dimmed the lights.

"Who are they, dammit?"

Merlin ignored him, but Roosevelt Allison was more humane.

"Shooters."

"What?"

"Snipers," Merlin announced and blew smoke that curled into the chubby executive's face.

The theater was dark.

"Snipers? What do they do?" Lomas demanded.

"They snipe," Merlin replied, and the first frames of the film on the Martians flickered onto the screen. . . .

There were several seconds of silence when it was over, and then Merlin spoke in the blackness.

"Any questions?"

Lomas had several, but he held back out of pride and caution. After all, he was a senior official and he was supposed to know just about everything.

Roosevelt Allison had fewer ego problems. "This crowd, Merl—Lietzen and the rest—you want us to take 'em or burn 'em?"

It wasn't fair. The director had sworn to Congress and the press that the agency wouldn't even consider killing anymore, and now Merlin and his friends were forcing the CIA security chief to listen to their cold-blooded dialog on death.

"What do you say, George?" Merlin challenged.

Let the headquarters executives get a taste of what it was actually like out in the real cloak-and-dagger world, far from their computers and committees and staple guns. George Lomas would be angry, for he didn't want to hear any of this.

Good.

Let him sweat.

"I say we blow them away," the shotgun specialist volunteered, "unless you need them for something, Merl. Why take chances with a bunch of mothers who've burned twenty or thirty cops and a gang of other people?"

"Save the taxpayers a piss pot of money," Budge agreed.

"We'll play it by ear," Merlin said—and everyone in the theater understood that the terrorists whose faces they'd seen on the screen were now targets.

"Any more questions?"

"Mr. Wasserman?" It was the sharpshooter captain, a careful man.

"Yes?"

"Could you please roll that film again?"

Lomas felt a little better, a trifle less bitter. It was reassuring to think that the marksmen would shoot only the right people. Killing the wrong ones might reflect poorly on the agency.

33

"Yes, Comrade General," Duslov said.

"Of course, Comrade General," he agreed into the phone when the torrent next subsided. "You know, Comrade General, we have an excellent connection. Direct land line."

"And what the hell does that mean?" Zimchenko roared.

"It really isn't necessary to shout, Comrade General."

"One of our best sources badly wounded and lying in one of *their* hospitals, you moron, and you tell me not to shout? Are you out of your mind, Duslov? Don't you realize how important Victor is, you imbecile?"

Duslov was holding the telephone a full two inches from his ear, but the noise was still jarring.

"I do, Comrade General."

"And stop that Comrade General shit, you effete hypocrite. I know you hate my guts, Duslov. Well, I'm not too crazy about yours—and I'm in command. Keep that in your sophisticated mind, art lover."

Most of the insults left Duslov unmoved, but "effete" was certainly uncalled for. He'd have to bring that up sometime—after this crisis.

"I appreciate your frankness, general. To return to the current situation, there's no evidence that either the Amerikanski or the Maoists know anything about Victor. I'm convinced that the Maoists were after the Yankee station officer, and since they're prone to casual violence—"

"You said all that, Duslov. Now pay attention to what I'm saying. I want you to do three things. First, get someone into that hospital and check on Victor. Are they treating him like a friend or an enemy?"

"I've already started on that."

"Finish it, and report immediately. Second, I want that Lietzen-Stoller mob wiped out. Pull out all the stops. I've got enough problems here with wheelers and dealers without worrying about some cheap thugs injuring our operation in Germany."

Duslov had heard the rumors about the son of a Central Committee member maneuvering for Zimchenko's job, guessed that the political infighting was contributing to the KGB general's rage.

"And third?" the man in the East Berlin cellar asked.

"Bury that clever Wasserman or whatever his name is. I'm fed up with him too. You got that?"

"Of course, general. *For the record,* that will not be simple. We will do it, but—*for the record*—the price may be high."

The phrase "for the record" was carefully chosen.

Zimchenko's phone had a tape attachment, and Duslov was reminding him that a similar device was working here at the KGB bunker in East Berlin. Shrewd, quick and lucky, Merlin had outlived a number of agents—including three of China's best—who'd tried it in the past. If the liquidation of Merlin cost many lives, the responsibility would be the Comrade General's.

"Are you afraid of him, Duslov?"

The stupidity of the question was depressing.

Only a fool—or an arrogant general—could ignore Merlin's savage skills and achievements. Maybe Zimchenko was getting too old for the job after all.

"No, general. Anything else?"

"Get moving."

Duslov promised to report daily, and when the conversation was over he ordered a duplicate of the tape for his personal file. After that he began to select his assault team. If Victor had been discovered, an armed attack on the hospital to rescue him might be necessary.

Many others were interested in the kidnapped woman and the man who'd been shot, but that was hardly surprising since it was on page one of every paper in the Federal Republic. The story got more space than the concert-riot of Torn Knickers, the famed British rock group whose Hamburg fans had half-destroyed an outdoor stadium the previous night. The press reports didn't mention the CIA, but a number of people in

West Germany knew, and wanted to help. Merlin had never received so many offers of assistance in his life. It was extraordinary, and he managed not to laugh at any of them.

Karl Grad was the first. He was waiting in Merlin's hotel room when the American returned from the movie-theater briefing, all gray and all politeness as usual.

"I hope you don't mind the intrusion," he said, "but I thought we ought to talk."

"Good thinking. Have my fine friends of the BND any leads?"

"Not yet, but the terrorists are still in West Berlin. We sealed off the city five minutes after your associate telephoned, and we've moved in a special detachment to press the search. Every policeman in the town—and every border guard—has her picture, and it's on all the television news broadcasts."

Merlin didn't ask how the BND had secured a photo. It didn't matter. He was concentrating on his plan, the scheme he hadn't discussed with anyone.

"We'd like to cooperate fully," Grad continued.

Translation: What's your plan?

"Sure. Once we get her back—"

"You'll pay the ransom?"

"What else can we do?"

Grad didn't believe it for a minute. Paying the money was, theoretically, the safest move, but Merlin never did the logical thing. He always did his own thing, and while Karl Grad found that disturbing he couldn't help but admit that Merlin's odd thing usually worked.

"We're counting on your people, Karl. After we've made the exchange and she's safe, we're relying on the BND to nail them. It's your turf, and we know you can do it."

Was he lying—again?

Probably.

It was true that a U.S. diplomatic courier had reached West Berlin with a pouch containing $1 million in used tens and twenties as the kidnappers had demanded, but Grad couldn't accept the idea that the tricky and ruthless man who faced him would deal on the terrorists' terms. Maybe the decision had been made in Washington. Yes, the higher-ups there would be more sensible.

"I've been authorized to promise—that's an official commit-ment—any help that you may require," Grad announced stiffly.

"I'll let you know when we get delivery instructions," Merlin promised. "We'll need six or eight of your best men to convoy the money to the exchange."

"A dozen if you want."

Grad gave him the telephone number of the local West German intelligence center, and five minutes after the compe-tent BND executive left, Merlin descended to find a street telephone to call Cavaliere at the hospital. As he stepped out of the Hilton, someone tugged at his sleeve. It was one of those huge woman wrestlers who worked for Blue Bernard.

"He said to tell you that the admiral's widow wants to see you," she declared as she handed him a slip of paper. Merlin glanced at it, saw the address was one in a fashionable neigh-borhood two miles away.

She looked better without the mud, but she was still a vast woman.

"Are you the math teacher or the other one?"

"The other one," she replied in a sweet, shy voice. "I'm studying at night to be a dental technician. Uncle Bernard wants me to make something of myself."

"He's your uncle?"

"How else could I get a good job like this?"

She liked the mud, and whatever else Blue Bernard dreamed up for her. *Right,* he'd called her kinky.

Merlin thanked her. But he didn't get to the house for almost forty minutes. It took that long to shake the two followers, one probably Grad's and the other a faithful retainer of either Lomas or the Sovs.

The house was a house. To be more precise, it was a cat house/house of prostitution/brothel/bordel/crib. It was not a house of ill repute. Among local bankers, television stars, brokers, politicians, industrialists, corporation lawyers and proctologists, it had a wonderful repute as one of the finest sex parlors in the nation.

Big potted plants, deep Oriental rugs, Tiffany lamps, brass-topped tables, flocked red velvet wallpaper and dramatic silk drapes all testified that someone—with a lot of money—had chosen to re-create an elegant Berlin brothel of the 1920s. The

women who sat reading in the salon—a meaty blonde who
looked Dutch, a splendidly curved black whose features were
Ethiopian, two Japanese who might be twin sisters, a leggy
redheaded Texan much admired by Arab gentlemen, a strap-
ping Welsh lass who'd picked up enough Spanish to chat with
Latin American diplomats, and a sensible Bavarian brunette
who'd played clarinet in a jazz band until she discovered how
these talents could earn more—were all dressed in simple expensive gowns. The liveried footman-butler who let Merlin in
went nicely with the period decor, and even his glass left eye
seemed appropriate.

The two men mounted a carpeted marble staircase to the
next floor, and Merlin smiled as he noted that each room had
its female occupant's name engraved on a brass plate attached
to the dark wooden door. There was one portal without such
a sign, and the butler rapped on that one—three times.

"How good of you to come, Herr Wasserman," the chicly
dressed madam said as she waved him to a pink love-seat. The
elegant sheath, perfect makeup and erect posture made her
look like a very attractive forty-eight or fifty, instead of the
sixty-one she was. She probably exercised every morning, had
a daily massage, took lots of vitamins and hormones, and
screwed her brains out, Merlin guessed.

He was right.

"How kind of you to invite me," Merlin replied as his eyes
swept the room. It was furnished in the same lush style, aside
from a large color TV set and a stereo-tape-phonograph rig
that cost more than $2000.

"The television? One of my amusements," she explained
with a girlish giggle. "There are concealed cameras in the bed
chambers, and when I'm bored I—*peek.* Naughty, I'm afraid."

"I can't imagine that you're bored very often."

He was really *quite* charming for an American who was
heterosexual. She gestured with the jeweled holder, and the
scent of the marijuana reached Merlin.

"May I offer you some grass, or a spoon of coke, perhaps?"

She was the perfect hostess. Merlin sensed that if neither of
those drugs appealed to him, he could have a glass of sherry
or a pair of human ears or a nine-year-old Finnish virgin. He
made his choice.

"Sherry, please?"

How nice.

A gentleman—an old-fashioned gentleman.

She poured the Amontillado into cut crystal glasses, and then she got down to business.

"I'd like to help you, Mr. Wasserman, and I think I can. Are you still looking for that Karla Lange woman, the terrorist whose pictures you showed?"

"Very much so," Merlin replied. "Excellent sherry, Frau Admiral," he added truthfully.

"Thank you. You may be amused to hear that I think I know where she is. There's a doctor—he examines my ladies each week. He's quite popular with several of Bernard's friends."

An underworld physician.

Karla Lange was the woman Merlin had wounded during the kidnapping.

It figured.

"Please go on, Frau Admiral."

"Call me Lotte. All my friends do, and I'm sure we're going to be friends. Well, my doctor was called to treat a woman who had burn scars—just like Fraulein Lange. Burn scars and a fresh bullet wound in her hip—a big hole caused by a large-caliber bullet."

She paused to sip at her sherry, and then she took a powerful "hit" of that costly Thai stick— class grass.

"She may be left with a permanent limp," the madam announced casually.

"How unfortunate."

"Not really. There are men who find limping women especially attractive. Now where do you think this Lange woman is?"

"Where?"

She picked up a pair of bejeweled opera glasses, giggled again. "Right *there!*"

She pointed out a window. There was a passage between the two buildings behind hers, and through that opening Merlin could see a four-story gray stone private residence. She handed him the binoculars, and he raised them to his eyes.

"The others are with her. I've been peeking with my glasses, and I've seen two of them today. The big fellow who blows up things, and another one—the Falkenhausen woman."

"Number fifty-three, is that it?"

She laughed and nodded toward her four-poster bed. "You can stay here if you want, and watch them," she invited slyly.

"I'll be back. I've got to talk to some friends, and I'll bring the fifty thousand marks."

She walked to the bed, sat on the edge smiling. "Pleasure's more important than money. Remember that, liebchen. Come back soon."

"I will. By the way, does Bernard know?"

"Only you, liebchen. You're my kind of gentleman."

Even stretching charitably, no one could call Blue Bernard a gentleman. He'd asked her several times why she wanted to see Herr Wasserman, but she'd lied adroitly, hinting at lust as her motive.

"And he believed me."

"So do I," Merlin said and he kissed her hand, rather gallantly, before he made his escape.

When he got to Amerika Haus, Lomas was seated at the station officer's desk.

"They called. They want to make the exchange at five o'clock, day after tomorrow, on the edge of the Grunwald Forest."

"And what do you want, George?"

"I want to help you get her back, Merl."

Lomas wanted to help and Grad wanted to help and dear Lotte was more than willing to help—among other things.

"You do intend to make the swap, don't you?" Lomas asked cautiously.

Merlin's answer was somewhat oblique. "George," he said, "I need six TV cameras, and a remote truck—the kind directors use on location. Can you help me with *that?*"

"What?"

"And a helicopter—an army chopper equipped for photo recon—and a baby carriage."

It sounded like something out of a Woody Allen movie.

"Whatever it is, can I watch?" Lomas demanded sarcastically.

Merlin shook his head, explained the scheme.

"Have I *ever* liked any of your plans?" Lomas asked after he'd heard it all.

"Never."

"I like this one. Merlin, it's daring and it's—creative. Very—well, contemporary. A dynamite idea."

" 'Preciate that, George."

"Dy-no-mite. Of course I knew from the start you had something up your sleeve. You wouldn't need all those shooters and the Band if you intended to pay. Okay, I'll gamble with you. I'll keep my part of the bargain. How about yours?"

Merlin put his right index finger to his lips. "No names," he instructed.

"We've just swept the whole place for bugs, Merl."

"Humor me."

Lomas took a pad, wrote one word.

Victor.

Merlin borrowed the ballpoint, wrote under the name.

Jeff Anderson.

Lomas winced. This was a personal blow, for Anderson was one of his own people.

"Are you sure?"

"Absolutely," Merlin answered as he tore the top four pages from the pad. He ripped them into strips, heaped them in a large ashtray and set them ablaze. Through the curl of smoke, Merlin could see the rapid eye movements that said Lomas was thinking out all the details of the many things he had to do. Identifying Victor's contacts, spotting his lines of communication, checking and digging very quietly to ascertain how and when and why Anderson "turned"—or was this Anderson at all? Those items alone would involve thousands of hours of work. This was the sort of thing George Lomas did well, and when the final report was written—perhaps in two or three years—it would be an account of victory for the agency's internal-security branch.

"How did you figure—"

"Animal intuition," Merlin interrupted.

Lomas reached forward, carefully destroyed the charred flakes in the ashtray. "I'll get that stuff for you," he promised.

Merlin turned to leave.

The betrayal of American operatives in East Germany was over, and now the United States would start picking off *their* agents.

"Good job, Merlin. . . . I guess I never said that before. Good job."

"Thanks."

Merlin walked out, and Lomas called in an aide to order the strange equipment that the daring plan required. If it worked, the West Germans would be outraged, and the director would like that.

34

In the small hours of the night while most of Berlin slept, Merlin and Freddy Cassel celebrated their bodies in the large bed in her apartment. Only a few miles away men were establishing a command post in a flat not quite directly across the street from the building where the terrorists had been seen. Radios, laser-beam listening devices and other expensive new surveillance gear were installed and tested. The telephone lines to the military hospital, the house where the kidnappers were and—just to play it safe—the brothel were all tapped. Overhead in the blackness, a photo-recon helicopter droned almost inaudibly as its crew shot scores of infrared pictures of the target area.

The alarm clock went off at 7:50 and Freddy Cassel sat up in bed, and Merlin said "Don't."

"Don't what?"

"Don't get out of the sack. I want to talk to you."

"We 'talked' twice last night," she reminded him.

"I really mean *talk*. This is very serious."

"I've got to get to work."

"Call in and say you're sick. It's important."

She looked at him curiously, wondering whether he finally trusted her enough to discuss his secret mission. It would be a terrific feather in her cap. On the verge of success, she tensed with the awareness that she had to be extra careful.

"Frank, what's this all about?"

She exposed a bit of one breast to emphasize her sincerity. Nice touch, Merlin thought.

"It's about the woman who was kidnapped. We want to get her back."

"Can I help?"

Welcome to the club.

Merlin nodded, looked at her as if he were trying to make a difficult decision.

"What have you got to do with this, Frank?" She shifted, giving him a free flash of the other mammary.

"Freddy, I'm not a private detective. I work for the U.S. government, and we need your help."

"The government?"

"Yes, it's all secret. We're supposed to deliver the ransom and pick up the woman tomorrow, and I want you to help check out the exchange point first. They're less likely to notice a woman."

"Will—will it be *dangerous?*" She didn't overdo the widened eyes, the touch of tremor in her voice.

"Not for a professional like you, honey."

"What?"

"Cut the crap," Merlin instructed as he pulled an envelope from the inner pocket of his jacket on the nearby chair.

"Frank!" she protested.

No, "innocence" wasn't her best number.

He dropped the envelope on her lap. "I think you're better at the screwing. What I want to know is whether you're just a bed commando, or are you a fully trained agent?"

"You're crazy!"

"Check the pictures, honey."

She opened the envelope, found a dozen excellent pictures Cavaliere had taken of her with two of her contacts. One of them was Grad.

"You've been monitoring our office at Amerika Haus for BND for nearly two years, Freddy, but that's standard stuff. Can you shoot as well as you screw?"

"Better. You didn't say anything about shooting."

"I will. Make some coffee, and I'll tell you all about it."

Merlin explained when and where the exchange would be made, and Freddy Cassel swore she'd tell no one. She didn't have to. Her BND colleagues listening in the apartment below smiled at the naïveté of the American, and they promptly relayed the schedule for the ransom payment to Grad, who called for maps of the woods as he began planning to saturate the entire sector with German agents. Credit for the capture of the terrorists would help the BND in next month's budget hearings, and it wouldn't hurt Karl Grad's career either.

Just because nine different gangs of terrorists have danced around West Germany as if it were a hotel ballroom doesn't mean that the BND isn't good. It's a lot better than many intelligence outfits, but—as Joe E. Brown said in the final scene of *Some Like It Hot*—nobody's perfect. So the BND missed a few things now and then, and among those was the arrival of the TV cameras and the "remote" truck.

While Grad was spending his afternoon with maps of the payoff zone, Angelo Cavaliere was busy with other charts of the streets near the brothel. Then he actually walked the area to confirm his ideas. After that he went over the blowups of the infrared photos again.

Merlin's plan was set. All it needed was fine tuning. If no one meddled, it was going to work. The trick was to keep people —the wrong people—from meddling, and to make sure that the right people knew precisely what to do. At 5 P.M. Merlin phoned Blue Bernard to say that he'd need those machine gunners at 3:30 the next day.

"Shall I pick them up or do you deliver?"

"For an old friend, we deliver. They'll be outside the Hilton in a black sedan."

"A black sedan?" Merlin wondered.

"I'm a traditionalist," Blue Bernard confessed.

"Someone has to maintain the standards."

Bernard thanked him for the compliment, and forty-five seconds later telephoned Duslov to report that the Americans were about to make their move. The KGB officer sat silent for an hour, doodling as he wondered why Merlin would need hired hoodlums when he could draw upon the substantial CIA and—probably—BND units in the area. The ransoming of the woman was probably involved, but it didn't make sense.

Something funny was going on.

That was no surprise.

Something funny was always going on when that damned Merlin was in the game.

The only thing Duslov could do was send a carload of men to follow Merlin from the Hilton rendezvous—and recheck the situation at the U.S. military hospital. Thus far all the signs indicated that no one suspected Victor, but there could be something funny there too. Why couldn't Merlin do things like anyone else? Even his deviousness was irrational and different, odd stunts and strange surprises that—what was the expression?—yes . . . came from left field. Merlin's tricks came from out of left field, as the Amerikanski would say.

Duslov merely jostled his food at dinner, too fretful to ingest more than fragments. Merlin ate like that proverbial horse—with Freddy Cassel at his side. She'd been near him, within his sight, since they got out of bed that morning. She realized he wasn't taking any chances that she might phone Grad, and she played along with his illusion that his secret was safe. She even offered to help again.

"You really want me to shoot tomorrow?" she asked as they left the restaurant at ten o'clock.

"It might be necessary."

"Then get me a weapon."

"Name your weapon, lady," he invited amiably.

"Shotgun."

"Holy shit!" someone said behind them.

"This is—what the hell are we calling you this week?" Merlin asked the man who stepped out of the dark doorway.

"Bonomi," Cavaliere said.

"*Lieutenant* John Bonomi," Merlin corrected.

"He's out of uniform."

"You've got to do something about that, John," Merlin joked.

"Why did you say 'holy shit,' John?" she asked.

"I always do when I meet ladies who work shotguns," Cavaliere snapped testily.

"What else does he do?" the German woman asked.

"He drives. Let's go."

The Band and the team of sharpshooters were waiting when they entered the U.S. Army theater, and a number of the men eyed Freddy Cassel approvingly. A few of them measured her, and a couple lusted as simple folk often do. None of this bothered the practical fraulein, who had often found the admiration of males useful—sometimes even fun.

"Only want to run this two or three times, so pay attention," Merlin sang out briskly.

He looked around, began to count. "Everybody here?" he asked.

"Godfather's busy, Merl, but he's sending you a present," Roosevelt Allison announced.

Fraulein Cassel filed away the name "Merl," smiled at the black man.

"Present?" Merlin asked.

"Little Lou—for the carriage."

Now Merlin smiled, and he introduced the woman to his associates. "Freddy Cassel—she's with our good West German friends, the BND . . . sharp chick . . . been casing our Berlin station for nearly two years."

"Wooo-wee!"

That was Country Binks, doing his redneck thing.

"Godfather won't like that," Allison predicted.

Something in the tone of the conversation was starting to bother her. Let them be rude. She'd have the last laugh.

"Freddy, I'd introduce you to those quiet fellows in the back," Merlin ambled on, "but I don't know them too well. They're shooters, fine shooters. The noisy crowd up front is— let's see . . . Ed . . . Luther . . . Rosie . . . Country . . . Don . . . and Jesse. You ought to get along nicely with Jesse. He digs shotguns too."

Maybe it was their common interest, but she thought Jesse McAlester was clearly the handsomest and the smile he got was double-strength. He grinned back, awkward but interested, and he waved the shotgun in greeting.

"Moving right along," Merlin continued as he lit a fresh corona and automatically handed one to Allison, "we have found the Martians' hideout. That's the Lietzen-Stoller mob, honey."

Fraulein Cassel blinked and sat up very straight, and wondered whether the BND knew about this.

"No, they don't," Merlin said, reading her thoughts, "but I've been too busy to tell them. Okay, here's the drill. All past evidence convinces me that the Martians will take the money and kill our woman. I figure we'll burn them first."

He'd said it—loud and clear.

"The drop at the Grunwald? The million dollars?" she blurted.

Merlin snapped his fingers. "Knew there was something I forgot—three things. Fellow I know—one they called the Godfather—will deliver the cash at five *if* we don't blast her free at four. We're going to take them as they come out of their house—ambush. Latest thing in ambushes. You'll love it."

"Yes?"

"Second, I didn't mention it back at your place because I knew your flat was wired from the day after I met you."

Smug bastard.

"Third, stick real close. We work family-style. Wouldn't be right if you tried to call Grad about our little change in plans. Wouldn't be loyal."

Or healthy.

She understood, and she hoped that Karl Grad would. She felt better when Merlin urged her to consider this "a joint CIA-BND operation" in which she was representing West German interests, and promised her that most of the credit would go to the Federal Republic's counterespionage forces.

"Okay, Freddy?"

"Okay."

Cavaliere brought out the street maps and the aerial photos, and Merlin assigned the duties and street positions. The shooters were given nearby rooftops or high apartments with clean fields of fire. The film was screened again, and Merlin explained how the street would be sealed by a squad of agents handpicked by the Godfather. Lomas wouldn't want his name mentioned in her presence, and Merlin saw no reason to provoke him unnecessarily. He told Freddy Cassel what she was to do, nothing more.

"Split-second timing and absolute command control every second, every step of the way, are our only chance to get her out alive," Merlin said. "Perfect coordination—like the Radio City Rockettes or the TV coverage of a big fast ball game. I'm going to be watching all the plays from all the angles, and I'll be calling the shots. Listen carefully to exactly what I say, and trust me."

"My men follow orders," the sharpshooter captain announced with a trace of soldierly pride.

Ed Budge flashed his thumbs-up ratification, and the explosives expert beside him called out "All the way, Merl." The rest of the band merely nodded. They knew the game and the rules. They'd played with Merlin before.

"Just like Athens?"

"Just like Athens, Rosie."

"That was baaad," the black man recalled admiringly.

"Same headsets?" the shotgunner asked.

"Headsets, flak jackets. One thing different—we're military jets. On the radio, I'll be Charlie Leader and you'll each have numbers. Charlie One, Charlie Two. The shooters will be Baker flight, with Captain Rodriguez the Baker leader. Any questions?"

The only voice that sounded was female.

"When do I get my shotgun?"

"Jesse, be nice to the lady," Merlin instructed.

It turned out that the young German woman was not only intelligent, professional and busty but also quite knowledgeable about the hand and shoulder weapons of the major powers. McAlester was delighted to find that her interest in shotguns was genuine, and he lit up when she asked for the same brand and model that he favored.

It was a pleasure to meet a pretty woman who really appreciated fine shotguns, he thought.

It was wonderful to meet a man who respected her professional skills as much as he admired her beauty, she thought. This was a man to whom she could relate, and she hoped that he wasn't quite as shy as he seemed. They talked animatedly about shotguns for six or seven minutes while she watched his face for some sign of personal interest.

Nothing definite—yet.

Then they discussed the fine points of shotgun loads, ammo pouches, bandoliers and other gear for another five minutes, on a friendly but not truly personal basis. She began thinking of how she might encourage him—just a bit.

It wasn't necessary.

All of a sudden, it happened.

"Fraulein," he said with a boyish-charming smile, "what're you doin' after the ambush?"

35

Typical setup.

Six small screens set in the video panel, with gauges and dials below and beside the frosty glass rectangles.

Jutting out beneath the black knobs, a Formica-topped shelf decorated with the inevitable half-filled ashtray and half-empty carton of tepid bad coffee.

Tense but competent director in a swivel chair, leaning forward compulsively toward the microphone that squatted between the dying coffee and the dead cigarettes.

Typical television control room.

As usual, the director was in his shirtsleeves with no tie and a look of concentration. There was something unusual about this man, however. Very few of the TV directors in Hollywood, London, Rome or other large cities wear .357 Magnums in belly holsters, and hardly any keep 8.8 pounds of Uzi submachine gun across their laps. It may catch on later, for Merlin was always a trend setter.

"Want some more coffee?" Cavaliere asked.

"Do I look crazy?"

"Yeah, and damp too."

Even with the air conditioning blowing steadily, it was hot in the closed truck as the afternoon sun beat down fiercely. The "remote" truck was parked some forty yards from the brothel, a block away from the house where the enemy was entrenched. Observers equipped with night scopes had reported sandbags inside two of the second-floor rooms and one on the third. That made Merlin's scheme even more logical, for with such barricades the *only* place to take them was as they came out into the street.

Four of the screens showed views of different parts of the street near number 53, and that was because four of the cameras installed before dawn were focused that way. A fifth was aimed at the front of the house, and the sixth at the rear.

"Sweep," Merlin said to the engineer seated three feet to his left.

The technician began to turn dials, and the first camera started a slow horizontal pan. After it swung about forty degrees to scan the three houses to the right of number 53, he adjusted another knob to move the lens higher and search the upper floors. Camera One was zeroed in on the front of number 53, and the excellent image got even better when Merlin ordered "Zoom."

"Okay?" the engineer asked.

"Okay. Now the next one."

It was the ninth sweep since noon, and Angelo Cavaliere was bored. He knew that these scans and tests were necessary, but he found himself increasingly impatient with the process. No point in mentioning this to Merlin, who seemed completely fascinated as each camera covered and re-covered its observation zone.

"Thanks, Irv," Merlin told the engineer, whose Rolling Stone T-shirt looked odd with the shoulder holster and peaked baseball cap. He told people that he always wore it because it was his "lucky" hat, but everyone suspected that the real purpose was to cover his bald spot.

"Communications check."

"You're on, Merl."

"This is Charlie Leader to Charlie One. Do you read me?"

"Charlie One—loud and clear," Roosevelt Allison replied. The rest of the Band called in from their concealed positions, and then Merlin spoke to Captain Rodriguez.

"Charlie Leader to Baker Leader. Give me a flight report."

"Patrol on assigned flight plan. Twenty-four thousand feet. All our birds are healthy and happy, Charlie Leader."

"How's your visibility?"

Merlin could see it in his mind's eye, the shooters in their lofty perches peering through their sniper scopes. Each of their worlds had a diameter of three-quarters of an inch, divided into four by cross hairs.

"Visibility fine up here," Rodriguez assured.

"Roger, Charlie Leader. Over and out."

Cavaliere thought it sounded silly, like one of those dumb cop shows on TV with lots of high-speed auto chases and handsome young method actors named Kent and Gregg. Merlin must have been thinking along the same lines, for he immediately checked the CIA cars and trucks to make certain that they were in position and ready to roll. Then he looked at his watch.

It was 3:49 P.M.—and no sign of activity.

"Anybody want to split a braunschweiger on pumpernickel, huh?" the engineer asked.

"With mustard?"

"No mustard, Angie."

"Never mind," replied Cavaliere, who wasn't hungry anyway.

Irving Sherman—who was always hungry but blessed with a marvelous metabolism—shrugged, and took one big bite.

"Hey," he said with his mouth full.

It wasn't the sandwich. He'd seen what Merlin and Cavaliere had—the front door of number 53 was opening. He glanced up at the row of photos taped to the wall above the screens, read aloud, "Grawitz."

"Stand by. This is Charlie Leader. Wheelman's on his way out, maybe more," Merlin advised.

Paul Grawitz was the specialist who stole and drove cars for the terrorists, so it made sense for him to emerge first to bring up their vehicle. He studied the street as he paused to light a cigarette, and then he nodded to someone inside who stepped out to join him. It was Fritz Kammler, the deserter who served as the Lietzen-Stoller weapons expert.

"He's got company, and they're heading toward Charlie Three."

"I see 'em," Budge reported.

"Hold your water, Charlie Three. Let's see where they're flying. Mobile surveillance, pick 'em up at the corner."

"In my sights," one of the shooters announced in a matter-of-fact voice.

"No way. That's an order."

"You're the boss, Charlie Leader."

Grawitz and Kammler walked north two blocks—right past one of the CIA trucks—and then turned west. A rooftop ob-

server reported that they got into a gray BMW, and nine minutes later one of the "mobile observers" radioed that Grawitz
had stolen a blue VW van.

"Heading back your way, Charlie Leader. They keep looking around and taking extra turns—checking for company."

Merlin ordered another surveillance unit to leapfrog the
first, and a dozen minutes later the gray car and the blue van
cruised into view of Camera Five. Some forty seconds after
that Captain Rodriguez radioed in an even more interesting
position report.

"They're only a block and a half from you, Charlie Leader,
and they're heading your way."

Irving Sherman reached down for his bulletproof vest,
strapped it on and then donned a steel infantryman's helmet
—all in thirty seconds.

"You nervous, Irv?" Cavaliere asked as he handed the engineer an M-42 submachine gun.

"Certainly not. Just don't want to catch a cold."

Merlin swiveled in his chair, pointed the Uzi at the rear door.

"They've stopped right behind you—dead stop, maybe
fifteen yards away."

"Thank you, Baker Leader," Merlin acknowledged.

Still facing the back door, he spoke to the engineer. "Still got
that half-sandwich, Irv?"

Gordon passed the food to him, and Merlin ate it with one
hand while the other pointed his automatic weapon at the rear
portal. "Would've been better with mustard," he said as he
chewed the last bits and stifled a belch.

Son of a bitch hadn't even said thanks.

"Thanks anyway," Merlin added suddenly, and then Rodriguez told them the terrorists had driven on at last. The engineer put down his machine gun and Merlin reached for the
half-carton of bitter liquid.

"Thought you didn't want any coffee," Cavaliere said.

"I don't."

Merlin sipped, scowled at the taste.

There they were. The two vehicles slowed in front of number 53, halted. Kammler remained at the wheel of the car, but
Grawitz climbed out of the van and opened its rear door. He
waved at Kammler, who hit the horn of the BMW twice.

"This is it. Charlie Leader to both flights. I think this is it. Let's go, Freddy."

Down at the corner, a woman appeared pushing a baby carriage slowly toward the van. Now the door of number 53 opened, and two men emerged carrying a large straw hamper. One of them was a stranger Merlin had never seen, but the face of the other was familiar. It was Werner Buerckel, the demolition expert.

She was almost surely in the hamper, but where the hell was Willi Lietzen?

What about Marta Falkenhausen and the wounded Lange woman? Were they staying behind?

"Charlie Leader to Baker flight. Keep those goddam windows covered. I don't want any surprises. Watch your step, Freddy—don't move too close."

The BND agent, who had a headset under her wig and a transmitter in her bra, answered immediately. "I'm moving as slowly as I can." She stopped, leaned down to fuss with the "baby."

As Buerckel and the other man neared the van, Marta Falkenhausen and Lietzen stepped out into the sunlight. The wary terrorist chief glanced up and down the street, started toward the car—and froze. He stared up at the roof of number 44, and Merlin sensed that Lietzen had spotted one of the army marksmen.

"Seal off the street. Go," he ordered.

Trucks and cars idling a block or two away roared into gear, raced toward their assigned blocking positions. Lietzen shouted something, pointed. The other terrorists grabbed for their weapons.

"Open fire! All Charlie and Baker units, open fire!"

One of the shooters put two bullets into Paul Grawitz, the first in his stomach and the second opening his throat with a gush of red. Another drilled Werner Buerckel through the chest, spinning him back against a parked car. The explosives specialist wasn't done. Only half-dead, he groped for the two sticks of dynamite he'd fashioned into a bomb and fumbled to untape the contact detonator. He was weaving as he struggled to heave it, but moving targets had never been a problem for

Country Binks. His first round killed Buerckel, who fell atop his charge.

That's when it exploded, blasting chunks of Werner Buerckel two hundred feet in all directions. One piece almost hit Rodriguez on the roof of number 40, but the captain ignored the distraction and kept shooting. Everyone else was too. Lietzen and Budge were exchanging fire at almost point-blank range. When the Californian stood up just a bit for a better shot, Marta Falkenhausen got off a round that shattered Budge's right forearm.

Kammler tramped on the BMW's gas pedal, and Merlin computed instantly. There was a chance—just a small chance —that the fast luxury car could blitz through the intersection before the heavy truck plugged that exit.

"Take him, Rosie!" he shouted.

Roosevelt Allison stepped out of an alley between two houses, pointed his antitank weapon and fired. The rocket demolished the front of the car, setting it ablaze. Another vehicle—only a few feet from Buerckel's explosion—was already burning fiercely. Merlin could see all this quite clearly on his six screens.

The trucks were finally in place at both ends of the block, but the terrorists weren't about to yield. Another man, who looked vaguely Arab, inched out of the back door. He had a Walther MPK submachine gun stolen from a West German military depot, and a determination to leave this part of the city. A blast from Jesse McAlester's shotgun tore away his weapon and an impressive number of ligaments and blood vessels.

A bullet from somewhere gouged the sidewalk beside Allison as he crawled toward number 53, and then another slug hit Luther Lartensen right in the gut. He fell, and if it hadn't been for his body armor he'd never have risen. As it was, he had a pain in his belly, most of the wind knocked out of him and a terrible desire to hurt whoever had shot him.

He never got the chance.

The enemy marksman in the third-floor window leaned forward to find another target, and became one. Three of the crack U.S. Army shooters saw the movement and the glint of the gun, and they all opened fire simultaneously. Karla Lange slumped forward, swayed and fell to the street. Merlin saw the impact a moment before Lietzen and the Falkenhausen woman threw their gas grenades. Acrid clouds bloomed abruptly, and now they were nowhere on any of the screens.

"Can you see them, Freddy?" Merlin called out urgently. She was the nearest to them, but not near enough.

"No, but I'll move in," she replied.

Merlin leaped to his feet, grabbed up his Uzi.

"Call the meat wagon, Angie—and take over!"

Before Cavaliere could answer, Merlin was out of the "remote" truck and into the battle. He dog-trotted toward the alley beside the brothel, the brick-walled passage through the block to the street where the fighting raged. As he approached the mouth of the alley, he looked ahead and didn't see Lietzen step out from between two cars behind him. The terrorist chief raised his gun to shoot Merlin in the back, took careful aim—

"Willi!" someone shouted from the alley.

He spun in reflex reaction, catching the blast from Freddy Cassel's shotgun full in the face. His weapon clattered to the sidewalk as his hands flew to his ruined face. He was screaming, half-blind and in serious need of about $25,000 worth of plastic surgery. Merlin watched as she walked slowly toward the wounded terrorist, and he saw her reload the empty chamber. When she was some eight feet from Lietzen, she spoke.

"In the name of the Federal Republic, I arrest—"

His rush at her—the hopeless lunge of a crazed animal—ended her legal remarks. Her shotgun ended Willi Lietzen, two rounds at eight feet. He was literally thrown up on top of an elegant Porsche, dying all over the $13,000 vehicle parked only twenty minutes earlier by one of the brothel patrons.

At the other end of the passage, Marta Falkenhausen had found a hostage. She'd seized the abandoned carriage, seen the baby and guessed that the infant might be her ticket to freedom. They wouldn't dare risk the kid's life. She pushed the carriage for about twenty-five feet, suddenly stopped. The shooters staring down saw her raise her hands. They laughed.

The midget in the carriage kept his .38 pointed precisely between her eyes. Little Lou looked odd in the baby garb, but the way he handled the pistol left no doubt as to his ability to shoot professionally. She began to curse him, and she was still swearing when two members of the Band disarmed her. By this time Merlin and Freddy had pushed through the tear gas to the straw hamper.

She had to be inside.

Was she dead or alive?

He jerked up the lid, looked down at a very attractive black graduate of Yale. Her wrists, ankles and mouth were all taped and her clothes were a mess. Her skirt was up well above her knees, exposing saucy, candy-striped bikini panties. She appeared to be unhurt, for no woman who'd been injured would have eyes like that. He lifted her out of the hamper, felt her shaking in his arms. After holding her for several moments, he realized the impropriety and removed the tape from her lips as painlessly as possible.

"I knew it was you!" she accused.

"You okay?" he asked as he tugged at the tape on her wrists.

"Soon as I heard all that goddam shooting, I knew it was you! Oh, my God!"

The scene she surveyed was undoubtedly disturbing. Two cars were burning and a number of bodies were strewn about, and pieces of a corpse were scattered around like red confetti. A man with a shattered right arm was cursing in English, and a woman somewhere across the street was swearing in German. When the still disoriented CIA station chief glanced that way, she saw a *baby*—a large *baby*—holding a .38-caliber revolver and smoking a thin black cigar. For one moment Diane McGhee thought she was in the middle of a Fellini movie, but decided that there was too much gore.

"It looks like World War Three," she said as Merlin ripped loose the tape binding her ankles. She tottered back a step and Merlin grabbed her. She'd almost tripped over the remains of Karla Lange, and in this state of mind such an accident might upset her.

She saw several men—all wearing headsets and body armor and automatic weapons—walk slowly to Merlin. One of them was tall and black, and he spoke first.

"You want us to take the house, Merl?"

"It's probably booby-trapped. Leave it for the BND demolition crew. Should be along soon."

Allison nodded, then listened to the voice in his headset. "Shooters want to know if they can climb down," he reported.

"Not yet. Tell them to cover the windows till the cops arrive. . . . What's the score?"

"Budge has a broken arm and Luther caught one in the

abdomen. The armor took the impact, but he feels terrible. May toss his cookies."

"That's a fifty-mark fine. Oh, Di, I'd like you to meet Mr. Allison. He's one of the people who risked their asses to blast you free. And this is Fraulein Cassel."

"Who's one of the women you've been shacking up with recently," Ms. McGhee jeered.

"Up yours, lady," Freddy Cassel countered jauntily as she strode off to find McAlester.

"Freddy's with the BND, honey," Merlin said, "and she's been looking up your skirt at Amerika Haus for the past two years."

The black woman winced.

"Good agent," Merlin continued. "Pretty fair with a shotgun. Just blew away Willi Lietzen."

She nodded, heard the horns of what had to be several police cars. "Looks like a battlefield," she said.

"Crash Dive. You wanted to know. This was Crash Dive," he replied with a sweeping gesture.

"A slaughter."

"I didn't shoot any of these people," Merlin said truthfully as he lit a cigar. "I didn't do this."

Kammler was still alive. He'd been hurt when the bazooka demolished his car, but he wasn't dead. He rolled out from beneath a parked Mercedes, pistol in hand—and Merlin shot him four times with the Uzi.

"*That* I did," Merlin admitted.

The flames flickering in the rocket-wrecked BMW reached the gas tank, and it exploded. Everyone recoiled at the noise, and Diane McGhee saw—for the first time—the corpse of plain dead Karla Lange only ten inches from her feet.

"Take it easy, honey. It's all over now," Merlin soothed.

Then—for some reason—the head of the Berlin station of the Central Intelligence Agency began to cry.

36

Seven police cars.

The first man out of the first car was the same sergeant Merlin had met at Amerika Haus. He surveyed the carnage, shook his head.

"I'm glad I'm not in the furniture business," he declared.

"You wouldn't like it. It's seasonal. That's the rest of the Lietzen-Stoller gang. Oh, there's one stretched out behind number fifty-three, and Willi Lietzen's on top of a Porsche up there."

"Dead?"

Merlin nodded. Allison walked up to "borrow" another cigar, and the sergeant eyed his headset and other combat gear.

"Furniture salesman?"

"No, sarge. He's a musician."

The sergeant looked around, saw the others in similar outfits.

"What the hell was this—a concert? *Lieber Gott*—it looks like Vietnam."

"Vietnam was much worse," Allison recalled.

"What's *his* name?"

Merlin shrugged. "Leonard Bernstein," he offered.

"Leonard Bernstein is short and Jewish, and he has gray hair."

"I dye it," the black man confided.

He turned to Merlin. "Can the shooters come down?" he asked. "One of them has to take a leak—real bad."

"There are marksmen on the roofs," Merlin explained casually. "They're covering number fifty-three until your demolition people get inside. There may be booby traps, or even somebody up there with a grease gun. You'd better call Grad."

"*Scheiss,*" the sergeant hissed.

"That's German for shit," Allison translated.

"No shit, Rosie? Okay, tell everybody the party's over. The West German cavalry has arrived and we can go home."

The sergeant scanned the burning cars, the corpses.

"I've never seen anything like this. This is German territory. Who the hell do you think you are?"

That was a perfectly valid question.

"Friends of the Federal Republic. We're crazy about the Federal Republic." He groped in his pocket, found the scrap of paper with the local BND number and handed it to the sergeant. "Here—call Grad. He's in town."

Then he took off his bulletproof jacket, sighed. "Those things make you sweat," he complained.

Now the sergeant noticed the sobbing woman sitting on the sidewalk.

"The one they kidnapped, Herr Wasserman?"

"Right. Heroically rescued by the Berlin police and BND—great bunch of men. Ought to get medals."

This American was unbelievable.

"Is she well?"

"Tip-top. It's her birthday. Always cries on her birthday."

At that moment the sergeant saw four men in coveralls emerge from a truck at the end of the block. They were carrying a stretcher and kits marked with red crosses.

"Your own medical unit, Herr Wasserman?"

"Wouldn't want to impose on the Berlin taxpayers. We could —*you* could—use a hearse or two, though . . . and maybe a fire truck."

Cavaliere wandered out of the alley, M-42 in hand.

"Lead guitar," Merlin announced. "Used to tour with Elton John."

"There's a fat guy back there hollering about his Porsche, Merl," he reported, "and Irv wants to know if we can leave now—Hi, Diane."

Merlin asked him to "keep an eye on her" while he "straightened out a few details" with the sergeant, and while the two men walked back to the radio car Cavaliere sat down beside the crying woman to comfort her.

"It's okay, Di. The war is over. You're safe."

The weeping continued.

"Take it easy. Merlin saved you."

The sobbing slowed.

"He's crazy. He's still crazy," she lamented wearily.

"Crazy about you."

"No, crazy about guns," she moaned and the tears poured down her perfect ebony cheeks.

"Crazy about you," Cavaliere insisted and hugged her comfortingly.

"Why didn't *he* do that? Why couldn't he put his arms around me?" she gasped.

" 'Cause he's crazy—and shy. Merlin doesn't show his private feelings in public, Di. You know that."

The crying began to subside, and a minute later she was drying her face on Cavaliere's handkerchief.

"I don't really believe you," she said defiantly.

"Take a look at this street. You think Merlin would lay on a whole damn war for anyone? Listen, whether you believe it or not—and he isn't willing to admit it either—this man needs you."

She was completely unconvinced, but she began to fix her hair. She looked around at the team that had rescued her, found no familiar faces.

"Who are they, Angie?"

"The Band—that's the Varsity. Merlin made Lomas fly them in—just for you. Merlin forced the army to give him their best sharpshooters—those guys on the roofs—for you. Think about that."

She'd heard about the Band.

No, you couldn't believe anything Merlin said.

You certainly couldn't count on him.

Grad arrived with three carloads of BND men and a look of icy fury, an expression that thawed only somewhat even after Merlin told him that the German security forces would get all the credit.

"I don't enjoy being tricked," he said stiffly.

"Who does? Name of the game, fellah," Merlin joshed as he punched the BND executive's arm familiarly. "Say, Karl, can you handle the rest of this?"

"What?"

"We'd like to split. My boys have a plane to catch in about an hour. You mind, kiddo?"

That was when Karl Grad—one of the coolest heads in West German intelligence—blew his stack.

"An hour? I'm giving you five minutes—not a second more —to get your men here and your snipers and your trucks—the whole damn outfit—out of this area. Is that clear?"

"We don't stay where we're not wanted. See you."

Merlin hurried back to where Cavaliere was talking to Diane McGhee, who was looking a lot better. "Tell everyone to bug out," he ordered. "Get the Band and the shooters, the truck and the cameras—everything—to the airport. Lomas will lay on a special flight for them."

He turned to his ex-wife, spoke very gently. "Would it be okay if I took you home? You could probably use a decent meal and some sack time."

She stood up, began walking with him—stopped. "Sack time? I hope you don't have any funny ideas," she warned.

"I give you my word, hon. There's no such thought in my mind."

After a hot bath, a good dinner and some wine, Diane McGhee discovered that her former husband had been lying —again. She wasn't the least bit surprised. She was an extremely intelligent woman, and Merlin had never fooled her for a minute. He was still a fine lover, and—as every progressive female knows—that is nothing to sneeze at in today's world.

Yes, she thought contentedly, there was only one Merlin.

The planet probably couldn't handle two.

This single evening didn't mean anything permanent, of course. It was good to be with him again, but there were still many important things to be discussed—frankly and fully and in a mature and adult fashion—in the morning.

She slept like a baby.

37

"That wasn't very nice," Blue Bernard complained.

"What wasn't?" Merlin asked.

"Standing up my two men was bad enough, but they waited an hour and a half for you outside the Hilton and got a ticket for double-parking."

Merlin put down a hundred-mark note.

"Money doesn't cover everything," the pornographer argued—and took the bill.

"Bernard, it's too early in the day to bicker."

It was 10:50, less than an hour after he'd left his sleeping ex-wife sprawled out in the big bed and smiling in some secret dream. A scream sounded from the next room, and the "other one"—the woman who'd delivered the madam's message—appeared in the doorway. She was carrying a whip and wearing high boots and a vague smile—nothing more. Bernard gestured, and she walked out of sight.

"She likes you," Bernard reported.

"I wouldn't want to interrupt your picture."

Bernard shrugged expansively, smirked. "She's terribly versatile."

"Some other time. I came to pay you the remaining thousand marks for the machine gunners—even if I didn't use them."

Blue Bernard was visibly impressed. "You know," he confided, "you may be a tricky bastard, but you aren't cheap."

"Not like the Russians?"

The affluent criminal coughed—twice.

"Bernard, I know you sold me out to the Russians."

"Of course. I *knew* that you knew. You don't think I'd have done it otherwise, do you? You wanted them to concentrate on the Hilton while you were way across town chopping up Willi Lietzen, right? Very *shrewd*."

Merlin smiled.

You might hate Blue Bernard, but you couldn't dislike him. His total cool, his ability to improvise effortlessly and his marvelously Levantine mind were entirely engaging. This man could have run a television network in any country on earth. Yes, Blue Bernard was a stylish survivor.

"You knew that I knew you knew?" he asked Merlin.

It was difficult not to laugh. "Absolutely. I never doubted you for a minute," Merlin assured him with a straight face.

"Listen, if you'd prefer Helga—"

Merlin shook his head, pulled out a cigar.

"Put that away," Bernard ordered imperiously. "Have a Havana. That was *some* job you did on those scummy terrorists —*some* job."

Merlin accepted a dark Upmann corona, lit it.

"The box is yours. Take the box. The good people of Berlin owe you plenty for getting rid of those gangsters, even if they don't know it."

All the newspapers, television and radio stations had given the credit to German police, and a cabinet member had made a sincerely patriotic speech about the incident in the Bundestag.

"Nice cigar," Merlin judged as he glanced at his watch. "Before I go, I want to thank you again for your crowd's help in finding their hideout. Never could have done it without you, Bernard."

For a moment, the pimp/pornographer/cocaine dealer was choked with emotion. This kind of appreciation, this old-fashioned courtesy, was all too rare in Berlin these days. Bernard swallowed, dabbed at his right eye with a lavender-scented handkerchief of the best French lace.

"Everything's okay," Merlin assured him.

"No hard feelings?"

"Course not. Gotta split. Meeting your pal Duslov in forty-five minutes, and he gets nasty when I'm late."

Bernard tensed, shoved the box of cigars at the American. "You know, those Russians are—well—you know."

"Cheap?" Merlin tickled.

"For sure, but also—sort of hot-tempered."

"Bernard, I won't tell him a thing. I'm your friend, remember?"

Merlin didn't start chuckling until he got into his car.

"What's so funny?" Cavaliere asked as Merlin slid behind the wheel.

"The Heerstrasse Cemetery," Merlin thought aloud.

"You've got a weird sense of humor."

"That's not a joke, Angie. That's where we're going, now."

Located close to the historic 95,000-seat Olympic Stadium where Hitler capered obscenely for the world's newsreel cameras in 1936, the Heerstrasse Cemetery lies near the banks of the Havel in the western part of the city. One might say the western part of the western part, which isn't the Communist eastern part—known as East Berlin. If you're crazy about landscaping, you'll love the Heerstrasse Cemetery.

"Scenic, isn't it?" said Duslov when Merlin met him just inside the main gate.

"Creepy. I think I preferred the crapper in that restaurant."

They walked on among the graves, hundreds and hundreds set gracefully in the greenery. They talked about the ambush, and they speculated on whether any fragments of the Lietzen-Stoller organization might have survived.

"I don't know," Merlin said truthfully. "We blew up everyone we could—even some damn Arab we never heard of before. They were all crazy, I guess."

"There are always plenty of crazies," Duslov brooded.

A philosophical KGB officer.

That's all I need, Merlin thought.

"We'll burn them too," he promised irritably.

"All over the world?"

"Right—just like the Israelis. They don't take any crap from anybody. They learned the hard way, and now they're teaching us all."

"Education with a nine-millimeter?" Duslov speculated.

"It beats finger-painting and U.N. speeches. Anyway, I'm not much of an orator."

They strolled on in silence for ten seconds before the Russian, selecting his words carefully, sighed and spoke.

"So there's no end to it? The killing goes on until all the fanatics are dead?"

"Until the killers are killed, or locked up in a damp place with bad food and scratchy sheets—for a long time. Even in the workers' paradise, you don't let homicidal maniacs run loose."

They turned, started back toward the gate.

"Maybe we should have met at the museum again," Duslov said. "Not the Dahlem, the Egyptian Museum in Charlottenburg. I'd like you to see the bust of Nefertiti."

"Thirteen seventy B.C.," Merlin recalled to Duslov's amazement. "Great chick, but dead a long time."

The KGB officer lost his temper. "You will be too. As a matter of fact, until an hour and a half ago I was under orders to kill you. Bury you—those were the exact words. Fortunately for you, the man who gave those instructions was relieved of his command last night—and the orders canceled."

Merlin looked ahead, saw the KGB trio in the Red Army staff car parked only twenty yards from Cavaliere's sedan.

"Fortunately for *you*, Andrei," Merlin said.

The Russian smiled sadly for just a moment. "We cannot be friends, American, but I like you. You're a man of spirit, not just a cog. Tell me, why must you be so *macho*—so savage? Even in our brutal business, you are—well, ferocious."

They were at the gate.

Cavaliere drove the car up, and Merlin sat down beside him.

"You don't fool me," Duslov said good-humoredly through the open window. "You may be tough, but you're not the worst American agent I ever met."

Merlin looked up with a pleasant expression of utter candor. "Yes, I am," he answered truthfully, and then Cavaliere put the car in gear and they sped away.

38

"Fifty thousand marks?"

"Fifty thousand marks," Merlin replied as he speared a final tidbit of creamed eel.

It was 1:35 P.M. and Merlin and Lomas were lunching in the charming restaurant that now fills the 158-year-old Nikolskoe Blockhaus, an historic log "cabin" with a superior view of the Havel River.

"I promised fifty thousand for a good tip on Lietzen," Merlin reminded, "and the Frau Admiral delivered his head on a plate."

Lomas scooped more potato onto his plate, grunted. "You're a big tipper, Merlin."

"I keep my word."

"To whorehouse madams?" the fat man jeered as he refilled his face.

"Especially whorehouse madams. I wouldn't want to lose my credit rating, George. It was a bargain at fifty, and you know it."

Lomas swallowed almost half a glass of beer. "Maybe we could get up twenty-five," he bargained.

"Don't get me angry, George. If I get mad, I'll break all your Wedgwood and set your mother on fire."

"Want some dessert?" Lomas asked hopefully.

"Fifty thousand marks—by four this afternoon. You want people to think we're cheap like the KGB?"

That stung.

"How do you want it?"

"Nice. No stunts. Used fifties and hundreds, no counterfeits. If there are any tricks, it'll be your ass, George."

Lomas finished his beer. "Strudel looks good," he volunteered.

"On you, not me. One more thing."

"Yes?" asked Lomas, who'd always expected to pay the fifty thousand.

"Leave a decent tip."

Merlin was halfway to the door before the counter-espionage executive realized that he was being stuck with the check, an event that was hardly surprising since Merlin made a habit of sticking other people with bills, bodies and assorted burdens. Grad had been most unpleasant about all the corpses and other debris left in the street after the ambush.

It was 2:10 when Merlin reached the apartment house where Ms. McGhee lived, and he was pleased to see two CIA operatives seated in a car nearby. He recognized them as part of the team Cavaliere had sent to Amerika Haus after the kidnapping, and he walked up to exchange professional greetings.

"Everything cool?" he asked.

"Like ice."

"You got the back covered too?"

"What do you think?" the sentry replied contemptuously.

The man had a submachine gun and terrible diction, so Merlin broke off relations and went up to the flat, where Diane McGhee was looking rested and marvelous.

"Terrific," Merlin judged—and they kissed.

"I'm going to forgive you for bugging my room," he announced, "provided you've got a decent cup of coffee. I left Lomas at lunch before the coffee came."

"He was here."

"When?"

"Just before noon. Very nice. They're reassigning me to Washington. Promotion, too."

Merlin computed.

Lomas wanted his own man in to run the deception of Victor. Nice? Shit, Lomas couldn't spell the word.

"More money?"

"Four thousand more a year. I'll be making more money than you," she laughed.

"You deserve it. How about that coffee?"

As soon as she was out of the room, he telephoned Cavaliere.

"Don't talk, listen," he said. "This isn't a secure line. The Godfather will have a green package for you at four o'clock. Give it to the admiral's widow, with my compliments."

"Right. Anything else?"

"Yeah, the doctor. The guy whose phone I used?"

"What about him?"

"Out. I want him on a bird to the States within three hours. He's hot."

Cavaliere understood. If the Sovs got to speak to Margolis, he might innocently mention the sodium pentothal.

"What do I tell him, Merl?"

"National security, birdbrain. Call my pal in Heidelberg. He'll fix it. You got it?"

"I'm on the case."

Merlin put down the phone, lit a cigar as she walked back into the room.

"Water'll be boiling in a minute," she reported.

"Good. Sit down here, hon," he invited, tapping the couch cushion beside him.

She complied, caught the smell of the cigar.

She'd missed that familiar Merlin scent for a long time.

"I couldn't help hearing part of your phone call. What was that all about?"

"Sex," Merlin improvised instantly.

Lying was one of the things he did best, she thought affectionately.

"Scout's honor. Sex," he insisted.

"You know," she replied, "that's a terrific idea."

They didn't get to drink their coffee until half-past three.

Several thousand miles west, Greta Beller was sipping her tea and smiling hopefully at her husband. His progress toward recovery was encouraging, and the doctors all agreed that he'd probably be able to get around without the walker in another seven or ten weeks. Speech was still a problem. After all this time, the only word he could say was "Ernest." Still, dear Martin wasn't discouraged. In recent days he'd been struggling with a child's school pad and a pencil, fighting to communicate in writing. Dr. Esserman had said that the ability to write might return first, and Martin obviously had something —something choked up in him—that was important. His handwriting was awful, but it was getting better as he worked at it.

All of a sudden he handed her the ruled pad, pointed urgently. She studied the dreadful scrawl, finally deciphered the primitive kindergarten letters.

"Yes, dear. Yes, I will," she promised.

He pointed at the pad, jabbed it with his finger emphatically.

"Absolutely, Martin," she assured him.

She walked out to the living room, looked across Central Park at the lights of the apartment houses on Fifth Avenue. It was all so puzzling. Had the stroke affected his splendid intelligence?

Stop Ernest.

Now what could that mean?

39

Obscenity?

You never heard such language.

Even Merlin—who had heard plenty of such language—had never heard such language.

Marta Falkenhausen had what your mother would call a dirty mouth, and a big one too. She poured out a gush of filth that would bedazzle a marine sergeant, spicing the flow with political epithets, Maoist slogans and insolent idiocies by the yard.

"Why don't you throw her down the stairs?" Merlin suggested.

"We don't do such things in Germany," Grad answered starchily.

"Funny. You used to."

It was appalling that this American, who was only a "guest observer" at the interrogation, should be so provocative.

"That was rude," Grad said.

"No, dumb," the black woman corrected. "Behave yourself," she told her lover.

"I'll try. I still think we should throw her down the stairs."

Fraulein Falkenhausen went on screaming what she thought—about Merlin, the Federal Republic, capitalism and many other subjects that were definitely peripheral. She didn't get to the world food problem, the Stuttgart Ballet, the state of the British pound or whether homosexuals should be ordained, but she covered almost everything else, in filth. She waxed especially lyrical on Merlin's parenthood and the subservience of the West German government to American imperialist fascism.

After spewing a good half-hour of blue material you or I could never try out on either the Johnny Carson show or the

BBC, she paused briefly for station identification—and then denounced the Soviets with equal vigor.

"Maybe she could work Las Vegas, but only as a lounge act," Merlin speculated.

"Too dirty," Diane McGhee translated for Grad.

"She was worse yesterday."

"Sorry I missed it. How about throwing her *up* the stairs?" Merlin suggested.

She began cursing again, not as loudly but just as sincerely.

"Have you tried an enema?"

Grad wouldn't even answer that.

She resumed her litany, swearing and denouncing until she ran out of breath.

"Doesn't surprise me," Merlin said. "Any broad who'd ice her own father'll do anything."

She stopped the barrage.

"What?"

"You heard what I said, lady. A woman who'll kill her own daddy is strictly the pits in my book."

"That's a lie!"

"The pits! Tarantulas don't do that, baby."

Marta Falkenhausen turned her attention to Diane McGhee. "I have done many things you bourgeois call criminal," she admitted slowly. "I have destroyed banks and factories, attacked army camps, liberated large sums of money to finance the revolution. I have shot people—for my cause."

"Balls," Merlin commented.

"But I did not kill my father. I despised him, but I did not kill him. *I did not kill my father.*"

She spoke with great intensity. Then, after a pause, she asked, "When did he die?"

She hadn't known. Her face, her voice said that clearly.

Merlin told her where and when, still unconvinced and studying her carefully. The news seemed to sober her, and the loud semihysterical diatribes ended. She still recited chapter and verse of the Lietzen-Stoller bible, but now and then she answered the questions—usually indirectly and always incompletely. Bit by bit, a picture of the terrorists' movements and activities during the previous six months began to emerge. It was like a half-done jigsaw, just enough to give an image of the general subject.

"What do you think?" Merlin asked as they walked out of the police station into the early-afternoon sun.

"About what?"

She'd been a great wife with many excellent qualities, but one of her few irritating habits was answering questions with questions. Merlin had often accused her of talking like a goddam psychoanalyst, and here she was doing the shrink bit again.

"About whether her father's death really was news to her."

Merlin looked up and down the street, routinely checking on whether anyone was lying in wait to kill him.

"Hard to say for sure, but—don't laugh—my woman's instinct tells me she was telling the truth."

"I'm not laughing."

Her instincts had been right so often.

What if the Frankenhausen woman wasn't lying?

"What do you think?" Diane McGhee asked.

"I think we'd better go see Fritz Kammler."

The terrorist whom Merlin had shot four times was in the criminal ward of a large public hospital a mile and a half away. He was a lucky man, even if he'd never have full use of his right arm again and would be breathing with one lung for the rest of his life. Most of the people Merlin shot weren't breathing at all two days later.

Grad wasn't too eager to authorize the visit. "What do you want to see him about?" he probed.

"About fifteen minutes," Merlin replied with his customary charm.

The tired BND executive told himself that it just wasn't worth arguing about, and the guards at the criminal ward let them in as soon as Merlin showed his Wasserman passport.

There were bars on the windows, whose thick panes were plainly bulletproof. A BND agent in civilian clothes sat reading a sex magazine in an armchair, glancing up from the nude photos every twenty or thirty seconds at the pale man in the bed.

"Fifteen minutes," the security man quoted.

It didn't take that long.

Merlin told Kammler that he might get him a reduced sentence if the terrorist answered questions about a few details of the attack on the trainload of VWs, the demolition of the petro-chemical plant and the shooting of industrialist Heinrich Hessicher in the Frankfurt toilet.

"That was Willi's personal project," recalled the battered driver. Then he talked about the planning and execution of the rail and factory raids, minimizing his own role.

"You were there?"

"I won't deny it. I was with them on every job."

"Did you drive when they killed that Nazi up in the Hamburg prison, and when they gassed the woman?"

"The rich slob in the toilet? Sure, but I never heard of those others. You can't blame those two on us. The group wiped out a lot of imperialists and fascists, but don't try to stick us with every killing on the books."

"Maybe Willi did them alone?" Merlin pried.

"No way—we were always together—and he talked a lot. He was a good talker, a good leader."

"And a great corpse. One of the best stiffs I've seen in years."

Kammler stared at him, remembered.

"You're the bastard who shot me!"

"Right. And you're the bastard who tried to shoot me! Listen, Speedy, I'm going to check on what you said."

The wounded terrorist then suggested something else that Merlin could do, closed his eyes and yawned.

"So long, Karl," Merlin said for the concealed microphone just before the two Americans left the room, "and send me a copy of the tape."

"You know," he said at the elevator, "I may have been wrong."

"It doesn't matter," she assured.

"If those two are telling the truth, I've been dead wrong—and that matters. Matters to me. I'm going to go over all the transcripts, check every detail. If they didn't burn those Nazis, who did?"

An orderly wheeled by a pretty blonde woman in a chair, and a nurse with a remarkable rump rippled past—and Merlin didn't even notice. It was extraordinary.

"Darling, it isn't any of your business," Diane insisted. "You came for Crash Dive, and you did it. You did what no one else could. Isn't that enough? It's over."

She probably loved him, Merlin thought, but she still didn't understand him completely. He shook his head, cupped his hand affectionately under her chin.

"No. No, it isn't over," he said patiently. "It isn't over at all."

40

"You sound like Hitler," Cavaliere said.

"All I said was that the Jews probably did it."

"That's what *he* always said, Merl."

They'd been driving for five hours, and Cavaliere felt a headache growing.

"To be accurate," Merlin corrected himself, "the Israelis. I checked out every point, and those goddam Martians couldn't have done it."

"What am I doing here?"

"You're helping your old friend."

"Merlin, this isn't any of our business. We are in the glamorous world of high international intrigue—trench coats and spy-in-the-sky satellites. Local hits are beneath us."

"That's what she said—two days ago," Merlin remembered as he swung into the fast lane of the autobahn to pass a little Renault.

"You're just sore at her because she wouldn't listen to your joke about the gorilla in heat."

The effort to change the subject was too obvious.

"Nice try, Angie, but no cigar. Angie, these Nazis were totaled by experts—people who cut 'em down like surgeons. It had to be the Israelis."

"How about the Eskimos? Why the Israelis?"

Merlin flipped down the sun visor, sighed tolerantly. "They have the motive and the high-class manpower. The Mossad's one of the toughest little intelligence outfit in the business."

That was true. The Israeli Secret Service was slick, daring and ruthless. Jerusalem's Mossad had earned the respect of its big brothers, again and again. Cavaliere felt depressed as he faced the fact that the Mossad *could* mount such a large and lethal operation.

"They've got the nerve," he admitted reluctantly as Merlin turned off onto the ramp off the superhighway.

"And the imagination. Check the map again, will you?" the man behind the wheel asked.

They found the road, and they reached their destination twenty-five minutes later. Barbed-wire fences, cattle grazing and three men in cowboy outfits right out of the old western films—an odd vista for central Germany in the 1970s. The burnt-wood lettering on the crude sign—Cheyenne Ranch—was the final touch.

"Weird," Cavaliere judged.

"Out-a-sight," Merlin disagreed admiringly.

The beefy man in sombrero, chaps, denim shirt, six-gun and boots looked out from the shack at the gate, waved them down.

"Got a reservation?"

"We're expected. Tell Tex it's his friend Doug from Nairobi."

The guard spoke into an incongruous walkie-talkie briefly, gestured for them to enter. "Some imagination," Merlin celebrated as they drove the half-mile to the clump of low wooden buildings. "Who but the Israelis would run their German intelligence operation from a phony dude ranch?"

"Why not? It's *West* Germany."

"Not bad, Angie. Here we are, pardner."

He parked the car, and they entered the "saloon" just in time for the regular 3 P.M. shoot-out. The bar was filled with German "cowboys"—many of them businessmen who paid cheerfully for this fantasy trip—and the decor was strictly early John Wayne. Precisely on schedule, two of the "cowboys" insulted each other, the other customers scattered, and the antagonists pulled their six-shooters.

The Colt .44s roared, and a splotch of red dye blossomed on the plaid shirt of one of the gunfighters. Friends of the other man congratulated him as the loser in this fast-draw ritual wiped the stain from his chest and the victor sang out in the grand old tradition. "Red-eye for everyone!"

"It's bourbon."

The Americans turned to face a curly-haired man in the ceremonial attire of the 1880s gambler. He wore a thin mustache, gold watch and chain and a gun that—unlike all the others in the room—was loaded with real bullets. He reached out with a grin, shook Merlin's hand.

"Beautiful. That job you did on those mothers in the street ambush was just *beautiful*," he said as he held up three fingers to order drinks.

"Not as beautiful as Entebbe."

The Mossad executive shook his head. "You always say the right thing, Merlin. You're a *mensch*. Okay, not exactly like Entebbe—but beautiful."

Cavaliere's eyes wandered to a busty barmaid who amply filled—almost overflowed—a low-cut dress. She kissed a portly Swabian sausage tycoon right on his bald spot—just like in the movies.

"Entebbe's a classic," Merlin responded. "That's a textbook operation. Going to be studied in fifty different countries for years. A model—don't deny it."

"Merlin, enough is enough. That bit you did with the TV cameras? You think that'll be forgotten? That was first-class, amigo."

Now the barmaid came swinging her hips through the crowd, holding the tray of drinks aloft with her left hand and fending off assorted "slap and tickle" enthusiasts with the other.

"Aha, those must be the original Doberman pinchers. Tex, let me introduce my partner—John Bonomi."

"Pleasure. Can I call you John?"

"Angie. You wouldn't have an aspirin, would you?"

The voluptuous waitress arrived, bent low to put the drinks on the table. The view was impressive, and intentional.

"Got any aspirin for these dudes, Rosie?" the Israeli asked.

She reached into the cleavage, came up with a lukewarm tin of the tablets. "Take two before you go to sleep," she advised, "and if you can't sleep, call *me*." She winked, swivel-hipped away with a rolling gait that might make sensitive types seasick.

"Head of the Drama Club at the University of Haifa?" Merlin wondered.

"How'd you guess? Here's to the good guys, Merlin—that's us."

They raised their glasses, sipped some adequate bourbon

that wasn't ever going to make the Jack Daniels firm nervous.

"Can you stay a bit? We've got a nice little gunfight scheduled at a quarter to five down at the corral."

"The OK Corral?"

"What else? Merlin, you ol' varmint, tell me, what's on your
mind?"

Merlin swallowed the rest of the bourbon, wiped his mouth
with the back of his hand and pulled two of Blue Bernard's
Havanas from his shirt pocket. He handed one to his host.

"When Merlin gives away good cigars, look out! Let's have
it."

"I just want to ask you something. It's not official, and it's
only for my personal information. If you don't want to answer,
don't—and there's no hard feelings."

"That bad, huh? What's the big question?" Tex demanded as
he puffed on the corona.

Merlin told him about all the prison murders, and then asked
whether he knew anything about them.

"You're so refined, Merlin. It's a pleasure to talk with you.
You don't come right out and ask whether we killed those
momsers. No, you wonder if I know anything about them."

He signaled for more drinks.

"Merlin, if we had executed those monsters I wouldn't tell
you, even though I'm sort of fond of you. I wouldn't tell anybody. However, we didn't kill these degenerates. We have
better things to do. Hey, if you stay overnight you can get laid
and watch our terrific cattle stampede in the morning." The
Mossad supervisor nodded toward the "dance hall girls" in
very short red skirts who were mounting the stage. A white-
haired piano player sat down, began to thump.

"The truth?" Merlin pressed. "I won't tell anyone."

"Tell everyone. Not our job. Is it yours?"

"Not really," Cavaliere interrupted.

"Shut up, Angie."

The Israeli blew a smoke ring.

"Mr. Bonomi, you got rough friends. You know, I didn't
realize so many of those Nazis had been killed in the past five
or six weeks. If you find out who did it, let me hear."

"You'll give them all medals, I suppose?" Merlin speculated.

"And a free weekend here—with all meals. Now I'm entitled

to one question. If it's not official and maybe none of your business altogether, Merlin, what the hell will you do if you do find out who hit them?"

"Not if—*when.*"

"I'll pray for you. Right, when. When, what?"

The young woman with the eye-catching chest returned with the second round, each glass sitting on a cork coaster marked Deadeye Dick's. Merlin grabbed his, drank it all in one gulp. She put the other glasses on the table, winked again and twitched her tail skillfully back to the bar.

Merlin stood up abruptly. "Thanks for your hospitality, friend. Let's go, Angie."

"I *am* your friend, Merlin—so be careful," the Israeli advised. "Something about this whole *my-seh* doesn't add up right."

"My view precisely. Shalom, podner."

The piano player was pounding away loudly and the "dance hall girls" were kicking as high as they could, exposing patches of flesh and ruffled panties to guffawing "cowboys." Both CIA agents shook hands with Tex, who insisted that Cavaliere keep the rest of the aspirin in case the headache persisted. The raucous customers were singing loudly as the Americans made their way out, but Merlin didn't seem to notice. He was concentrating on something or somewhere else, and he didn't say a word until they were almost back to the autobahn.

"Goddam."

"Merl, you didn't answer his question. I thought it was a very good question."

The man behind the wheel didn't respond.

"Merlin," Cavaliere finally challenged forty seconds later, "what the hell *will* you do when you identify the killers?"

More silence.

"If the Israelis didn't do it," he wondered aloud, "who did?"

Angelo Cavaliere suddenly realized why the twice-asked question remained unanswered. Merlin didn't want to face it —not yet. Right now all Merlin cared about was finding out who'd make a fool of him, and he'd focus on that until he'd evened the score. Logical or not, Merlin was tracking.

No one could stop him.

Even after he returned to West Berlin, even after he drank

half a bottle of chilled Traminer and went to bed with the woman whom he cared for more than he'd admit, the obsession continued. He awoke at a quarter to three in the morning, wandered into the living room to stand by the French windows and stare out at the city.

It wasn't the Martians.

It wasn't the Israelis.

Who was it?

At 4:20 he glanced up to find her, sleepy-eyed and very beautiful in her ebony nakedness, watching him from the bedroom doorway.

"Go back to bed," he advised.

"It can't be sexual frustration, thank God, so what is it?"

"Dandruff. Go to sleep."

Her body seemed even more perfect than when they first fell in love, even more vulnerable and appealing.

"You're a very good-looking woman," he said.

"Then what the hell are you doing out here?"

She'd always excelled at relevant questions.

"Who do *you* figure did it?" he blurted.

She flopped onto the couch, shrugged. "I thought you'd never ask. I've been thinking about it—a lot. It wasn't the Sovs either. They don't give anything away, and they wouldn't go to all this bother because—if you get down to the nitty-gritty —they had nothing to gain."

"Check," he agreed.

"Run down all the governments—including Ecuador and those loonies in Libya—and you won't find one that would profit from killing those old Nazis."

"Check. Want a drink?"

"Club soda."

He brought two glasses of the bubbling water, sat beside her. She smelled good. It was the perfume he'd given her on their honeymoon. Christ, the woman was ruthless.

"Now let's try the terrorist groups. Left, Right, East, West, African, Asian, European, South American."

"Don't forget the Eskimos," Merlin reminded. "Angie thinks it could be the Eskimos, and he was Phi Beta Kappa."

"Screw the Eskimos. You want to feel sorry for yourself, or you want to make some sense out of this?"

A great mind as well as swell boobs.

Terrific at problem solving and contraception.

"Okay, we'll forget the Eskimos," he yielded and closed his eyes. He reached out for her.

"Just a second. That's nice, but let me finish the checklist. There isn't a single damn terrorist outfit in the world that—in your poetic terms—gives a crap about these war criminals. Everybody's forgotten about them, right?"

Merlin stroked her shoulder, and she shivered and purred. "You're distracting me," she whispered.

"I like to."

"Please. Please—we're almost done."

He stopped, but his hand still held her shoulder. "No, you're wrong. Everyone hasn't forgotten them," he announced.

"Right on. Every government and terrorist organization has written them off, but someone remembers. Maybe a couple of survivors of those death camps—a few individuals."

Merlin computed.

"Too old—unless they were kids. No government, no terrorist mob—okay. Private individuals? They'd have to be very good. Goddam very good. This was high-class work."

"Keep talking. You're doing fine."

He sipped at the soda. "What have we got? Somebody who speaks excellent German—with several different accents. Maybe an actor?"

She nodded, yawned. "Male?" she asked.

"All male. Hamburg, Frankfurt, Nürnberg—all the rest. Always one male, alone. Forged papers. Someone between five-nine and six-one, according to the witnesses—Hey, this is impossible."

"What is?"

"One man did all this—by himself? He'd have to be the superstar of homicide."

Merlin reached to the coffee table, picked up the Asbach Uralt bottle and poured an inch into his glass.

"Nobody's that good," he reasoned.

"He isn't nobody. He's somebody—with a special motive."

"And access to a lot of fancy stuff. Digitalis, curare compounds—you don't get that at Woolworth's . . . Wait a second. A chemist or a doctor?"

"You're doing even better. A highly motivated man—with a lot of nerve—who's a chemist or doctor or something like that, speaks German and plays different parts like an actor. Sometimes he's thirty-five, sometimes fifty. Pour me some."

Merlin did, and she sipped and snuggled closer.

"German?" she asked.

"Whoever he is, he knows how to kill. He's no mere hit man or soldier. German? Maybe not. Why did he wait until now? If he was German, he could have chopped them up years ago."

"Unless he was in a prison or mental institution himself," she reckoned. "German or a top linguist, and a fanatic. Totally obsessed, willing to risk his own life again and again. Avenging sword. Think he's Jewish? Maybe some ex–Israeli officer or Mossad grad they retired as a psycho?"

"Chemist or doctor," Merlin reminded. "Well, we've reduced the number of suspects from two billion to a lousy two hundred thousand or so. That's some progress, I suppose."

She stood up and stretched, marvelously. "In the morning," she said, "you can call the BND and tell them everything we've figured out. Let them try these facts on their computers, their lists of doctors and chemists and survivors of the Nazi camps."

"They won't want to listen," Merlin predicted. "They'd like to write the whole thing off as Lietzen-Stoller stuff. A lot cleaner that way."

He was still stubborn.

"You tell them, dear," she cajoled, "and you'll feel better. Let's go to bed."

That part went nicely, with lots of warmth and mutual respect and squeezing and lust. In the morning, however, Merlin's prediction came true.

"Grad advised me to stop making up fairy stories and to start minding my own business," he reported to his favorite ex-wife sourly.

"You tried. Don't feel bad," she consoled.

"I feel awful."

She understood immediately. "Don't be foolish!" she enjoined.

"I may be feeling even worse," Merlin speculated.

"Leave it alone. Come back to Washington with me next week," she pleaded.

He shook his head. "Not well enough to travel, hon. Think I'd better find myself a doctor."

The stubborn bastard hadn't changed a bit.

He probably never would.

41

It was a love affair.

What else could you call it?

They held hands as they walked together, both in Freuden-stadt and up on some of the 125 miles of "nature trails and footpaths" featured in the Chamber of Commerce brochures. The cool woods and the sunny green fields, the singing birds and the serene vistas were even more splendid than in the four-color photos of the Tourist Office leaflet—the one with the snapshot of the golf course and the picture of the two naked women in the wood-lined sauna.

They swam together, bicycled and rode horses.

They went to concerts, listened to her records and sang as they hiked and picnicked. They ate together, drank together, went to bed together and awoke happy—together. It wasn't supposed to be like that, and yet it *was* supposed to be like that because that's what young—and not so young—men and women dream will happen. If they believe in true romance and Hollywood, they expect that love will come along without warning and sweep them into the arms of some wonderful stranger.

But it wasn't supposed to happen to Ernest Beller, not now and not here and not with a German woman. The idea that he could become seriously attached to the granddaughter of a Nazi sadist—one of the savages he'd come to slay—was prepos-terous. Even though he knew that Anna Griese herself loathed the fascists and was one of the great number of young Germans born after the violent death of the Third Reich, he wasn't that comfortable with citizens of the new Federal Republic—ex-cept this one.

There was something unique and appealing about this young woman, and it wasn't her blonde hair or fawn-eyes or female contours. It was Anna herself, the interior Anna. He couldn't understand it or explain it, and even as it was happening during those first days he couldn't believe it. He told himself that he merely felt sorry for her, that it was simply compassion for somebody who had no one else. Even at the funeral, there had been only Anna Griese, the priest and the avenger who'd come nearly four thousand miles and more than three decades to kill the man being buried.

Now, eleven days after that last shovelful of earth was tossed, the doctor still marveled at what had happened. It had grown slowly and gently, but irresistibly. He hadn't even held her hand for three days, and the rest had followed so peacefully and logically that they'd hardly noticed the journey. He looked at her as she unpacked the picnic basket, seeming even younger than her twenty-four years in the summer dress.

"It's a wonder," he said as he ran his hands across the mountain grass.

"No, it's a miracle—and miracles don't have to be explained. Please open the wine."

He kissed her instead, several times, but then he put the corkscrew to work.

"It would have been unbearable without you," she said truthfully. "I was always so ashamed of him. Not everyone was. Some people said that the stories of the camps were lies."

"They were true."

He hesitated, tried to stop himself—and failed.

"My parents died in one of those camps."

He knew that he could trust her. She caught him in her arms, and she wept again. He was startled to find himself consoling her, for it should have been the other way around. She stopped, looked him squarely in the eye.

"That wasn't guilt, darling. There's plenty of hidden guilt and suppressed rage in this country. That was shame," she spoke softly, "and shared pain. My parents' dying in that auto accident wasn't comparable to the camps, but I know what it's like to grow up without a mother or father."

"I don't blame you for what happened, Anna. There were others—whom I cannot forget."

She squeezed his hand like a high-school girl. "Can you forgive them? I couldn't. I know the Bible says good Christians should, but I'm not that good a Christian," she admitted.

"No, I can't forgive them," he said slowly.

She started to put out the food. "They tell us that we should be saints, Kurt," she thought aloud, "but I don't know how."

"No, you could be a saint—but I couldn't. Being near you is probably the closest I'll ever come to sainthood."

She kissed him again, looked up lovingly. "You could be anything, Kurt. You're kind, generous and very wise. I feel so safe with you."

He stroked her hair gently. "I'll do my best for you, Anna, but don't expect perfection. You don't know everything about me."

"For me, you're perfect!"

His smile seemed sad.

"Anna, it's too late. I'll never be a saint."

He was suffering, and she wanted to help him—somehow.

"Then be an angel and pour the wine," she urged with a smile that was much gayer than her feelings. They drank the whole bottle as they ate and sunned, and they were both careful not to talk about anything serious for the rest of the afternoon. Each of them worked very hard to avoid anything that might pierce the other's happiness, and finally the wine and the sun and the love prevailed and the tension eased. It would be back and they both knew it, but now they enjoyed the miracle.

Merlin wasn't enjoying anything.

The BND had checked out every German physician and chemist who'd been in the murder camps, reluctantly but thoroughly. Half a dozen agents had worked for four days. The list of survivors wasn't that long, for almost all the doctors and chemists who hadn't died in Hitler's slaughter centers had migrated to other countries. Every single survivor—even the women—had been investigated, and all could account for their activities during the days when the war criminals were slain.

"Dead end. It's over. That's what Grad said," Merlin told Diane McGhee bitterly as he entered her apartment. She went to the kitchen, poured two large steins of cold beer and returned to the living room to thrust one at him.

"Thanks . . . That's what he said. Dead end. That's what he wants, of course."

He didn't even notice the see-through blouse.

He was that furious.

"You think he really checked?" she asked.

"Yeah. I went over the whole list with him. Ninety-two people, including a woman in a wheelchair in Tübingen, and a blind man in Lübeck."

"You curse him out?"

Merlin gulped the good light brew, shrugged. "I couldn't. The bastard had done what I asked. The one who really got me pissed was Fat George."

"You didn't get into a fight with Lomas, did you?"

Merlin drank more beer, unbuttoned his collar and threw his tie on the floor. It was all very familiar to his ex-wife, who remembered so many similar scenes.

"He wouldn't fight. Bureaucrats don't sink to such cheap emotion. That porky turd told me he was sorry my *theory* hadn't worked out. *Theory?* I should've belted him."

The difficult aspect of the situation was that she sensed that Merlin was probably right. Headquarters executives such as Lomas had always resented Merlin's extraordinary gut instincts and illogical logic, largely because it was correct more often than their computer analyses.

"Then Lomas told me to go home," Merlin announced and finished the beer.

"I'm going home in six days," she reminded.

She wanted him to return with her so much, but she knew that he had to make that choice without obvious prompting.

"I told him to stick it—sideways. I don't work for Lomas. He's probably on the Teletype now, getting some deputy director to order me back. Those desk farts all hang together."

She handed him her half-filled glass, and he drank deeply.

It had never been easy to calm Merlin. Sometimes even going to bed had only a temporary effect.

"Don't be discouraged, hon," she advised. "Maybe it wasn't a German at all. Lots of people were in those camps. Angie could have been right."

"*He's* going back day after tomorrow too. . . . Right about what?"

"The Eskimos," she reminded brightly.

Why the hell wouldn't this ridiculous man come home?

Suddenly he looked thoughtful, and she knew that he was computing.

"Yeah, the *Eskimos*. Thanks. That could be it."

He was impossible.

"What could be it?" she demanded.

He didn't respond for ten or fifteen seconds.

"Di," he asked with an earnest smile, "do we have any more cold beer?"

42

Grad could have been angry—at least annoyed.

Transient foreign agents such as Merlin—violent field operatives who attracted attention—weren't supposed to know that this stockbrokerage firm was the cover for the BND in West Berlin, and they certainly weren't supposed to show up uninvited and walk in off the street without warning.

It was rude.

Just the sort of thing one might expect from an undisciplined and inconsiderate American gangster like Merlin, who always mocked the amenities.

But Karl Grad wasn't angry; he was surprised. In contrast to the CIA man's previous behavior, Merlin was actually trying to be polite. With the stock tickers clattering away in the big clients' room outside Grad's office, the BND executive studied Merlin warily.

"I can't believe it," Grad announced.

"Karl, believe it. Be reasonable. I'm asking you for a favor, *please.*"

Grad had never heard him say please before, and it made the German nervous. There might be a trick in this. An aide rapped on the door, walked in and handed Grad a strip of paper torn from the Teletype.

"Nothing serious?" Merlin asked.

"No, the usual. Another coup attempt in Ethiopia, and somebody blew up a Syrian airliner with a hundred and three people aboard. Nobody you know."

"Thank God," Merlin replied. "Listen, Karl, I need your help—as an old friend."

"What's this all about?"

"The Eskimos. I think some of the Eskimos did it—not any decent, law-abiding Germans."

Was he insane, or just teasing again?

"The *Eskimos?*" Grad asked incredulously.

Merlin's chuckle was a masterpiece of macho joviality.

"Not the real Eskimos. You knew that, you old fox. Just using the word to describe all the different kinds of foreigners. Foreign doctors or chemists, who entered the Federal Republic between, say, May first and the day that person was killed in the Hamburg prison. Male, Caucasian, between thirty and forty."

Now *this* was interesting.

Perhaps some insane group of homicidal foreigners had conspired to commit these murders. Grad had a certain fondness for conspiracies, although nothing to compare with U.S. journalists and free-lance social critics of both Left and Right who saw conspiracies under every gooseberry bush and dog dropping. Some of them were still gathering evidence to expose the bastards who stole that apple and framed Eve for the sin.

"There can't be that many," Merlin pressed.

"I don't know. It's the beginning of the tourist season."

"Forget the psychiatrists, chiropodists, brain surgeons, dermatologists and nutrition experts. Just the kind of guys who might have the skills for these fancy hits. You can do it!"

Grad considered, nodded. "Maybe the Tourist Office keeps records. Perhaps there were some conventions," he speculated.

"There were! One was swinging in Berlin the day after I arrived in June. Can we check on this? Please?"

Grad weighed the request, and hesitated. "We are not friends, Herr Wasserman, we are colleagues. I respect your work, and our governments are allies, but we are not friends."

Merlin shifted his attack instantly. "You're right, but I'm not asking this out of goodwill. Strictly business. Do this and I'll owe you one—a big one. No sentiment. It'll be in your account, like a bank."

The Tourist Office and the passport-control people would do all the work, and not an hour of BND time would be invested. Two or three phone calls ought to do it. With a little luck, Grad could avoid putting anything in writing—leaving an escape route from blame if anything went wrong.

"This is an official request from your agency?"

"Absolutely," Merlin lied briskly.

That was another piece of insurance—the kind that capable survivors like Grad always assembled.

"Sehr gut. I will do what I can, Herr Wasserman. Strictly business. I should tell you," he said as Merlin stood up, "that —if I may be blunt—I have always found you and your methods somewhat disturbing."

Merlin's expression of hurt surprise was only a trifle overdone, but rather good considering his closest connection with the Actors Studio was a blonde TV starlet who'd proven her sincerity during a wild weekend in Honolulu.

"I don't blame you, Karl. It's big of you to do this, and I won't forget it," he improvised creatively.

Brando could have done better, but no spy service in the world would meet his price. Merlin left and Grad made two telephone calls, and a lot of clerks and data-processing technicians in Bonn and Berlin were working on the matter less than two hours later. In the great tradition of bureaucracies and office management everywhere, no one told them what this "job" was all about—and they didn't care.

Ernest Beller cared a great deal. Alone in the apartment while she was out buying milk, he looked at the pictures again —and he hated. But it wasn't the same, for now there was another feeling that had come with his love for Anna. He knew that it was his duty to punish these murderers, but the nine more on his list seemed like strangers, more like ghosts than devils. There could be no doubt that this was the time of reckoning, but he wondered what might happen to Anna if he continued his dangerous crusade.

Would he be caught or slain, leaving her alone?

Would the dead forgive him if he stopped?

He heard her key in the door, relocked his attaché case and faced her in the doorway. Just seeing her was a delight, and the anger began to fade. By the time they went to bed that night, the bitterness was changing to something less fiery—a heavy burden of obligation. Long after she put out the table lamp and slid off into sleep, he lay awake in the darkness beside her warmth—wondering.

He made up his mind as he was shaving the next morning. He couldn't put it off any longer. He would have to go to that place, to confront the horror face-to-face. He had dreaded it so long, feared the reality that might tear him to pieces. He told her while she refilled his coffee cup twenty minutes later.

"I have to go away for a couple of days," he said as calmly as he could.

"I'll come with you," she volunteered.

"No, it's business. My book. I'll be back on Saturday night."

She accepted, smiled and lit up the whole man.

"Where are you going?"

"Munich."

It wasn't entirely untrue. He'd have to pass through Munich on his way to a quaint old Bavarian town twelve miles to the north, described as a "gay-hearted place" in the Fodor guide-book, which noted that it was "much frequented by landscape painters for the beauty of its scenery."

Dachau.

43

It was half-past one when Beller parked his car near Munich's gabled "new" City Hall, but he wasn't the least bit hungry. His mind, not his stomach, told him that he should eat. He walked across the Weinstrasse to the Donisl, recalling that it was the oldest beer hall in the Bavarian metropolis. After that, his attention drifted and he was barely aware that he was chewing as he mechanically cut and ingested two mustard-covered veal sausages and a dense dumpling. He didn't taste the draft Löwenbräu either, for he was half-numb with the apprehension that had been growing and hardening within him for so many hours.

When he wandered out into the August afternoon, he paused to focus on the flow of cars and trucks that could kill him. It wasn't easy, for the fear affected his sight and his senses —even his depth perception. Concentrating very hard, he forced his way through the streets to the railway station. He had made up his mind even before he left Freudenstadt. His parents had come to the camp in rail cars—cattle cars crammed with human fuel for that giant incinerator—and he, too, would go by train. He didn't know why, but the ritual was important.

His train was the number 2 S–Bahn, the commuter run out in the direction of Petershausen. Fare, one dollar. The other passengers were local people, for almost all the tourists who came to look in awe at the murder factory—not that many after all these years—traveled by bus with sincere guides who could talk calmly of the massacres in several languages. Beller heard only German in the modern and comfortable train.

After twenty-five minutes he got out and found a Dachau city bus. He boarded a number 6, paid his thirty cents and wondered whether he would faint before he got there.

He didn't.

Somehow, as he got nearer he grew stronger.

He forced himself to be stronger, to prepare for the impact of facing the nightmares he had never let himself dream. Even so, he wasn't ready for the shock of that small white sign.

KZ-Gedenkstatte.

KZ—that meant *Konzentrationlager*.

Concentration camp.

He literally gasped, and the other people who got off the bus with him turned at the sound. There were five of them—a pair of college boys in UCLA T-shirts, a middle-aged French couple, and a thin old man in black who walked with a cane.

"You speak German, mister?" the taller of the students asked.

Beller nodded.

"Gedenkstatte? What's that?"

"Memorial," the doctor translated.

They thanked him, walked toward the gate.

From the outside, the camp seemed unchanged. The big compound—990 feet wide and 1980 feet long—was still ringed by that barbed-wire-and-concrete barrier, and over there, outside the perimeter, stood four of those ovens where the bodies had been burned up so efficiently. One thing had changed. There were no armed guards at the gate. Instead of S.S. sadists, a polite young woman—a civil servant, no doubt—was selling guidebooks at fifteen cents. He saw the Californians buy one, stroll slowly into the "memorial."

"You've just missed the film," the woman at the gate said.

"Film?" Beller wondered numbly.

"In both English and German—twenty-five minutes long. We show it every day at eleven and three. Every day except December twenty-fourth, the afternoon before New Year's and Shrove Tuesday. That's when we're closed. It's free."

The stunned survivor walked past her, and saw that almost all the buildings were gone. The avenging Americans—or was it the embarrassed German authorities?—had leveled the barracks years ago, but two duplicates had been built so that visitors could see what the quarters had been like. Beller walked slowly to one, entered and stared at the empty silent chamber.

Something happened.

The room was filled with gaunt prisoners in that familiar uniform—for just a moment.

Then they were gone.

He turned, started across the compound to the museum, originally the headquarters for the camp's administration. A weird wind was blowing from somewhere, making a moaning sound like the voices of a thousand men and women in agony. And children.

Just like that.

There he was, a little three-year-old boy knotted up with terror. Gunfire. Tank cannon, machine guns, bazookas, shouting, screaming, engines roaring—the sounds of war.

The sounds of that awful-wonderful-unbelievable and fiercely unforgettable day when the Shermans smashed in and broke the murder machine. The noise was terribly loud and confusing, and the little boy turned his head.

He was looking into *that* pit, the one with all the emaciated corpses. There—that face belonged to his mother, and that hand sticking up out of the heap of human debris had once been part of his father. The clatter of the tanks drowned out everything—even the screaming—and now a metal monster appeared. The soldiers who manned it were oddly familiar too, even if he couldn't remember their names. The child pointed at a nearby barracks, and one of the Americans shot a sniper out of an upper window.

It all stopped.

Just like that.

Dr. Beller was walking toward the museum, saw the tourists and their guide—and turned away. He didn't have to look at the pictures and other "memorabilia," so he turned to stare at the open tower, the Catholic expiatory chapel named Christ in Agony. The Protestant commemorative chapel flanked it on one side, the Jewish memorial on the other. The Nazis had killed men and women of all faiths and nationalities.

And children.

Hundreds of children.

Tons of children, slaughtered for the incinerators.

Now people were emerging from the Catholic chapel, real-today people following a sober-faced guide. They couldn't hear the screams and noises that filled Ernst Beller's head, but they were plainly affected. They trailed the guide in total silence,

and one woman—a nun—was weeping without making a
sound. Beller saw her dab at her eyes with a handkerchief, and
thought of his Anna.

His eyes closed, and he was looking at those American soldiers climbing back onto their tank. The young one—the man
who'd shot the S.S. sniper—gave a book to a small boy, and
then an older man handed the child several packs of cigarettes.
The engine noise swelled to a roar, and the soldiers waved as
their armored machine moved away—leaving the child all
alone.

Alone.

The doctor must have blacked out, for he remembered nothing until he found himself in a bus entering the city of Dachau.
He'd ridden too far, or had he? No, the train station was just
ahead. The two American college students got out with him.

"Going to the festival?" one asked.

"Festival?"

"Starts tonight. Big celebration. It's an annual thing in Dachau. Traditional costumes, feasting, beer and ox races."

Beller looked back toward the camp, and even though it was
miles away and impossible to see he saw the pit again—and he
knew what he had to do. He hoped that Anna would understand.

One more.

"Ox races?" he asked. "No, I've got an appointment in Berlin."

One more, and then he'd be able to rejoin Anna and live in
peace—at last. He'd have paid his debt. He'd call her from
Munich to explain the brief delay, and then he'd go on to
Berlin for The Big One. It had to be The Big One, he thought
as he boarded the train. When that was done, he'd stop. The
people in the pit would understand. He was tired of killing,
and he wanted to live safely and warmly with Anna.

He smiled in anticipation, unaware that bored civil servants
and mindless machines were hunting him hundreds of miles
away. The threat was no longer the guards at all those German
prisons, or the BND that had alerted them. No, it was the
computers that were closing in—minute by minute.

The net was tightening.

44

"I won't do it," Diane McGhee repeated as they walked through the air-terminal crowd toward Gate 4.

"I'm not asking you to do it. I just want you to phone Bill Frost at State and tell him what I need," Merlin cajoled.

"Bill Frost hates you."

"No, he dislikes me, but he doesn't hate me. He'll do it. Look, Grad doesn't like me either, and he cooperated. Very nicely. Found out one thousand, two hundred and eighty-four foreign doctors entered West Germany in the five weeks before the first hit, eliminated the women and shrinks and golden-age crowd, found all but six had left the country before the last job in Düsseldorf. Now I'm going to check on the two Englishmen, the South African tropical-disease expert and those French immunologists. All I want you to do—"

"Is one American. Dr. Ernest Beller, New York City. You told me, seven times. It isn't my business, your business or company business."

"You've said that—seventeen times. Please, phone Frost when you get to Kennedy—and try Rudin in the Pentagon. Maybe this guy was in the Army."

"Rudin doesn't like you either, and he says so."

Merlin relit his cigar.

"That's just his manner. Really a sweetie-pie, and he loves to help people. Bill Frost at State, and Rudin at DOD, okay?"

"Never. I'll never do it, and you'll never change. It's hopeless."

"Honey, it's going to be okay. I'm crazy about you."

"No, just crazy. I must be crazy, too, to get involved with you again. You're a great lover, but—well—hopeless."

Merlin looked at her with visible admiration.

Of course, it could have been a sham.

"When I get back, baby," he said, "let's see if we can put it back together—the way it was."

That was when she raised her purse to hit him. The argument raged right up to the minute when she left him to head for the plane, which took off at noon—exactly sixty-one hours after Beller reached West Berlin.

The phone call from New York awakened Merlin at the Hilton shortly before 2 A.M.

"We were both right," she said.

"Where are you?"

"Central Park West—the apartment of Dr. Beller's uncle and aunt. Frost hates you—just as I said."

"Did he do it?"

"Yes. That's how I got here. The uncle and aunt are listed on the who-to-call-in-emergency-next-of-kin part of the passport because Dr. Ernest Beller's parents are deceased. You want to guess where they died?"

"Auschwitz?"

"Dachau. Class of forty-five. He was there too. He was three years old when our tanks broke in—it's in his immigration file."

Merlin shook his head, surprised to find more pity than triumph within himself.

"You there?" she asked.

"Keep talking. *Three* years old. Jesus Christ!"

"Jesus Christ!" she agreed. "He was in the U.S. Army—in Germany. Assigned to a Special Forces outfit. Took the damn hand-to-hand-combat and demolition courses just for laughs."

"Jesus Christ."

Merlin didn't know what else to say.

"There's more. His uncle—he's an analyst—had a stroke in May. Can't talk. Been trying to communicate something for weeks—in writing."

"What the hell is he writing, Di?"

"Three weeks ago—'Stop Ernest.' His wife couldn't make any sense out of it. Yesterday he wrote something else. 'Ernest kills—police.' She was wondering whom to tell when I arrived."

"How much did you tell her?"

"Very little."

"Good. She might have a stroke too. Who'd you tell her you worked for?"

"State—Hang on a second. . . . Listen, Mrs. Beller just remembered they got a card from him three days ago. It's postmarked—let's see—F-r-e-u-d-e-n—Freudenstadt."

"I'll find it. Freudenstadt, right."

"You've *got* to find him," she appealed.

"What?"

"You were right. It's our business. I'm putting a picture and bio on the wire to you tonight."

There was no immediate reply.

"Maybe *you* were right," Merlin finally answered. "This guy's a goddam genius. He's doing what we'd all like to do."

"Not me. Don't be crazy."

"Those murdering bastards should have been wiped out years ago, Di."

"Please—please, don't play God. Send him home before someone gets hurt. I beg you."

Before Ernest Beller gets hurt.

Or killed by some prison guard.

She didn't say it, but Merlin could hear it in her voice.

"I'm counting on you," she pleaded.

She still knew exactly what worked, Merlin thought admiringly.

"Okay, I'll do it—but I think this guy ought to get a medal."

"For me."

"I said I'd do it. Anything else?"

"When are you coming back?"

He tried to compute how long it might take to find one brilliant avenging angel in the middle of 62,000,000 West Germans and perhaps 750,000 summer visitors—somewhere in a nation covering 96,000 square miles.

"Two, three weeks. Soon as I can. I'll give you enough notice so you can change the sheets."

Her tone changed abruptly. "What?" she challenged sharply.

"I like fresh sheets."

"If you think you're moving in with me again—in my apartment—"

"*Our* apartment, Di," he corrected.

"Never. We haven't really settled anything. You're too damn cocky, mister."

"Honey," he cajoled.

"Never!"

She slammed down the phone, and he sighed as he reflected on her complexity. She'd always been so romantic, so unpredictable despite her splendid mind. After a minute he picked up the telephone to call Cavaliere, whose return Lomas had delayed so they could organize the Victor watch. If there was anyone in West Berlin who'd know where to find a big map of the Federal Republic at two in the morning, it would be Angelo Cavaliere.

Hell, he was a walking atlas. He probably knew where Freudenstadt was without even looking.

Then Merlin recalled the unpleasant question that he'd avoided in the car as they left the dude ranch, the same one that the Israeli had asked. Merlin hadn't wanted to face it then, and—despite his trans-Atlantic exchange a minute earlier—he didn't want to confront it now.

Why the hell should *he* hunt down the doctor?

Merlin had identified him, and was no longer irritated by the puzzle and his own mistake. Only a day earlier the woman who was begging him to pursue Beller had been pleading with Merlin to leave it all to the Germans.

Why not?

They'd turned a three-year-old kid into a homicidal avenger, so why not let them cope with him now? After all, they were competent and they'd find the executioner sooner or later. Later might be better, Merlin brooded. Let him wipe out a few more of the monsters, the creatures who frightened everyone because they reminded us all of the horrors that men and women were capable of committing. It wasn't just the Germans who were ashamed of the mass murderers. Even Merlin felt queasy at being part of the same species as those butchers.

Queasy and angry.

Angry and conflicted.

She'd been right, and that made him even more bitter. Merlin should never have gotten involved in this mess, this desperate dilemma created by a moralistic madman. What the hell was that quote from R. D. Laing that Cavaliere kept mouthing every couple of weeks? Yeah, "Madness is a state of grace in this crazy world." Merlin had always brushed it off because Laing was a British shrink, and it was infuriating to think that the psychotherapist might be correct.

Merlin could always tell her that he hadn't been able to find Ernest Beller. After all, even the best agents failed sometimes. Huge population, one tricky fanatic who spoke good German and knew the scene—almost impossible to catch. Merlin sat on the edge of the bed, annoyed with himself and Diane McGhee and that Old Testament avenger out there somewhere, smiting so skillfully and righteously.

"No," Merlin said aloud.

Screw Freudenstadt.

Screw Ernest Beller too.

It wasn't going to be Merlin who hunted him down. Merlin reached for the phone, hoping that someone was on duty at Pan American at half-past two in the morning. Merlin had done what he'd been asked to do—*more*—and he was going home to his woman.

The Pan Am reservations clerk told him to get to the airport by one o'clock the next afternoon, assured him that the "gold" American Express card would do the trick. Less than a minute later, Merlin tossed his suitcase onto the bed and began to pack. One of Merlin's survival skills was knowing when to leave, and he was suddenly and utterly certain that it was time for him to get out of Germany.

Maybe Beller would too.

45

This one would be the most dangerous of all.

The most heavily guarded prison in Germany.

The most famous Nazi alive.

The Big One.

Rudolf Hess, Hitler's handpicked deputy führer.

Hess was the only fascist still in Allied custody, Beller thought grimly as he dressed, and security would surely be tight at the strange and special Berlin prison that held him. Spandau Citadel was massive, reportedly impregnable. Its seventeenth-century stone walls and tower had survived the Anglo-American bombing, the Soviet shelling and the ferocious ground fighting as the Red Army clawed and hammered its way—yard by yard—through the last Nazi fanatics in a burning city.

That was more than thirty-two years ago, and all the high-level fascists whom the War Crimes Tribunal had sent to Spandau were released or dead—*except* Hess. The bitter Russians —who had such good reasons to be bitter—insisted on keeping this one symbol imprisoned in memory of their massacred millions. The Soviets had suffered five times as many casualties as any of their allies, and they weren't about to forget. Brushing off "humanitarian" appeals that it was hardly worth a million dollars a year to isolate this sick and weary old man who'd been a prisoner since May 1941, when he flew to Scotland, the Russians insisted that he remain in Spandau.

Good—for Ernest Beller.

Sitting target.

There was something fitting in this. Hess had to be somewhat removed from reality thirty-six years ago when he tried to persuade Churchill to join Hitler in a crusade to obliterate Red Russia, and Beller was certifiably insane. A madman to slay a madman—there was a nightmarish Kafka logic here. Beller was unaware of the irony as he adjusted his tan tie before the mirror, pleased that his army uniform still fit so well. That clothing was a key part of his plan. The BND had alerted all the *German* prisons about the threat to war criminals, but not Spandau. It was run by the Big Four powers. The British, French, Russian and U.S. governments rotated in running Spandau, and this month the Americans were in charge.

Good—for Ernest Beller.

With a U.S. Army Medical Corps uniform.

With old I.D. he could alter and the experience in military terminology and forms needed to forge orders.

He rechecked the contents of the GI doctor's bag he'd carefully kept hidden since leaving the army, looked lovingly at the snapshot of Anna on his bed table and picked up the envelope addressed to his aunt. He knew that he might have to lay down his own life to destroy Hess, but the letter was a cheery one that spoke of his plan to return to New York soon—perhaps with a fiancée. His aunt would like that, for she'd been urging him to "get married and settle down" for almost two years.

He put a stamp on the letter, stared at Anna again.

She was so beautiful, so tender, so *right*.

He sighed, smiled at her and forgot about the Nazis—for a moment. Then he scooped up the medical bag and the letter, descended to the hotel lobby and took a taxi to the U.S. Army Hospital, where armed secret agents watched the armed secret agents who watched Victor. He felt safe and assured as he entered, for he knew all about the layout from earlier visits and nothing about the dangerous men and women—more than a dozen cunning operatives—who walked these corridors disguised as healers.

"Is my staff car here yet?" he asked the nurse at the reception booth testily.

"What?"

"I'm Major Keller, and that damn car was supposed to pick me up twenty minutes ago."

"I'll call the motor pool, sir."

The khaki military vehicle pulled up twelve minutes later, and Beller slammed the door in noisy outrage as he bounded into the back.

"Jeezus Christ!"

"Sorry, major. Someone must have screwed up," the driver apologized.

"What the hell are you guys in the motor pool doing—beating your meat? I'm supposed to be at Spandau in nine goddam minutes."

"Do my best, sir."

"Softest damn duty in the whole army, and you guys sit around smoking grass and goofing off. *Someone* screwed up all right, and *someone's* going to get his butt bored. You can bet on that, soldier."

"Wasn't me. Don't blame you for being sore, major," the skinny Nebraskan behind the wheel soothed—and smiled at the possibility that Sergeant Hance would be the one to get the reaming. Teach that Dixie dick a lesson.

Twenty-two minutes.

Traffic wasn't too bad, and that's how long it took to reach the walled citadel.

"Sergeant Hance—he's running this shift at the motor pool," the vengeful Nebraskan volunteered hopefully.

"Fix his ass. I surely will," Beller promised nastily.

There were two armed sentries visible at the gate, both surprisingly alert for a post at a prison whose lone inmate was almost forgotten.

"Major Keller, Edward O.," the cool madman announced.

It had worked so far.

The guard glanced at the staff car, looked at his clipboard for several seconds, and hesitated. "Don't see your name, sir."

Killing him wouldn't do any good, but Beller tensed as he considered alternatives.

"Look again," he ordered.

No, the other sentries inside would cut him down before he crossed the courtyard.

"Right, here ya be. Edward O.—sir. Welcome to Spandau."

The senior officer on duty—Lieutenant Colonel F. M. Rich —wasn't quite that cheery. "Only got the call hour'n'a half ago. Why can't you medical hot shots give us more warning, dammit?"

The deadly doctor shrugged. "Don't ask me. I take orders just like you do."

Rich continued complaining as they walked. "What's this all about?"

"Blood pressure check. You want to do it? I won't object."

"Doesn't Pinney usually handle him?" Rich wondered as he nodded to another pair of sentries.

"He's got the runs. Too much beer, I guess. Nice guy, but no sense about beer or pussy."

Lieutenant Colonel Rich laughed in macho agreement, signaled still another guard to open a steel door into the courtyard. He noticed Beller's roving eyes. "First time here, huh? Damn dull duty. He takes a walk in the garden on mornings when he feels okay—and that's it. I'm bored out of my skull."

Perfect cue.

"Medical duty in Berlin's worse," the executioner grumbled deftly in the great military tradition. "Some twisted ankles, an appendix or two and a ton of clap. *That's* boring, chum."

Would there be metal detectors?

Body search?

They entered what seemed to be the main building, took five steps—and bells rang. More armed men jumped out of corridors on either side of the passage, pointed their short-barreled carbines.

There *were* metal detectors.

Beller squeezed out a smile, grunted and reached for his trouser pocket. Now the carbines pointed right at his stomach.

"Easy, easy. Just a Swiss Army knife my girl gave me last year," he announced as he produced the red-coated tool.

Rich stared at him. "Don't panic, doc," he advised as his face blossomed with a grin. He waved at the carbines. "Hell," he added, "nobody's goin' to shoot you for a lousy pocketknife. I'll hold it for you."

Beller handed him the knife.

"Scared you, huh?" the security officer joked.

"A bit—for a second."

"Crissakes, doc, we're careful but we're not that trigger-happy."

They started walking again, and suddenly Rich stopped.

Body search.

Beller knew it before a word was spoken.

"Gotta check out your medical bag. Open it, will ya?"

As he obeyed, Ernest Beller hoped that there wasn't going to be any trouble. His mind was made up, had been for days since the impact of revisiting Dachau. They weren't going to put him in any place like that again. He'd die first, and he'd take them with him.

"Let's see. Stethoscope, good ol' blood pressure . . . the usual crap. Tools of the trade, right?"

"Tools of the trade," the homicidal healer agreed.

Now Rich eyed him oddly, and he seemed to smirk. "You like boys, doc?"

Was it a trick?

"What?"

"I asked whether you dig boys."

The sexual implication was clear.

"No, women."

"Me too, but I've got to frisk you. S.O.P. for everyone. Didn't want you to misunderstand," Rich leered.

He stepped forward.

"I'm wearing a brace," Beller volunteered. "Strained my back playing tennis."

Rich nodded, tapped Beller's armpits, thighs and lower legs. He came close—*very* close.

He missed it by an inch and a half, two at most.

"Okay, doc. One brace and no guns, knives or nuclear devices. . . . You know, my brother had to wear a brace coupla years ago. Wrecked his sex life for three miserable months."

He handed back the medical bag, and they headed toward the stairs at the end of the corridor. Chatting away briskly about such popular subjects as sex, food, sports, the weather, sex, the army and sex, Rich had no idea how close he'd come to another subject that people rarely discussed.

Death.

Up the steps to the third floor, fourth cell down.

Rich slid back the bolt on the heavy metal door, pulled out a ring of keys and inserted one in a wholly modern lock.

"Max security, doc. Put in a coupla years ago—just in case some of his old buddies tried to spring him," Rich explained.

Then he opened the door.

"Hey—Hey, Herr Hess. Dr. Keller's here to see you."

The cell was large, sparsely furnished. The thick stone walls kept it cool despite the August heat, and if there was any major drawback it was probably the limited light that came through the small barred window.

Hess was either deaf, tired or moodily ignoring them. He sat at a small table, reading by a crook-necked lamp. His back to the door, he didn't turn, move or speak.

"Herr Hess," Rich said more loudly.

There was no visible response.

"When you're finished, knock on the door, doc," the military police officer suggested, and announced that he'd check back in five minutes.

Beller heard him lock the door.

Five minutes alone.

Good.

No, perfect. The curare—just as in Hamburg.

He'd tell them that Hess was sleeping and shouldn't be disturbed, and by dusk Ernest Beller would be on a plane out of Berlin. He opened the medical bag, took out the hypodermic and uncovered its tip. Hess still stared down at his book, and Beller stepped forward.

The white-haired old man looked so bent.

So vulnerable.

So worn after thirty-six years of imprisonment.

To his own astonishment, Beller hesitated—for the first time uncertain. Was it really necessary to kill this sick and weary old jailbird?

Click . . . click . . . click.

The pictures flashed across his mind like a series of newspaper photos, stills from front pages of the past.

Hess with Hitler.

Hess with Goering, Himmler and the butcher Bormann.

Hess and Hitler and the rodentlike Goebbels.

The doubt and the pity vanished, and Beller moved closer, looking for a place to plunge the needle. Five or six feet away from this final target, Beller raised the hypo—and the man in the chair turned.

"Don't!" he said in a strong young voice.

There was a .357 Magnum in his fist.

"If that's curare again, don't waste your time. I've got the antidote right here."

The man with the gun pulled off a wig, and he wasn't Hess at all. He was much younger, spoke like an American.

"Where's Hess? I came for Hess."

"Gone."

"Who are you? You're not the man," Beller complained. He

gestured angrily with the lethal hypodermic, and the impostor
pointed the big gun directly at him.

"I work for the U.S. government, Dr. Beller, and I understand your efforts to punish the murderers," Merlin soothed.
"After all, retribution—"

"Justice," the boy from Dachau corrected.

"Of course, justice. Now put down the hypo, and we can talk.
. . . Please, put it down. You don't need it. Hess isn't here."

The physician looked around the room as if he hoped to find
the old Nazi hiding somewhere in the shadows, and then his
expression changed. He seemed much calmer, much more
rational. He didn't have the look of a homicidal maniac at all.
He sighed, put the hypodermic back into the medical bag and
closed it.

He smiled—almost cheerfully—and Merlin felt a lot better.
He had no desire to hurt Beller, only to stop him and get him
into psychiatric treatment. Merlin smiled back encouragingly,
rose from the chair.

"I'm your friend, Dr. Beller."

"I don't even know your name."

The physician was backing away now, just a bit.

"They call me Merlin."

"Take me to Hess."

It was going to take some talking and cajoling to get him out
to the car, and Merlin decided to make a conciliatory gesture
to show his goodwill. He put the gun on the table.

"I'm afraid I can't."

"You'll have to."

Merlin didn't quite understand—for about four seconds.
Then Beller unbuttoned his jacket, and Merlin froze.

In an odd-looking harness, there was a battery and a small
box and some wires that led to eight sticks of dynamite.

Eight goddam sticks of dynamite.

Enough to smear the two of them across the walls in a nice
even layer, about one-quarter of an inch thick.

Merlin wasn't frightened, however.

He was merely scared shitless.

46

The crazy son of a bitch really was crazy.

Rich had screwed up on the body search, and now Merlin was locked in this cell with a brilliant lunatic and a bomb.

Merlin looked at the device and the man, shook his head. Best fucking security in Western Europe, they'd said, and here he was, alone with a goddam homicidal maniac and eight goddam sticks of dynamite.

How crazy was he?

"You all right, doctor?" Merlin tested.

Not surprisingly, that puzzled Beller.

It was supposed to.

"What?" He blinked as he responded, but his fingers didn't move away from the black box. Merlin made a mental note of what he was going to do to Rich if Beller didn't kill him.

"I asked if you were all right. You look tired. Want to sit down?"

The pathologist considered this very carefully, and sighed. "No, thanks. I want to see Hess."

Cool and slow, Merlin calculated.

That was the only way to survive, and to bring the doctor home alive too.

"Hess isn't here," the stubborn CIA agent repeated as he started to reach—quite automatically—for a cigar.

"No tricks!"

Merlin froze again, hand in midair. "Sorry, doc. It's a bad habit. Mind if I smoke a cigar?"

"You inhale?"

"Sometimes," Merlin confessed.

"Not too good for you," Beller scolded. "Cigarettes are worse, but take it easy on the inhaling."

The man who might kill him was offering free medical advice. It was, beyond doubt, insane. Merlin lit his cigar, took care not to inhale and relaxed—just the tiniest bit.

"It's time to go," the walking bomb announced.

Wherever they went could be an improvement, for the blast would be much less deadly out in the open, anywhere outside the compressing walls of the cell. Merlin rose, walked slowly toward the door and tried to think of some way to disarm the thing that the deranged doctor had strapped to his chest. He half-turned, estimated the distance to his foe and eyed the device.

"No tricks, Mr. Merlin. I'm quite willing to detonate, you know."

He probably was.

Merlin banged on the door, and it swung open less than fifteen seconds later.

"You got him?" Rich demanded eagerly.

"Not exactly. We're coming out. Stand back—he's got a bomb."

"Goddam!"

"My view precisely. Just stay out of the way, and Ernie and I'll work it out."

They stepped out into the corridor, faced a semicircle of seven armed soldiers—and Angelo Cavaliere.

"You okay, Merl?"

"Terrific, Angie. Just terrific. No sweat. Taking a walk with Ernie, that's all."

Nobody moved.

Then Cavaliere saw the dynamite device.

"Yeah, it's a goddam bomb, Angie. Good old Ernie made it himself. Neat, huh?"

"Jeezus."

"Why not? Listen, you guys get back and go pray."

Cavaliere and Rich exchanged glances, waved the guards to retreat.

"That's good," Beller judged. "And now I want Hess."

"We moved him out. Take a look for yourself. Check the other cells if you want."

With Rich's men trailing some eighteen or twenty yards behind, Beller and Merlin walked slowly down the passage, looking into every chamber. They were all empty.

"Not here, right? Now listen, doc—"

"Later. We'll look on the floor below, if you don't mind."

"Course not. Whatever you say."

Merlin now had the beginnings of a plan. He would work the walking bomb out of the building into the open, and then he'd try to wear him down or divert him. It was important to keep talking, and to avoid wetting one's pants. If that goddam thing went off, they'd need a vacuum cleaner to suck up the fragments of both men.

Goddam the bomb.

Goddam the woman who'd pleaded with him to stop Beller.

Goddam the Nazis who'd made the nightmare.

"And goddam me for not taking that Pan Am flight home," Merlin thought.

Fortunately Beller didn't hear, for Merlin was in no mood to explain. Right now, he hated almost everyone he could think of and he was particularly furious with himself and the crazy doctor. As they reached the head of the stairs he glanced around, saw that none of the guards was within twenty yards and hoped they'd maintain that distance. As long as the MPs stayed away, there was a chance.

The two men started down the stairs, only a yard apart.

It happened eight steps down.

One of the soldiers leaped out of a recess in the stone wall, lunged for Beller to take him by surprise.

Merlin hurled himself in between, punched the guard in the stomach as hard as he could. When the MP doubled up, Merlin kneed him in the groin and shoved him down the stairs.

"Is he hurt?" Beller asked solicitously.

"I hope so. If that dumb bastard had reached you . . ."

It took the doctor a few moments to comprehend.

"Yes, I'd have detonated, of course."

Merlin's hand shook just a bit as he relit the cigar. Then he roared his rage at the man below. "Rich—Rich, you idiot! You hear me, dummy?"

A voice replied from the foot of the stairs. "Wasserman?"

"You almost killed us both, moron! Leave us alone! Angie, clear the goddam area!"

It was cool in Spandau, but Merlin was sweating. His whole torso was wet and his throat was dry, and his mind seethed with thoughts as homicidal as any Beller had ever conceived. He puffed on the cigar, trying to control his fear and fury.

Being afraid only made him angrier, and he knew that he couldn't afford to yield to either emotion.

Eight goddam sticks of dynamite.

"Can we look at the cells on this floor, please?" Beller broke in, and once again Merlin led the way.

Hess wasn't on the second floor, or on the first either. When they'd checked the last cell and the last room, Beller's brow furrowed. He was disappointed, puzzled.

"Where is he?"

"Maybe he's out in the garden."

Yes, Beller recalled, the lieutenant colonel had mentioned that Hess often went to the garden. Merlin swung open the door, then blocked it with his arm. That bastard Rich might have marksmen out there, and Merlin had promised himself that he'd bring Beller in alive.

"I'll go first, doc."

Merlin stepped out into the sun, scanned the courtyard and then the upper windows and roofs. Nothing . . . nothing . . . nothing . . . nothing . . . Son of a bitch! There—up there! And on the other side—there! Gun barrels, pointing at the door. Infuriated, Merlin strode forward and shook his fist. "Angie! Angie! Call General Brieant! Get those snipers out of here! Do it! That's an order! Do it!"

He walked back inside, where Beller waited with his fingers a scant inch from the firing mechanism. It was disturbingly obvious that the dedicated and desperate doctor wasn't bluffing. He'd do it. Merlin wasn't surprised at that, but what did seem odd was the fact that he wasn't angry with Beller. It wasn't pity, but something like compassion—and that was startling.

"Take it easy, doc. We've got to wait a couple of minutes while my friend straightens out those clowns. Won't take too long."

Christ, there was no way to guess what Beller was thinking. He might do anything—at any moment.

The whole situation was insane.

All of them—including the shooters outside—were crazy, and this idiotic prison that held only one man because four great nations were bickering was crazy too.

"What friend?"

Merlin looked at him, saw the question was sincere.

"His name is Angelo Cavaliere. We work together—nice fellow. You'd like him, doc. He's very decent, well educated."

More frightening silence.

"What do you do?"

What the hell. Why not?

"We're spies. Secret stuff, all over the world. Doesn't make much sense for grown men, huh?"

"As much as a lot of other things."

Beller wasn't *completely* crazy.

"For the American government?" he asked.

"Yeah—the CIA. Spooks—that's what the hot-shit journalists call us. Spooks, not so nice, huh? Anything lousy goes down anywhere on earth, they say we did it. Half the time it's the other side that did it."

"What other side?"

"There's nineteen other sides, maybe thirty-seven. Who cares?"

Still more silence.

"Are your parents alive?"

Startled, Merlin nodded.

"Mine are dead."

Merlin wanted to cry, and that made him angrier.

"I know, doc. I know a lot about you—that goddam camp . . . your aunt and uncle in New York. All kinds of things."

Suddenly Cavaliere's voice boomed over a bullhorn. "Merlin —Merlin, it's okay. You can come out. It's okay."

Merlin stepped through the door, scanned the roofs and windows slowly, just in case. No harm in double-checking.

"Okay, doc, let's see if he's in the garden."

It wasn't really that safe, for those marksmen weren't too far away. Rich wasn't the sort who'd give up that easily. He was one of those achievement-oriented bastards, trained by the army to handle every contingency, and in situations like this the goddam manual said *act.* If necessary, *kill.* Couldn't blame Rich too much. That's what the book said, and light colonels in the military police went by the book. It was bitterly ironic that the book could destroy Merlin, who'd always hated such books.

They walked out into the courtyard, then turned toward the garden. It wasn't that large, but the flower beds were colorful and rather lovely—and Hess was nowhere in sight.

"Where is he?"

"Must be out here somewhere," Merlin stalled.

Hess was in the cellar with eight guards, who'd shoot Beller to pieces—literally—before he got within fifty yards.

"I don't see him. Is this a trick?"

As they say in official communiqués, the situation was deteriorating, and Merlin didn't have the slightest idea of what to do or say next. Beller was getting tense again, and those snipers were almost surely creeping up or taking new positions.

"Maybe he's taking a leak, doc. I could use one myself."

This would be a stupid way and a dumb place to die.

"You promised me Hess, and you lied."

"Would I lie to you? I'm trying to help you. I don't like Hess either."

The expression in Beller's eyes said that Merlin had failed. He'd run out of tactics and time, and there was nothing left. He watched the madman's hand move to the detonator box.

End of the line.

47

Merlin didn't reach for a weapon or plead.

He zipped open his trousers.

"Go ahead, Ernie," he said with a shrug as he began to urinate onto the dark earth between two yellow flowers.

"What—what are you doing?"

"I don't lie. Told you I had to take a leak, and I can't wait any longer. Be finished in a couple of seconds, and then I can die comfortably."

Baffled and incredulous, the doctor watched the stream fall and fall and fall. It didn't make any sense at all for a man to do this as his last act.

"That's better," Merlin announced truthfully.

Then he zipped up his pants, took four steps to a neat patch of grass and sat down with a sigh. He puffed on the cigar again, looked up at the puzzled executioner.

"Okay, Ernie. Blow us up."

Beller's finger moved to the box, stopped.

"I can't kill a man sitting down on the grass. That would be—well—wrong."

"You sit down too. We can both go out in comfort. One big bang and so long, Diane. So long, Anna, too."

Was this spy cunning—or insane?

"Who's Diane?" Beller asked—and he sat down.

"Great woman. Not as great as she thinks, but goddam great. Used to be married to her. She's waiting in New York, at your uncle's place. Like a cigar?"

"What?"

"Take it. It'll only be wasted when you blow us into dog meat. Enjoy your last two minutes, Ernie."

It was irrational and childishly innocent.

"No, thanks," Beller answered politely. There was something about this man he didn't understand. "I'm going to detonate."

"Course you are. Nothing can stop you. You're one of the best killers in the business—and I ought to know. Same line of work, Ernie."

Perfect smoke ring.

It smelled good, reminded him of the cigars Uncle Martin enjoyed after dinner.

"You've killed many?"

"More than you, Ernie—but not as cleverly. You're a smart fellow. Must have been one helluva doctor."

Merlin leaned back on the grass, yawned.

"Did you—like the killing?"

"No. Nice guys like you and me don't enjoy that kind of thing. Only creeps do. You do it because you have to or because you're angry, but—hell, you can't talk about it. You never told Anna, I bet."

Another smoke ring—*almost* perfect.

"How do *you* know about Anna?"

Merlin told him how they'd found his aunt, about his uncle's terrible concern and how the postcard had led them to Freudenstadt, where they'd shown his photo around and finally found Anna.

"She said you were here, and I figured out—guessed, I suppose—that it had to be Hess. Pretty shrewd, huh?"

"Is Anna all right?"

"No. Worried. Worried sick about you, Ernie. Crying, the whole bit. Gonna miss you, Ernie. That's love."

"You're pretty cynical, aren't you?" Beller replied sharply.

"Yup, and not too thrilled about dying so young either. Damn shame. Two sweet guys like you and me—boom!"

He heard the buzz, looked skyward and computed.

Beller didn't notice. He was remembering that he'd forgotten to mail the letter home, and he thought about the woman waiting in Freudenstadt—alone.

"You know, Ernie," Merlin said with an odd half-smile, "I came here to save you. To stop you from killing any more, and I succeeded—in a funny way. After you blow us both up, you won't kill anybody else."

Beller's mind was still on Anna. He didn't answer.

"Ernie, tell me—as one pro to another—how did you figure out all these hits?"

"Medicine is my profession." The pathologist sat up to explain, and went on to describe how he'd planned and carried out all the executions. As each minute ticked away, Merlin began to think that he might—with a great deal of luck—possibly survive.

"Ingenious," Merlin complimented. "Bet you were one helluva doctor. Too bad. . . . Say, what's going to happen to Anna and your aunt and uncle?"

"She'll be all right!"

That was it.

The emotion in his voice signaled that he cared deeply about the woman in Freudenstadt, and Merlin knew what had to be done.

"Hope so, Ernie. She's all alone, you know. Your uncle's getting better, and he's got your aunt to look after him, but Anna's got no one. No family, nobody to care—but you. Man, is she scared!"

Beller was breathing hard, clearly in pain.

"Full of shame about her goddam grandfather," Merlin went on, "no parents or sisters, and she falls in love with a terrific guy—stranger-in-the-night routine—who's everything she dreamed about. One week of magic, just like in the movies, and he takes off to kill some old politician who's probably going to die in a couple of months anyway."

"Please."

"Then the idiot blows himself up. What a lousy ending."

There was a long silence.

"I don't like you, Merlin," Beller whispered grimly.

"Or yourself—or you wouldn't do this dumb number. Why don't you think with your head instead of your guts, doctor?"

The buzz in the sky was a bit louder now.

Not much time.

Merlin had to make his move. He saw the tears welling in the doctor's eyes, decided.

"Ernie—Ernie—stop it now—for Anna—you just can't do this to her, Ernie. Please, it's her only chance—and yours."

Beller's face showed his torment, and his love.

After nine or ten seconds that seemed like half an hour, he groaned and sighed and groaned again, and stood up from the grass. "Anna, Anna," he agonized.

Merlin rose too, nodded. "Okay. . . . Okay, Ernie—you're doing the right thing, for Anna. Come on, let's get you out of that damn harness."

Beller hesitated and the noise grew still louder, and Merlin wondered whether to tell him. The troubled physician slowly struggled out of his officer's tunic, reached for some catch to release the straps. His fingers brushed the black box. A clicking sound broke the silence.

"What's that?"

"Time fuse. I'm afraid I tripped it," the dazed avenger mumbled.

Merlin rushed forward to help him get free.

"How long? Ernie, how long?"

"Minute."

"Shit!"

Merlin ripped and tore at the webbing, snapped the catches and glanced up once at the helicopter that was boring in fast. Goddam chopper—police or army—was swooping down fast, and the armed men aboard would try to pick off Beller in a few seconds. As Merlin finally jerked the last catch loose, he had a desperate idea. He grabbed the whole harness, swung it around his head and threw it as far as he could—in the direction of the charging helicopter.

The bomb hit the ground some fifty or sixty yards away, and Merlin knocked Beller to the earth just as it exploded with a tremendous blast. Great chunks of earth were hurled high in the air in a brown geyser, and the shock waves bobbled the chopper in midair. The helicopter veered away. Merlin could hear shouting, and when he stood up he wasn't surprised to see Cavaliere and a squad of soldiers running toward him.

It had worked.

The long-shot scheme of diverting the airborne marksmen with the bomb had succeeded, at the last goddam second. Beaming as he brushed the clods of earth and dirt from his face and clothes, Merlin waved to the approaching men to signal that everything was all right. Then he reached down to help Dr. Beller to his feet.

"It's over," Merlin said victoriously.

He swept the earth and debris from Beller, put his arm around the blinking doctor's shoulders reassuringly.

"Ernie, it's time to go home."

48

There was an argument when the special plane carrying Merlin and Cavaliere and Beller and the army psychiatrist arrived at Andrews Air Force Base near Washington. A typical Merlin argument. Everything had gone smoothly until then, with both the West German and U.S. authorities cooperating eagerly to get the killer of the Nazis out of the Federal Republic as quickly and quietly as possible to avoid political embarrassment. The argument arose when Lomas sent five armed CIA security men to Andrews with a straitjacket and an ambulance to take Ernest Beller.

"No way," Merlin announced. "This man isn't violent, and there's no way you're going to knot him up in that jacket."

"He's homicidal," the senior security man insisted.

"Only if you're a Nazi war criminal. Just hold it right here, sonny, while I call Lomas."

It was while Merlin was in the phone booth that the annoyed security agent spoke to Cavaliere.

"Does he always make scenes?"

"Almost always. He shoots people too."

"What's his name?"

"He's got lots of names," Cavaliere replied, "but I call him Merlin."

The reception team was plainly stunned. They knew.

"Holy shit!" two of the agents said in unison.

Merlin used even cruder language to Lomas, ordering him to "Get your animals out of here or I'll send *them* out in your goddam ambulance. You know what hell this guy's gone through since he was three fucking years old?"

"Take it easy," Lomas urged without much hope.

"Up yours. Hope your tape's rolling. Up yours—sideways. Beller's going to Walter Reed with me, in a taxi. No straitjacket. He's going with dignity. In a couple of days we'll move him up to a good private hospital in New York where his aunt and uncle can visit."

A private hospital would save the government money, Lomas reasoned, and he didn't want any more trouble with Merlin right now. He might need Merlin's unique talents again.

"Put Maloney on the phone, please."

Merlin stepped out of the booth, gestured. "It's the Boston Strangler—for you."

After they left Beller at Walter Reed Hospital, Merlin drove to the apartment of a beautiful and intelligent black woman in Georgetown—and he was not disappointed. Despite all she'd said, there were fresh sheets and much warmth and mutual appreciation. She wasn't disappointed either. It was two days before she tenderly reminded him that he ought to check in at the agency.

On the next afternoon, several excellent doctors at the Columbia-Presbyterian Psychiatric Institute overlooking the Hudson River began to "work up" the case of Ernest Beller. Everyone gets good care up there, but the nephew of a noted psychoanalyst receives even better treatment. For seven months they gave him their best shot, top people and latest methods and newest drugs.

Good results. Seven months and three days after Ernest Beller was admitted, a team of four of the best therapists in New York congratulated each other on the splendid achievement and agreed with Dr. Naiman's report that all traces of homicidal tendencies were gone, the rage was drastically reduced and the patient had achieved a "good social adjustment." Dr. Judith Temchin—who had a $400,000 federal research grant and a body that still caused a lot of eyestrain at Fire Island every summer—predicted that, barring regression, the patient would be back at work in the medical examiner's office in nine or ten weeks.

Upstairs in his twelfth-floor room, Dr. Ernest Beller said good-bye to his aunt and uncle and leaned back in the easy chair to read the fat Friday edition of the *New York Times*. He was feeling a lot better. Anna would arrive next week and Uncle Martin's speech was almost back to normal, and everything was going to be all right. Ernest Beller was flipping through the bulky paper for the crossword puzzle when he spotted the small item on page twenty-eight.

Dateline: Bonn.

The notorious "Butcher of Breslau" had been sentenced to twenty years for World War II atrocities, and would serve his time at the new prison in Essen. Dr. Beller smiled as he tore out the article and carefully put it in the pocket of his pajama jacket.

He found the crossword puzzle on the next page.

It was easy.